A RATHER VENGEFUL ACCORD

A RATHER VENGEFUL ACCORD

DANIELLE KNIGHT

◆ Daphne Press

First published in the UK in 2025 by Daphne Press
www.daphnepress.com

A CIP catalogue record for this book is available from the British Library.

Hardback ISBN: 978-1-83784-084-7
eBook ISBN: 978-1-83784-086-1
Illumicrate Exclusive HB ISBN: 978-1-83784-083-0
Waterstones Exclusive HB ISBN: 978-1-83784-118-9

The authorised representative in the EEA is Authorised Rep Compliance Ltd
71 Baggot Street Lower, Dublin, D02 P593, Ireland. Email: info@arccompliance.com

Printed and bound by CPI Group (UK) Ltd, Croydon CR0 4YY

MIX
Paper | Supporting
responsible forestry
FSC
www.fsc.org
FSC® C013604

To Alfie

Content warnings and a glossary can
be found at the back of the book

1

A VILE, IMPERIOUS ENERGY

When the moment of truth arrives on a gorgeously grey and horrible morning, I haven't even tried to sleep. Instead, I stand in the Fenlands that border Withersham Hall, mired in the worst of Preyburn's weather.

Come autumn, the air around Withersham is at once cold and humid. It's like wearing a damp, mildewy towel over your head. As if we weren't spoiled enough already, we also have fog to contend with. It gathers thick as unspun cotton about my knees, too dense to see more than fifty paces in any direction. Fortunately, I'm not missing much.

A good seventy per cent of Preyburn is fens, and when you've seen one, you've seen them all. They are vast, peaty wetlands rife with creatures both natural and eerian. The air buzzes with damselflies and midges and that dark, swampy funk that comes from stagnant water. It's common to see apparitions in the fog, so when a flustered prefect comes tromping towards me, I ignore her. The more attention you pay the fog's tricks, the more attention they pay you.

'Hal, what are you doing out here?' Only now do I look Miriam's way. Thankfully, the fog's apparitions don't speak. 'I've looked everywhere for you.'

With my *Compendium of Glyphs* open in one gloved hand, I wave the other towards the donations. They form a five-corpse star in the mud, heads together, feet angled out.

'Practising,' I say, voice muffled by the graver's mask. To protect me from death's stench, it boasts a large, unhandsome nose stuffed with pungent herbs: Balverian lavender and menthol.

Mine isn't the only face hidden. The donations wear shrouds of decorated cloth to preserve their dignity, secured with string about the neck so they don't flutter off in the wind.

'The day of admissions?' Miriam says, incredulous.

'I couldn't sleep.'

I unholster the graphium from my belt. Its nib glows with sorcerous heat, the brilliant orange of hot iron in a forge. Graphia hold no ink. Where I press mine to the dead bloat of a donation's belly, it hisses like pork loin searing in a pan. Each glyph-stroke I draw is a curve of branded flesh.

Glyphs must be inscribed into corpse-flesh, and this is the most effective way we've found. Our Lady used to do something similar with her own fingernails, which were famously long and sharp enough to rend femurs.

With each inscribed glyph, I get closer to completing the epitaph that will break down the donations' bodies, reforming bone and sinew into something new: an effigy under my control.

'The abettors are here,' says Miriam.

I stop dead. 'Since when?'

'Since first bell. Limbridge is trying to stall them with pastries and chitchat, but... well, you'll see why she's had trouble soon enough.'

I lift my mask to see Miriam better. The lenses in the graver's mask lend everything a greyish tint, but now her cheeks turn pink with fret. All that time we waited to hear back, agonizing over whether the abettors would come, and now they've been here since first bell.

After a full night's catastrophizing, I'm strangely numb to this slice of bad news. Instead of hyperventilating, bursting into tears, or any number of sensible reactions, I holster my graphium. I have to get back to the dorms and change into my spiring garb.

When Miriam starts marching to the school, I follow, abandoning the donations to the fen. I don't do this lightly, especially after the effort it took to procure them. Gravers around here spend half their time hunting for the most pristine bodies, many of which are past usefulness with blunted skulls, shattered legs, and punctured lungs. Infestations by pulpmoth larvae are just as common. You're not a real graver until you've spent an afternoon scrubbing viscera from your boots. The donations we receive here at Withersham are better than the calibre in Crippleditch, but not by much.

A new figure appears in the fog. Miriam slogs straight past him like she doesn't see him looming over us like a monolith. Malice gleams in his abyssal eyes, which is no less than I'd expect. I'm about to humble him in the training hall, after all.

When we find Limbridge, her eyes are bloodshot behind her lenses. Even more telling, homebrewed scotch sweats from every pore. Just the thought of a whisky hangover in this weather makes me feel ill, but my mentor's voice is full of forced good humour.

'You're all set. Fabulous.'

Her bleary gaze falls on the spiring attire I've changed into. Officially, Withersham doesn't teach spiring, so officially it has no spiring attire. What I wear now is a recent design by Limbridge and the headmistress, using our frankly tragic school colours. A spiring jacket is always stiff, waist-length, and high-collared, but rarely seen in dour grey with kelp-green accents. If the vest, breeches, gloves, and boots were ever meant to be white, they promptly soured to the colour of old milk.

'Have the others…?' I trail off when she starts nodding.

'Gone already.' A grim expression takes her corvine features. My classmates' auditions evidently failed to impress. 'We need you now, I'm afraid.'

My spiring mask hangs from my fingers, staring emptily at the mould-speckled walls. The mask looks like marble, but it's made of petrified grave pulp – thin as paper, harder than steel – with openings for the eyes and nostrils. Its perfect, glazed surface is meant to echo the face of Oldrac. He varies from one depiction to the next, but every artist agrees upon the deep-set eyes, square jaw, and smug, swollen mouth. Of course, wherever there is Oldrac, there is filigree. It's present on every edge of my mask, obscene and gold and gloating.

'I'm ready.'

Limbridge presses her lips together, pats me on the shoulder, and shoves a sheath into my right hand. Inside the cold, smooth metal is a two-handed longsword – my spire.

'Remember,' Limbridge tells me, 'no matter the airs they put on, these are just the provost's underlings.'

We walk the desolate void that is Withersham's post-term halls, where even Limbridge's croakiest of voices sounds loud, without interference. School without the full cohort has been a real treat. As the last cohort on the abettors' list, we six candidates had to remain with only each other and the sullen groundskeepers for company.

In all fairness to the groundskeepers, it can't be easy trying to keep Withersham Hall from her spirited descent into ruin. Our school is an avid collector of dust and mould. She stands marooned amid a vast, rust-coloured ocean of fen-pocked countryside. On a clear day, that's all you should hope to see from any window. On every other, the milky green fog, like an ill-mannered guest, settles in overnight and won't leave. Her carpets are threadbare, her floorboards spongy in places, her walls stained with humidity and rot. A hot, ripe summer has left her reeling, sticks of pale yellow wax stooping sideways in her candelabras.

It's eerie, being at school when all the schooling has stopped. Without life to busy her halls, Withersham is revealed for what she is: decomposing.

'You should have seen the looks on their faces when I insisted they trial some other pupils first,' Limbridge says. 'They were *stupefied* with outrage. But we mustn't let them intimidate us.'

A wild thing to say. When you govern one of the Commonwealth's regnant colleges, and therefore the realm itself, you've a right to intimidate through your underlings and anything that represents you.

'Two lordly little shites is what they are. Barely past graduation, neither one too shy to let us know how *lucky* we are they made it out to us at all.' Limbridge sighs. 'If you get into St Penderghast's, I hope you'll be a bit more gracious about it.'

If. If I even get offered the chance to enter admissions. We all know the abettors agreed to come out to Withersham only because they couldn't *not* trial a Faulton. Were Alastair anywhere else, they would have replied to Limbridge's appeal the same way they had done every previous year: with silence.

We stalk a series of windowless halls, each one gloomier and fustier than the last. The sconces are twitchy, spitting light at the high ceilings and strangely narrow walls. Where one hall crosses another, we find my competition.

Alastair – an utterly pedestrian Faulton scion descended from Oldrac himself – meets us with one hand holding his own spire and mask, the other buried in his pocket. His face is impassive, as if abettors turn up to see what he's made of every other day.

Like all scions, Alastair is less a person than a painstaking, centuries-long curation of his bloodline's traits of choice. From the tips of his dark gold hair to the toes of his anti-stab boots, he looks primed and hideously expensive. Even after five years of boarding here, he still manages to clash with everything around him.

His attire makes mine look like a cheap party costume with loose stitching. Where his is perfectly tailored, mine is badly cut. The Faulton sigil – Oldrac's sibylline eye beneath a Choir Knot, supported by two spires – sits on emphatic display over his left pectoral. The same patch on my jacket lies bare.

Limbridge rewards Miriam with a single, weary nod. 'Alastair – come.'

Miriam inclines her head as I pass her. 'May Our Lady sustain you.'

'Thanks, Miri,' I say.

Alastair locks into step beside me. He takes one look at my purple-shadowed, pink-rimmed eyes and, in his chasmically deep voice, says, 'Nervous?' There's no smirk on his face, but I feel like he's hiding one.

'And why should I be nervous?'

'You shouldn't. I've no interest in dragging this out.'

'Oh, how gracious of you,' I say beneath my breath and, hopefully, Limbridge's hearing.

Alastair scoffs. 'Fine – hostility it is. You can't say I haven't tried to be civil.'

'You haven't tried to be civil, you cream-faced little tart. You've tried to be condescending and succeeded magnificently.'

He opens his mouth again, but Limbridge beats him to it. 'Downed gods, you two, don't start! Today is *not* the day.'

True to form, Alastair's feeble interest disappears as suddenly as it came. On his loveliest day, he could give lessons to blocks of wood on how to be rigid and humourless. He defaults to charmless brooding, and we go the rest of the way in silence.

When we reach the training hall's heavy elm double doors, Limbridge stops dead in front of them. Instead of pushing through, she stands there with her back to us. At first, I think she's going to throw up, but then she speaks. Her voice is quiet and even. 'Do you remember what you both promised me?'

Limbridge facing the doors is a good thing. One look at my expression would tell her I've no clue what I promised. I go mute with panic, like I've stumbled into a surprise exam.

Then Alastair says, 'A good clean fight,' with all the deep feeling of a Zsietian machine responding to input.

Limbridge says, 'Exactly right,' before I can argue how unlikely that is, both that I would have promised it and that it will happen.

She inhales sharply through her nostrils, seizes the janky door handles, and leans hard enough to swing the elm forward. Damp, cramped gloom gives way to the grey, amorphous light haemorrhaging through the training hall's lancet windows as we follow our preceptor.

Between a distant fan vault ceiling and a naked stone floor lies a cavernous space. It wasn't made for spiring, but it'll do. My eyes adjust to the new light, picking out two unfamiliar figures, one male, one female. They stand in starched splendour on the makeshift judges' platform, so wildly out of place that they could only be the provost's abettors.

While every graving pupil, including myself, must have short hair as part of our uniform, this lady's gone one step further, flaunting a fully shaven head. Her partner, a man, has gone for an intriguing choice of hat: tall, conical, and brimless. Both sport the exquisite tailoring and richly embroidered fabrics of St Penderghast's alumni, and twin moods of gilt-edged impatience. Brocade creeps from the hems of grand, shin-skimming capes like the growth of a stately, golden vine. The overstated collars and forceful shoulder lines give the attitude of graving commanders, offset by the heeled shoes.

More than that, there is something classical and dreamlike about them. It's as if they've been ripped from an old fable, flung into the real and present day. It's how Alastair looked when he first arrived from Glimwick. How he *still* manages to look.

As Limbridge hurries towards them across the vast room, her worn brogues echo on the stone. 'I *am* sorry to keep you waiting,' she gushes, sweeping Alastair and me forward like so much dust. Her face, when she glances back at us, has hoisted up a smile. 'May I present Withersham Hall's final candidates: Alastair Bartholomew Faulton, and Hal.'

I slide a reproachful look Limbridge's way, which she luckily misses. The abettors probably think I'm only in the room because Alastair can't duel with himself, that I'm little more than a sentient practice dummy for him to demonstrate his moves on.

They look less than impressed. They look as though they've never had the sensation of being impressed in all their twenty-something years of living. Although neither deigns to speak, one of them does gesture curtly to the floor. The message is clear: *Get on with it.*

Limbridge takes this in stride, clapping her hands together. 'Places!' she says, heading for the steps beneath the platform.

Alastair and I cross to the centre of the training hall floor, a rectangle with rounded corners and gallery seating along each length. There's no audience today but the abettors and our preceptor. If this were a proper spiring school, today we'd be fighting eerians, wild creatures made and driven by the Eternal Spite of Our Lady.

The Spite is a fundamental concept of Our Lady made manifest, much researched and little understood. It's primarily known for fashioning eerians out of corpses and pulp, although its influence is far greater than that. Its power can be channelled, allowing gravers to create effigies. Thanks to pioneering research by a certain Master Graver, the Spite is now understood to be the closest power we have to a deity, with the ability to take physical form. Since the day Our Lady returned to the firmaments, there's been no entity in the world more powerful, nor longer lasting.

Regrettably, Withersham doesn't have the facilities to hold eerians. Even if we could have hunted one down, subdued it without killing it, dragged it in from the fen... where and how would we have kept it?

Thanks to Alastair, the abettors have made a concession. We'll be allowed to demonstrate our spiring prowess on each other.

Alastair and I exchange a look. I know what's needed now. This is my chance to charm the abettors with a show of fellowship – of *oneness*. They like that sort of thing in Glimwick. I could offer to shake his hand, or give him a friendly pat on the shoulder. Instead, I glare straight into his hollow black eyes with all the threat I can invoke.

I won't lie. Alastair *does* intimidate, not only due to the history of his lineage but from the sure flow of muscles beneath his exorbitant clothes, his precise cut-glass accent, and his height. He's always looking down on me, literally and figuratively. And then, of course, there's the weapon itself.

Both our swords meet the basic description of a spire. Both are longswords, the crossguards between hilt and blade S-shaped, the blades double-edged and tapered. Both are styled after the spires atop Glimwickian cathedrals, designed to draw lightning in a thunderstorm. Pommels crown the hilts as finials crown the buildings, while the blades' fortes – the section below the crossguard – come lined with crockets like fine, gapped fangs.

I don't read menace in Alastair's gaze, only a grim sort of pity. I'm not worthy of pre-game menace. I don't have a legacy to threaten his.

With a look, I tell him how all that's going to change. I'll show him, and the rest of the cohort too.

We turn and take our paces.

If this were a just world we live in, I'd already know who's going to win. It would be the person who deserves it, who's worked the hardest for it, and to whom it would mean the most. For me, earning a place at St Penderghast's means the chance to study under the greatest graver of our age. I'm not exaggerating. First Graving Master Mortritis has more accolades than I could comfortably fit in my room.

Alastair, as far as I can tell, has no such aspirations, nor does he admire anyone more than himself. He simply radiates a vile, imperious energy. He'll attend St Penderghast's because it's what Faultons do. And if by some strange slap of luck he doesn't get in, he'll wind up in another, marginally less prestigious college, like St Caladyne's. No doubt there'll be a few stern chats at the next family gathering, but any long-term effect to his career? Doubtful.

We're in place by the time Limbridge reaches a safe distance beneath the judges' platform and the stone-faced abettors. We don our masks. My hands tremor slightly as I fasten the clasp at the back of my head. Alastair, inscrutable at the best of times, now looks utterly inhuman and pitiless for it. He does some lazy flourishes, disturbing glimmers of dust motes with his blade.

Facing each other does mean we won't have to demonstrate the full, consummate power of a spirer. Just like the architectural spires they're patterned after, combative spires attract lightning – a violet charge about the blade called Oldrac's Acclaim, or, if you're a Glim, *Our Lord's Acclaim*. If you're going to play the Hallowed Game, it's a necessity.

I've never achieved Acclaim, and likely never will. It's a gift Oldrac bestows upon those aligned with the Radiant Principles, a bit of positive reinforcement for his disciples. Pulp-made creatures – namely, eerians and effigies – are weak to it, and without it spires aren't nearly so effective. Apart from atrophers, Acclaim is the only thing that can disrupt the active glyphs that hold these creatures together.

I'm not entirely sure what effect Acclaim would have against another spirer, but thankfully I won't find out today. The abettors haven't asked to see it, which means I still have a chance of winning this.

With every thump of my heart, want throbs in my gut. I *burn* at the thought of Alastair taking my place at St Penderghast's.

Limbridge says, 'When you're ready, you may beg—' and doesn't even get the sentence out before Alastair kicks off with a flying lunge, like an arrow shot from its bow.

2

ANOTHER STUPID MISTAKE

Inevitable is the word I'd use to describe a duel against Alastair. His strikes are inevitable. My ability to evade them is not. Even though I'm ready for him, even though I know what he's about to do before he does it, there's only so much I can do to compensate for that kind of speed.

In case I had any misconceptions about how this duel would go, Alastair's burning black eyes are little more than a spire's length from mine before I can even take a breath. The blade doesn't catch me – not this soon into the duel; wouldn't *that* be humiliating? – but he strikes the ground beside me with an ugly strength that might have cleaved me in half.

The thing is, the world isn't just in the sense of cosmic fairness where everyone gets what they deserve. Hard work absolutely can, and often will, amount to nothing. But my only alternative is to give up, taking my chances from slight to naught.

There's a chance I can beat Alastair. There's a chance I get to try for admissions to St Penderghast's. Beyond that, there's a chance I'm awarded a place there, and Mortritis takes me on as her proxy, and I create a new effigy that opens up an entire nebula of possibilities for the Commonwealth's military.

But let's not get ahead of ourselves. Grind Alastair into the dirt now. Revolutionize the field later.

I recover as best I can, which is to say, without grace or style. Perhaps to show the abettors he's a decent sport, Alastair gives me the few moments I need to regain my form. I could never afford that kind of charity, and his giving it to me is an insult. The millisecond I've regained my balance, he vaults forward, giving me just enough time to block with my forearm before he opens it up.

A stupid mistake.

I want to say that I grunt with pain like a big, butch hero. In reality, it's more of a cry.

I only get any space at all because he so generously gifts it to me, because he steps off to admire his handiwork, eyes glinting like dark marbles in a fire. Thanks to the charge in my blood, I barely feel what he's done, but I see.

Bright crimson weeps from the slash in the arm of my jacket, in the scaling and skin beneath. I'm no fainter, but seeing your own blood is a shock to the senses, a foul omen.

This is no way to look in front of the abettors.

Shoving his next strike aside with my spire, I force myself to focus. Fights with Oldrac's pure-fleshed brats must be ended as quickly as possible. Their strength is too brutal, too relentless. It's a stamina I can't hope to match; the attempt brings the taste of copper to my mouth after a while.

I parry again, but clumsily, and when I retaliate Alastair swats my blade aside as if it were a bug.

Sweat veins my forehead. I'm heaving for breath when he comes at me again, point angled towards my core, towards my vitals—

I'm realizing, as I just barely evade him, that my concentration is fading in the face of this onslaught, my momentum spent already.

I'm bleeding *quite a lot*, actually.

Which means, for all my efforts, I still can't hold a candle to him. If I don't do something now, I'm going to lose this. I'm going to lose St Penderghast's.

I do the only thing I can think of. I get a decent grip on his collar and yank him in for a kiss. Except, instead of kissing him, I tuck my chin so his nose meets the thickest, boniest part of my masked skull. It is, frankly, gorgeous technique.

That does the trick. Maybe not the most heroic way to fight, but you can't argue with results – the crack in Alastair's mask, his off-kilter nose spewing thick runnels of blood, the satisfying '*Mmmpff!*' sound he makes as he stumbles backwards.

Just like that, I like my chances better.

I go with him, robbing him of even a moment's recovery, taking advantage of his shock. And he is *shocked*, the whites of his eyes gleaming. Oldrac's broken face slips from his own, exposing a battered nose. Pain tells him to protect it, offering me a free shot at his middle. I take it.

I'm too close to use my spire, but my gloved fist must connect with his liver, because the impact almost floors him.

My heart leaps so high, I have to stop myself from laughing. I'm *winning*. Actually winning! Alastair's buckling like a rickety chair, right in front of me, right in front of Limbridge and the abettors, and all of a sudden everything's within my grasp – admissions, my place at St Penderghast's, Mortritis, my legacy.

Almost.

I want the punch to drop him so much that I believe it will – another stupid mistake. In my moment of celebration, he recovers, because *of course* he does. He always bloody recovers. He bounces back on one foot, getting the distance he needs to swing the blade up one-handed, so fast and so close he couldn't possibly miss.

I neither dodge nor parry. The flat of his blade smacks into my ribs, clouting the breath from me, and in that instant he drops me.

The next thing I know, Alastair's towering over me, his cheeks pink, his hair a mess, his body rigid and seething. All semblance of composure gone. This morning, picturing such emotion on his face would've been a struggle. Blood slides over his lips and teeth and chin, thick and dark like chocolate.

I realize my spire's loose in my grip in the same moment that he boots it away. It shrieks across the stone, well out of reach.

I have the horrifying thought that for the past two years we've trained together, he's just been going through the motions. Now, for the first time, I have the full force of his attention.

I see Alastair winding up and realize what he's going to do.

From my place on the ground, I say, 'Wait! You can't!' and curl in on myself like a human woodlouse, because he can and will.

Limbridge's voice bounds off the walls like thunder roiling in clouds. *Alastair, don't you dare!*

Alastair, showing impressive restraint, stops after one well-angled boot to the ribs.

Or at least, I only feel one before the world goes dark.

3

THE NECESSARY ARRANGEMENTS

I awake to find myself slumped in a high-backed armchair. Along with a dull, rising panic, the sting in my arm brings me round a little faster. So does the ache in my ribs. Every laboured breath squeezes my lungs like a fist.

I try to lift my head, but the movement requires too much effort. I sense, or think I sense, someone else in the room with me. Someone who watches as I begin to stir.

Even this tiny motion makes me dry-heave, and it's no wonder. In the last day, the only things to touch my stomach have been a bowl of watery porridge and my own blood. The world turns and turns.

My eyes close…

When they open again, the world isn't turning anymore. Painfully lucid now, I roll straining eyes to the figure in the chair next to mine. It's the victor, both nostrils crusted with red, split lip swelling, and a broken, blood-streaked mask in his lap.

I take a moment to savour this look on him; it gives his face some much-needed character. Sadly, it won't last long. Scions are like roaches, damn near impossible to break.

'Feeling better, are we?' he says. If anything, he looks embittered by his win.

We're in a parlour I've never seen before, some refuge for the preceptors. The velvet furnishings reek of stale smoke from their pine-tar cigarettes, and crystal decanters of amber whisky huddle together on a side table as if for warmth. There are windows, but the light struggling through their dusty panes does little to lift the umbrage.

I grimace at the roses of blood over my ribs and forearm. Gingerly, I reach under jacket and vest to inspect the damage. All I find is broken scaling, bruised skin, and crusted blood that flakes off at my touch – reminding me that I, too, am a roach. Brief wounds are a sure sign of Oldrac's litter.

I don't know if it's the lack of sleep, the pain, or the fact that I was soundly thrashed in front of St Penderghast's abettors, but I feel a choke rising. This only brings new misery. My gullet feels as if I've spent the last full bell gulping down handfuls of glass.

'I—'

I cough up blood with my words, spattering the chest of my already ruined jacket before I can even think to do anything about it.

Alastair looks at me as if I've just urinated in the nearest porcelain vase. 'Had you not headbutted me in the face, you utter villain, I might even feel sorry for you.'

If I wasn't in so much pain, I'd have some clever riposte. As it is, I just sit there, scuffed and beaten, while Alastair spins an armillary ring on his index finger. If not for his compulsive fidgeting, I could've been fooled into thinking he was relaxed.

Any moment now, Limbridge is going to come barrelling through that door to give us both a legendary tongue-lashing –

and it won't end there. Next, she'll go barrelling into her office to dash off letters to our parents. My mother's reply will make Limbridge seem cheery by comparison. How will I face her when she finds out I've failed?

I take this moment to drink in just how completely screwed I am.

Then, to complete my misery, I start to cry. Not out loud, obviously, but my eyes sting badly enough that I rub them.

Alastair looks bewildered. 'You're not *crying?*'

'Shut up,' I try to say. My tongue feels like a scabby creature living in my mouth and doesn't shape the words properly, but for a saintly moment Alastair does as I ask.

Then he says, more quietly, 'I shouldn't have kicked you. That was bad form.'

'I don't care about that.'

'Clearly.'

'I care about St Penderghast's.'

'There are other colleges that will take you, I'm sure.'

My stomach twists, threatening to upchuck blood and porridge all over the balding carpet. 'Of course you wouldn't get it. You've been guaranteed a place since your parents negotiated the terms of their engagement.'

'Do you honestly imagine they'd admit me without skill, purely because of my family?'

'I was going to study under Preceptor Mortritis,' I say, my voice small and miserable.

Alastair stops turning his ring and looks at me with total attention.

'I was going to be her proxy.'

There's a pause. Alastair uses a knuckle to scrub at the crust of blood round his nostrils.

'She's already retained her son for that position,' he says.

'People can change their minds.'

'You're deluded.'

I start to sit up but stop when the pain shoots from a plaintive wail to a high-pitched scream. 'And you're a vacuous cad who puts too much product in his hair.'

Alastair instinctively pushes his fingers through it, saying, 'Mortritis isn't *people*. She's a St Penderghastian preceptor – not the sort to make decisions lightly, and certainly not the sort to renounce them.' There's no malice in his words; these are cold, hard statements of fact. 'You can't believe she'll take a stranger over her own flesh.'

'Even if her own flesh were to have a nasty accident?' I say, mostly joking.

Alastair gives a little shake of his head and says, 'You don't have it in you.' As if it might be a sensible option otherwise. 'What *is* your fascination with Mortritis, anyway?'

'What's my fascination with the greatest graver of our age?'

Mortritis practically conceived modern graving, not least through her research on the Eternal Spite. Before her seminal paper 'Characterisation and Structure of the Eternal Spite: emergent behavioural phenomena in the Blood of Preyburn', people thought it was as mindless as the wind, but no. Centuries after Our Lady was snatched from us, it continues to forge eerians with intent, cunning, and strategy.

There are experts in the industry who are uncomfortable with this theory. They argue that any of the Spite's human characteristics were instated by Our Lady, making it no more conscious than a programmed machine. They're wrong, obviously – mindless forces do not create avatars of themselves or seek to communicate. Alastair, of course, will understand none of this, much less appreciate it.

'Who wouldn't jump at the chance to learn from her?' I say. 'Except those who take their chances for granted, of course.'

'Pinning all your hopes and dreams on a woman you've never even met...' Alastair lets out a short, ugly laugh. 'You set yourself up for a fall long before our duel.'

'How comforting. Thank you.'

'Better hard truths than comforting lies.'

The door swings open, hinges screeching, and in stalks Limbridge. She takes one baleful look at each of us before backtracking, though she doesn't go far; moments later she re-enters with the abettors in tow. The pair of them glide into the room on a cloud of expensive cologne that conspires with the stale, smoky air to worsen my headache.

From this vantage, they seem almost too big for the room, as if the behatted abettor might have to swerve the pendulous circlet of lights overhead. But this is a St Penderghastian trick, borne of dramatic apparel and impeccable cheekbones. I hadn't thought I'd see them again, but it's hard to focus on my alarm through the stress of my own nausea.

Limbridge barks, 'Up! Now!' with such ferocity that Alastair tuts and drags himself up to full height. I don't move, and Limbridge's glare could incinerate. 'Both of you!'

'My rib's broken,' I say, sounding every bit as pitiful as I feel.

Limbridge isn't moved a jot. I've broken a cardinal rule, more important than my rib: I've discredited the school with shameful tactics in full view of the abettors. Shameful tactics are perfectly fine – desired, even – but only when you aren't seen to use them.

'Get. *Up.*'

The shaven-headed abettor smooths a bejewelled hand over her scalp, saying, 'It's quite all right, Preceptor.' Her accent sounds just like Alastair's – big, broad vowels and extra consonants. It's something like mine, too, though filtered through a relaxed jaw and rounded lips. 'No need to injure your pupil further on our account.'

I suppose I should be grateful for the reprieve, but I'm too busy feeling sorry for myself.

Limbridge's voice, in harsh contrast to the abettor's, is full of desperate assurances. 'Forgive her, Your Learnedness. She's not nearly so frail as she appears.'

Once the abettors are done with staring at Alastair, while he in turn stares impassively at the far wall, they come over to stare at me. The intensity of their twin gazes, their irises yellow as yolk, makes me self-conscious – so much so that I can't find it in me to stare back, instead finding solace in the carpet's patterns.

Since Alastair's the one Glim I've met before today, yellow eyes are something I've only read about. It means the bearer inherited Oldrac's gift of prophecy. The closer they are to a person, the more accurately they view their future. If that person's present actions correlate to what the abettors wish to foresee, even better. It's a handy trick in an abettor's line of work – and, indeed, every other – and it makes me squirm to think these people might know exactly what's in store by looking at me – *might* being the operative word here. Pulp was designed to stifle every Oldracian gift, including foresight.

'Her fragility does not concern me,' says the behatted abettor, 'so much as the unsporting behaviour.'

I sink a little lower in my seat, cheeks heating.

'Not just the girl,' says the other. 'Scruples were lacking on both sides. I expect better from a Faulton.'

Her partner nods, giving up on me to face Limbridge. 'Oneness,' he says, 'is vitally important to St Penderghast's.'

I had wondered how long it would take that word to crop up. Oldrac believed his separation from Our Lady was a fundamental wrong. Oneness was his rationale for a centuries-long battle to reunite with her, and it's been the Glims' rationale for many daft ideas since, hosting gravers and spirers side by side at every regnant college being just one of them.

'Dirty schemes and wanton practices have no place in our institution,' the abettor continues.

Limbridge hovers fretfully in their orbit. 'Oh, but I couldn't agree more.'

'And if what we saw today are the sort of tactics we're to expect from Withersham Hall pupils...'

'The match you saw was far from typical. The oneness in Withersham's cohort is profound.' Limbridge just keeps stuffing every pause with as many nonsense words as she can. 'But you know how it is – where there's talent, there's ego, and ego makes them competitive.'

The shaven-headed abettor sighs. 'And where unwieldy ego accompanies reasonable talent, Her Sagacity's instructions are clear.'

It takes me a moment to remember that *Her Sagacity* is the correct way to address a provost.

Her partner says, 'You must know today's provost would *never* admit two pupils who couldn't put their differences aside and collaborate.'

'Oh, but they could!' says Limbridge. 'Of course they could. Friendly rivalry is all it is. They think nothing of their duels; they forget any pain taken or inflicted as soon as it's—'

'If you don't mind,' says the behatted abettor in tones of *will you please shut up?*, 'I'd like to hear that from your pupils.'

The abettors' gazes fall back on Alastair and me.

I squint up at them. 'Hear what from me, sorry?'

'Are you willing to put your differences aside,' he says, 'and collaborate?'

Limbridge hisses, 'Are you prepared to work together for the sake of admissions?'

Alastair rubs at his breastbone, agitated. 'Meaning what?'

'Bluntly, we would not consider any of the *surprise* pupils foisted upon us today.' The behatted abettor flicks a pointed glance at Limbridge, who pretends to look chastened. She'd do it all over again in a heartbeat. 'What we would offer, if you were willing, is a chance at admissions in an accord with each other.'

My stare is blank, so they keep going.

'An accord is a professional or, in this case, academic partnership between two people.'

'A successful accord,' says the shaven-headed abettor, 'will prove you are aligned with St Penderghast's principles.'

'The Radiant Principles, taken directly from Oldrac's teachings.'

They explain this as if I might be ignorant of such things. As if I hadn't been forced to read and report on the Choir's insipid drivel since my first year at Withersham. We may not follow the Principles here, but we learn the theory inside out.

'We understand Preys have... exclusive ways of thinking,' the shaven-headed abettor goes on. 'But in Glimwick, accords are held in high regard. They are a sign of oneness.'

Glims believe that, as Our Lady brought the Eternal Spite to our world, so Oldrac brought compassion. They reckon it's an invisible but powerful force that's lingered long after their departure, one that works towards the oneness of everyone and everything in existence. The issue I have with this concept is that the Eternal Spite's vestigial power is easily seen in the eerians. If Oldrac's compassion has any power here still, its effects must be subtle indeed. The Choir will argue about the essential goodness in humanity, but you won't see much of that in Preyburn.

'Right,' I say. 'But what does it mean in practice, please?'

'It means you would be competing to share a single place at the college,' says the shaven-headed abettor.

'Either you both get in, or neither of you do,' says her behatted colleague.

I choke a little, my ribs complaining with the force of it. When I glance at Alastair, he doesn't look back; he's too busy glaring at the carpet. He's lapsed into one of the stubborn silences for which he's known, cementing his image as a handsome brick with zero charm. It'll take more than a prompting look to bait him out.

Naturally, my gut instinct is to tell them I'd sooner be disembowelled with a broken bottle than work with Alastair – but what will that get me? Some entertaining looks and a single moment of smug satisfaction, closely followed by despair.

The offer's far from ideal, but compared to what it was a minute ago – abject disgrace and rejection – I feel things could be looking up.

Behind and between the abettors' fine clothes, Limbridge makes wide, staring, *say-yes-you-risible-fool* eyes at me.

'I'm willing,' I say slowly, turning again to Alastair.

He seems reluctant to look at anyone, and for a moment I wonder if he could be so vicious as to say no. Alastair is, after all, a Withersham pupil. Turning down their offer for the pleasure of my pain? I wouldn't put it past him. I wouldn't put it past *me*.

His silence has a severe, almost physical pressure. But then, through a tight jaw, he says, 'As am I.'

To say Limbridge looks relieved would be an understatement.

The abettors lock eyes with each other, and the behatted one says, 'There is one more issue to address.' He turns to me. 'Naturally, no spirer would be foolish enough to attempt St Penderghast's admissions without Our Lord's Acclaim.'

I keep my face completely straight. *They know. They absolutely know.*

'And naturally,' says the shaven-headed abettor, flicking her gaze to Limbridge, 'no preceptor would dare waste our time by putting them forward.'

Despite having spent most of this morning doing exactly that, Limbridge laughs. The sound is quite unnatural. 'Well, of course—'

'We *trust*,' the behatted abettor cuts in with almost painful enunciation, 'that we will see Acclaim on Halen's blade in the arena.'

'Naturally,' Limbridge and I say together. And why not? I won't make it to the arena. The moment I get to St Penderghast's, I'm switching to the graving conspectus.

'Then the matter is settled,' says the shaven-headed abettor. 'We'll have the roster changed accordingly.'

'The admissions process starts in five days' time. Please make the necessary arrangements,' the other tells Limbridge.

'Thank you, Your Learnedness. I cannot tell you how thrilled I am – how thrilled *everyone* will be.'

Neither abettor seems to have an opinion on this. They simply sweep from the room, capes flaring in theatrical fashion as they leave all three of us speechless.

4

THE BIG PICTURE

Alastair and I reconvene in Limbridge's office that afternoon. Ordinarily, having to see his leaden face more than once in a day would poison my mood, but right now nothing can.

I'm going to St Penderghast's admissions! I'm going to meet Mortritis! And when she accepts me, I'll start on her conspectus in two months. The future's never looked so bright.

We've scrubbed the blood off and changed into our uniforms. For me, that means a knee-length, heavy linen skirt over woollen tights, relatively inoffensive blouse and jumper, and disgusting, trout-brown loafers. Arguably, the skirt looks no worse for the ink stains from my fountain pen. The jumper is lichen grey, with Withersham Hall's sigil embroidered on the left breast – upper left, a graphium; upper right, a fen heron, Preyburn's national animal before we were lashed into the Commonwealth; lower right, *The Compendium of Glyphs*; lower left, three pulpmoths, chosen to evoke 'the spirit of sacrifice and service'.

Alastair gets to look infinitely less prim, as all Withersham boys do, in pleated trousers, dress shirt, and blazer. Nobody ever tells him off for undoing his top button or rolling up his sleeves, but if I turn up to class with so much as a penny-sized hole in my tights, that's an instant demerit.

Though we might be forced to wear the uniform, nobody's going to bother with demerits outside of term time. Even if they did, I wouldn't care, because *St Penderghast's*.

Limbridge sits behind a mahogany desk with her head in her hand. Framed by damp-blistered wallpaper and shelves of crusty, umber tomes, she's found herself a pair of dark glasses and a snifter of whisky, neat. She meets our entrance with the grim determination of a woman beginning an endurance test. If she spares even a scrap of pity when I limp in with my mending rib, she hides it masterfully.

'Hal, stop that. You leave in two days' time, and so help me, I will see you off prepared,' she says. Pine smoke fills the air like a eulogy, the hand curled around the snifter also pinching a cigarette. She sucks on it drearily as we approach, looking as though she'd rather be anywhere else.

'*Smoking*, Preceptor?' I say, waving off ribbons of acrid grey. Together with the mouldy-paper funk, it's nauseating.

Limbridge glances at the cigarette in surprise, as if someone stuck it there without her noticing. But then her eyes dull and she says, 'Yes, Hal, smoking. But you're quite right. Not good for my star athletes.' From a desk drawer, she pulls out a glass ramekin overflowing with stubs and adds her latest.

I take one of two fiddle-backed chairs facing the desk. Alastair takes the other.

'First things first,' Limbridge says. 'What to expect from the admissions process. Once the abettors have fed back to Penders' preceptors—'

'Are the preceptors really going to take their word for it?' I ask. 'Shouldn't they see what we can do for themselves?'

'Hal.' Limbridge's face is a stiff mask of patience. 'Preceptors are exceptionally busy people. They don't have time for a grand tour of every school in the Commonwealth. What they *do* have is lots of lovely resources so they can pay minions to do that for them.'

Alastair flicks a glance at me. 'So eager. And here I thought you'd be scared to go again.'

'The only thing that scares me is how drowning a Faulton in a mud puddle might look on my report card.'

'Another fantasy. If you'd bested me even once, maybe your clumsy attempts to—'

'Would you like me to leave the room so the two of you can be alone?' Limbridge takes a throat-incinerating swig of whisky without so much as an eyebrow twitch. 'No? In that case, *I* speak, *you* shut up and listen.'

We absolutely do. Limbridge has a wonderfully long fuse but a diabolical temper. In her fragile state, it's not wise to push.

'Once you arrive at Penders, you will be introduced to the preceptor whose patronage you're bidding for. Then you will be tested against the other admissions pupils. The results will decide who gets a place and who's cut...'

Limbridge trails off. She holds herself very still for a long while, and as she raises a fist to her mouth, I wonder if we'll see her throw up this time.

'Can I get you a vase, Preceptor?' Alastair says.

Limbridge waves a hand – *no*. She takes a deep, quivering breath and stabs a button on her tarnished desk fan. As it shudders to life, she lifts her voice over its rattling and ruffling sheets of paper.

'There will be trials spread across ten days, culminating in a final exam where the preceptors make their selection. No more than five pupils will receive patronage from each preceptor.'

'Meaning,' I say, 'the preceptors choose who passes? Not the provost?'

'Nothing happens in St Penderghast's without Her Sagacity's say-so, dear. But what sort of provost would force unwanted pupils on her staff? She'd have some very bitter people on her hands, and she already has her fill of enemies.'

Alastair lets out a grim chuckle, making me feel as though I've been left out of some private joke.

'Does she?' I say, glancing between them.

'I'd suggest doing your research,' Limbridge says. 'She's something of a controversial figure. Now, the preceptors sponsor your acceptance to the institution and, in so doing, stake their reputation on your ability. Your successes will be their successes; your disappointments, their disappointments. This system of patronage forces them to think long and hard about which pupils to support. Which *means*...'

'We have to impress them,' I say.

'Precisely. This year, only Edusa and Mortritis are open to new pupils. Alastair, Edusa's your natural fit. He'll want to see strong physical constitution, combat strategy, and *artistic flair*.' Said in the same tones as *insufferable theatrics*. 'Hal, I understand you have designs on Mortritis...'

I give a forceful nod.

Alastair says, 'To put it lightly. She's made Mortritis the store for all her hopes and dreams.'

'Yes, well,' Limbridge says ruefully, 'as it happens, you will be bidding for the same preceptor.'

I bristle. 'What? Share Mortritis with—?'

Alastair tuts. 'Be serious. We bid for Edusa.'

'I'm not bidding for Edusa, you fen-sucked eel.'

'You already have.'

I glare at him.

'Really, Kilchoir,' he drawls. 'You can't be this oblivious.'

'What are you prattling on about now?'

Limbridge groans loudly, pushing her glasses up on her head so she can massage her temples. '*Volume.*'

'Think about it,' Alastair rumbles on. 'Why would the abettors present you to Mortritis when they've only seen you spire?'

'That's just to get through the door of the admissions process. I'll change to the graving conspectus once I arrive. Limbridge, tell him.' When Limbridge doesn't immediately jump to my defence, nor even feebly crawl towards it, I level my hardest stare at her. '*Limbridge.* You said—'

'I know, I know.' She sighs. 'Hal, what you have to understand is that Alastair was our most likely to succeed. He had to spire with someone, and I couldn't very well put him up against a graver, could I?'

I take this in like a knee to the gut.

'I *am* a graver.'

'A graver without Oldrac's traits, then. Spiring is out of the question for everyone else at this school. We would've had a murder on our hands. Graver or not, your body heals quickly. Equally, you wouldn't be allowed to give two auditions.'

'So you lied to me?'

'All right, yes. I lied to you. Happy?'

'Happiness isn't even in the same constellation as what I feel right now. Alastair's already guaranteed a place, and still you risked my chances to better his – and you won't even pretend to be sorry about it! With the greatest respect, that is utter pig shit.'

Maybe I won't become Mortritis's proxy. Maybe I'll become an abettor instead, and I'll come strutting back here in ridiculously fine clothes to snub Limbridge and cackle at her tears year after year.

'Everything to suit Alastair *bloody* Faulton! Playing to *his* strengths, making *him* look good, ignoring the fact that *my* talents lie elsewhere!'

'Hal, you're shouting,' Limbridge says.

I lower my voice to a hiss. 'I'm a soldier, not a ruddy gladiator.'

'You have the capacity to learn, especially in Edusa's redoubtable hands.'

'And Alastair doesn't? If he's such a genius, why didn't you tell him to hit the books?'

Limbridge draws in breath as if gathering the very last relics of her patience.

'It's not a case of genius, you imbecile. Mortritis needs pupils deeply read in the branches of science, occult and common, relating to effigies. Alastair – how much do you know about glyphs, effigies, the processes of death and decay, et cetera?'

'Very little.'

'You see? Even if he spent every bell reading until you leave, he still wouldn't know what you know.'

A little thrill goes through me when she says this, but then I remember it's a point against my argument.

'Obviously it's too late *now*,' I grit out. 'But he had two years to learn, same as me.'

'Ignoring the fact that Alastair would never have consented to such a deal—'

'Nor would he have been duped into it,' Alastair puts in.

'—the abettors would have baulked at a Faulton graving.'

'And a Kilchoir spiring?' I say. 'That isn't baulk-worthy?'

Gravers take *Kilchoir* for their last name. It means 'with the Choir's blessing', a sign of our pledge to live by the Choir's religious doctrine. Our family's middle name – Foulblood – used to be our last name. Now it's just a way to identify us from all the other Kilchoirs.

Limbridge says, 'Your heritage yields some degree of pliability.'

Exasperated, I glare up at the ceiling, where someone went to the trouble of painting a map of the Commonwealth. Like everything in Withersham Hall, it's discoloured and peeling, with a lavish water bruise swelling across Preyburn. Glimwick is less damaged, so I can still read the names of the five regnant colleges that mark its regional capitals.

There's only one that matters to me. Some five hundred shanks away from Withersham, St Penderghast's lies in the city of Balver, the proud, cold capital of southern Glimwick and neighbour to the Champion's Roost Mountains.

'What good is pliability if it just means shaping myself to suit pouting wastrels?'

The pouting wastrel in question sits with his arms crossed and his eyes closed as if the sound of my voice pains him. Limbridge simply looks baffled.

'Evidently the good is that you might just pass admissions,' she says. 'Which would you prefer? To gain acceptance by Edusa, or no acceptance at all?'

'I will be accepted,' I say through locked teeth, 'by *Mortritis*. I've been following her for years.'

'Steady, Kilchoir,' Alastair says. 'There are laws against that sort of thing.'

'Shut *up*, you invertebrate. Limbridge, the whole point of going to St Penderghast's is so I can develop as a graver. I want to make monsters, not slay them!'

'Tumbled gods,' she mutters. Then, more loudly: 'You aren't looking at the big picture. Once you have St Penderghastian credentials, the world will be yours for the reaping. Five to seven years under Edusa and—'

'*Five to seven years?!*'

'—you'll have the connections, the wealth, the *clout* to develop whatever you damn well please.'

Admittedly, this piques my interest. 'Oh, yes?'

'Acceptance into the school is the least Edusa's patronage brings. He's insensibly rich and extraordinarily well connected. Both will be leveraged to slingshot his victors to stardom.'

'The victors also take a share in his riches,' Alastair says. 'To start, Edusa finances them from his own bottomless coffers – not out of generosity, you understand; it's an investment. Once the victors are established in the spiring circuit, he'll easily recoup his losses through their ticket sales, interviews, gifts, sponsorships, appearances, and so on.'

'You see?' Limbridge cocks an eyebrow at me. 'All that, and you'll be a bloody good combatant of the Hallowed Game too.'

As much as I like the sound of bottomless coffers, there's a larger issue we've yet to address.

'Why are we even having this conversation?' I say. 'Your mad scheme was doomed to fail the moment they put us in an accord!'

'Such fatalism,' Limbridge replies. 'Your accord is a snag in my mad scheme, nothing more.'

I glare at her, incredulous. 'Like the abettors said, to compete for the spiring conspectus without Acclaim would be *lunacy*. It's the only effective weapon against eerians. I'd need to have some sort of humiliation kink to enter the arena without—'

'You can achieve Acclaim,' Limbridge says. 'In fact, it's now imperative that you do.'

I scoff. 'Be serious.'

'She's right,' Alastair says, and for a moment I'm too shocked to glare at him. Only for a moment.

'In what world would Oldrac ever bless me?'

'One where you align with the Radiant Principles – honour, compassion, prudence, courage, honesty, loyalty, faith, and above all, oneness.'

I blink. 'Have you met me?'

'You have it in you, even if it's only to win.'

'If I act honourably only in order to win, how is that honourable?'

'The Principles forgive our thoughts. *Everyone* has foul thoughts.

It's human to wish bad things for those who have wronged us. We aren't judged until we act upon them.'

There's a knock on the door, prompting Limbridge to groan. 'Come in.'

In comes Prefect Miriam with a tray bearing bitterest coffee, a doorstop sandwich, and what could be two massive blood clots. These are in fact eggs, hard boiled and pickled in beetroot vinegar. Miriam bypasses our chairs to shimmy the tray in between the stacks of humidity-wrinkled paper on Limbridge's desk. 'How's your head, Preceptor?'

'I've never had any complaints,' Limbridge replies, but wearily, as if exhausted by her own joke.

She tips what's left of her libations into the mug and takes a delicate sip. Personally, just the thought of caffeine on a hangover gives me acid reflux, but Limbridge's stomach is made of sterner stuff.

Miriam turns to Alastair and me with her hands on her hips. 'So,' she says. 'St Penderghast's, eh? Congratulations, both.'

'Thank you, Miriam,' Alastair says, pinking her cheeks.

I like Miri well enough, but she does lose points for turning up to watch Alastair train in her free time, and for insisting his Glim accent with its swollen vowels is sexy. That alone makes me want to take her by the shoulders and shake sense into her.

'No, Miriam,' says Limbridge. 'Their trials are just beginning. When they've got through admissions without shaming the institution, *that's* when you congratulate.'

Miriam bows her head a little. 'Did you still want to go through those reports?'

'Oh, nothing would give me more pleasure.' Limbridge slips her glasses back onto her nose. 'Right. I think that's enough bashing my head against a brick wall for one day. Out, both of you. Get packing. And while you're at it, see if some form of truce isn't entirely beyond you.'

5

A FALSE IMPRESSION

The next morning, I have to leave the dorms. It's pulp collection day. Besides that, the air's been pressing in all week, thick and stale as the crypt, and my only company has been the radio. All it talks about is war.

'Under the charge of Commander Nettlefold, Commonwealth ground forces invaded the north-western coast of Zsieti this morning, bringing Prey troops and a legion of effigies into the heart of the Zsietian Ascendancy...'

The resulting claustrophobia makes me desperate to get out.

Before I leave, I drag the locker from underneath my bed and work the combination lock. A backlog of pulp physicks lie entombed within, their polished pewter flasks collecting dust. The Choir's sigil, the Choir Knot, is etched onto each one. It's a circular pattern of astral motifs, all interwoven, no beginning or end, to represent the oneness of all things.

When I unscrew a flask, a familiar grey smell crawls into my nostrils, wadding at the back of my throat. I sip the foul sludge and it coats the inside of my mouth, sticking to tongue and teeth like chocolate.

The backlash is immediate. My stomach lurches as if insulted by Our Lady's gift, and I spend the next minute retching out of the window. I used to down physics like milk tea, but they've stopped agreeing with me.

The obvious solution would be not to drink it, and if only it were that simple. Grave pulp contains the lingering essence of Our Lady, the Eternal Spite, in concentrated form. Every day I go without, I draw farther away from her favour and power. I've tried to force a little down whenever I can, but lately even that's become impossible.

Even if I currently have enough pulp squirreled away in my locker to fuel an entire regiment for a week, I still have to collect my allowance from the Choir. Otherwise, everyone will know I'm not taking it anymore. When it comes to finding reasons to torment and scorn me, the cohort's well versed. No need to give them more ammunition.

On my way out, I stop by the mailbox. Sure enough, there's an envelope bearing my name in Mother's trembling but determined hand. Some days, her illness is so severe that she struggles to hold a pen, yet here my letter is.

I slice open the envelope with my thumbnail and unfold its contents. Limbridge telephoned my parents to say I'd be going to admissions instead of back to their house in Crippleditch. Underscoring her gift for lies by omission, they've assumed I'm going there to grave.

Mother's words leave me queasy. It isn't just Withersham's confines that have been gnawing at me; it's the question of whether I leave for St Penderghast's tomorrow. If I do, it'll only be a matter of time before my parents realize I'm there to spire. They don't know I have Oldracian traits. I only discovered it myself two years ago, when I broke my arm and it healed in a matter of days. I spent some weeks bluffing with a sling before the nurse ratted me out to Limbridge.

My mentor, with undisguised joy, blackmailed me into spiring lessons. Either I began training with Alastair or the whole school would learn I'm some Glim's bastard. My parents are both laypeople, and Mother's illness means there's little chance I was secretly adopted. Thus, the identity of my natural father is a mystery.

I've never asked about it for two reasons. Firstly, a love affair with a Glim would stir ridicule in Crippleditch. Secondly, it'd mortify Father to realize Mother had been unfaithful. She has no idea I'm not her husband's natural daughter, and that would mortify her too.

I fold the letter into my coat pocket and set out. The fog's no lighter as I inch through the disfigured wrought-iron gates that mark the edge of school grounds. Later still, I step onto the Fenway, the treacherous wooden walkway that connects Withersham to Burymeadow. Wide enough for a single motorcar and perilously sunken in places, it's the only way across the fen unless you plan to swim. From each stepped-on slat, silky sludge wells up like blood from a mortal wound.

The Fenway usually takes ten minutes or so to walk, but I'm still sore from the duel, and all the sorer for having lost. But despite moving with the speed of a slug climbing a mound of salt, I do eventually reach Burymeadow. All the streetlamps have been left on due to fog.

Burymeadow businesses are lovely outside of term time, utterly desolate. The pubs are dark and silent – no drunken songs, no scotch-bellied booze-hounds staggering out into the streets, stinking of tar and sweat and liquor, pissing against walls and rattling each other in the alleys. Today, leaving Withersham for Burymeadow is like escaping a prison cell, only to realize an apocalypse has wiped everyone out. A lavishly peaceful dream.

I wind my way through the grotty, haphazard lanes until I find the coffee house. My clothes are damp by the time I push through the door, finding it empty but for the teller. I buy coffee and a wodge of candle cake to go, leaving immediately for Old Burymeadow Chapel at the town's fulcrum. It stands apart for being so well kept, its lawn freshly cut and its windows still secured on their hinges. A murder of crows take wing as I pass its lopsided gates.

Inside the chapel door, the citrusy wood polish of the pews undercuts the floury odour of dust. I expect a long queue to collect my pulp allowance, and the day fails to surprise me. The pastoress must be fetching more physicks from the back, because she's nowhere in sight and the chapel's filled with huffy, unimpressed silence.

I join the tail end of some thirty people and distract myself with goodies. The cake is fresh, bready sweetness, the beeswax cream only a little sweaty, and the coffee more an afterthought to cold, sugary milk – exactly how I like it.

Then I turn to see cold, lightless eyes staring out of a bleakly symmetrical face. Alastair looks clammy. Mizzle dews his forehead, throat, and jaw, and glistens on the dark wool of his coat. My expression says he's as welcome as the pox, but he joins me in the queue anyway.

'I've been thinking,' he says.

'Well done.'

'Save your snide remarks for someone who cares.'

'So I have to suffer your thinking but you won't take my snide remarks? Hardly seems fair.'

Peering around the man in front, I see there's still no pastoress. The queue won't move until she returns, so who knows how long I'll be stuck with Alastair?

I look for solace in my cake, but can't bring myself to eat the rest. After a while, it's like eating lipstick, melted and sweetened. Instead, I drag my fingertip through the last glob of beeswax cream and put it in my mouth.

Alastair's gaze drops from mine to track the motion, fixing on my lips before he looks away. It's a strange moment that I won't take personally. Withersham's isolation sometimes gives rise to bizarre, unthinking aches. They don't linger.

'I'm worried you might do something rash due to a... a false impression.' Alastair sheds his coat, deciding he's more sweaty than cold. I allow myself to notice his bare forearms, flecked with fine blonde hairs and leanly muscled from spiring, but only for a moment. 'It occurred to me that Preys – *you* – might not understand how someone becomes a scion versus a graver.'

'Will you ever piss off? I've known that since I was seven.'

'Tell me then.'

I give him an acid look. 'Scions inherit the abilities of Oldrac, which are passed down purely through flesh. Graving becomes possible via pulp. The mother has to drink enough as the child grows inside her.'

'And you know I wouldn't be able to charm corpses into monsters just by studying and taking pulp, right? After your question in Limbridge's office—'

'*Obviously* I was being flippant.'

'So.' Frustration fills his sinkhole of a voice. 'You know it's impossible for me to compromise, but still you behave as if I'm being difficult. Why?'

I take a cold, miserable sip of my coffee, gritty with sugar, and say nothing.

'We both know there's only one solution, Kilchoir.'

My mother started training me to be a graver when I was four. Some of my first memories are of going to collect donations from Crippleditch Chapel's mortuary, her bony hand fastened around mine. She likes to tell people I was squeamish, that she soon hammered this out of me with a training schedule of her own ruthless design. Thanks to practical lessons from the private tutor she hired, I got used to bodies. Cold, loose skin. Cloudy, sightless eyes.

Limbs stiffened by rigor mortis. Pools of stilled blood. The stench of intestinal decay.

The living are naturally disturbed by sensations of the deceased, not least the odours of decomposition. Gravers, however, don't have the luxury of being disturbed. We are practical, reasoned – the antithesis of spirers. Looking at Alastair's pristine hands, his perfectly square nails and intaglio wax seal rings, it's hard to imagine them wrist-deep in gore.

'I've already come to the same conclusion,' I say finally. 'Even if you did have the knack for it, you still wouldn't have the stomach.'

He gives a gentleman's snort. 'Keep thinking me the gutless priss if that's what gets you to a compromise. I only care that we reach one.'

'I don't know that we can, lordling. Five to seven years is too great a chunk of my life.'

Finally, the pastoress emerges from some backroom in the chapel. I'm in luck – it's Flaypenny, all ivory curls and pillow-ruffled blouse. Alastair's got a thing for her, and he's hardly alone. Thoughts of the pastoress have taken many a mind after lights-out in the dorms.

There's nothing strange about finding a pastoress in a chapel. What's strange is who she's with: a man and woman in liver-brown clothes who slink off like they've been rumbled mid-coitus. As Flaypenny tucks a hand into her robes, I realize why: she's holding an envelope, fat with what is likely cold, hard pud. She doesn't even bother to hide it.

I *knew* she was too fresh-faced and sweet-natured to be real. The only pastoress I'll trust is one who looks like she's been pulled from the antiques cupboard and had the dust blown off her.

But at last, the pulp can be handed out, and the queue begins to shuffle forward.

'You act as though you wouldn't be allowed to keep graving outside of class,' Alastair says archly.

'Oh, I'd somehow have to. If I don't grave as much as I spire, I'll lose the ability. Oldrac's traits supersede Our Lady's.'

'Naturally. But for someone as obsessive about graving as you are, surely there's no chance of it?'

'Don't pretend I'll have the time or energy for anything besides Edusa's stupid training,' I say. 'I'll have to put in thrice the amount of work as you will, just to keep up.'

'What's your solution then?'

'Accepting one of my back-up offers.'

St Penderghast's isn't the only place I applied to, so I do have options in Preyburn: Stuckgorge and Narrowhere. If I can't get Mortritis's patronage, it makes more sense to accept an offer from a college where I can study what I actually *want* to – what I'm good at. I feel almost sick with the thought of missing out on St Penderghast's altogether, but Limbridge insisted I look at the big picture. This is it. I'll sacrifice Penders to study my craft.

Alastair says nothing at first. He simply stares. But then he laughs – a deeply sinister sound. 'I told myself even you couldn't be so vindictive, but deep in my gut, I knew it. You're doing this to punish me.'

I barely resist an eye-roll. He *would* make this about him. 'For what?'

'You know what. Let's not pretend this is anything better than your latest move against me.'

'This may be hard for you to hear, but it's not about you.'

'What else would it be about? You'll do anything to have the last laugh.' His eyes centre on mine, huge and dark and inevitable as the void. 'We both know Penders is the breast of the breast—'

Had Alastair not cut himself off mid-sentence and turned scarlet, I might not have noticed this delightful slip of the tongue. As it is, a savage smirk takes over my face. I don't wear bras on non-training days because I don't need to, and nobody ever notices – at least, I *thought* nobody noticed.

Poor thing. He must be getting *very* lonesome in the boys' dorms if he's sliding rough looks at me of all people.

'What was that, Faulton?' I say, horribly smug. He's really left me no choice but to tease him; his mortified face says that if a portal to the abyss opened beside us, he might simply throw himself in. 'I think you may have meant to say the *best* of—'

'You know exactly what I meant to say,' he snaps, all the fiercer for being caught out. His whole face is bright as a flame. 'You won't get another opportunity like this, and neither will I. Are you seriously going to throw your chances away just to spite me?'

I make a point of inspecting my nails. Unfortunately, they are grubby with ink, along with the rest of my hands. If I'm doing this to spite anyone, it's the cohort. None of them believe I'll become a graving master, and nothing will bring me more pleasure than proving them false. If I could capture the look on each of their faces when they learn of my success, I'd have them framed and hung in my house.

But I can't tell Alastair that. It doesn't exactly counter his claims about my character. Instead, I say, 'The opportunity to throw your chances away is the icing on an otherwise rancid cake. If I was basing my decision on you, it'd be the sponge.'

His glower only intensifies, and when he speaks the timbre of his voice reaches depths hitherto uncharted. It drops from *man with deep voice* to *man possessed by an eldritch horror who now uses him as a mouthpiece.*

Frustratingly, my body cannot help but respond to this sound, so much like the untold abyss we all yearn for. A tingle thrills up my spine, making me stand a little straighter. With all his tedious, conventional good looks, it's easy to forget that Alastair does possess *some* attractive qualities…

'This isn't a joke. Do you have any idea what my mama will do when she learns I've been denied admissions?'

…and then I listen to what he's actually saying. It's like biting into a warm, sugary jam doughnut only to realize it's filled with glue.

I sigh. 'Cut you off, leaving you chastened and penniless? In any case, it's a *you* problem.'

'Wrong. It's very much an *us* problem, which will become all too plain when she hears the reason why.'

'You're not seriously trying to scare me with Mummy's wrath?' A scion throwing their lineage around surprises as much as finding pulp in a pulp flask, but still. 'What's she going to do? Send heavies across the border to break my kneecaps?'

'You lack imagination. My family take petty grudges and reprisals to an art form.' Alastair's best attempt at inflection still sounds like a stone slab feels, but the blush in his cheeks and throat says he's getting worked up again. 'If your own welfare doesn't move you, what about *your* mama?'

'Again, piss off.'

'She's a laywoman, no? It must have cost her a great deal to get you into Withersham, and not just the funds to have you tutored.'

'There's no need to play coy,' I say, pretending a smile. 'If you want your nose smashed in again, just say so.'

We're almost at the front of the pulp line. I'm minutes from escape.

Alastair leans closer. He looks feverish, words tumbling from his lips with uncharacteristic urgency.

'You're first generation. I've seen what happens when laywomen give birth to gravers,' he says, causing me to flinch. 'Their muscles atrophy. Bones turn brittle as a sparrow's. Your mama didn't sacrifice her health for a daughter that falls foul of my mama, or worse, *chooses* mediocrity. She must have been so proud to hear you got into admissions. Surely you can't drop this disappointment on her now?'

My face goes hot. He always knows exactly where to stick the knife.

It's true. My mother's a laywoman. If you're born without Oldrac's gifts – something that can be acquired only through ancestry – you're fen-mired without a lantern. Scions get the best education, the highest salaries, and every perk that follows. The rest of us fight tooth and nail for the scraps.

There is one way you might improve your standing, and it starts with a lengthy application to the Choir. As long as you can write, seem healthy enough for children, have no record of your criminal offences, and might conceivably afford the tutelage, the Choir will dole out grave pulp like it's going out of style. Get enough of that down you and there's a chance your next child will be worth something. There's a chance they'll be able to grave without dying.

Graving and dying used to be one and the same. To use Our Lady's gifts, you need grave pulp in your blood. Pulp is mortally toxic. For centuries, gravers lasted only as many years as it took them to waste away.

Thanks to the Choir, things are different now. They invented physicks that laypeople can drink for six years or more before they start to wane. If a laywoman conceives in this time, her child will be able to use pulp and Our Lady's gifts without sickness, and so will their next generation. This undertaking spoils the mother's health forever, but her family will be elevated to the class of gravers, filtered from the dregs.

It was Mother's ambition for me to attend St Penderghast's. My success will be the payoff for years of incurable pain. After all she sacrificed to give me the best chances in life, how could I bear to disappoint her?

Moreover, how can Alastair wield this against me so shamelessly?

I wait until he's done talking, and then do the only rational thing. I take the lid off my cup, say, 'Is this disappointing enough for you, you dead-eyed curse?' and dash the contents in his face.

He cringes as the coffee hits him. Had it been hot enough to scald, it would've satisfied a little fantasy of mine.

As Alastair wipes the gritty milk from his eyes, the man in front of me collects his pulp and leaves, bringing us face to face with the pastoress. Behind her, brown paper bags and polished pewter flasks crowd a table whose oily polish and cracked wood give a strangely leathery appearance.

Blinded, Alastair grabs the back of my collar as I step forward. It snatches tight against my windpipe. 'Listen,' he snarls, 'you can't just—'

He sees who's stood in front of us and chokes more than I do.

Flaypenny speaks in her high, soft voice. 'Alastair. Hal.' No matter who she's talking to, she always sounds as if she's reading a bedtime story to a child.

Alastair releases my collar, staring at Flaypenny with an attentive, almost nervous expression.

She lifts her eyebrows, both so blonde as to be invisible. 'What are you two still doing here? I thought term was over.'

'Both of us leave for St Penderghast's tomorrow,' I say. 'Alastair came to say goodbye.'

'Oh, Alastair, that's incredible news. You must be so excited to be going back to Glimwick.'

Alastair responds to the trap snapping down on him with a tight jaw and pink cheeks. 'I—yes...' Ever since the rumours of Alastair's love for Flaypenny reached their peak, he hasn't been able to bear her company for more than a moment. He must want her something chronic, to be so agonized by her presence.

As I hoped, Alastair loses his nerve. Eyes that are black as the fen on a starless night leer at me as he takes a step back. 'We aren't finished,' he intones, his low voice beneath Flaypenny's hearing. 'I'll see you back at Withersham.'

Despite this highly valid point, my smile is gloating as he turns and stalks from the chapel. This round is mine.

Flaypenny flips through the register, scribbles a mark next to my name, then takes a fresh paper bag for the flasks of special, non-lethal pulp. She bags the first flask slowly, indifferent to the queue behind me. 'I take it you'll be spiring at St Penderghast's?'

'What?' I say, alarmed.

'Well, forgive me for noticing, but you have a scion's features.'

'What do you mean? Which features?'

Flaypenny adds a second flask to the bag, going on in her silky cream voice. 'Did you think fair hair would be the only tell? It's in your build, your hands, the shape of your face.'

My stomach sinks. *Are my differences so obvious?*

'I find it easier to tell than most Preys. And as a pastoress, I practise discretion above all things.'

'My parents can't know.'

'Why not?'

'If people in Crippleditch found out, our family would be shunned.'

The *obviously* goes unsaid, but Flaypenny frowns. 'Why shunned?'

'Because it goes against everything Our Lady stands for.'

A little laugh escapes her, startling me. 'Oh, I doubt they'd be so sentimental about it. All Preys understand pragmatism. There's no shame in survival, wouldn't you agree?'

'Of course,' I say, frowning.

'You've done well to hide it all these years. But then, how often do your parents see you?'

'Only in the holidays.' *And even then, we don't spend much time together.*

'Well, then it's their own fault for not paying attention.'

For a moment, Flaypenny looks at me and I look back at her, not sure what's going on. Something in her expression sets me on edge, but I couldn't say what.

'Here's hoping everything goes well for you at admissions – and that you won't forget your old pastoress.' In a strangely intimate move, she puts a delicate hand on my shoulder and squeezes. 'If you find things haven't worked out quite as you hoped, you ought to come back and see me.'

'Yes?'

'Yes,' she says, hand still on my shoulder in a way that grows creepier by the moment. Flaypenny's a tiny slip of a thing. She couldn't be less imposing if she tried, and yet my heart starts to thud as if facing off against an eerian. 'I'd have work for you, if you found yourself in need.'

I hesitate to ask, but: 'What sort of work?'

'Contract work,' she replies, as if that answers my question.

She leans towards me a little, sweetened condensed milk and browned butter usurping the damp in my nose. I fight the urge to lean back. She's still holding the flasks in her other hand, and I can't leave without them.

'*Outrageously* well paid. You'd easily set yourself up for whatever venture you fancied next.'

A lump forms in my throat and I try to swallow it. Judging by the dodgy meeting I just saw, I take it she doesn't mean pastoress training. Probably she wants me to be some sort of runner for her – drugs, or illegal tech she wants smuggled in from the Ascendancy. Maybe she needs a heavy to shake down her debtors. No doubt she'd find all sorts of uses for a scion's abilities, all of them criminal. I don't want any part of it, but I don't want to piss off a crime boss either.

'Thank you,' I say. 'I'll keep that in mind.'

Flaypenny smiles, gives my shoulder one last squeeze, and thankfully drops her hand. She gives me the bag of flasks, which is my cue to exit the chapel as quickly as I can without offending her.

6

AN ACHIEVABLE PLAN

The problem I face now is that there's nowhere to hide from Alastair. Coal-black clouds gathering above the chapel menace me out of Burymeadow and back to school. A flash lights up the sky as I make my way back, followed by a groan of thunder that I feel in my chest. I see Alastair several times along the Fenway, but every leering apparition is a trick of the fog.

Withersham Hall's a confusing sprawl, but pupils reach the last of their five years with intimate knowledge of every nook and cranny. Every mushroom trumpeting from the walls, every act of vandalism, every loose floorboard under which to hide skin mags, booze, and other contraband.

I take the long way round to the girls' dorm via a vast, swampy field that Limbridge forces me to run laps of. I'm about to go through the refectory doors when a peculiar scent catches my attention: petrichor, the scent warm graveyard earth gives off after cold rain. It's too pungent to be natural.

Curiosity gets the better of me, so I strike out across the field with the mud sucking at my boots. Before long, I can make out figures in the fog. Four pupils stand in drenched gravers' uniforms around a five-corpse star in the mud – heads together, feet angled out. I have to assume they're donations.

Gravers' belts sit at the pupils' hips, a place to holster their Compendiums and graphia. Until you've memorized all 1,063 glyphs, you'll be wanting to keep *The Compendium of Glyphs* on you throughout your training.

I can't see their faces thanks to their gravers' masks, but I know who stayed to bid for Penders: Stripthicket, Gretch, Cecilia, and Ramshaw. Two are brandishing their graphia, the nibs searing hot.

By accident, I once branded my hand with a graphium, although the thin white scar vanished before my eyes two years ago. When I got it, Mother berated me until her voice thinned to nothing, saying no school would take a clumsy graver. I wasn't clumsy. I was nine.

A third pupil handles the Compendium, guiding her peers to different parts of the donations' bodies, dictating which glyphs to brand them with. 'D three, left palm, *obash*. D one, above the navel, *heth*.'

A fourth, probably the lookout, glances up and notices me watching. She lifts her mask – it's Gretch, smiling – and then a gloved hand as she waves me over. As far as my dealings with the cohort have gone, Gretch has always been a neutral party, neither ally nor aggressor.

I'm reluctant to move closer, but since the waving only gets more insistent, I go against my better judgement.

'Heard you got through to admissions.' She lifts her gloved fist as if holding a glass in toast. 'Congrats.'

'Thanks,' I say, because anything else would only invite more bitterness from everyone here.

'D three, right inner elbow, *mhure*.'

'Show me,' Ramshaw says.

Cecilia flips the Compendium around so he can copy the glyph. She turns her head towards me, voice muffled by her mask. 'Miri says you've bid for the spiring conspectus.' She keeps her tone light, as if this is no big deal, but every muscle in my body cringes.

The cohort connected my regular absences to Alastair's private spiring lessons ages ago, but nobody had any proof and I've always denied it. There's a reason why I keep the glut of pulp under my bed secret. Never mind how the cohort would retaliate, reports could travel back to Crippleditch, to my parents.

But the look in Gretch's unmasked eyes tells me there's no point lying now. They know. They know because I wasn't with them when they all auditioned for the graving conspectus together. So, after a too-long pause, I say, 'Yes.'

'*Wow*,' she says. 'I didn't know you could spire.'

My cheeks heat a little.

'Cecilia,' Stripthicket says, impatient and poised with his graphium. 'D one, right hand, first knuckle of the ring finger, *odelpox*.'

'It's not what I planned,' I say. 'Turns out dear old Limbridge led me astray somewhat.'

'Led you astray?' Gretch's smile is deeply unpleasant. 'Everyone knows you've been training with Alastair. What else could you've planned for?'

'Graving,' I say. Now the heat's spreading to the tips of my ears. *Stupid, stupid, stupid*. 'I thought she just needed someone for him to practise with. She said I could switch conspectuses.'

Stripthicket lifts his mask to see me, or perhaps so I can see him. His face is all disdain, hideously shadowed like a gargoyle.

Cecilia's tone is even less comforting, somehow. 'But spiring's the sport of champions! Soon you'll be in arenas, courting the press, winning the hearts and purses of the Commonwealth... D five, base of throat, *hakliss*.'

'Slaying Our Lady's creations for sport,' Gretch chimes in. 'Much more glamorous.'

Ramshaw stays quiet, refusing to engage.

'I never wanted glamour,' I say, bristling. 'I wanted to study under Mortritis, same as you.'

'Are you certain, Hal?' Gretch's voice is sweet, but her eyes are fierce. 'Maybe the life of a graver's not for you. Too lowbrow.'

'Too difficult,' says Cecilia.

They are, all four of them, simmering with hostility, their voices so insincere it makes my collar itch.

It's unfair, but inevitable, that spirers are more celebrated and recognized than gravers. Gravers are the greatest minds of the Commonwealth, but few laymen get – or, indeed, want – to see the work we do. We make monsters from human corpses. Some find that distasteful.

Spirers, on the other hand, are flashy, charming, and widely seen in public performances called stages. Are they heroes who saved lives in the war? No. They are puffed-up performers, making the most imbecilic use possible of their divine gifts. Even so, the Commonwealth encourages this obsession with spiring for the wealth it brings.

Now my cohort thinks I aspire to the same. They think I chose a life of vain frivolity over one of humble substance.

'I never asked to be taken from graving studies,' I say, sounding petulant even to my own ears. 'I only spired because Limbridge made me.'

'Yes, because training with Alastair has been such a nightmare for you, poor girl!' Cecilia says. 'You must be gutted about your accord.'

Tripped gods, is there any detail Miriam left out?

Now Ramshaw speaks up. 'Her what?'

'They've been offered a shared place,' Stripthicket says. 'Meaning they'll spend even more time together. But I suppose this is some sort of tragedy, is it, Hal?'

'I wouldn't say it's ideal,' I say, voice clipped.

'*I* would. If you're clever, you might be able to ride Alastair's coat-tails all the way across the finish line.' He lets out a hard little laugh. 'And if you're brilliant, you won't need to.'

'Say what you want to say, Stripthicket.'

'Don't be like that, Hal. I'm trying to help you.' He crosses from one donation to another, careful not to slip in the mud as he steps over them. 'Play the right cards and you could have yourself a little Faulton Junior.'

This conjures images in my mind so abhorrent that it begins to malfunction.

'Even the black sheep of that family can set you up for life,' he continues. 'The only kind of labour you need worry about then is the kind you do on your back. How's that for ideal?'

My heart squeezes tight like a fist. Is this what they really think of me? Surely I've made it perfectly clear that I'd sooner rub gravel into my eyeballs?

'Ready? *Dagnoth* to trigger. Order is D three, D two, D five, D one, D four.'

All of them don their masks again. One by one, Ramshaw and Stripthicket tear off the donations' shrouds to inscribe *dagnoth* on each forehead. Epitaph complete, every glyph begins to wake, whispering to each other like leaves in the wind. The sound comes from everywhere and nowhere.

The donations shiver as the glyphs ignite on their skin, rising to a blinding brightness that forces me to turn away. It'd hurt to watch without a mask's protection, but I know what's happening. The glyphs break down their hosts, reforming bone and sinew into something new. The donations spasm and drag together, flesh coupling with flesh, to form an effigy – an imitation of Our Lady's creations, the eerians.

When the glyph-light dulls, we stand in the shadow of a behemothic, clawed biped with features both cervine and lupine. Its maw, when it snarls, displays two rows of spiny teeth that would look more at home in the mouth of a deep-sea creature. They jostle for growing room in its pink, swollen gums. Horns of bone decorate its head, which is dwarfed by its broad shoulders, the thick straps of muscle that make up its neck. It is a witherbrute, and it moves on four legs as often as two, lending ferocious speed *and* intimidating height.

Stripthicket removes his mask and the rest follow suit. He dusts his hands off, celebrating a job well done.

Only Ramshaw has the grace to look uncomfortable. The girls look vindicated, as if Stripthicket's said perfectly what they've been wanting to for a long time. Apparently anything goes now that I've been accepted to admissions and they haven't.

But I already predicted that. I already knew how sharp the people at this school can turn when they feel slighted. Insults demand answers.

'Marrying rich might be *your* goal,' I say, wiping rain from my brow, 'and if it is, more power to you – but it's not mine.'

'I see,' Gretch says. 'We thought you might've used your wits, masterminded the whole thing... but no, of course you didn't.'

'This is where you fall down, Hal.' Stripthicket taps his temple. 'No foresight.'

'Right, because marrying rich is such an amazing, well-thought-out plan.'

'It's an achievable plan. What's the likelihood of you getting through admissions? Realistically, will you even last a day?'

'*Maybe* the college will be so desperate to keep the Faultons' contributions coming that they'll accept some extra baggage,' Gretch says. 'But what about afterwards? How do you expect to last once Alastair's finally shucked you off?'

She pauses, waiting for my defence. All she hears is rain pummelling the roof tiles and bubbling up from the mud, because I don't have one. I'll back my skills as a graver, but not as a spirer. And now, thanks to Limbridge's deception and my own ignorance, spiring's the only skill Penders will measure me in.

Stripthicket nods. 'If I were you, I'd start being nice to Alastair, as many times as you can, while you still have his attention.'

Cecilia says, 'Assuming you make it to St Penderghast's, that is.'

The witherbrute snarls with every dreadful tooth, its beady, black eyes fixed on me.

Both effigies and their wilder cousins, the eerians, are controlled by their makers. As the eerians' maker is the Eternal Spite of Our Lady, a force we can't change any more than we can the turn of the planet, they may as well be feral.

Effigies, on the other hand, are controlled by the gravers who create them. In this case, my lovely classmates hold the reins.

I take a step back.

'Insults demand answers,' Gretch says.

'You are joking?' I say, but I can see it in their faces, Ramshaw's shame and everyone else's glee. They're not joking at all.

Why am I surprised? This is the cohort. This is how it goes.

Still, I say, 'Have you all lost your minds?' and take another step back.

'In the spirit of your craven god,' Stripthicket says, 'we'll give you a ten-second head start. Aren't we nice? One... two...'

I turn and bolt for the back doors of the refectory as fast as my injuries will allow. If I can get inside, there'll be a nook to squeeze into, somewhere its teeth and claws can't reach, makeshift weapons. Out here, I'm as good as savaged.

The witherbrute beats me to it, charging around on all fours to block the doors, saliva stringing from its teeth.

I could die here. A pure-fleshed scion might recover from the ravages of a witherbrute, but I certainly won't. My body only heals if it has time, and if the 'brute's necrotic bite doesn't finish me off, the claws will.

With few options, I whirl from the blocked refectory doors and pelt along the building's side. There's nobody here. Every window's dark and shut. I'm too far from the dorms, and Limbridge's office is on the other side of the school. The 'brute will catch up to me before I even get halfway. The main gate is my best bet, but even that's a gamble.

Straightforward running isn't going to work, either. I may not be the sharpest knife in the drawer, but surely I can outsmart a thick-witted 'brute…

Sadly, whatever brilliant ideas my brain is seeding don't get their chance to bear fruit. The 'brute crashes into me from behind, my knees hit the mud. I scream as jaws clamp down on my shoulder with grisly strength, teeth almost to the point of meeting.

But far worse than shredded skin and muscle is the poisonous saliva working its way through my system. The burn builds to crematory heights in no time, spreading like wildfire in a gale through my veins. The panicked-hare pace of my heart only quickens the poison's flow.

Driven entirely by fear, I tear myself free of the 'brute's teeth, only to stumble and fall again moments later. The excruciating pain says I've left a chunk of shoulder behind.

The witherbrute chews on my shoulder meat, watching as I contort in the mud like a netted fen eel. It feels like I'm being immolated, and I don't need mirrors to know what's happening to my bitten flesh. I can smell it putrefying.

Now the 'brute moves in for the *real* savaging. I can do very little, except notice that the bastard cohort have followed to watch.

Its jaws stretch wide, showing off those hideous spiny teeth, and I brace myself for the next bite – but it doesn't come. Instead, the 'brute jerks as if struck, unloosing a pitiful howl that goes right through me.

I can't make sense of it, until Alastair leaps onto its back, his spire incandescent and crackling with Oldrac's Acclaim. He lances the 'brute's shoulder and it frenzies.

I grimace. He couldn't have timed this better if he wanted to.

The 'brute tosses Alastair from its wet-furred back, but it's blinded by pain and panic. He takes but a moment to recover, skidding in the mud to bowl onto his feet.

They circle each other, the 'brute never taking its eyes off the Acclaimed spire in Alastair's two-handed grip. The sounds it makes terrify in the way that only a god's blessing can. It's the rumble of a close storm, the crackle of live wires with enough voltage to scramble your guts.

Alastair advances on the 'brute, jaw tight. When his next strike misses its flank, violet light jags free of the blade, arcing to the nearest lamppost. The bulb blows in a silver flare, spitting glass and sparks. All its neighbours round the school pop in the resultant power surge, plunging the field into darkness.

Not that it's ever been a worry for me personally, but we aren't supposed to seek Acclaim here. This is the opposite of safe. It's one thing to wave a lightning rod about in Glimwick, but in Preyburn we use all sorts of electronics, just asking to be blown up when—

Shit! My radio!

The 'brute takes advantage of the sudden darkness. Only by the violet light of Alastair's Acclaim do I see its claws stripe him across the chest. The blow sends him staggering, but with his spire raised, fending off any follow-up.

The issue with Acclaim, according to Limbridge, is how physically gruelling it is. All that power puts Alastair's body into a constant, furious state of healing, meaning it can't ease the hits he takes in a fight. Any injuries he gets are there to stay until he loses Acclaim.

Alastair charges with a flurry of slashes that sends the Acclaim into a frenzy. It drives the creature back, cringing as veins of lightning thrash from the blade like a flog.

With the 'brute good and cowed, he lunges with his spire's point, and through sheer luck – I refuse to believe it's skill – skewers the 'brute's left eye.

Its howl is raw as Alastair snatches his spire back from its skull and a hissing whip of blood lashes the mud. The 'brute weaves left then right, its fried brain still working its jaw long after its howl has died, to collapse in a shaggy heap in front of its awestruck gravers. The stench of burnt fur thickens the air.

Alastair stands over it, breath punching in and out of his chest. He frowns at his spire. Acclaim spent, the lightning dulls and shrinks, then disappears altogether. My eyes take a moment to adjust to the darkness it leaves behind, yellow spots dancing across the field.

Reaching into his trouser pocket, Alastair shakes a handkerchief loose and runs it along the blade. Only then does he turn and walk towards me. He thinks he's so bloody slick.

'If you've fried my radio with that little stunt,' I snarl, 'you'll be buying me a new one!'

Alastair rises over me like a six-foot-plus obelisk and, in the voice of the abyss, says, 'I would have thought you preferred living to your radio. Especially since you won't be allowed to take it across the border.'

I glower up at him. 'As I said earlier, I won't be crossing the border.'

Alastair bows to look at my shoulder, as if I might need to be reminded of the bite. I don't have the same relationship to pain as I used to, having shrugged off all sorts of training injuries that would spell death for a regular Prey. Nothing hurts for long, and knowing I'll function as normal soon enough dulls the fear.

Mercifully, my veins aren't burning anymore, but the skin is badly lacerated. Still, the damage I find isn't nearly as terrible as I'd imagined. If not for my hybrid blood, the flesh would be dripping down my sleeve by now.

Happily, my shoulder's more or less whole, and I still have enough movement in it – however excruciating – to get up. I ignore Alastair's extended hand, along with the seams of pinkish-white scar tissue that now run the length of his forearm. They fork across his wrist and fingers, the pattern of blood vessels, but wilder. It's as Limbridge said about Acclaim's tax on the body: the longer a spirer uses Oldrac's gift, the more scars they'll get; the more scars they get, the closer they come to exhaustion.

Alastair sighs. 'Kilchoir, I'd appreciate it if—'

'All right!' I say wearily. I can hardly argue now; I'm too mortified, not to mention drenched and shivery. 'Can we do the rest when we've sat down?'

My limbs are stiff as I limp around the 'brute, glaring at the cohort over my healing shoulder. They glare back, no doubt gutted their efforts amounted to nothing. There's not much they can do about it now. The four of them might be able to take me without an effigy, but they haven't a kitten's chance in the abyss of taking on Alastair. Even if they could, the consequences of a Prey succeeding against a Faulton would be dire.

We push through the back doors of the refectory, a cavernous maw of hammerbeam trusses and wainscoted walls. Despite the room's scale and emptiness, and the opened back doors, the air sticks to me like a crowd's breath in a tight space. The stained-glass windows are large but lightless, the rain falling past them in slanted sheets. When the sky is black, as is often the case, the job of brightening the room is left to candelabras. They aren't up to the task.

I sit at a long, gaunt table on the far side of the room, feeling lightheaded. The refectory balters around me and my pulse hasn't slowed at all. Alastair takes the seat opposite and lays his spire down. His wounds continue to weep through his slashed shirt, which has turned awkwardly sheer in the rain. I pretend not to notice the way it clings to his abs. His ego's big enough already.

'You have to tell Limbridge about this,' he says.

I sigh. 'Five years at Withersham, and you still don't understand how the cohort works. Maybe snitching's routine in Glimwick, but we don't do it here.'

'I think this is a bit different than the other times, don't you? They could have killed you.'

I force a shrug in my good shoulder, even though my nerves are still quaking.

Alastair's brows pinch together. 'You still want their approval, still follow their craven rules, even when they wouldn't care if you died and they were responsible. I don't understand it.'

'Listen, you dizzy-eyed strumpet. Even if I did tell the preceptors, do you think they'd care? Or would they say, *If you can't even handle your own cohort, what chance will you have on the battlefield?*' How many times have we all heard them say something along those lines? Tough guts are rewarded here, not spilling them.

Perhaps hearing the truth in this, he takes a deep breath. 'I think you might be in shock, but have it your way.' He pulls forward a little, dropping his voice. 'I'd appreciate it if we could speak honestly for a moment and leave off the unpleasantness. Are you seriously considering a back-up school?'

'I am seriously considering a back-up,' I say, looking him straight in his sharp, black eyes. 'More so now than ever.'

'Graving means that much to you?'

'Can you imagine a world where someone values a grim, peasant science above the unparalleled glamour of gutting Our Lady's creations to thrill a crowd?'

Alastair doesn't so much as flicker. 'I did say about the unpleasantness.'

'So you did.'

His gaze shifts from my right eye to my left, hunting for any sign of a lie. I refuse to look away. Finally, he takes a deep breath.

'In that case, I have a proposition.'

'Oh?'

'I suppose you wouldn't know this, but Mortritis is a dear family friend.'

'Slander and lies.'

'I can get you a personal introduction when we arrive at Penders. If she likes you, she may allow you to audit her conspectus.'

'To *what* her conspectus?'

'Audit. To take her classes without receiving credit. You'll still be spiring, but you'll be graving too. Will that do?' He says this last bit tersely, because it certainly *would* do... if only he weren't lying through his tiresomely perfect teeth.

'You don't know Mortritis,' I say. 'You're trying to manipulate me, and not for the first time today.'

'I've known her as long as I have memory.'

'So why've you never mentioned it?'

'I didn't realize you were obsessed with her. Come to St Penderghast's and I'll prove it.'

I do and don't want to believe him. I want it to be true, but I'm afraid to get my hopes up. Private access to Mortritis is a dream too fantastic to be real.

But what if it *is* real? What if I don't have to disappoint my parents? They'll find out about the spiring, of course, but now that it's out at Withersham, it'll work its way back to them anyway. People can hardly say our family has broken faith with Our Lady when I'm auditing Mortritis's conspectus, can they? If proving myself to a graving master doesn't bring pride back to our family, nothing will.

But then there's the issue of my ability to consider. Training for the spiring conspectus will put my graving at risk. Every day, I'll have to practise glyphs or Oldrac's traits will grow over-bold from the spiring. The more I use his abilities – the reflexes, the strength, the healing – the more glyphs I'll need to write to balance myself out. Graving's the only thing that can restrain Oldracian flesh.

I've had to do this the past two years, of course, but at secondary-school level. The mere thought of carrying it on at collegiate level exhausts me.

Whether true or false, I should walk away. But how could anyone walk away from a meeting with Mortritis?

'You'll say nice things about me?' I say. 'Put in a good word?'

'Of course.'

I mean, this *is* incredible. I almost feel the urge to thank him, but as it rises within me, I kick it back down into the dark, where it belongs. Only Alastair could make someone want to thank him for offering a deal. Scions are a nightmare.

'I want a meeting within the first two days,' I say instead.

'Be reasonable. I have no idea what her schedule—'

'Or I'll be getting the next train back to Preyburn.'

'I—fine. Within two days.'

The problem with all this is that I'm proving Stripthicket right, using Alastair's connections to elevate myself. There's no pride in that. But pride, compassion, honesty, valour – these are luxuries Preys can't afford. In this life, you have to do whatever you can to get your foothold. My parents always say you have to fight tooth and claw.

Alastair's eyes are fixed on me, waiting. 'Do we have a deal?'

'Actually, we do.'

He releases a held breath, which is the closest he gets to emoting throughout this conversation.

'My takeaway from all this,' I say, 'is that you find coffee-in-face to be an excellent motivator.'

Alastair's eyes return to their usual deadness, devoid of light or soul. 'See what it motivates me to do next time you try it.'

7

THE LONG GAME

The next morning, with Miriam in the passenger seat, Limbridge drives us to Burymeadow Station. It marks the very end of the tracks and endures only to bring freight and Withersham-bound people in and out of town. The lone ticket office camps like a hermit beside a single dilapidated platform, so lopsided as to look stepped on.

Alastair and I climb out of the back seat with our sheathed spires. I didn't even want to get in the car with him; electronics don't fare well around scions. The same gift that makes their bodies conduits for Oldrac's Acclaim also causes electrical shorts. This might be managed if it happened only when spiring, but Alastair's broken more appliances than I can count simply by trying to use them. I was sorriest to see the toaster go. They didn't bother to replace it.

On the platform, Alastair slings an embossed leather belt around his hips and buckles it in place. He laces two straps to the suspension rings on his sheath with thoughtless finesse, leaving his hands free for luggage. Where Alastair's spire is thoroughly decorated, mine is of a blatantly cruder make. His crossguard ends in snarling eerian heads, there is a flourishing design to the outside of his knuckle-bow, and the name Ivo Helel – a celebrated Glim sword maker – inscribes his fuller. The difference is downright cruel.

It's the first time I've travelled with a spire, so it's the first time I've had to wear a spire belt. I copy Alastair's movements with half the confidence, adjusting to its weight on my hips.

Limbridge pulls me aside for a private word, leaving Miriam, Alastair, and our luggage under a wonky umbrella. She shelters us with another, raindrops pattering against it.

'Hal, listen. I didn't want to say this in front of Alastair, but I'd be remiss as your mentor if I didn't say it now.'

Ah, my apology. Better late than never, I suppose.

'The truth is,' she says, 'I didn't just lie to you for Alastair's sake. I also did it to help you. The fact is, if you *had* auditioned for graving, the abettors wouldn't have asked you to admissions.'

My jaw drops. 'Are you—?'

'Despite just two years' training, you're a decent spirer. Despite putting in more effort than any pupil I've had, you are a mediocre graver. On a good day.'

'How can you say that!' My voice rises to an indignant squeak. 'My report card's got more ticks than a stray hound!'

'Your theory's excellent, dear, but your practice is the stuff of nightmares.' From the look on my face, her voice softens. 'Forget about graving. Forget about sticking it to the cohort. You'll do more harm to your own life than you will theirs. You're not cut out for war, and you could have quite the career as a professional spirer.'

'Limbridge,' I say, 'you've given some rotten pep talks in your time, but this… this really does take the teabag.'

Rather than looking admonished, she looks at me with pity. *Pity!*

'I hoped to talk sense into you, but alas, you're like every youth

I've ever taught – determined to make the same mistakes for yourself. Say what you like about scions, but living as long as they do gives perspective, exposes patterns.' She sighs, pulling a small drawstring pouch from her lock-top handle bag. 'Who knows? Maybe your account will be different. Either way, may Our Dark-Crowned Lady sustain you.'

'And you, Dorothea,' I say warily. She's not averse to being called by her first name when it's just the two of us.

I accept the pouch from her as though it might be the next blow. Inside, a polishing cloth, three cartridges of ink – Burnished Copper, Balverian Lavender, and Oldsfall Pine – and a brown leather pen roll. The leather is supple yet well structured with a smart snap closure, and stamped with a company name and sigil that makes me feel all fluttery inside. Within, there's a smaller drawstring pouch, this one of velvet, holding a bona fide Skimmington pen. Walnut-barrelled in an elegantly tapered cigar shape. Gorgeously weighted. Sterling-silver trim. Nib of a blisteringly classy design. *Skimmington* is engraved on the cap band, lest anyone forget how expensive it is.

'It's called the Prelate's Archivist. I wasn't sure what nib you prefer, so I got you a medium.'

'Limbridge,' I say, wondering if she hasn't lost her mind. This pen must have cost her a month's wages. 'I don't know what to say. You really shouldn't have.'

As if hearing my thoughts, she says, 'A gift from the institution, dear,' with one eyebrow cocked above her dark glasses. 'The headmistress hopes you won't forget us at Withersham amongst all the glitter of Glimwick. Also, we dread to think of our representative roaming St Penderghast's halls with ink stains up and down her.'

I should be flattered that the headmistress thinks I'll see enough success to afford donations to the school – and I would be, if she believed I'd do it by graving.

'I'm getting mixed messages here,' I say. 'Give up on writing glyphs, but also, here's a sickening pen to write glyphs with?'

'Well, we could hardly afford to get you a posher spire, and there are things you can write besides glyphs. Letters to me, for example.'

Perhaps to hide the fact that my eyes are stinging, I throw my arms around her and squeeze. 'This is *everything*,' I say, cheek mashed against the itchy, fog-dewed wool of her coat. 'I won't forget it, ever.'

Limbridge pats me on the head several times. It's a gesture of such high affection that, when I pull away to see Alastair watching us with his cold, dead eyes, it turns my face hot.

On the train, I shove my carryall into the overhead rack. It's much lighter without the radio. I debated trying to smuggle it across the border, but the penalties for bringing illegal tech into Glimwick are strict. Ultimately, bringing the radio wasn't worth the risk – especially when I realized it'd be too far from Preyburn's transmission towers to get a signal – so I gave it to Miriam to look after while I'm away.

Withersham can be a lonely enough place, but the radio dulls the ache. If Miriam had better company, she wouldn't have come to watch Alastair train all those times, or spilled all that gossip to the cohort. She just likes having people to talk to.

The train's seat cushion wheezes dust when I take my place by the window. There are several suspicious stains on the tufted upholstery and a smattering of dodgy-looking characters who size us up as we board. It makes me glad to have my spire with me.

I wave goodbye through the window as our train grinds out of the station, headed north-west for Glimwick. Miriam waves back with unabashed enthusiasm. Limbridge props the cigarette between her lips to spare me two downward flicks of her fingers. Her voice is muffled by the glass and the chug of the train. 'Try not to strangle each other before you get there.'

Alastair, sat opposite me, is as cold and remote as a distant glacier.

Not even a flicker of feeling at having to leave. I suppose he couldn't wait to scrape this place off him, and why not? Why should any of it matter? Everyone here will be dead before he gets his first wrinkle.

On the bright side, it's lovely when he goes full taciturn like this. I can read my now-stolen library book, *An Elementary Treatise on Latter-day Graving*, in peace. The school library has a wealth of excellent graving books, though most are sadly powder or mush, depending on how damp their section is. Even this one's on the decline. I read at arm's length due to the dank, fungal smell of its spine. Every time I catch Alastair out of the corner of my eye, I pretend he's a malignant presence that's chosen me for a haunting. He's almost good company that way.

Before long, Withersham Hall is little more than a black smear on the glass, the kind a squashed beetle would make. The town where I've spent the better part of five years slips away from me, streaking past the glass at ever-hastening speed. Soon, I will have lost sight of the province where I've lived my life to date.

I get the melancholies whenever I leave a place, never mind how much I detested being there. I was the same leaving Crippleditch for Withersham. But who knows? If things go *very* badly, I could be heading back this way in a matter of days.

The train's route takes us along Preyburn's western edge, the Smudgecoast. Fenside towns whip past the windows in huddles of gaunt and wounded buildings, their windows thrown wide as they gasp for air.

Preyburn sits on a peninsula of sorts, surrounded on all sides by the Fenlands. To the south, the Greater Fenlands fill a thousand-shank gulf between Preyburn and the Zsietian Ascendancy. To the north, a bridge of solid land connects Preyburn to Glimwick, pinched tight by the Northern and Western Fenlands. Funnelling out of that bridge, stretching towards Glimwick like a beggar's open palm, is the Embankment.

As a direct line from Burymeadow to Balver doesn't exist, our journey is longer and more complicated than I'd like. After nine bells' travel, the first train brings us to Narrowhere. We wait three exhausting bells in the station until a sleeper train's ready to board. Alastair and I proceed down a slender corridor to a slenderer cabin with bunkbeds and a sliver of floor space for manoeuvring – barely enough to squeeze past each other. Since he led the way, Alastair edges in first. He slips straight into the bottom bunk as if I never had a choice. I'm too tired to fight over it, so I take the top bunk and whatever sleep I can while the train rocks and rattles around me.

Morning arrives well before I'm ready, and the sleeper disgorges us onto one of Embankment Hinge's many busy platforms. Glims come here for a cheap good time and Preys come here to bleed the rich, gullible Glims for every last penny in their pockets. Bleeding Glims is not only necessary to live but excellent for morale. We change here, as our journey isn't over; Limbridge said it'll bring us into Balver late tonight.

We step off the train, each of us shifting a single carryall and our sheathed spires at our hips as we try not to get swept away in the currents of other travellers. I've never seen so much of anything in one place. All the noise, all the people – the Hinge is suffocating with them. Outside the station, cranes loom over buildings half finished, their wooden beams like bones waiting for skin. Unlike Withersham, the Embankment is growing. It feels like it still has a pulse.

The announcement sheets, which Limbridge said I could use to navigate myself around the Hinge, are a confusion of letters and numbers arranged in no order that I can decipher. Fortunately, Alastair seems to know where he's going, so I follow him.

Ten minutes to a quarter-bell later, he brings me into what I might call a taxi rank, only instead of motorcars, there are horse-drawn carriages. An unusually well-dressed driver holds a cardboard

sign with *Withersham Hall* scrawled across it. Before I can ask what
is probably a stupid question, Alastair strides over and presents
himself. I greet the driver, let him take my luggage, and climb into
the carriage.

I don't know why I thought we'd be boarding another train to
Balver. They don't have trains and motorcars and suchlike in Glimwick;
if scions can't use them, the laypeople don't want to either. Scions,
at least, have the luxury of time. Who cares if it takes a week to get
somewhere when you'll live more than a century?

I'll need to brace myself for more absurdity. Limbridge always
said travelling across the border was like travelling backwards in
time.

As our carriage trots out of the courtyard to join the traffic of
the Embankment's streets, I get a good look at the people. Just as I'd
heard, they are a jumble of Preys and Glims. I've met three Glims in
my life – one before the abettors – so it's hard to imagine a city where
oil mixes with water.

But then, I remind myself, oil *doesn't* mix with water; oil always
rises to the top, and nowhere in Preyburn could this be more obvious
than it is outside my carriage window.

The Embankment's in the business of entertaining Glim tourists
who come to misbehave where their actions won't have consequences.
We pass a strip of smoking houses, eateries, bars, betting shops, the-
atres, soap rooms, and whatever else they have here. Squiffy tourists
stand outside crowded pubs with their arms around the waists of
local girls, knocking glasses of amber liquid together.

Thanks to Oldrac's Principle of Oneness, Glims don't see anything
wrong in consorting with Preys. The wealthiest among them even have
an interest that goes beyond morbid curiosity, although that's certainly
part of it. When you live a blessed life, isolated from the rest of the
world and its problems, a bit of Preyburn grime must seem exciting.

Would Our Vengeful Lady truly support this place? While Oldrac pursued reunion, Our Lady felt rather differently. Oldrac blamed the Condemner, a malignant entity of the abyss, for corrupting Our Lady's mind, but I can't help thinking she'd rather we did away with bleeding Glims, casting off the Commonwealth's banner to reclaim our independence.

Our Lady's people seek solitude while Oldrac's seek oneness, but solidarity also means control. Despite our ostensible autonomy, we're a vassal state to Glimwick. It could easily crush us if we defected, cutting off our supply of non-fatal pulp before they set the scions on us. Preyburn could never risk it. It's a relief when we're finally out of the city, heading for the hills.

I've just cracked the spine of my book when Alastair says, 'You should use this time to prepare.'

'Prepare how?'

'With information. Despite saddling Penders with all your fantasies, you somehow know next to nothing about Glimwick, the preceptors, or the admissions process.'

'What do you mean, *somehow*? I'm a born-and-raised Prey and a Kilchoir. No line, no connections, no Glimwickian holiday homes. And in case you've forgotten, Limbridge wasn't exactly forthcoming with the details.'

Alastair scoffs slightly. 'Perhaps you should stop reading graving books and start reading the room.'

'I'm sure that sounded clever in your head, but I've no idea what it means.'

'That's no surprise,' he says.

Dammit. I walked straight into that one.

'You whine as though she's betrayed you. Limbridge wasn't forthcoming because you didn't question her. The slightest interrogation would have exposed the truth.'

'Right – it's my fault for taking her at face value. Silly me, thinking the mentor who trained me these last five years would have my best interests at heart.'

'Listen to yourself, Kilchoir. Your interests are by the by; Limbridge wants what Withersham wants.'

I shouldn't expect Alastair to understand. Limbridge isn't just my preceptor and mentor; she's my… well, she's been my one friend at Withersham.

'I still can't believe she'd sell me out just to make the school look good.'

'She also sold you out for the funding. You do know Penders doles out grants for every pupil they take?'

I don't reply, but my blank face gives me away.

He tuts. 'This is exactly the thinking that will cripple us in admissions.'

'What are you blathering on about, foul reptile?'

'Short-sightedness and inattention. The first I can forgive – it's hard for Preys to think long-term planning with life expectancy so short—'

'Yes, thank you for that reminder.'

'—but the second is inexcusable. You've got to question everything and plan to the end.'

When Alastair says this, my mind harks back to that envious ghoul Striphicket and his frankly horrendous suggestion of what a farsighted person might do in my position. These thoughts rock my stomach. Fortunately, I doubt that's the sort of thing Alastair has in mind.

'Take no one at face value,' he goes on. 'Everyone has their own motives, and it's up to you to wrest them out. Otherwise, they'll take advantage of you, and your negligence will be to blame.'

'As if! Most Glims wouldn't know guile if it bent them over a barrel.'

Alastair looks at me as though I've just left the restroom without washing my hands. 'Must you be so vulgar?'

I roll my eyes at him. If he thinks I'm vulgar, he should meet my parents.

'Yes, exactly. You're all about virtue and sincerity and pretending to be better than everyone else.'

'Thank you for bringing me to my next point: you'll want to change how you talk about Glims, scions, and spirers.'

'Will I now?'

'Yes, you will – for the same reason I didn't go around Withersham saying all gravers are sickly, ink-sniffing creeps. Even if your real interest is Mortritis, don't forget whose patronage we're actually bidding for.'

'Thank the firmaments you're here to guide me, Faulton. Otherwise, I would've walked straight up to Edusa at the first opportunity to tell him what I think of his conspectus.'

'I'm not just talking about Edusa. The staff, the competition – anyone can and will feed information back to him. Even Mortritis.'

'But if I don't tell Mortritis, then how—?'

'Eventually, Kilchoir. I know you'll find it a challenge, but exercise a bit of patience for once. Play the long game.'

'If I didn't have patience, Faulton, I would've thrown that coffee into your eerily blank face so much sooner.'

Alastair's eyes burn black. 'You mistake blankness for keeping one's emotions in check. If you expect to last, it's one of many things you'll need to learn.' He pulls a tight, thick roll of papers from his bag, held in place by string, and holds it out to me like a baton. 'Every periodical with society pages featuring Edusa in the last quarter. Read.'

'Since you asked nicely, I'll do my very *breast*.'

For all his composure, Alastair's helpless against the wrathful blush that takes his face. Perhaps he thought I'd forgotten about his slip-up in the chapel. No such luck.

I put my book aside to take and uncurl the papers. 'Would you say this is *required* reading?'

'The serious candidates will know everything that can be known about Edusa. They will have been front and centre at his stages, dreaming of the day they could win his patronage.' He leans forward and taps his finger on the page. 'Not only is this required, it's also not nearly enough.'

I sigh, resigned to the fact that I will be reading every insipid feature instead of my book, starting with a timeline of Edusa's highly public, highly disastrous affairs.

8

AN ⊕BSCENE DISPLAY

Outside the carriage, the Embankment's clammy mists retreat from Glimwick's squalling winds. The temperature plummets and the overcast skies split open, lancing the fields with cold sunlight. Before long, white flecks the wind. This is snow country.

It's my first time seeing snow, and I can't say I'm a fan. It grows thicker and heavier, and by the time I've finished reading, the silver crust on the ground is constant and bright enough to singe the eyes. Our breath turns white and heavy in the cold. I shouldn't have packed my coat away.

Beyond the hills lies the city of Balver. As soon as I see it, I recognize it as the old fable from which the abettors and Alastair were ripped. A network of interlaced, pastel-hued residential and commercial estates hosting every business you might expect to find in one of the Commonwealth's wealthiest cities. Its roofs are steepled to prevent cave-ins from heavy snow, so that the skyline is indeed a cluster of spires silhouetted against a mauve evening sky. All looks eerily perfect, like a hallucination.

St Penderghast's claims the tallest spires, positioned on a hill that overlooks the buildings before it, itself overlooked by the Champion's Roost mountain range. Although its snowy, scalloped tiers give the air of a cripplingly expensive cake, St Penderghast's is imposing in the way that only the realm's regnant colleges can be, the magnum opus of the great layman architect Eger Wyche.

The stone façade is cool-toned white where it catches the sun and parchment-coloured in the shade. Its texture varies from so lithe and sinewy that the sweeping arches, columns, and sculptures look like draped silk to reliefs as sharply defined as shaved bone. Best of all, since it's illegal for any other building in the city to be brighter in colour, it appears to radiate light.

You'd think Alastair would be delighted to see Glimwick again, but as he takes in the view, his cheeks are livid, his posture tight, and his dark eyes hot with rage. Then he sees I've given up on the periodicals and snaps out of it.

'How was the reading?'

'Oh, thrilling. My opinions on spirers have completely turned around.'

The articles read like the sort of thing I might write about the Condemner. Each account of Edusa's riotous parties, romantic entanglements, and slanging matches with other spiring luminaries comes cluttered with lengthy, self-gratifying descriptions of his *Oldracian abs* and *smouldering eyes*. If these so-called journalists are to be believed, Edusa always comes out on top and even better loved than he was before. Perhaps he is simply too powerful to publish anything negative about.

Alastair appraises me. 'Nobody cares about your opinions, just your behaviour. You have to be able to hold a conversation with Edusa's most rabid fan: himself.' He pauses. 'What medal did he receive at the Grand Mêlée of '94?'

'Are you joking?'

'Wrong answer. Give me the name and birthplace of his second wife.'

'Aren't you going to tell me what the right answers are?'

'If I give you the answers, you won't remember them. His favourite colour is…?'

'Blue?'

'Be specific.'

'Bright blue?'

'Zero out of three,' he says – words that chill me, even though this isn't a real test – and nods at the sheaf of periodicals. 'I suggest you hold on to those.'

As the carriage draws into the city proper, I can't help but stare at its careful sprawl of classic architecture. It's just as Limbridge said. The buildings appear to belong to some bygone century, and yet they are pristine. There are no cars, not even a bicycle, and instead of lamps, the fire-glow of lanterns and braziers lights the streets.

I take a deep breath to calm my nerves, but it pains my lungs. Here, the air is as cold and dry as Alastair's personality, and so thin that I wonder if I'm breathing anything at all.

The citizens, too, are dressed for a different age. The same long cloaks I saw on the abettors seem to be the fashion here: fur-trimmed with theatrical length, rich embroidery, and impractically heeled boots. Handsome but sepulchral faces are mostly hidden by parasols that are steepled like their roofs – and for the same reason; snow falls like sugar through a sieve. Unlike the fiercer flurries we saw on our journey, here the flakes are too small to stick.

Glims are known for two things: the foundation of the Choir, and an abundance of intensely charismatic, physically striking redheads. Why so charismatic and striking? All the better to convert heathens to the Choir, mass peddler of the Radiant Principles.

Alastair falls outside the stereotype. For all his physical virtues, nobody could accuse him of being charismatic – and for anyone thinking five siblings an abundance, his parents must hate each other by Glimwickian standards. Over a hundred years of fertility plus the wealth to support numerous children equals some very large families indeed.

As we go, Alastair hurls more impossible-to-answer questions at me.

'But I don't even know these things about Mortritis,' I protest, 'and I've followed her work religiously.'

He waves his hand. 'It's different. The society pages document every detail of a spirer's personal life because all of Glimwick will pay to read it. Fewer people want to read about gravers.'

My mind is so busy trying to remember anything I spent most of the journey reading, anything at all, that I forget to notice how exquisite everything is. I'd always known life in the Commonwealth would be different outside Preyburn, but I hadn't quite realized how vast the divide between us really is.

For anyone who doesn't know the history, it may seem strange for Preyburn to have joined the Commonwealth directly after the Zsietian Ascendancy declared war on it, especially given our past. We had our own conflict: the Reunion War. Our Lady taught Preys graving for the sole purpose of destroying the Glims, of ending Oldrac and his brood. We didn't manage it. The Glims could have squashed the Preys like earwigs, but of course they're all about forgiveness. Instead, they left us to wallow in our downfall for a few centuries, then offered us a deal. We weren't in a position to refuse it then, and still aren't today. Ruin from a failed war aside, the fact that only the Choir knows the secret to manufacturing non-fatal pulp keeps our loyalty. Whatever their methods are, it's proved impossible to replicate.

While most Preys tend to forget the ins and outs of their capitulation, the Glims' one clear demand was that gravers handle the war against the Ascendancy. And so we have, year upon year.

As much as I despise the Glims, I have to appreciate their cunning. Just look at all they've been able to achieve by co-opting Preyburn. *Their* war consumes *our* country while they enjoy paradise.

Paradise takes on new meaning as we get closer to Penders. The grounds that encompass the college are a ramble of well-groomed gardens across gentle slopes. Flagstone pathways meander around fussy topiary, gazebos, mazes, a lake, and marble fountains covering thrice the area of the buildings at their core. The same curious shrubs that were spiking from pots in the city proper have entire lawns to themselves here, whole swathes of powder blue somehow enduring the cold – the famous Balverian lavender.

We draw through the literally golden gates of St Penderghast's and into a vast courtyard. Here, the buildings' ornamentation becomes so rich that trying to work out what details I'm looking at gives me vertigo. I have to give up and refocus on the whole, at which point I get sucked into the details again. The effect is mesmerizing to the point of disturbing.

A lone figure crosses the courtyard towards us, wearing the college's informal uniform. They use this apparent contradiction to mean the attire worn by all pupils while on the grounds but not in class, which, of course, would require that they wear either spiring or graving attire.

Having read the prospectus, I already knew St Penderghast's uniform could make our school weep envious tears. No annoying tie, no ugly shoes, just beautifully made apparel that make the young man in the courtyard appear half scholar, half royalty. He wears a fitted jacket with a standing collar in robin's-egg blue, embroidered with swirling foliage and Glim hares in the same gold silk as the abettors' cloaks. Lest the outfit get too busy, this is coupled with a crisp cream shirt, pleated trousers, and dress shoes.

His yellow eyes would be impossible to ignore at the best of times, but the gold thread makes them striking. He must have Oldracian foresight, like the abettors. Only the best pedigree inherits Oldrac's more unusual gifts, so he's likely someone special. He bears the magisterial look that all scions perfect before they leave the womb.

As we climb out of the carriage, Alastair says, 'Watch for ice.'

'I'm not an idiot,' I say, even though I actually hadn't considered ice at all.

'Did I say you were an idiot? I thought I said *watch for ice.*'

Snowflakes catch and melt in my hair as the driver unloads our bags. I expect the boy in front of us to come out with some sort of welcome. Instead, he throws both arms around Alastair. *A curious way to greet strangers*, I think.

I watch him try to cave in Alastair's ribcage without much success. Alastair is carved from concrete.

'How was the trip?' asks the boy. Although he releases Alastair, he keeps a hand on his shoulder. It's a relief to know I won't be his next target. I wouldn't be able to handle that sort of affection from people I've barely met.

'Tedious,' Alastair replies.

'I'll bet.' The boy grins. 'Too used to rushing around in your Prey machinery and whatnot.' Then, evidently remembering that two of us stepped out of the carriage, the boy turns to look me up and down. 'The abettors said there'd be two of you, but I thought they'd fudged the paperwork. How did you manage to find another spirer in Preyburn?'

'He didn't,' I say, an edge to my words. 'I'm a Kilchoir.'

'A Kilchoir?' the boy says, dropping his hand from Alastair's shoulder. 'But you're in an accord?'

'Don't worry,' Alastair says. 'She likes to pretend otherwise, but she spires.'

'Well, she'll have to,' the boy says, looking unconvinced.

'Who are you again?' I say.

Finally, the boy remembers his manners. 'Tieran Sebastian Faulton.' He nods to Alastair. 'And before you say it, I'm two years his senior.'

I see the obvious truth in this statement. It's hard to know which similarities come from Oldrac's flesh and which come from family, but it would be deeply strange for so many people in Glimwick to look quite as similar as these two. He's at least a finger shorter than his younger brother, with a corona of chaff-coloured hair and eyebrows I'd call distinctive. His face is more boyish than Alastair's, but he does have two things in his favour: he has a wide, genuine smile and eyes that show the spark of a soul.

I can tell just by looking at him that he's used to everyone behaving as though light was invented to shine on him.

'Welcome to St Penderghast's,' he says. 'I'll show you to your accommodation.'

The grandeur of this new environment and the presence of two Faultons keeps me from asking questions. Luggage in hand, we follow Tieran into the building.

Every inch is exhaustively decorated, the moulding worked with complex tracery, twisting columns, and hare motifs in the Glimwickian style – an obscene display of wealth, and a route so labyrinthine that, within minutes, I couldn't hope to find my way back to the entrance.

St Penderghast's provost watches our progress from several paintings. While her pose and attire vary from frame to tawdry frame, she bears the same steely countenance in each one.

'I take it this is your first visit to St Penderghast's?' Tieran says.

'It's my first time out of Preyburn.'

'Truly? I'm dying to hear more about Preyburn. *This* one never writes. Have you seen many eerians in the wild?'

'In Preyburn, eerians can only be seen in the wild. We don't catch them and put them on display.'

'Right, of course.'

'And yes, a few – around my home in Crippleditch.'

'Is that near the Embankment? Some of my friends got to go there last summer.'

Of course they did. 'How did they like it?'

'From what they could remember of their drunken stupor, they liked it very much. They lived like gods for a pittance.'

My look is withering, but Tieran doesn't notice. 'How lovely for them.'

'I was desperate to go, but Papa forbade it.' Tieran's bewildered tone at being told no says he usually gets whatever he asks for. 'I'm hoping he'll let me go to the site of Our Lady's Last Stand after I graduate. He travelled there after he graduated.'

'I've never seen it myself,' I say. 'Our Lady's Last Stand isn't anywhere near Crippleditch or Withersham, and the route there is said to be crawling with eerians. The aggressive kind.'

Because of this, spirers have turned the route into a sort of pilgrimage. To them, battling their way through the most virulent eerians, keen on handing Oldrac's brats a miserable, humiliating death, is a chance to earn bragging rights.

Tieran has a glint in his eye. 'Well, isn't that half the fun?'

I could do with hearing a bit less from Tieran, not just because of what he says but because I'm so tired. I wonder if Alastair wants his brother to shut up as much as I do.

We pass through a set of doors into vast, open space, acres of botanical gardens cut by roads swept clear of snow. Night has well and truly fallen, the sky navy and star pricked. The temperature has dropped further, so much so that the cold now ignores my airy Prey-weather clothes completely. It could be some sort of meteorological illusion, but the moon over Glimwick seems brighter and fuller than the one that lurks over Preyburn.

Towering at the gardens' axis, some distance away, is a curved stone wall of epic proportions. This can only be Penders' spiring arena – all roads lead to it. Withersham has no such facilities, but I've seen illustrations in the papers and a diagram Limbridge chalked out on the blackboard.

'Our arena seats thirty thousand spectators,' Tieran says, acting the tour guide. 'They had it refurbished last year.'

What an eyesore. All fringing buildings, pathways, and topiary bow to its shape as if snared in its gravitational pull. As we skirt around it, I think how much larger the park would be without it. It takes up an uncharitable amount of space, foiling the view, dashing its vainglorious shadow across us. This might not be such a crime if I didn't suspect, from studying the prospectus's campus map, what awaits us on the other side: Thumbarrow campus, where all the gravers board and train.

'And the library?' I ask.

Tieran indicates to our right. 'Next to where you'll be staying – the main building, Dunchester House.' We round on one of the arena's less maligned neighbours. 'Staff are on call day and night. Anything you need, just ask.'

If I thought the exterior was boastful, the interior is worse. Everywhere I turn, I'm slapped in the face with grandeur. We walk through a hall lined with veined marble busts of – according to our escort – every sneering fop to hold the office of St Penderghast's First Spiring Master for the last 300 years. (I'm paraphrasing, of course.)

As if this wasn't tribute enough, several dramatic, chiaroscuro portraits of the same decorate the walls on filigree-edged linen canvases more than six feet tall. Thanks to the periodicals I was forced to read, I recognize at least one of them. As the reigning master, Edusa's portrait takes pride of place where this hall meets the games hall's opening, where he can pout and smoulder, in oil form, down at all who enter. Posing emphatically in mid-lunge and spiring gear, mask under one arm, spire striking from the other, he could be halfway through either a stage or a dance routine.

Farther on, Tieran points out the common room, a princely vault bordered by panelled walls in robin's-egg blue and elaborate, gold-framed mirrors. It's already decorated for Oldsfall, the ceiling bedecked in hanging garlands of conifer, holly, and eucalyptus, woven together with orange ribbon, dotted with tiny glittering stones. I glimpse a few pupils looking pompous in their armchairs.

'All the admissions pupils for the spiring conspectus will be in these dorms, so you'll have your potential future cohort for company,' says our escort.

Joy of joys.

A curved staircase takes us up three flights of stairs that make no sound. Not only does the palatial white marble fail to groan beneath our weight as Withersham's steps do, but the runner of bombastic blue-and-gold carpet silences our boots.

Eventually, our escort stops in the middle of a long hallway, gesturing to the two doors either side of us. 'We try to keep pupils from the same school together,' he says, handing us each a key. 'You'll be neighbours.'

He then launches into a well-practised spiel describing the facilities, including directions to rest- and washrooms; the common room we just saw, where meals will be served until term starts; where we can ask for help if we need it; and what times to expect the housekeepers. I wonder if he does actually give tours. Penders has dominated spiring for the best part of two centuries, so the stages bring tourists here in droves.

Finally, he says, 'Edusa wants you down in the games hall at second bell tomorrow morning. No spiring, just orientation. He'll tell you everything you need to know.'

I leave the two of them talking. Or rather, I leave Tieran talking Alastair's ear off. I'm sure they have a lot to catch up on if he hasn't been writing.

'See you at second bell,' is all I say before vanishing into my room.

Overwhelmed by a day's travel, Tieran running his mouth, and the single day I have to acclimatize before admissions begin, I turn in for the night.

9

THE DUST OF OBSCURITY

First bell is striking. My eyes open to the walls in my room, which are a soft and powdery violet. I lie buried in a grand bed, heaped with throw pillows, swaddled in covers and blankets that I dread leaving. The last nights at Withersham were so warm, I could barely stand to have a sheet over me. Not so in Glimwick.

I labour my way out of the lovely warm nest and the chill brings my skin out in gooseflesh. Poking my head through the drapes, I see a cold, bright day. The sun rises past the rimed glass, obscene in its brilliance, sharpening the snow-dusted treeline of the pines and stirring the sky to a peachy delirium. Last night's snow was heavy enough to stick, and now it's like being trapped inside a titanic snow globe.

I turn back to the imposingly large armoire, hand painted with naked, cavorting figures in a mountain hot spring, and remember it stands empty. I went directly to bed last night, so all my clothes are still in the suitcase.

Dread turns my insides to liquid as I don my spiring garb. In the mirror, the shadows under my eyes are the same colour as the walls.

Despite my exhaustion, I lay awake last night, imagining every possible misfortune the next few days could bring. What if I don't last long enough to meet Mortritis? What if Edusa takes one look at me, knows me for a square peg in a round hole, and boots me out of admissions?

Shuddering half from the cold and half from a humiliation yet to happen, I slip on the new jacket Withersham provided. It's fleece lined to ward off the elements. For all its newness, the fabric still manages a gross, fusty smell of soggy pencil shavings and the ghost of pine-tar smoke, courtesy of you know who.

I leave the room to find Alastair waiting in the hallway with the air of a cat outside a butcher's shop. No jacket for him, but he has banded a kerchief around his brow to keep his curls off it. His abyssal eyes take in my kit.

'You can't wear that,' he says. When I frown pointedly at his own spiring attire, he adds, 'I mean the jacket. It's not uniform.'

'Faulton,' I reply, 'I appreciate you may not realize this, being a reptile, but we warm-blooded creatures need to keep our blood warm.'

'Not how reptiles work. Also, we're not even going outside.'

'Yes, and it's still freezing.'

He scoffs. 'Are you going to fight me through this entire process? You know I'm only trying to help you. Help *us*.'

'How does me catching a cold help us in any way?'

Alastair's mouth goes tight, but he says no more.

As we make our way to the stairs, we pass at least six housekeepers, busying about. Provost knows how many people it takes to keep this place not only functional but pristine. They've got fires to feed, towels to deliver, surfaces to dust.

'I'm sorry about my brother,' Alastair says in a low voice. 'He doesn't mean to offend. He's just the golden child.'

I'm surprised Alastair thought he'd said anything wrong. 'Golden child?'

'The favourite, the eldest son. Remarkable win-loss. He always gets his way.'

The knowledge that Alastair, the golden boy of Withersham, has an even more powerful golden boy to deal with shows how low down the food chain I really am.

Moments later, Alastair strides onto the polished porcelain floor of the games hall with an enviable composure, while I trail glowering two steps behind him. The hall has none of the crumbling charm of Withersham's equivalent – no gloomy respite for your eyes, only tyrannous radiance and splendour. It's all too much.

We enter on the ground floor of a vast, curvilinear room the height of two floors, capped by a glass domed roof that exposes the sky's wispy clouds. Above and around us is a gallery, where people can spectate the action on the ground floor from behind a balustrade. Sculpted tympana cap every window and entrance. Each bears a scene that depicts Oldrac facing down Our Lady's ferocious creations with spire in hand.

Swaggering fabric scarfs the windows in gold and cream while spiring-conspectus sigils are pinned to the walls between them like medals. The sigils show a Glimwickian hare springing over a wreath of blue and gold – St Penderghast's colours. Beneath, two spires cross a spiring mask between twin columns. I imagine these are supposed to be stone, but their twists of cream, gold, and robin's-egg blue evoke marshmallow. A scroll at the bottom displays the college motto: *In passion, glory.*

This could be a ball- or banquet room, but instead of dancers or dinner guests, we find the competition. According to Tieran, there are forty-eight of us in the running this year.

Ugh. Look at them all.

It goes without saying that everyone in this hall has over and above the desired fitness level of a spirer. I've never seen so much athleticism in one room, all geared up in immaculate spiring uniforms, marked for various schools.

Physical fitness isn't quite as vital for gravers as it is for spirers. Depending what role you take in the forces, a graver's labour could be mostly intellectual; effigies take care of the fighting. Thanks to my sweet tooth, I used to be a little heavier too, but that changed the day of Limbridge's blackmail.

In Withersham, sucking pilfered pine tar in the copse of trees behind the boys' dorms and booze in the girls' toilets was the best we could look forward to – the preceptors didn't even try to catch us. But then Limbridge told me that if she caught the palest whiff of smoke in my hair, or stout on my breath, I'd be reprimanded in assembly before the entire cohort. Most poisons pass through scions like water, but alcohol is uniquely toxic to them, by which I mean it can still get them drunk.

More cruelly still, she told the cooks to halve my desserts! It's like she did everything in her power to ostracize me. And don't think there weren't sly glances every time I declined to puff on a cigarette or pretended to sip from a bottle. An abstinent graver sticks out like a hammered thumb. Gravers *indulge*.

What I mean to say is that I'm not in the worst shape I could be, but I'm nowhere near as fit as this lot. Nor do I have any Oldracian traits beside the basics of healing, strength, and dexterity. No divine foresight, no voice, and no Acclaim.

It also goes without saying that everyone in the hall bar me is a Glim. Some of them are probably from the school Alastair would have gone to, along with all five of his brothers. Not to mention his father and uncles and myriad cousins and so on, through every generation. In Glimwick, he would have enjoyed all the luxuries that a pupil of his family's great legacy can expect. Instead, he's been slumming it in rural isolation with the likes of me at Withersham. Even for soulless statues, that has to sting.

If any of them are at all concerned by the trials ahead, none show it. Every smile and gesture comes as easily as if they were passing time between classes in their own school.

How I long to slink back to my dark, blissfully empty room. The impulse to do exactly that seizes me so powerfully, I have to clench my gut to ward it off. By contrast, Alastair's look is keen and ready – and why wouldn't he be? He belongs here. Never before has this been so obvious.

He scans the crowd of Glims with an attentiveness that makes me wonder if he knows anyone here. I can't tell which families they're from, but lineage is eagerly documented among scions. By the time Oldrac left Glimwick, he'd fathered over a hundred scions. He was prolific with his affections.

Our Lady wouldn't dream of such degeneracy. When she enlisted the Preys in her fight against Oldrac, she used her wits to empower them. Evidently, all Oldrac had to empower the Glims was his nasty little stub.

'Well!' booms a rich, sonorous baritone. 'This is *quite* the turnout!'

All faces tilt sharply upwards, prompting mine to do the same. A new figure stands up on the gallery with one gloved hand resting on the balustrade, looking down on us all. The puffed-chest pose is simply the beginning of all that I despise about spirers. After that, there's the bleached, smarmy grin, the big poofy shirt sleeves with added flounce.

There's no mistaking this stranger. Edusa wears the garb of St Penderghast's First Spiring Master: cream blouse, breeches and shoes, sleeveless jacket in robin's-egg blue, and princely gold finishes. Through narrowed eyes, I see he's shadowed by none other than Tieran.

'In fact, I'll be damned if it isn't the largest turnout I've seen in all my years of experience. My conspectus grows in popularity every year – and you know what *that* means.' He chuckles. 'To impress me, you'll need to work harder than any admissions group before you.'

As the periodicals foretold, he possesses a rare Oldracian trait. Pure-fleshed scions may inherit Oldrac's Divine Voice, the very weapon he used to humble Our Lady. Its perks aren't limited to spiring; it allows him to project his words farther than ordinary humans. Oldrac's Voice fills every corner of the room.

His hair is oiled to a sharp crease of auburn, a fashionable moustache shaping the bow of his mouth. In the making of his spiring jacket, no expense has been spared – it is thoroughly quilted, with a family sigil I don't recognize embroidered in gold thread over the right breast.

Whoever painted Edusa's portrait over the entrance clearly knew which side his bread was buttered – when it came to the lower half of his face, he evidently just made it up. While the figure in the painting boasts the sort of jaw to have its own name and postcode, the man it supposedly depicts tries to hide his lack thereof with a sharp, structured beard.

If it wasn't already clear to me how desperately everyone in this hall wants to impress, seeing every spirer pulling themselves up to full height would set me straight. Although they affect airs of confidence, they can't hide the hunger in their eyes.

I curse Limbridge for setting me on the path that led me here.

'But what does it take to impress *Edusa?*' He strolls along the balustrade, forcing everyone on the ground floor to turn with him. 'Well, my spirelings, your task is simple: you win.

'Winning makes you worthy. Winning makes you rise. That's all it takes to become a champion...' He pauses for effect. '...is what a preceptor who had *not* received gold in the Grand Mêlée seven times might tell you.'

He chuckles again, evidently entertaining himself if nobody else. I bite my top lip to keep it from curling. Downed gods, has anyone loved anything more than this man loves to hear himself speak?

'Spiring cannot be reduced to a binary of win or lose. This thinking misses the craft of the Hallowed Game, the reason behind our fair Commonwealth's love affair with it.

'But Edusa, I hear you ask, surely winning equals success? Well, history tells us otherwise. How many excellent spirers have been cast aside for their technically inferior rivals? Fans don't just care for technical skill, and it is *they* who decide a spirer's success.'

I cast a surreptitious glance at the other pupils to see if they find this man as insufferable as I do, but alas I see nothing but ravenous, eager gazes all around. *I should be in the graving class*, I think miserably, *surrounded by my peers.* I should be nose-deep in some rare, first-edition graving book, gorging on anatomical diagrams of effigies on yellowed paper.

I try to tune Edusa out, to pretend I am inhaling the glorious perfume of ink and binding glue, the Prelate's Archivist perfectly weighted in my hand as I scribble Burnished Copper notes.

'It is *they* who lift you from the dust of obscurity. And why should they do such a thing? What must you do to earn their love?' Edusa braces both gloved hands on the balustrade, surveying his captive audience. 'Who here believes winning will be enough?'

Again, I glance around. They all just stare back at him like reverent cultists.

'Just so! Spiring aficionados are lovers of drama and spectacle. They are romantics. They want to *feel*. A dramatic loss that stirs up emotion can serve you better than a predictable win.' He resumes his stroll. 'Consider my so-called defeat in the semi-finals of the Grand Mêlée of '87. The people *adore* an underdog, while the spirer who wins his every stage with ease inspires no one!

'A stage should tell a tale. A series of stages should tell a saga – redemption, loss, betrayal, vengeance, desire, sacrifice... Of course, spiring is as much about what happens around the stage – what the fans and society columnists imagine – as what happens within.'

Already, this is worse than I ever could have imagined. I expected smarmy pricks being ridiculous. I did not expect the preceptor to wax lyrical for what feels like an epoch on the poetry of stabbing Our Lady's creations with metal sticks.

I swear on all the gods yet to fall, if this man doesn't stop talking, I'm going to lose it.

'As you compete, I will be asking myself, who here has the beginnings of a long and thrilling saga within them? And for those hoping to hide the most shameful parts of themselves, remember: the worst you could do is bore me. We enjoy villains here – the *right* kind, that is – but dullards we do not tolerate.'

Just when I'm starting to think it'll never end, he draws to a stop, a smile quirking his lips as his eyes catch on someone in the crowd.

'A wealth of potential graces this hall,' he bellows. 'In one year, the scions of no fewer than *four* great bloodlines seek my patronage. Priel Cofferspyre of Thundermark—' He gestures to a flossy-haired strawberry blonde with a dour face. 'Ransley Liverich of Harehollow—' Copper haired, athletic, and foully smirking. 'Lourdes Spendlove of Lordslake—' Tall and lean with white-blonde hair slicked back from her angular features. '—and one other...'

My gut clenches when Edusa gestures towards us.

'One who might have the beginnings of a saga already. The prodigal Faulton, Alastair Bartholomew of Copperfont, returned from exile in darkest Preyburn!'

There's a second shudder of excitement in the hall. Pupils crane their necks to look at Alastair.

'Oh, come, come. You didn't think my proxy's own brother could slip into my admissions class unnoticed, did you?'

Now I join in with the curious looks. Bigmouth Tieran is Edusa's *proxy?* How did he manage that? A preceptor's proxy is supposed to be the cream of the cream *of the cream*, a pupil they think capable of acting as their representative. In their absence, a proxy has the authority to make binding decisions on their preceptor's behalf.

But even now, with his face and posture locked straight, it's hard to imagine anyone would trust Tieran to play that role for them. I wouldn't trust him to make a sandwich. Then again, Alastair did say he's some spiring prodigy, and unlike his exiled brother he will have received the best instruction since his little hands were strong enough to hold a spire.

Alastair responds with stubborn quietness and a demeanour as stern as his brother's, but their combined effect is utterly undermined by the blush in his cheeks.

'And aren't you a sly one, Miss *Kilchoir*?' Edusa gives me a co-conspirator's wink. 'Good for you.'

I clench my fists, but then, remembering Alastair's pep talk yesterday, force myself to flex them.

Edusa backs off the balustrade to complete his loop of the gallery. 'Exiled Faulton returns from Preyburn in accord with a scion's love child!' he thunders, as if selling a headline in today's periodical.

My resulting cringe is so violent, I immediately taste bile.

'But can she *spire*?' Edusa goes on, and on. 'No doubt there are lesser preceptors who'd let this go for a Faulton's sake, but Edusa is not that man. No room for passengers in *my* class!'

'I'm not his bloody passenger!' I snap, my voice so loud it strains my throat.

My bravery lasts as long as it takes all of Edusa's cultists to turn their hard stares on me, all of them stunned that I should speak out of turn. In the resulting silence, their outrage becomes a physical pressure, and the bright lights of the games hall intensify 'til my eyes burn.

He could throw me out of admissions right now, just for that. He could—

Edusa gives a shout of riotous laughter. 'Oh ho! *Very* good! But it's going to take more than Preyburn charm to win *me* over! So as not to waste your time, or, more importantly, mine, you will have the great privilege of stepping into the arena first thing tomorrow. Now, I don't want the rest of you to fret – your chance for glory will follow, one by one!

'My schedule allows four days' recovery before you take the arena again. If you haven't been cut by then, St Penderghast's will host you over Oldsfall. You may avail yourself of the city's festivities, and for those lucky enough to be invited, I even host a little soirée of my own.

'After that, the Crucible! Finalists shall prove themselves worthy of my conspectus by battling one of the most ferocious eerians a spiring novice might face! Survive the next ten days with flair, and my patronage is almost certainly yours.'

Almost certainly? So he can put us through ten days of pain, and then decide not to take us? On a whim?

He lifts his gaze to the grand glass ceiling, as if addressing the firmaments. 'Have courage, my spirelings. *In passion, glory!*' With that, he sweeps from the room.

The Faulton brothers exchange inscrutable looks, before Tieran dispels the mystery by winking. Then he turns to follow his master from the hall.

Within seconds of Edusa's exit, conversation bubbles up from everyone in attendance. I feel as though all eyes are on me. They look formidable. They look *credible*, something Limbridge's ramshackle classes always lacked. When we got together on those dark, stuffy Withersham mornings, either in the training hall or out on the field, there was never more than the three of us, and we all knew Alastair was the only one with professional training.

With her knowledge of spiring, Limbridge was the most qualified out of all the faculty to train us – or rather, the least unqualified.

Provost knows Withersham didn't have the pud to persuade a real spiring tutor to spend any amount of time in Preyburn.

Everyone else in this hall has been properly trained by former champions turned educators since childhood. They've likely all achieved Oldrac's Acclaim. While I was practising glyphs, they were learning to strike.

It feels like my lungs are shrinking with every breath. It was one thing to spire when nobody had a reason to notice me, when none of them knew who I was or where I came from. But now, thanks to Edusa, I have an audience of people who already know that I shouldn't be here. I can't do it. I'm off.

Halfway to the door, the sound of my name in Alastair's voice only makes me move faster.

10

A VOLCANIC TEMPER

As I depart the games hall, I'm struck by the wealth of new... not *hiding places*, but private ones that are available to me at Penders.

The last time I was fleeing – that is, *quickly leaving* – Alastair, I knew it was only a matter of time before he sniffed me out. Here, I could probably hide for months. That's at least half the time it'll take me to get over the disgrace of being called a *love child!*

Where I go is less a conscious decision than it is automatic. Like an effigy commanded, my body gravitates towards the building that holds St Penderghast's centuries-old collection of graving books. This involves a spell of icy unpleasantness as I cut from the door of the main building to the one right of it.

One glance at the blinding white scenery is enough to give me vision spots. The powdery, icing-sugar snow is gone; now it pelts from the sky in fist-sized clumps. If I thought it was cold outside when we arrived yesterday, today's air goes in like a punch to the chest. I wrap my jacket around me and sprint.

It's eerily quiet, as if I'm the only thing alive for miles. Even so, I'm holding out for a Balverian snowcat sighting. I've often fantasized about befriending one and sneaking it up to my room for snuggles, only it'd probably gore my leg with its massive claws when it made dumplings.

Running in the snow doesn't feel too much different from running in the mud around Withersham. Snow doesn't try to suck the boots from your feet, but it's uneven, demanding smaller steps than I could take on firmer ground, and the ice on the flagstones is treacherous.

Rather than having two libraries for the two campuses, all their books are kept in one enormous space. Meaning, the graving pupils must trek all the way over to the Dunchester campus to get their books. According to the prospectus, this is because Penders was a hallowed arts college first and a military academy second. It hardly seems fair – how much can anyone really have to say about the Hallowed Game?

I enter the library's atrium, and the sight of tall, lovely stacks is a balm for my frayed nerves. It's empty but for a woman sorting through gorgeous fabric-bound books with cream gloves. She sees my spiring garb, offers a perfunctory smile, and goes back to what she was doing. Relieved to have escaped questions as to who I am and why I'm here, I check the map on the wall nearby.

As it happens, there are enough books on the Hallowed Game here to clog up the first and second of three floors. I shouldn't be surprised. If the people to document spiring are anything like Edusa, I imagine they tend to ramble.

The shelves are even taller than Mortritis, or so I hear, meaning each row comes equipped with stepladders. Far from the gorgeous dark wood I've come to expect from bookcases, these are a painted powder blue. The reliefs – gold, all of them – narrate the theological and political work of various prelates throughout history.

I take the stairs, and the banisters are lousy with ornamental carvings of hares, foliage, and more Choir officials. No points for guessing who paid for all this.

Penders holds many rare and valuable editions, which I'd need the appropriate permission to request. Today, I'll be content to read the common books. Anything legible is an improvement over Withersham library's mould-riddled tomes.

The sound of people coming down the stairs as I go up startles me. A glory of gravers descends, patterned light falling across them through the diamond-leaded glass. I'm struck with envy over their uniforms. Gravers take navy for their outfit, with gold-and-cream finishes, jackets of fine navy wool lined with cream-silk twill, buttoned with gilt metal, and worked with eerian embroidery. Capelets of the same cover their right shoulders, St Penderghast's sigil etched on every button. They pass in a breeze of dark, resinous tobacco. I'm not subtle in my interest, but their gazes coast straight over me as if I'm invisible. If I were wearing their uniform, perhaps I would've gotten a nod of acknowledgement, even a smile. My spiring gear sets me apart. They probably think I'm another Edusa cultist with a particularly dishevelled uniform.

What they're doing here between term times, I don't know – maybe helping Mortritis with some special project? I should be with them, soaking up her wisdom. It simply isn't fair. Alastair's about to reunite with his kindred, slotting right in like a puzzle piece, while I'm being kept from mine.

I stare after the gravers a moment, then continue up to the third floor. My steps barely make a noise on the unrotten wood no matter how heavy they are. As I submerge myself in the stacks' shadows, a moan in the dark tells me I'm not alone here either.

I spy another couple of gravers, not quite hidden away in an alcove. One boy has another pinned to the wall, their tongues in each other's mouths. The one pinning wears a hulking, double-breasted wool overcoat that conceals both their bodies, and I blush to think what's going on underneath. Even the Withersham cohort wouldn't have braved such depravity. Fun is fun, but a library is a sacred space.

As if sensing my gaze on him, the boy in the overcoat turns his head slightly. He leaves his companion flushed, mouth kiss-swollen like an overripe plum. I scurry off down the aisle, but of course they both saw me lurking like some voyeur. One of them calls after me, throaty and amused, 'If you want to watch, I'm afraid I'll have to charge you.' I throw a dirty look over my shoulder to see it's the guy in the overcoat talking, eyes glinting in the dark. 'Ten gilts for a half-bell. Does that sound fair?'

I keep going, mortified, until I can't hear the other boy's snickers. What an outrage. *They're* the ones getting off in a public place, and *I'm* the one made to feel like a creep.

I push the incident out of my head, combing the fabric spines of heavy tomes until I find one to pick out. As libraries seem to swallow most sounds, I don't hear anyone follow me down the aisle, and I don't realize anyone's there until the book is plucked from my hand. I start, turning to face Alastair as he wanders over to the window to get some reading light, a slice of late-afternoon sun turning his edges gold.

'How did you find me so fast?'

'I knew you wouldn't be able to resist the siren's call of crusty old books.'

Far from crusty, the books here look and smell to be in pristine condition.

'They're glyphs.' Apparently this needs pointing out. But as the seconds tick by, Alastair's eyes aren't just looking at the glyphs on the page but drinking them in. 'You can read them?'

'Some.' He lays the notebook out on the windowsill and taps one of the fiddlier, more obscure glyphs. 'This one doesn't want to be read.'

'When did you learn *any* of them?'

His frown shifts into a smirk. 'You've really never looked into my line, have you? Even here—' he gestures to the army of bookshelves fencing us in '—with all the almanacs you could ever need at your fingertips, it still hasn't occurred to you.'

'Stumbled gods, your ego! You think I've the time or appetite to research your family history?'

'Of a person I have to work with? Certainly. Family history can tell you a lot about a person's values and motives. Especially a scion.'

'Right. So what would I have found in the Faulton almanac that links you to gravers?'

'You would have found,' he says, 'that my mama is a Moppeton.'

I gawp at him. 'You're not serious?'

'Didn't you wonder how my mama and Mortritis were involved?'

'Not really. I just thought…' I don't know what I'd thought. 'They probably hooked up at some high-society party and the rest was history.'

He shakes his head.

'But you're pure-fleshed,' I say, looking him up and down. Apart from the eyes, every inch of him screams *Oldracian brat*. 'And why would a Faulton risk his legacy to marry a Moppeton?'

Oldrac's flesh metamorphoses over time. In a child born to both a scion and a mortal, the Oldracian flesh from their scion's side will gradually take over before they reach adulthood. That's why scions look so similar – they look like Oldrac. A god's corporeal makeup is simply more potent than a human's.

Scions further their bloodlines by coupling with ordinary people, knowing their own heredity will take dominance in any children. This becomes less certain, however, when their partner is Prey, and even less so when they're a graver. Descendants of Oldrac and Our Hollow-Hearted Lady stand to inherit both sets of gifts, but one will have conquered the other by puberty's end. Just as Our Lady spurned Oldrac, so her gifts spurn his flesh. That's why the glyphs will confound me if I don't grave as much as I spire.

'He did it to prove the strength of his lineage,' Alastair replies grimly. 'Scions often pursue marriage to gravers to mark their status, especially in Copperfont. If their children become scions too, it means Our Lord's flesh is so strong in their lineage that it will even smother the pulp of a graver.'

I grimace, but why should I be surprised that a Faulton would go to such lengths to flatter his own pride?

'So Mortritis is your aunt?' I say.

'She is.'

I don't know how to feel about the fact that Mortritis's blood – Moppeton blood – runs in Alastair's veins. How can this soulless abomination come from the same family as the most brilliant woman alive?

'In that case, you could have graved...' My mind whirls. 'If Limbridge had actually told you to hit the books, you could have auditioned for the graving conspectus. I suppose that's why you kept it quiet.'

Alastair scoffs. 'Of course not. When I try to read this page, even the basic glyphs writhe around. I can recognize them if I put all my concentration into it, but the more advanced ones are nothing but a blur.'

Hearing my greatest fear spoken aloud, I barely suppress a shudder.

'How long has it been since you practised?'

'Five years. My mama taught me a little when I was a boy, but I haven't touched it since I came to Withersham.'

'Surely Withersham would've been the perfect place to learn? Well, not perfect, but... I mean, you're a Moppeton. You could've been a *stellar* graver. Why would you ever give that up?'

'Because I'm a Faulton first,' he says, that familiar stiffness coming back into his voice. 'Faultons spire.'

'But you had the choice. You could've been a Moppeton first.'

Then I remember who I'm talking to. Alastair would never stoop to graving when he could spire instead. The fact that he goes by his father's Oldracian last name rather than his mother's makes his choice clear. He's cast off his maternal heritage. He's his father's son. Oldrac's son.

Alastair looks deep in thought, using his thumb to spin the silver band on his sphere ring. 'Papa didn't want me to grave,' he says, his words rumbling up from some farther depths. 'Spiring is his legacy. We can trace our line back to Our Radiant Lord. It's riddled with champions, almost all of them schooled here. Balver's Museum of Spiring has our great-great-grandfather's spire collection on display. Even one graver out of six children was too many. We *all* had to be scions. When he found out Mama was tutoring me in secret…'

He pauses, taking a deep, uncomfortable breath. Even though he speaks with all the emotion of someone reading out an essay they paid someone else to write for them, I feel the weight of his words.

'Papa has a volcanic temper. He forbade me from my studies; I threw a hideous tantrum. I repeated what Mama told me, that it was my heritage too. If I'd thought he was furious before…' He shakes his head. 'He said that when I got to his age, I'd be able to see vicious cycles.'

Despite knowing next to nothing about Alastair's father, my guess is he's tragically old. While most Preys will be lucky to hit sixty – this number isn't helped by all the crime, war, and pulp sickness – the oldest recorded scion died at one hundred and ninety. She didn't look a day over fifty.

I have wondered what this means for me. If I become pure-fleshed, no doubt I'll outlive every member of my family still breathing today, including my young cousins.

'He knew where my graving would lead,' says Alastair. 'He sent me to board at Withersham to see what's become of that heritage. As soon as I saw how people live in Preyburn, I knew what he meant.' He gives me a little apologetic grimace.

Wanting to hear the rest of the story, I decide to let this jab against my beloved home go. Besides, it sounds like the lesson Alastair's father wanted to teach him was less about where graving leads and more about where defying the Faulton patriarch leads.

'So you stopped graving to appease your father?' I ask, and Alastair nods. 'But he still kept you at Withersham?'

'Like I said: volcanic. Even when the lava cools on the ground, the poison remains in the air. I doubt he even knows what I look like now.'

'But I thought you went back home between terms?'

'I did. Every time, he refused to see me. No matter what I said or did, he always insisted I return to Withersham – with the gravers.'

'But you're of age now. What's to stop you from going back if you want?'

'Papa said I wouldn't return home permanently unless I got into St Penderghast's spiring conspectus. He's the head of my household, don't forget. If I disobey him, he'll have me cut off. I'm hardly independent.'

Getting cut off is no trivial matter. He'd be utterly alienated from the upper echelons of society with little hope of climbing the ranks. He has to obey his father to keep his status, like I have to obey the Choir if I want them to keep sending me physics...

'But,' I say, 'you could always apply to the Choir. As a Moppeton, they'd be guaranteed to send you pulp. It may not be too late.' Seeing his face, I add, 'I suppose you can't think of anything worse.'

He tenses straight away. 'It's not just a lifestyle choice. I've hardly seen my family in five years. If I don't get into Penders, that's the way it's always going to be.'

'You miss them.'

'Of course I miss them,' he snaps, a brick-coloured flush rising on his cheeks and throat. 'No matter what names you like to call me, I'm not a reptile, or a statue, or a soulless abomination. Just because I keep a hold of myself—'

I wince. 'That's not what I meant.'

He takes a breath to calm himself. 'I never told anyone at Withersham about this. Not even Flaypenny knew the whole truth of it.'

'Why tell me?'

'I thought I'd try appealing to your humanity.'

'Also known as a guilt trip.'

Alastair draws closer, looking at me with an intensity that makes my face prickle. He smells of a deep woody cologne and freshly washed skin, which makes me conscious of my own scent – sweat and existential terror, most likely.

'I came to help,' he says. 'So why don't you tell me what you need?'

When it's in his interests, Alastair can be as charming as a cat that wants feeding. He can turn his voice from a block of wood to melted chocolate drizzling on a pancake stack. This shift has all the subtlety of an anvil dropped from a great height, because he so rarely bothers. Why would he? Everyone falls at his feet no matter how unpleasant he is.

'I am profoundly offended that you think I want or need anything from you.'

'Unless you no longer want or need to meet Mortritis, I'll wager you're wrong.'

My toes curl. He's got me there. 'Did you see what we're up against in the games hall? There's no way I can compete.'

'If that were true, do you think I would have agreed to our accord? Or would I have saved myself the bother?'

'You've always said I'm a terrible spirer.'

'Two years ago, that was true. Now, I say you're a decent spirer with a sloppy attitude.'

'You seemed pretty confident you'd trounce me in our audition.'

'*Decent*, I said. Not better than me. Don't give me that look – it should be a comfort. You won't have to take the stage alone.'

'I don't know, Faulton... I want to meet Mortritis more than anything, but I don't think I can do this. How will I fight eerians without Acclaim?'

'As I said, you can achieve it. You just need—'

'I need time we don't have, at the very least. You heard Edusa. We're first up in the arena tomorrow.'

'Tomorrow's eerian will be the easiest. We'll spend today training, but in the event that you lack Acclaim come morning—'

'The *inevitable* event.'

'—I'll have figured out a strategy. Trust me; if I thought our only option was failure, I wouldn't set foot in the arena.'

I suppose that's true. He needs nothing to risk my humiliation, but his own is another matter.

'You can't go home before you've even tried. That's pure cowardice.'

He's right, of course. I hate to admit it, even in my own thoughts, but scurrying back to Preyburn with my tail tucked between my legs after simply glimpsing our competition would be cowardice.

'Come on,' he says. 'Afterwards, we'll go to the common room for lunch.'

So, with my gut still roiling, I let him lead me from the library's comfortable darkness back into the searing lights of Dunchester House.

11

THEIR STRANGE
CHOREOGRAPHY

It's the day of our first stage, and despite Alastair's increasingly frustrated attempts to train me yesterday, I don't have Acclaim. In fairness to myself, he makes a terrible preceptor. Aside from our constant bickering, Limbridge always says you should never take instruction from the naturally talented. Often, they don't know why they succeed. They simply do.

Alastair's wielded Oldrac's Acclaim since he was a child, uncorrupted by the world's cruelties. All he's had to do is hold on to it. He doesn't know the first thing about acquiring it later in life, when you've designed and committed acts you're not proud of. I might not be able to stomach Our Lady's pulp anymore, but I'm still her daughter, a graver at my core. Oldrac sees this, even if Limbridge and Alastair don't want to.

When our mutual chagrin hit its peak, Alastair agreed to abandon the idea that I'd achieve Acclaim – at least for this stage – in favour of a new plan.

I sit in the common room beside Alastair now, squinting at a breakfast so fancy I can't believe it's free. A typical Withersham breakfast is pork sausages, black pudding, kelp bread so hard you could club a man to death with it, shavings of hard, sour-sweat cheese, rubbery eggs, and brown ale if you're over the age of fourteen. A St Penderghast's breakfast is a knot of warm, squidgy Choir loaf made with saffron, various jams in flavours I've never tasted before – quince and apple and pumpkin – fresh fruit, a toffee-top rice pudding, and, to drink, strong black tea aswirl with orange peel, cinnamon, and cloves. Thanks to my nerves, the tea is the only thing I can stomach. Maybe it's for the best; I'll only give myself a stitch if I go into the warm-up with a full stomach.

I alternate between watching Alastair eat and watching the ceiling. A painted mural narrates Oldrac's gloating return to the firmaments with Our Lady. I have to admit, the artist has captured her beautifully: sharp, gleaming teeth, flesh-rending claws, and fury of cosmic proportions. In spite of his triumph, Oldrac must fight to drag her thrashing, black-gowned, and lightning-burnt body to the feet of their godly kin, his golden muscles bulging like poxed animals.

As I explore the mural, I can't help but overhear a low conversation from the next table over. It's difficult to say whether they think everyone else's low murmuring hides their voices, or that I'm deaf. Perhaps they don't care who eavesdrops.

'I've never even heard of Whittle-sham before.'

'*Withersham.*'

'Is that a surprise? Some pit in the depths of Preyburn?'

'Well, what in the name of the provost's favourite garter was a Faulton doing there?'

'Exile, remember? He had an almighty row with his papa. Withersham was the result.'

'Row over what?'

'Well, *I* don't know. Apparently he was wayward.'

'Seems to have levelled out now.'

'Five years in Preyburn will do that to you. Sober you up, build character. He's probably *seen things*.'

'Yes, with those terrifying eyes of his.' She makes it sound like a bad thing. Alastair's terrifying eyes are one of his few charms.

In a quieter hiss that still doesn't escape my hearing, another says, 'Something to do with his aunt, I'll bet. Her *experiments*…'

I don't get to hear the rest because Alastair rises from his seat. This is no mean feat; the armchairs are the kind that try to swallow you, and I have to wriggle out of mine.

With movement, the carved metal of my atropher scrapes gently against my upper chest. I'd almost forgotten the graving tool was there. Snug between skin and scaling, the plate's warmed to body temperature and perfectly hidden. Good – I need it for our stage, and using it for spiring would likely count as cheating. I'm certainly not going to ask.

We spend the next quarter-bell warming up in the games hall. Although we don't exchange more than a wary glance with them, we share the space with the pupils who'll follow our stage.

The babble of a distant crowd reaches me before we've even left the building. Families with children trickle down each path to the arena. Admissions stages, it turns out, are open to the public. I'm surprised anyone would care to see amateurs spire, but then, a failure can entertain as much as a victory.

As we join them, people take note of our spiring garb. They turn to stare, nudging each other and pointing. Some of them call out to us: '*In passion…!*'

I stare, blank-faced and sore-eyed from the brightness, until Alastair thunders back: '*Glory!*'

The crowd replies with a cheer. This back-and-forth carries on all the way down to the arena. I don't join in.

Preyburn has nothing like this arena. It grows grander and more intimidating the closer we get. What began as a trickle of people thickens to a river as Glims of all ages flow into the entrances to claim their seats.

Alastair and I take a slightly different path, to an entrance that's slightly out of the way. Tieran waits for us outside. He beams when he sees Alastair.

'How are you feeling? Nervous?' he asks. When Alastair shakes his head, he says, 'What about you, Kilchoir?'

It sounds strange to have someone else call me by that name. I shake my head too, though it's a blatant lie.

Once the last of the spectators have taken their seats, Edusa's thundering Oldracian voice starts to welcome them.

'Gentlepeople of Balver! May I present our first stage of the day to thrill and obsess you!'

I can still hear him with impressive clarity as Tieran leads us into the bowels of the arena. We reach what appears to be a waiting room, needlessly glamorous, with benches and refreshments. I suppose spirers wait for their turn to participate here.

Tieran gestures us towards the yawning entrance of a dark tunnel. 'I've got to get back to Edusa. Just wanted to wish you luck.' He claps Alastair on the back. 'Remember you're a Faulton. Eerians don't stand a chance.'

Alastair replies with a cold-eyed nod, which somehow provokes a smile from Tieran. He leaves us to walk the agonizingly long tunnel. Just when I think it's never going to end, light slants in and, moments later, we emerge from one side of the arena.

The crowd cheers as we walk out. The arena floor itself is a wide disc, two-thirds surrounded by tiered seating that is far from full, but far from empty. Flags bearing the spiring conspectus sigil drape the walls. Where the snow has melted, there are stone slabs in a circling pattern, some decorated, many chipped or outright shattered. Blades of hardy Balverian grass spike from the cracks.

Edusa sits beneath the silk awning of the judges' platform like a monarch. Dressed in full regalia, he's ready to observe and judge. Tieran appears behind him, hands clasped at his back.

'Alastair Bartholomew Faulton, son of the legendary Aiden Faulton! Any spiring aficionado should know that name. He is returned to us from exile in darkest Preyburn, seeking redemption in the arena...'

I stop listening.

Facing him, a colossal statue of Oldrac stands victorious over a fallen eerian. Like every Glim statue of Oldrac I've seen, he is ridiculously handsome and muscular, driving the point of his spire down on his foe. It leaves much to be desired. Preyburn prefers to see statues of eerians towering over Oldrac, sinking their teeth into his shoulder while he cringes in pain.

Black poles thrice my height and silvered with frost jut upwards from the stone ground at irregular intervals. They look like the bars of a wrought iron gate, thick and twisting with arrow-shaped railheads at their tips. There's enough to cover every stretch of the arena, like a copse of dark trees, none more than ten paces apart. In all the illustrations I've seen, these have not been a feature.

I look to Alastair, nodding to them. 'What are these for?'

'They'll be specific to the stage – to the sort of creature they want us to spire. We won't know until we see it.'

'...Halen Kilchoir! Yes, you heard correctly – a Kilchoir that spires! An accord that crosses provinces! For those of you who have wondered how a Prey might fare in the Hallowed Game, you are mere moments from finding out!'

'Get on with it, you jawless has-been,' I mutter. The rage of any eerian will be better than listening to him witter on all day.

Edusa shouts, 'Release the eerian!' to the staff manning the portcullis.

My heart picks up pace as the latticed metal rises with the noise of the crowd, exposing the gloom of the tunnel behind. Alastair and I take stance, ready for some horror to present itself.

It doesn't. I glance back at Edusa. I'm ready to ask where it is when there's a soft thudding on the stone. It's the movement of something hulking and graceless inching its way along the tunnel.

Several hands' worth of fingers curl over the walls and spiked metal teeth of the portcullis. The eerian's strength impresses right off the bat as it heaves the dense, ripe bloat of its body into the light. More hands reach out, their fingernails gripping the stone-cracks.

My eyes struggle to make sense of it. It looks as though it's been cobbled together from people and thick globs of candlewax. That pale, jaundiced pallor is a telltale sign of Our Lady's earlier, less refined designs. I've researched a number of such creatures in Eerian Studies. Regardless, it is a privilege to witness.

What eventually wriggles free of the tunnel is an enormous boulder of flesh, sewn with straining mouths and flanked by tangled limbs.

My eyes begin to sting as I take in the creature. The motion of pressing tears from my eyes causes Alastair to glance at me in alarm.

'What's the matter?'

'Nothing, I— It's just so beautiful.'

'*Beautiful?*'

Remembering who I'm talking to, I scoff. 'I wouldn't expect a spirer to appreciate Our Lady's genius. This privilege is wasted on you.' After a beat more of Alastair's baffled stare, I say, 'It should be a crime to ruin such a masterpiece. Like spoiling a famous painting.'

He surprises me by saying, 'We needn't kill it,' in a leaden voice. 'Not if it concedes defeat. Our Sweet Lord teaches mercy, after all. Look at all the eerians he left alive.'

Even though I suggested it, this defies logic. If you defeat someone, you must destroy them. Leave them alive and sooner or later they'll have their revenge. But the thought of killing a beast that Our Lady fashioned with her own hands… If I don't have to do it, I shouldn't.

Every limb is an arm. While the arms disagree on how many elbows is too many, each one ends in a hand. It flattens its palms on the stone and hoists its body off the ground like a great, lumbering spider – a toddler's attempt to draw a spider, that is: lopsided, every leg a different length and thickness. The effort of lifting its body makes them all tremble like a stray hound doing its business.

'Yes, my friends! Your eyes do not deceive you! Something special for this year's only accord. One of the most hideous, revolting creatures ever twisted into shape: a pulp-flesh ancestor!'

That's when its fungal odour hits me, a nauseating miasma of curdled milk, festering wounds, and skin folds that have gone months without soap. If the arena walls had any paint on them, its stench would peel it off.

Alastair gags a little, and I can't blame him – even a maggot would gag at this. Then he says, 'Remember what I said?' in a choked voice.

'Fools rush in,' I say, although I'm dying for a better look.

'And our strategy?'

I rap my knuckles against the metal plate hidden beneath my scaling, reassuring him I've not forgotten. Since I failed to achieve Acclaim before our stage, as we both knew I would, Alastair will lead offence. My task will be subterfuge, finding a sweet-but-discreet spot for the atropher.

Atrophers are brands containing *ezorhox*, the glyph of atrophy – as essential to a graver as an eraser is to an artist. You can't always get it right first time, and even if you do, effigies lose function through time and damage. Without atrophers, we'd have to dismantle each unwanted effigy by hand, at least until its components could fit inside a cremator. Atrophers take care of that for us, their use so regular that *ezorbox* demands ready-made brands. Heat them, toss them on the effigy, leave them to work. Effigies and eerians work on similar principles, so the same rules should apply.

I squint at the approaching creature, trying to read the glyphs inscribed on its flesh. I need to find the best place for the atropher, but the ancestor's too far away to read its epitaph.

'I need a closer look,' I say.

As much as I detest everything about the spiring conspectus, I have to admit that this is sickening in the best way. Had I gone into the graving conspectus as planned, I might've gone my entire life without seeing a pulp-flesh ancestor up close.

I have to savour every moment of this.

It shrieks – the shriek of fifty people at once – and I feel the collective wince of the crowd. Its cry contains men's voices, women's voices, young and old, furious and joyful and frightened. Truly exquisite.

Every lurching thump of the ancestor's limbs judders up through my boots. I hope it'll scuttle towards me, but it seizes the nearest poles instead, testing them against its weight. It struggles to shimmy up them, and not just because of gravity. Its hands have trouble gripping the ice-slippery metal.

Fifty mouths groan with the effort, sinews flexing grotesquely in its arms. Their strange choreography is mesmerizing.

Once the ancestor raises its flabby bulk over the poles, it begins the awkward task of manoeuvring across them. It has plenty of mouths, yet only one pair of eyes that I can see: a baby's face that marks the creature's axis as it lurches and reels towards us.

It gathers momentum, poles flexing beneath its weight as it bulls off them. Its shadow falls across me, so big it blocks out everything but *it*.

I run my gaze over its skin, hunting for conjunctions.

In eerians, glyphic epitaphs behave almost like a nervous system. Humans have brains at the centre of theirs, transmitting signals around the body. Eerians' brains, so to speak, are external; they're powered by the Eternal Spite. Just as the best way to stop a human's functions is to sever their neck, severing its connection to the Spite is the best way to fell an eerian. Spirers accomplish this through Acclaim, which ravages glyphs and the pulp-flesh they're bound to like nothing else. An atropher does something similar, but it's limited and less spectacular. By placing the atropher on a key glyph – a conjunction – that connects the eerian to the Spite, I can make up for my lack of Acclaim, supporting Alastair in a stage meant to challenge two.

Unfortunately, complex as they are, glyphs are difficult enough to read on a page. Now, inscribed on the flesh of a lumbering creature in faint and shivering glyph-light, it's a real struggle.

What I can tell straight away is that the ancestor's epitaph makes the witherbrute's look like a toddler's shape-matching puzzle. I knew that would be the case; the more powerful the creature, the more sophisticated the epitaph needed to craft it. But actually *seeing* the intricacy, almost comically elaborate in the way of Dunchester's décor—

'Kilchoir!' Alastair yells from a safe distance away. 'That's too close!'

I scramble away moments before the ancestor hurls itself down, slamming the ground behind me. The impact pelts my back with snow. A moment later, it would've crushed me.

Edusa's voice rings out across the arena.

'Almost!' he booms, half laughing. 'Luckily for our little Prey hopeful, she's inherited the reflexes of Our All-Glorious Lord!'

While I back away, putting more space between myself and the ancestor, several blobby lips moan in pain. I still don't know quite what I'm seeing, but the horror of it sets my heart racing with excitement.

The ancestor lifts itself up, the mouths on its underside spitting slush. A confusion of hands reach for me, fingers unfurling like pudgy petals – too many to fend off all at once.

At its fulcrum, the chubby-cheeked baby gives a beastly smile.

'Get the traitor!' it squeals, turning my blood cold as its hands draw near. 'Her half-flesh offends Our Lady!'

'Her mother is a treasonous harlot!'

'Abomination! Gut her!'

Ah, so that's why it wants me. I should've known. If there's anything eerians despise more than scions, it's defectors to the scions' camp. Our Lady ensured that Oldrac and his brood would never use her craft against her through pulp's rejection of their flesh. As any union between her people and his is a betrayal, a Prey holding a spire *would* be an abomination in eerian eyes.

So would a graver's descendent-turned-scion. Luckily for Alastair, his faults are trickier to detect. His Moppeton heritage has recoiled, chased off by Oldrac's features, whereas my Preyness still shows.

A slash of Alastair's Acclaimed spire sends the arena's shadows into twitching hysterics. He slashes again, and again, a barrage of blinding cuts that drench him in arterial spray. The ancestor's reaching hands come to a stop in front of my face, quivering.

I move as fast as I can without taking my eyes off it – no mean feat with all these damn poles in the way. What's more, they seem to pull at Alastair's Acclaim; lightning arcs from his spire to the nearest poles. *Are they weakening his attacks?*

Still, Alastair chops every limb that crosses his lightning-tressed blade. They fall at the elbows, wrists, and knuckles, leaving only the stubs wiggling. Arms lash at him blindly; the ancestor's little eyes remain fixed on me, smiling despite all the crimson staining the snow. Such a great beast has plenty to lose, and unlike the witherbrute it doesn't seem a bit cowed by Acclaim. It shambles back up the poles, where Alastair's spire fails to reach, and manoeuvres itself towards me again.

It hardly seems fair that *I* should be the one to pay for Mother's crimes against Our Lady. But then, this could work in our favour...

'Have you found anything?' Alastair yells.

'I can't get close enough to read the glyphs,' I yell back. 'I'm going to bait it down. When it's grounded, use the opportunity to strike!'

After a moment's consideration, he yells back, 'A decent plan!'

It's so pathetic I don't even want to say it, but this tiny hit of praise gives me a rush.

The ancestor thrashes its way towards me with the strength to warp every pole it shoves out of its way. I keep my eyes on it, moving back, but not as fast as I could. My pulse is wild as the creature prepares to catapult itself at me.

I pause, letting it think it has me while I search its countless lumps for conjunctions. If the creature wasn't so girthy, there wouldn't be so much ground to cover. As it lets go of the poles, I dart aside.

It lands on the ground beside me with an almighty thud. Alastair wastes no time and rains down dazzling blows on its back, but I don't quite clear it. Fingernails rake at me, making a fist of my spiring jacket.

I twist and swing for the offending arm. My un-Acclaimed blade does absolutely nothing, bouncing off the ancestor's skin as if it hasn't a sharp edge. The sight drops my stomach. I knew my spire would be less effective, but I didn't think it'd be *useless*.

With no other options that I can see, I frantically slip out of my jacket. The ancestor can have it. I've plenty just like it in my bag, and my scaling for modesty.

Alastair hacking away, blunted limbs flying every which way, is a sight to see. Dismembered hands litter the ground, slick with blood and twitching like chopped eels. I'd say I was jealous, but then I'd have to hit myself. He must be starting to do real damage, because a cacophony of foul language leaves the ancestor's mouths.

An even longer arm lashes out and gets lucky, hooking gnarled fingers on my scaling's collar. I bring up my spire to sever it, but a second many-jointed arm follows the first. The crowd gasps as it grabs my other hand by the wrist, then roars as a third plucks my spire from me.

'Tut-tut!' Edusa calls. 'Our Prey hopeful has allowed herself to be disarmed!'

While four of the ancestor's arms go to work on my spire, applying muscle enough to warp it, I struggle to get free. It isn't working. I dig my heels in as the ancestor drags me towards its many shorter arms, hands upon hands grabbing for me. When they reach me, they will curl my ribs inwards until they snap and pierce my lungs, forcing haemorrhaged blood up and out, thickening my screams to a gurgle. A magnificent death, but one I'm not nearly ready for yet.

Raw panic takes me as the ancestor tosses my spire aside, disfigured beyond even pretend use. For the first time, all its voices reach a consensus, chanting, '*Open the traitor's belly!*' in unison.

Alastair comes sprinting through the snow as fast as Oldrac's flesh allows.

With one hard, downward slice, he halves the arm holding mine, blinding me in the process, then stabs the second. The first arm retreats, but the second retaliates, latching onto Alastair's forearm and squeezing.

There's an audible, visceral crunch. The whites of Alastair's eyes gleam through the holes in his mask. He manages to shear off the attacking limb at the elbow – which is lucky, because provost knows I've got no defence to offer – but the damage is done.

All remaining limbs make a temporary retreat, but only so they can drag its soft, vulnerable parts off the ground again. They leave both of us uncrushed but trembling, eyes levelled on the blundering mass of anatomy as we stagger out of range.

'My scaling,' I say, breathless and reeling. It's ripped, the skin shredded beneath. Then, seeing Alastair's spire wilt in his grip, 'Your *arm*.'

'Broken,' he says, matter-of-fact.

'But you're the damage-dealer! Even if I could use Acclaim, I don't—'

'I can spire one-handed.'

When he takes the spire with his other hand, I can honestly say that I've never felt so useless in my entire life. Alastair's the only one of us that has Oldrac's Acclaim, and now a weapon. He's going to fight the ancestor with a broken arm while I... what? Try to stay out of his way?

Right now, I *am* his passenger. What am I contributing to this stage except failures?

'What should I...'

I trail off at the look in Alastair's eyes. It's all Mother's and Limbridge's disappointments concentrated into one, along with exhaustion, pain, and fear. If he's afraid, I should be terrified. The cost of Oldrac's Acclaim is plain; tributaries of raised, pinkish-white flesh creep up from his collar. He's scarring – a sign of his body's ability to heal edging towards its limit.

Even with two working arms, he couldn't do this alone. This eerian was meant to challenge *both* of us, meaning whoever designed this stage thought it impossible for a solo spirer.

We're going to lose this, and it'll be my fault.

'Good grief!' says Edusa, massaging the wound with salt. 'With only one spire left to *spire* with, we could be saying goodbye to our cross-province accord in this very first stage. A pity!'

Alastair doesn't have time to reassure or even direct me. He has to meet the ancestor, which has shimmied up onto the poles to come for us again. Anyone can see he's flagging, his form wrecked by fatigue.

It could be my imagination, but I hear the crowd mocking me. Not even in Withersham's training hall was I so humiliated before so many people. It's the scathing disdain of Withersham's cohort times a hundred, Stripthicket and all the rest jeering from the sidelines as they await my next failure. If this gets mentioned in the papers, my humiliation will be indelible.

I watch Alastair whacking at the ancestor's remaining limbs and know I must do *something*. Otherwise, I'll never meet Mortritis and all these Glims will leave the arena thinking Preys are soft. I simply can't have it.

But I've searched every inch of the ancestor's flesh I can see without finding a single conjunction.

Which begs the question: what of every inch I *can't* see? What about its crown? The ancestor could have more reasons to lumber on top of the poles. It's a stab in the dark, but one guided by logic. I need to ground it permanently.

I follow the fight, staring the ancestor down, thinking furiously, watching how it moves. Even when it first came out, it was clumsy. Now, it's downright blunderous. With fewer limbs supporting its great weight, even changing direction is a task.

Yes. The ancestor could have more reasons to use the poles – and the stage designer could have more reasons to give them to us.

The moment an idea hatches, I move in, stealing underneath the creature. With only two eyes to see by, its vision's limited to Alastair and his flashy Acclaimed spire – the only discernible threat. When its shadow falls across me, I reach up, grazing the fingertips dangling from its underbelly. They clasp me on instinct, and I, them.

I fix my other hand to its sinewy forearm, brace my heels on the edge of a cracked stone slab, and heave backwards with every scrap of Oldracian strength I inherited. It feels like my shoulders pop from their sockets with the strain.

All this barely has an effect, but the ancestor jolts with the shock of being yanked in the wrong direction. The ice on the poles and gravity do most of the work for me. The sudden, unwanted leverage forces it to throw more hands out to stabilize itself. Those hands slip.

If I don't get out from underneath it, it'll crush me. It lets go of me in a frantic bid to save its balance, to no avail. It rolls sideways, squealing, and lands directly onto a pole.

The crowd releases a collective vocal grimace as the pole pierces the middle of the ancestor's soft, fleshy sac of a body, impaling it. A panting Alastair watches from the other side as it slides to the ground, leaving the pole bloody and even more slippery than before. Trembling hands attempt to pull *and* push itself up, but I don't fancy its chances.

'At last, a bit of initiative from our Prey hopeful!' Edusa bellows. 'That's what we like to see!'

The crowd roars back at him.

The ancestor's too huge for its crown to be clearly visible, but as an arm lifts, the skin on its shoulder undulates and there it is: a conjunction. It burns no brighter than the rest of the epitaph, but I recognize its dense knot of strokes all the same.

I yell at Alastair, 'Strike now! Get to its shoulder!'

With our opponent freshly pinned, confidence returns to Alastair's stance. He lifts his spire, not with desperation but conviction, and begins turning limbs to stubs. He must clear a path to the conjunction.

I get as close to the frantic, sweating creature as I dare. Moving with Oldracian speed, I whip the atropher from my scaling's collar to fling at my target. My aim's true enough, and as soon as it leaves my hand, I point, as if flagging something to Alastair. With any luck, this little manoeuvre will have been too quick and far away for the crowd to analyse.

As Alastair gores the clump of bodies at their centre, paying special attention to the topmost flesh, Oldrac's Acclaim crackles. Its heat triggers the atropher, scorching *ezorhox* into the ancestor's skin. A rotting, burning-flesh smell rises all around. The pole that had once kept its vitals out of range now acts as a conductor for the lightning, cooking the poor skewered creature from the inside out.

Several screams leave the ancestor's many mouths as Alastair carves a wodge of flesh from its shoulder, yelling, 'Yield, damn you! Yield!' like a blood-crazed fiend – justice for his broken arm. The ancestor's own limbs start to go dead, glyphs shrivelling on its skin around the atropher.

One of its voices wails, 'A nurse! Get me a nurse!'

It's not dying, I don't think, but it *is* hurt – bruised and punctured and de-limbed, weeping blood.

'You'll pay for that, you little shit!'

'No, please! Don't hurt me!'

'Waste them! What are you waiting for?'

The baby's face darkens like it wants revenge, but with so many voices screaming different things, it's hard to know what it'll do.

'No more,' seethes the baby's voice. 'We yield.'

A yearning shudder takes my body. Then I shut my eyes tight as I try to commit every part of it to memory. As long as I live, I may never meet another ancestor. Today is a special day.

When I open them, Alastair's going at it again.

'Leave it, Alastair,' I snap. His eyes glower at me. 'It's finished. Oldrac teaches mercy, remember?'

With no small amount of reluctance, Alastair backs off. Then he stabs the creature three more times, and backs off for good. I know he's done when the Acclaim fizzles out.

I glare at him. 'Was that really necessary?'

'You have a tender heart, Kilchoir. The world will be a better place when all these horrors are gone.'

The ancestor's remaining hands scoop up the blob Alastair sliced out, cradling it to its body. It bears half a dead conjunction; the atropher glows white-hot on the ground where it had been. It's evidence, but it'll burn our hands off if we pick it up.

In a move almost too fast to catch, Alastair kicks the atropher into a crack between the stones. If not for the fact that it's vanished, I couldn't guarantee it happened. We might actually get away with this.

Alastair unfastens his mask, and I do the same, gasping for breath but not getting enough as the crowd's roar rises around us. Acclaim scars skirt along his jaw, pink and splitting like veins. His face is tense with pain, but exultant.

There was no crowd to watch us in Withersham. I would have hated that, but here I don't mind it so much. It feels like getting an A+ on your last essay. Cheers, whistles, and of course applause. Edusa wouldn't be in this game if there wasn't applause.

'Well, well! Balver – what did we think of that? Do they pass or fail?'

Edusa cups a hand to his ear, listening for the crowd's input as if he values any judgement but his own. Downed gods, I cannot stand him. When I look at Alastair, his face flushed and the bones in his forearm fractured, he's staring hard at Edusa, vicious with anticipation.

If it weren't already obvious from Tieran's broad smile, the gesture Edusa makes tells us – tells everyone – the verdict.

12

THE DEALS PREY
W⊕MEN MAKE

To counterbalance my time in the arena, I spend the next day practising glyphs. I would have started yesterday, but as I feared, my body needed time to mend. If spiring was all I had to worry about, these four rest days before our next stage would feel generous. Unfortunately, I'll have to push myself. Of course, it would only worsen if we got Edusa's patronage and he began training us. I still wonder if it's even feasible to grave and spire, but I won't know until I try.

When I think back on yesterday's stage, my gut roils. My lacklustre performance put Alastair in the infirmary, but the memory of the ancestor is a soothing balm. I can only hope it's in my nightmares again tonight.

The scent emanating from my notebook is another comfort – bitter, pungent, and metallic. The Prelate's Archivist stays in its fancy pen roll. I've been dying to test it out, but every time I think about it,

I remember what Limbridge told me at the station: *Give up on graving.* I couldn't deny the gift, but I can't bring myself to use it.

So, just as she feared, I am walking St Penderghast's with ink stains up and down me. By the time I finish, there are dark green fingerprints all over the page. I've been working my way through a cartridge of Preyburn Fen-Kelp, a dark, greasy green that makes it seem as though I've developed some exotic rash. I don't care how I look, so long as I retain my graving ability.

On the way to the common room for dinner, I see a familiar figure coming towards me down the hallway. A coltish woman in her twenties with an exaggerated collar, sculpted shoulder lines, and fully shaven head. She stops, so I stop too.

'I must congratulate you on winning your first stage,' she says in her silvery voice.

'Oh. Thank you, Your Learnedness.'

'Credencia,' she corrects, surprising me. I didn't expect to reach first-name terms with an abettor. 'Forsaking Acclaim to create drama – rather daring.'

I fight to keep my face straight, just like the last time I lied to her. I swore I'd use Acclaim in my first stage, and now that I haven't… She knows, doesn't she? She knew all along, but now it's proven. I'm about to get—

'We look forward to seeing more from you, Laurentius and I,' she says, inclining her head. After a moment's shock, I awkwardly do the same, and she strikes off again. I thought for sure she was going to expose me, have me escorted off the premises for deceiving her, or worse… but I'm still here, meaning she really did stop to congratulate me. To give me her name and, I assume, her abetting partner's.

When I enter the common room, the admissions pupils skilled or lucky enough to make it through their first stages sit clustered around tables. Tieran predicted more than half of the starting number would be cut at the first stage, so I shouldn't be surprised to find the place so sparsely populated.

It's hard to believe I made it through when more than twenty-five others – highbred scions with rare Oldracian advantages like Tieran – didn't. I can't help but feel more than a little smug about it. They've all done a fantastic job of pretending I don't exist. I'm an oddity, all the odder for still being here, and I suppose they don't know how to take me. That's fine. I'm used to silence and averted eyes.

Alastair's back from the infirmary, nursing his bad arm in a sling. He sits alone at his table, far enough from the carved marble fireplace that he's not being roasted alive. The delicate leading of the arched windows casts swirling foliage motifs across his table. I don't go over straight away.

His dinner is on the table in front of him and I watch as he struggles to cut a flank steak one-handed with the edge of his gilded fork. It's not as entertaining as it should be. I thought I'd see him mingling with the other scions, reacquainting himself with Glim society, but no. Every time I've seen him he's been alone, and vice versa.

As if sensing my gaze on him, he stops suddenly, lifting his to meet mine. I go over, heat from the fireplace lighting up my left side as I set my tray on the table. When I gesture for the fork, he first glances at the oily green stains on my hands, then gives it to me by the handle. I take up the steak knife and start cutting it into pieces.

'How's your arm?'

'Fractured, but everything's where it should be. It'll be set by morning.'

That's not his only injury. Up close, the scarring from Oldrac's Acclaim is still visible. His shirt is open at the base of his neck, exposing the pale pink branches that scale his throat like ivy scales a trellis. He has a lovely throat.

Alastair notices me staring. I flick my gaze back to the steak a second too late and give myself a mental slap. I mean, perving on Alastair? What's *wrong* with me? I can't still be concussed.

'Thank the provost we've a rest day,' I say, partly to distract him.

His gaze weighs heavy on me. 'How are you?'

'I can't stop thinking about the ancestor,' I admit, a smile tugging at the corner of my mouth. 'The way the stone shuddered beneath me when it hit the ground. The gut-churning stench of its blood. The many-voiced screams…' As miserable as my situation is, I'm downright giddy over the chance to see more eerians. I could tolerate Edusa, the spiring crowd, all of Glimwick for that very privilege.

Alastair stares at me for a long time. Then he says, 'You are a worry, Kilchoir.'

I shrug.

'And how are you physically?'

'Not a scratch. I ran around like a dizzy hare while you did all the hacking.'

I set the knife down, putting the fork back in his good hand. I start on my own dinner before it cools, the same delicious helping of steak with apple sauce, caramelized potatoes, and greens I can't name. If we grow them back home, Withersham couldn't afford them.

I'm going back for dessert. They have warm, doughy sugar cookies and hot chocolate thick enough to stand a spoon in.

'An accord isn't about who does all the hacking,' Alastair says. 'How do you think it would have gone for me had you not been there?'

'It's a moot point. Alone, they would've given you a less dangerous eerian, like they did the others.'

For a moment, there's no sound but the pop and crackle of the fireplace. Then he says, 'I never thought I'd say this, but self-deprecation doesn't suit you. I won't pretend you performed *well*, but you did pull through. In the end.'

It's shameful, but this verbal pat on the head makes me all warm inside.

'But,' I say, 'the eerians will only get tougher. Do you really believe we can get through the next two stages when only one of us has Acclaim? We may not even have to worry about it if Withersham doesn't send out a spire before our next stage.'

'Do you have any idea how much your admission is worth to that school?' Alastair asks. 'Withersham will get a replacement to you if the headmistress has to deliver it by hand.' He pauses to smear a napkin across his mouth. 'As for Acclaim, you *can* achieve it.'

'So you keep saying.'

'And so you keep evading. The abettors wouldn't have brought you here if they didn't know it was possible.'

'What are you talking about?'

'Put two and two together, I beg you. They're *abettors*.'

'You think they've foreseen it?'

'Beyond a doubt. You obviously hadn't achieved Acclaim back at Withersham. Why else would you be here, unless they decided to bet on your potential?'

Hm. I suppose that *could* make sense.

'Even if that's true,' I say slowly, 'who's to say their bet will pay off? What if they've overestimated me?'

'I did say about the self-deprecation.'

'So you did,' I mutter.

Though he continues to eat, Alastair's knee brushes my thigh under the table. We never usually touch each other unless it's during a fight. I squirm and glance at the other admissions pupils.

In Withersham, the sight of Alastair and me in close conference like this would be enough to power the rumour mill for months. Each week, it'd churn out ever more lecherous and bizarre rumours about what the two of us *really* got up to in and around our spiring lessons.

Everyone delighted in them. Even the preceptors joined in the fun, which I found deeply pathetic. But I could always argue my case with total confidence. As far as evidence went, they had nothing but obfuscation and hearsay.

But this? This counts as evidence.

We're miles away from Withersham now. Nobody in this room, this building, the entirety of this college, would ever deign to step foot in Preyburn if they could help it. It's difficult to explain why I find myself shifting away from him.

Mercifully, Alastair chooses not to react. Perhaps he didn't even notice.

'I spoke with my aunt earlier today,' he says.

My ears prick up immediately. 'You did?'

'I did. She's invited us to her office tomorrow evening.'

'No,' I say in disbelief. 'Has she really? What time?'

'Last bell.'

'Tripped gods.' *I'll have to make myself presentable.* Seized by a joy so powerful, I don't know what to do with it, I say, 'This is stellar, Alastair. Thank you.'

He watches me carefully. 'You really are smitten with her, aren't you?' His knee nudges my thigh again, radiating heat. The pressure feels deliberate. 'This woman you've never laid eyes on before.'

'I don't need to lay eyes on her to know she's a genius. Without her effigies, tens of thousands of our countrymen would've been lost to the war. Surely you know that?'

'Yes, but I also know *her*. Don't misunderstand me, I would never discredit the work she's done for the Commonwealth...'

'But?'

'There are people – including the provost – who believe that if not for Mortritis's effigies, we might have been able to negotiate with the Zsietian Ascendancy.'

I snort. 'Negotiate? What sort of libertine nonsense is this?'

'Think about it. The Ascendancy send men onto the battlefield, and we send gravers. We don't just slaughter them. We desecrate their dead with foul sorcery, reshape them into nightmarish monsters they can't even comprehend. The Commonwealth becomes a faceless, inhuman evil against the laws of morality and nature.'

Still not sure what to do about the knee. Really, there's plenty of space under this table for both our legs, if only Alastair wouldn't take up so much of it with his arrogant lounging! If I were any less engaged in our conversation, I'd say exactly this, but as it is, I manage to extract myself by pushing my chair back – the diplomatic route.

'Believing we were human didn't stop them from invading in the first place,' I say. 'Why does it matter what they think we are? Anyway, it's not like Mortritis's effigies were the first.'

'No, but I'm sure we can agree they are more monstrous and far deadlier than the kind that came before her. More like eerians.'

'In other words, more effective.'

'Too effective. Too many dead, too quickly and too hideously. Now, the Ascendancy and its allies will always hate and fear us. They will always seek to destroy us, not to even the score but because we are the villains. Because of her actions, the Commonwealth is alienated from the rest of the world and will never have peace.'

'What are you basing that on? Everyone knows the Ascendancy's running out of resources. I'd say peace is well under way.'

'You're talking about beating the Ascendancy into submission. I'm talking about peace.'

'I didn't take you for a pacifist,' I say, revolted. In Preyburn, there are few dirtier words. 'Why would you want peace with the greedy rogues who started all this? If they didn't want war, they should've left us alone.'

'It's not about pacifism. It's about oneness.'

'Oh, save me. Not your religious piffle again.'

'Imagine if Our Lord and Our Lady came to the Ascendancy instead of Glimwick and Preyburn. Imagine if *we* were the ones hearing tales of unnatural, dangerous sorcery. Don't you think we would have tried to stop it? Besides, the people who started all this are long dead. Now, it's their heirs who pay.'

'What's your solution then? Withdraw our effigies from battle, send our countrymen to get slaughtered instead? Or don't you want your country protected? Maybe we should let the Zsietians invade?'

'I'm not saying I have the solution. I'm saying different beliefs about the war exist outside of Preyburn, that's all.'

'These are pointless hypotheticals, Faulton. You'd soon change your tune if the Council decided it was the scions' turn to fight. An army of Faultons trained for war would tear straight through the Ascendancy's soldiers. Of course, no scion will ever see battle because you're too rich and important to be pushed into it.'

'You're right. Instead, the Council and the Choir pushed *you* into it, a bankrupt country desperate enough to accept Glim strength for war service.' Eyes that rarely betray emotion now centre on mine with far too much feeling, the blush high in his cheeks. 'What they did was beneath contempt, and look what it's done to you all.'

'Don't you dare pity Preyburn,' I snap.

'I can't help it. You're all indoctrinated and beggared—'

Before Alastair can get any farther with that thought, both our heads are turned by the shadow creeping across our table. I recognize the boy standing over us from the games hall, one of the potentials Edusa pointed out during his speech, copper-haired, athletic, and blandly handsome in the way of other people here. Alastair's lucky to have his bottomless-pit eyes or I'd never be able to tell him apart. There is the difference in our spiring garbs, of course – this one wears lavender and pitch black to accent the whites.

'Sorry to interrupt,' the stranger says, looking as if he doesn't know the meaning of the words. 'I thought I'd congratulate you on a magnificent first stage.'

I'm not sure what to say to this, and my blood is still simmering from our debate. Fortunately, Alastair steps in with a simple 'Thank you.'

The other boy nods. 'Ransley Liverich,' he says, as if either one of us asked. 'You've been all the periodicals can talk about, the exiled Faulton paired up with a handshake baby.'

'Beg pardon?' I ask.

'I'm just saying, it's unusual. But I mean, good for you – good for your mama! They say Prey women have iron in their souls. You'd have to, sacrificing health and dignity to get halfway out of poverty...'

'My mother hasn't sacrificed her dignity, you venomous whelk.'

Ransley's lips twist into something between sneer and smirk. 'No, I suppose not. More likely there was nothing to sacrifice in the first place.'

As I grip the table edge, ready to push up from it, Alastair stamps the hand of his healthy arm on my thigh. The weight of it is so complete, my leg cannot even think of lifting from its position.

'If your intention is to rile us,' he rumbles, 'I'd give some thought to the consequences.'

Ransley scoffs loudly. 'If your Prey hound's fool enough to lose her temper over a bit of game talk, the consequences will be yours.'

The muscles in my leg flex. Alastair's fingers respond, biting deep into the muscle, though he keeps his stoic gaze on Ransley. His grip could be warning me not to rise to Ransley's baiting, or simply taking out his frustrations on me. The pain doesn't curb my anger, but it does redirect some of it towards Alastair, confusing who I want to cuff first.

'You might've forgotten what *Liverich* means down in the nowhere of Preyburn,' Ransley goes on, 'but trust me when I say not one person in Glimwick has.'

'Your game talk bores me,' Alastair says, at the same time as I say, 'Sod off, you absolute homunculus.'

Ransley's face quirks as if I've said something strange, but quickly defaults to looking impressed with himself. With one final, gloating look at Alastair, he turns on his well-bred heel.

I grab Alastair's wrist in warning, and feel his pulse against my fingertips. I'd never have guessed how quick it's beating just from looking at him – in fact, he doesn't look like he even *has* a pulse. He doesn't let go until Ransley's out of drink-chucking distance. My leg tingles as the blood rushes back in to fill the five hollows left by his fingers.

'Yuck,' I say. 'What did he call me? A handshake baby?'

'Ignore him.'

'Yes, but what does it mean?'

Alastair lowers his voice. 'He's referring to the... *deals* Prey women make.'

'What deals?'

Alastair gives me a look, as if my playing dumb is tedious. 'I didn't walk around Burymeadow with a blindfold over my eyes and the fen in both ears. The deals to make sure their child is a graver.'

I stare hard at him, cogs rattling in my brain as I rub the memory of his grip from my aching leg.

He seems to misinterpret my silence for anger, because he continues, 'It's not like I don't understand. It's logical, far more reliable than physicks alone will ever be.'

'What's logical, Faulton? I don't follow.'

'Flaypenny's deals. She puts Prey women in touch with scions. For a sum, they...' He breaks off with a sigh. 'Do I really need to say it?'

I think back to the couple leaving Flaypenny in the chapel. The envelope she slipped inside her robes. Then I realize what he's hinting at – Prey women bedding scions to conceive gravers – and my heart slams down into my stomach, instantly spoiling my appetite.

I've heard that Oldracian flesh helps laypeople to conceive, a feat that becomes more difficult with pulp. Without it, you can't possibly birth a graver, yet its toxicity brings complications. Naturally, people would use scions to overcome this issue, and naturally, people like Flaypenny would monetize it.

Not a love affair. A transaction.

But of course. What happened in my childhood to make me believe my mother would have stumbled into an adulterous fling? My mother never stumbles into anything. She's a woman of grim and uncompromising logic, and she's never cared about love. If she thought she'd fetch a decent price, Mother would've sold her own mother. Moving up in life is the only thing that drives her. Besides, where would she even have met a scion in Preyburn if not for Flaypenny's little side business?

'I'm sorry,' Alastair says. His unabashed sympathy makes me feel sick. 'I honestly thought you knew.'

If I'd done any digging at all, I would have. I never spoke about it to anyone. I couldn't, not without exposing my mother – or so I thought. But then there was Limbridge. She must've known what Flaypenny was up to, and how I came to be.

But this means Mother knew Oldracian traits were a possibility. By her sickness, she definitely took pulp for a time. Perhaps she tried both to better her chances. But because my abilities didn't show up 'til recently and I hid them from her, she didn't learn the truth.

'I mean,' Alastair says, perplexed, 'how did you *think* your mama—'

I get to my feet before he can finish, far too embarrassed to admit what I'd thought.

'I'll see you tomorrow morning for training,' I blurt, and I'm out of the common room before he can protest.

13

A PERSONAL INTEREST

The next evening, I stand with Alastair in the main building's vestibule, bracing myself to go outside. While he turns up the collar on his worsted-wool coat, I rearrange a careworn Withersham scarf to cover every inch of neck. St Penderghast's abundance of grand, lit fireplaces do an excellent job of generating heat, but on the other side of that door boreal temperatures await.

'They have trains from the Hinge to Crippleditch daily,' I say, 'in case you were wondering.'

'How wonderful,' Alastair says in his usual monotone. 'Can I look forward to regular updates on the train schedules going forwards? You've taken up spotting as a hobby, I suppose.'

'If you fail to hold up your end of the bargain, good word and all, rest assured I will be *on one*.'

Alastair leans on the door with his good shoulder. His other sleeve hangs loose, the arm still tucked against his chest. A bitter chill sweeps in through the rift, making my whole body cringe. I follow him out into the snow, our footsteps crunching. The sky is smouldering orange in one direction and navy in the other. These gardens are idyllic, but the dry, cold air makes my eyes water and appreciation difficult.

On the map, Dunchester is shaped like an upside-down teardrop, its gluttonous belly swelling over the centre of the grounds. Being that the good lady St Penderghast was a spirer – that is to say, the founder of the Commonwealth Cup – the spiring campus is the largest, oldest and most storied of the two. Thumbarrow occupies a squashed oblong in the north-eastern corner.

We cut a path through spiralling topiary, frozen fountains, and snarling eerians in statue form. All are buried by a white of such eye-gouging intensity that even at dusk Alastair dons shaded eyeglasses to go outside. They look spectacularly stupid, especially in Glimwick.

Up ahead, the Thumbarrow campus presents a regiment of grey-stoned buildings, their design unforgiving and severe. It's named for Rook Thumbarrow, inventor of graphia and celebrated glyph scribe, and is beset by hundreds upon hundreds of memorials. Headstones are posted with no obvious strategy around every dormitory, training field, and lecture theatre, though few are actually buried here. If I swept the snow away, I'd see names listed in tight, stunted inscriptions, people who donated their corpses to graving.

A thrill goes through me as we near the sombre majesty of Thumbarrow's main building. I picture glories of gravers stalking its halls, debating theory with eloquence and verve, and myself among them.

We shove through the main doors. My eyes take a moment to adjust to the light as Alastair removes his eyeglasses, folding them into a pocket. He leads me down the succession of tastefully decorated hallways that will bring us to Mortritis's office.

'Don't let her pressure you into a card game,' he says, 'or drink of any kind. A crippling hangover won't improve your spiring.'

'Is Mortritis a drinker?'

'She's a graver who spent a great deal of time in Preyburn.'

'Must you go on with these trite stereotypes?'

'Are you forgetting that I lived in Preyburn? It may be a stereotype, but it didn't come from nothing.'

'Yes, well, she can't be worse than Limbridge.'

'My aunt makes Limbridge look like a first year. She'll drink men thrice her bulk into a stupor without even a flicker of colic. Once you start, she won't let up until you're either comatose or bent over a toilet.'

'What a charming image,' I say, helpless to stop my grin. 'You speak from experience?'

Alastair pointedly doesn't answer as he stops outside one of many grand darkwood doors. My breath catches as he raps his gloved knuckles against it. A female voice calls from within, and my heart sings. *I'm hearing Mortritis's voice for the first time.* Alastair, with no such reverence, forges ahead into her office.

Before I follow him in, I take a moment to check my nose isn't running and smooth down my hair. With any luck, I enter looking halfway presentable.

At the room's farthest edge, Mortritis rises from behind a stately desk. Even from this distance, I know the illustrations haven't done her justice. In her portraits, she is always depicted as classically beautiful in the way of apocryphal queens, with skin like glass, expressive eyes, and a rich, shapely mouth.

No one can accuse me of blushing. My ears and cheeks were already burning from the cold before I walked in.

'If it isn't my beloved nephew,' she drawls, stoking an envious fire within me.

She closes the gap between the two of them with a grace that would shame even the lithest snowcat. The closer she comes, the taller she becomes – she's got *three heads* on her nephew. She wears a jacket and trousers of superb tailoring in the style of gravers' military uniform. It's an altogether different cut from the kind our troops wear, with finer material and a tasteful swell of bosom on display.

She pulls Alastair into a brief but spine-cracking embrace, succeeding where Tieran failed and forcing a grunt from him. The long nails against his back look marvellous. Each is filed to a point and painted the same colour as her skin to give the appearance of clawed fingers, like Our Lady.

She pulls back to scrutinize Alastair, a devilish glimmer in her eye. 'How should we celebrate? Whisky? I've just opened a new honey scotch that is simply divine.'

What had been at the back of my mind in the hallway makes its way to the front: *Who could say no to this woman?* I'd probably drink an embalming-fluid gimlet with a phalange garnish if she offered it.

'Tea,' Alastair says flatly, reminding me that he is pulseless.

Mortritis grimaces. 'Still a bore, then?' she says, her gaze falling on me. 'Maybe your friend is more fun?'

'Hal,' I say, dry-throated.

'And why not? A nice, straightforward Preyburn girl.' She dashes a sly look at Alastair. 'In that case, we'll each have a stout with a nice thick head of cream.'

Before I can ask where she'd get such a thing, Alastair says, 'We have admissions.'

Mortritis groans. 'Have it your way. You'll have to entertain me with stories of debauchery from farthest Preyburn, then. Sit!'

I sit. We take seats by the fireplace, sinking into armchairs even plusher than the common room's. While Mortritis readies the tea in a dimly lit corner, I'm torn between staring at her and everything around her.

There are no damp stains on the ceiling in *this* office. It's more like a private salon with upholstery of a deep, juicy purple, sensuous plants, and faceted glass that winks from every lacquered counter. Yet, despite obvious glamour, it has a moodiness that soothes in its familiarity.

At the far wall, the Moppeton sigil sits on a pedestal, carved from pulp. The maker went into excruciating detail, particularly around the three gravers' masks. It must be worth a prelate's ransom.

Mortritis brings over a tea set and fudge cake as black as sin. As she serves Alastair, seeing the two of them side by side draws attention to a familial resemblance I hadn't noticed before. Quite disturbing, really.

She brings the tray over to me, leaning close enough that I can inhale her perfume: ripe wild raspberries and luxurious rich chocolate.

'So Hal,' she says, 'how did you two meet?'

'We both schooled at Withersham Hall.'

'Of course you did. In that case, you must have all sorts of sordid anecdotes. I only want to hear the most depraved, and will award extra points every time Alastair begs you to stop. Begin.'

I take the teacup on its saucer and, when she nods to it, the wodge of fudge cake. I try to balance the tiny dessert fork while racking my brains for a cringeworthy story about Alastair.

'Hal's going to disappoint you. She doesn't have any dirt on me.'

'Hush, now,' says Mortritis. 'Hal's trying to think.'

'She didn't even know we were related until the abettors put us in this accord.'

'Ah yes, your accord!' Mortritis bowls her eyes up to the ceiling in such exaggerated fashion, it looks as if she's being possessed. 'Yet another of the provost's sentimental initiatives. She does so *love* to make things difficult.'

Abandoning the tray on the side, Mortritis sets herself up in the chair next to Alastair. No teacup, just a slab of fudge cake so mighty, I wonder where she's going to put it. 'The abettors try to rustle up a few every year to please her, whether it fits the situation or not.' She scrapes as much fudge as the delicate dessert fork can hold into her mouth, and talks through it. 'I suppose you were unlucky.'

'Perhaps,' Alastair says, shooting an inscrutable look my way.

'But a Kilchoir who spires!' Mortritis wears a devious smile. 'However did you manage that?'

My face flushes, remembering what Alastair told me about my mother. I still haven't been able to process it.

'Obscure heritage,' I say, and am rewarded with a winsome cackle. 'But I grew up graving. It was always my dream to...' I trail off at the look Alastair's giving me. 'How have the gravers' admissions been so far?'

Mortritis heaves a sigh. 'My problem is twofold. Talented gravers are in incredibly short supply. Most are taught to the standard of war fodder, which is to say, miserably. And then there are the abettors...' She pauses to take another mouthful of cake. She looks no less gorgeous for the bits of fudge in her perfect white teeth. 'Graving utterly mystifies them. With spirers, they need only recognize a pupil's last name. "Oh, he's a Faulton? In that case, get him in!" But when faced with gravers, how to separate the wheat from the chaff?'

'Can't they be... educated?' I say.

'Oh believe me, I've tried. The reality is, they've neither the time nor incentive to do better.' She pauses to suck fudge from under her talons, at which point my stomach tightens so much I have to look away. 'In other words, my admissions group is rather hit and miss.'

'That's down to the provost, surely? She should push the abettors to do better.'

'She won't care, poppet. She thinks we're overpowered as it is.'

My thoughts cycle back to my meeting with Limbridge in her office before we left. She'd said the provost has *her fill of enemies*, and it sounds like Mortritis might be one of them. That can't be fun for the provost. While Her Sagacity has one of the most influential positions in the Commonwealth, Mortritis is a commanding figure in her own right, especially with graving academics and militarists.

'I do have one promising candidate, who I'm sure would love to meet you. She has a special interest in *obscure heritage*.'

Mortritis slides her suddenly empty plate onto a side table and runs a pink tongue over her teeth. 'Would I be right in thinking you've a personal interest in my admissions group?'

My mouth opens slightly of its own accord. I fire a worried look in Alastair's direction. He glowers, daring me to agree.

'There's no need to play coy,' she says. 'You've had to forgo graving to suit Alastair, and now you hope to audit my conspectus, am I right?'

'Yes,' I say faintly.

Mortritis retrieves a pipe and lights it by match. With her next breath, I know she's smoking something quite a bit stronger than pine tar.

'Well, now it's my turn to disappoint,' she says on the exhale. 'Nobody audits my conspectus.'

I go very still. For a long moment, the only muscle that seems to move is the one thudding behind my ribs. I try to catch Alastair's eye, but he stares doggedly at the carpet. Did he know about this?

Then I say, 'But they *could*.'

Mortritis shakes her head. 'Successful audits are rarer than pulp-moths' teeth. More likely you'll exhaust yourself failing both con-spectuses.' She drops her voice to a stage whisper, as if sharing a juicy secret. 'Terrible for one's self-esteem.'

'It seems unfair to assume,' I say, fighting to keep my voice even, 'that I wouldn't be one of the pupils who succeeds.'

'On the contrary. It'd be unfair to assume you *would*. It's too much pressure to place on a novice.'

'But you haven't seen what I'm capable of,' I protest. 'Your admissions group is hit and miss, but you're happy to dismiss me without trial? You can't possibly gauge my value until you've given me that.'

'Well, I couldn't agree more, poppet... but you're in an accord with my sister's son. If she found out he failed admissions because of my influence? I can't risk it. Maybe when we were quarrelling, but we're enjoying a ceasefire at the moment.'

'The risk will be marginal. *Alastair*.'

I make eyes at him, attempting to transmit the image of me catching the train home from my head into his.

Mortritis turns to him too, shapely brows lifted. 'What do you make of it, beloved nephew?'

He takes his sweet time to answer, perhaps savouring the power he has over me. With a word, he can put down like a sick dog all hopes of studying under Mortritis.

Finally, he says, 'Withersham's preceptors considered Hal to be an exceptionally dedicated pupil. She deserves a trial.'

'Even though Edusa may take it as a sign she's not fully committed to spiring, and cut you both?' Mortritis asks. 'He always prattles on about how spiring is a jealous mistress.'

Alastair goes mute. I can't blame him. I don't know how to counter this either.

Mortritis turns back to me. 'Sorry, poppet. It's not to be.'

I swallow, my throat dry and silence loud in my ears.

'Now please, let's put this business to bed and get on with our evening. Are you absolutely certain I can't offer either of you a proper drink? It is rather rude to make a lady drink alone.'

'Actually,' I say, 'I think I'm ready for one now.'

Alastair shakes his head, his eyes flashing, but I ignore him.

My plan is doomed. I may as well enjoy myself.

14

SUCH WICKED THINGS

A few honey scotches later, I'm slumped in my chair, warm and dopey. It's dulled the sting of Mortritis's rejection a little, which is a mercy.

I can't stop staring at her. She truly is gorgeous. Her eyes glitter like the very firmaments.

'I still can't believe you don't have a tale for me. Not even a crumb of dirt on my nephew?'

I mine the deepest recesses of my memories. It might take some embellishment, but I *must* have a sordid tale that will please her…

The words slip off my loosened tongue before I can stop them.

'Alastair was infatuated with the pastoress.'

He tenses, face darkening with a rush of blood. 'That's a bald-faced lie. I can't believe—'

'Alastair!' Mortritis gasps. 'You demon! How old?'

'Fifty-something.'

Alastair scoffs. 'Forty-two. I know this must be difficult for you to comprehend, but my interest in Flaypenny wasn't sordid.'

'The first time we went to chapel,' I go on, 'he fell to his knees, grabbed both her hands, and put kisses all over them while looking her dead in the eye. I don't think dear old Flaypenny knew quite what to do.'

'Always so eager to put your ignorance on display,' he says. 'In Glimwick, whenever meeting or parting from the pastoress, it is customary to kiss her knuckles.'

'Is it also customary to follow her about all the time? And bring her gifts?'

'Seeking holy counsel, and offering tributes? Yes, it is.'

'What about the poetry you used to write her? Awful, dirty poetry that would even curl the toes of Preyburn's bawdiest lecher?'

'Alastair,' Mortritis says again in mock dismay. Although her head shakes in disbelief, the grin says she's enjoying this little glimpse into Alastair's time at Withersham immensely – however exaggerated it may be.

'Aunt,' he grits out, 'don't encourage her.'

'He had a shrine to her in his room, with a picture of her face – which he painted.'

'Are you certain you want to continue down this road, Kilchoir?' The firelight makes sparks in his dark eyes. 'I remember things from Withersham, too.'

'Finally,' I say, 'the rumours swirling around Alastair and Flaypenny got so bad that they had to stop speaking completely.'

'It was because,' Alastair says, 'the cohort made it plain that I wouldn't be allowed to worship as in Glimwick. Preyburn is a cold, repressed province, full of cold, repressed people for whom affection is strange and intolerable. It is a place devoid of oneness, everyone divided and desperately alone.

'When I first arrived in Withersham,' he continues, 'I knew nobody. Everything was strange. I could barely follow a conversation, and when

I spoke, my accent was ridiculed. The only thing familiar was the Choir. Flaypenny was there for me at a time when I had nobody else.' He flicks a look of violence my way. 'And then she wasn't.'

And doesn't the shame just come flooding in, thick and fast? Because although my first instinct is to say he's twisting the truth to make me look cruel and petty in front of Mortritis, I look back and see it.

Alastair, when he first came to Withersham, was treated like an exotic creature in a travelling carnival. Most of us had never travelled. We watched everything he did, including the preceptors: his fine but peculiar clothes; the looks we weren't initially sure how to feel about; the accent people felt compelled to copy, parroting everything he said. Not everyone wanted to make fun of him; it was almost a unanimous vote that the Glim accent was the sexiest thing ever, and he drew admirers the way honey does ants – but even that would have made him feel like something apart.

I sink even lower in my seat, cheeks prickling worse than they did under the abettors' judgement. Not only do I look like a nasty, vindictive idiot, but I look like a nasty, vindictive idiot in front of Mortritis. *Of course* it would've been difficult for him. It would've been rough for any thirteen-year-old to emigrate by themselves. It's been jarring enough for me, coming to Balver, and I'm five years older than he was.

What's needed in this moment is a sincere apology, both for the misunderstanding years ago and for dragging it up again now. Something that will assuage the writhing knot in my gut and redeem myself a little.

Instead, I say, 'Yes, I'm sure it was a real headache for you, being the only rich kid at Withersham Hall. However did you cope?'

Downed gods, how many of these have I had to drink?

Alastair stares at me as if struggling to grasp the depths of his hatred, while Mortritis giggles as if someone tickled her. She too is slumped, her cheek propped up on one fist.

'You two certainly like to tease each other,' she says. 'I too had a rival at college. Kieran Kilchoir – a real viper.'

My thoughts snag on the name *Kilchoir*. If he was Mortritis's rival, that makes him a Prey who got into St Penderghast's. Glim gravers get to keep their own last name.

'He maddened and obsessed me,' she goes on. 'After years of torturing and humiliating one another, it all came to a rather explosive head at the Winter Formal.' She pauses to finish her glass. 'One of our preceptors caught us going at it in the gentlemen's restrooms. He never did look me in the eye again.'

The image of a younger Mortritis with her ballgown hitched up around her hips, pressed into the tile by someone impossibly rugged and handsome, enters my head uninvited and unwilling to leave. My crossed legs press together.

Alastair also stares, but his look is unreadable. Then he says, 'In the restrooms?'

'Oh, give it a rest, Alastair! You are such a tiresome prude. It was glorious, mindless desire, as if we were both possessed by Our Ferocious Lord!'

Excepting the location, it *does* sound rather glorious.

'I'm far from a prude,' Alastair says. 'What you and your rival get up to in the intimate privacy of a public restroom is no concern of mine. I'm just surprised to hear such a charming story from my aunt.'

'Well, it was either there or the roof, and may I remind you, it was midwinter.'

'The ladies' would have been nicer, surely?'

'Too much traffic.' Mortritis tilts her head to one side. 'Incidentally, that's how your cousin Kiel came to be.'

The corner of Alastair's mouth tics. 'Has he heard this story?'

'Oh, no doubt he's been in the room when I've told it at one time or another.'

Alastair tries and fails to contain his smirk.

My stomach lurches and I am suddenly, painfully aware of myself – the glass in my hand, refilled one too many times; the late time; the close heat and gentle turn of the room. I set the glass on the table beside my chair and rise slowly, ungracefully to my feet.

'Thank you for... your hospitality, Preceptor,' I say. 'I think it's my bedtime.'

'Don't be silly. You just got here,' she says, even though we've been here for bells.

I hesitate. If she tells me to stay, I'll be powerless to resist.

Alastair says, 'What was that about not wanting to risk my chances?'

Mortritis points at me. 'Sensible girl,' she says. 'Alastair, you'll be a gentleman and escort her back to the dorms, won't you?'

Alastair says nothing but dutifully rises from his seat.

'I can escort myself,' I say.

'Without your spire, poppet? In the dark? After three glasses of honey scotch? Then I take it back – *not* sensible. We like to say the grounds are the safest place in the city, but incidents happen everywhere.'

Alastair kisses Mortritis on each cheek and then the forehead, and walks me from the building. Leaving is like climbing out of a deep, warm cave. It's the deepest bell of night, and the temperature's fallen with the day. Even with my scotch jacket on, the night cold slaps me in the face. Every deep breath brings a sharp pain to my chest that forces me to wheeze out. At least it isn't snowing again.

A trench of memorial stones and glistening snow stands between us and Dunchester House, the way lit by moon- and starlight and lanterns that line the footpaths. The honey scotch fuzzes my senses, but not so much I don't know to shiver. I walk hugging myself, unsteady in the snow. There's a sense of stillness – nothing to hear but the breeze tangling in the trees, the crunch of our boots in the snow, and our breathing.

I percolate in the aura of Alastair's dark mood. He has the air of a stovetop kettle silently reaching the boil. I should tell him I'm sorry now. I should apologize thrice: for the misunderstanding, for dragging it up, and for the heartless comment after he revealed the truth.

'You have to convince Mortritis to trial me.'

The breath leaves his mouth like steam. '*Have to* is a strong choice of words.'

'If you renege on our deal—'

'What did we agree exactly?'

'That you'd introduce me to Mortritis so I could audit her conspectus.'

'Wording, again. I said she *may* let you audit the graving conspectus. There were never any guarantees.'

I gasp ever so slightly. 'You knew she'd say no!'

'I had no idea what she'd say,' he says flatly. 'Either way, I've done my part. Unless *you* mean to renege on our deal, we're still in the competition.'

'You must be thrilled she shot me down.' My voice drips bitterness. 'You still resent me because of this business with Flaypenny. I might've contributed to the rumours, but I certainly didn't start them.'

He scoffs but doesn't reply.

'I didn't! Anyway, I had no idea the situation was... what it was.'

If anything, Alastair only looks more incensed, his jaw painfully tight. His silence deafens, and his stride's hard to keep up with since I'm half cut with drink.

'Slow down. Alastair—'

I catch his sleeve and he whirls on me so suddenly, there isn't time to step back. His face is in my face, tendons flexing in his neck. His voice rears up like a monster from a fathomless black lake to say, '*What?*'

I stumble back, hitting a memorial double my size. It wobbles like a loose tooth. Snow spills from its top and falls on my head, but I can't react. Alastair petrifies me with his void-like eyes in a way that daunts and thrills me. For a long moment, my heart is the only part of me brave enough to move.

Then he snorts and looks away. 'I don't care about the rumours,' he says, backing off. 'I didn't stop speaking to Flaypenny because of that.'

He turns and stalks off as if he can't bear the sight of me. If I knew any other way back to Dunchester House, I might take it right now. As it is, I have to follow.

'It was because of her side business. She was only there for me because she wanted me to... contribute.'

I momentarily lose the order my arms and legs are supposed to move. My last conversation with Flaypenny comes crawling back to me: *I'd have work for you, if you found yourself in need.* But Alastair wasn't even old enough for a brown ale when he came to Withersham...

So Flaypenny's a *real* villain.

'Did you?' The question tumbles out.

Alastair's eyes blaze like glowing coals in mortal fire. 'No. As soon as I realized what she wanted, I distanced myself.' He waves this away. 'But that's a separate matter. What I resent is this worthless feud that you won't let die.'

'Oh, right, yes – *I* won't let it die. It's all me. You've had no part in it.'

'I know I haven't been perfect, but I *have* been trying to end it. You keep finding ways to aggravate it. Whether it's fouling me in a duel, or making up stupid stories...'

I turn on him. 'Excuse *me*, but neither of those things was about you. One was about winning, and the other—'

'Was about blowing smoke up my aunt's arse. Yes, that was obvious to everyone.' Alastair drops his voice to a hiss, and I realize we've bickered all the way back to Dunchester House. 'If you really wanted an end to this, you wouldn't even have considered throwing me to the wolves like that.'

We slip inside the vestibule's warmth, stamping snow off our boots on the hall matting.

'Sometimes, I thought you did it for the cohort,' he says. 'Your desperation to match them is so pathetic, it gives me chills. If the rest of Preyburn started rolling about in the fen on a Friday, you'd dive in head first.'

'Shut up, you swollen tit sore. That isn't true.'

Alastair ignores this. 'Well, we're not at Withersham anymore, and I'm done humouring you. You'd make a piss-poor graver.'

He obviously enjoys the way those words taste.

I laugh. Not because it's funny; I laugh as Our Lady did when she first contacted the Condemner, an entity too terrible to understand. I laugh out of despair and wildness, my heart squeezing as I remember Limbridge using almost the same words.

'*What?* What would you know about it?'

'I happen to come from a family of saluted gravers, and I've seen you grave. Don't think you'll be another Kieran Kilchoir. You don't possess even a sliver of talent.'

Too stunned to come up with anything cleverer, I say, 'Silence!'

'Even if you did, do you really think a life spent labouring in obscurity would make you happy? You were ecstatic over the ancestor. Graving won't give you that.'

We mount the stairs, yelling in whispers.

'So what if I was? Gravers are selfless. We work to protect the Commonwealth, regardless of how it makes us feel.'

'You don't pursue graving because you're selfless. You pursue it because you're desperate to prove the cohort wrong.'

'And I will.'

'But what *for?* Why not admit you're a better spirer and that you enjoy it and be happy?'

'I could never enjoy savaging Our Lady's creations for sport.'

'Right – eerians should be left to riot around the countryside, savaging people instead.'

'If it were really about culling the population, you wouldn't need a crowd and trophies.'

'You ignore what spiring brings to the Commonwealth. The people don't just need soldiers; they also need distraction and joy.'

We reach the top of the stairs and turn into our hallway, still hissing at each other like cats.

'I still can't believe you're comparing sport to military service. Gravers dedicate their lives to—'

'I'm not saying they don't! I'm saying that if you really wanted to serve the Commonwealth, you'd serve her better in the role you're actually good at.'

I can already feel a choke rising in my throat. 'And if you really wanted an end to our feud, you wouldn't say such wicked things.'

Alastair's expression isn't without sympathy. Somehow that makes it worse.

'I don't say them to upset you. I say them because I care for you.'

I glower at him, although the effect is no doubt ruined by the tears.

He sighs. 'Look. I think we should speak in the morning. You're half cut and I'm dog tired.' He opens his door, pausing before he goes inside. 'Are you going to be all right? Do you want me to—'

I vanish into my room and slam the door, leaving him to stew in the darkened hallway. It feels like I've been gutted.

I draw the curtains, making sure not even an inch of moonlight slips past. Then I burrow deep under the covers and start sobbing. That honey scotch did me no favours.

15

A PISS-P⊕⊕R GRAVER

When I wake the next morning, my mouth is dry, the skin around my eyes puffy and sore. I feel positively polluted. For a moment, I lie in my warm nest of covers, blissfully unaware of last night's events. This doesn't last long.

There's so much to cringe over, it's difficult to choose what to focus on. Mortritis saying, *Nobody audits my conspectus,* and my lame attempts to argue with her. Alastair recalling the miseries of Withersham, then explaining the real reason why he stopped speaking to Flaypenny...

I'm still cursing myself as I return from the washrooms, sunlight stabbing at my eyes through the mullioned windows. This isn't just an opportunity for cringe, but something altogether more visceral. Flaypenny is, after all, a pastoress in her forties, a grown woman in a position of authority. The idea that she'd befriend an isolated boy, solely to lure him into... I'm still not sure what to call her racket.

I mean, this is child exploitation we're talking about. Alastair was in a vulnerable position, and too young to consent to the work she wanted him to do. I'd enjoy smacking her in the face.

I recall Alastair's face when we came across her in the chapel, and the pain that's settled behind my eyes intensifies. What I read at the time to be *flustered* might have been panic or dread. If I could have my time again, I'd never tease him about her. Even though he called my graving piss-poor.

If only I believed he was trying to hurt me. If only he was the first to admit they don't believe in my skills and probably never did. How am I supposed to take it?

Happily, I have two more rest days before our second stage. Outside the arena, every waking moment ought to be spent practising – with a graphium if not a spire – but I'm feeling rather delicate. Once dressed in my casual clothes, I make a quick trip to the common room to scoop up five cinnamon-and-clove pastries. I'm deep in my thoughts and not ready to see Alastair yet, so I plan to devour these in my room.

Before I can steal back out, however, I'm snagged by another admissions pupil, Lourdes. I've seen her around Dunchester since Edusa's speech, lounging in her debonair spiring garb – umber and charcoal grey accenting the whites – as if this were a holiday resort. With her angular features and slicked-back hair, she might be the handsomest girl I've ever seen. Do any of the admissions pupils suit Dunchester as much as she does? I must look like a goblin stood next to her, pinching food to hoard in my cave. She dazzles me with a smile I have neither the ability nor the inclination to return.

'Hal, isn't it?' she says, her voice unexpectedly husky.

'Yes,' I say, clutching my pastries. For a wild moment, I wonder if she might try to confiscate them. There's surely an unwritten rule about hoarding pastries.

'Compliments on a sensational first stage. Rare to see anyone recover from a broken spire, but you really spun fate.'

'Right,' I say warily. 'Thank you.'

'I confess, I didn't realize there *was* any spiring in Preyburn. I've never had the opportunity to go. Is it very popular over there?'

'Popular?' I almost sneer. 'It's reviled. We don't really go in for that sort of thing.'

'So you're a special case.' Lourdes smooths both hands back over her hair, although I doubt it's even capable of misbehaving. She appraises me a little too keenly. 'Listen, I've got a proposal for you. How about a little practice, just us two?'

I interpret this as any sane person would. Apparently my debatable success in the arena has made me a target for saboteurs. 'Practice that ends with me brutally injured before my next stage, I presume?'

Lourdes looks equal parts appalled and tickled. 'Er, no. That's not how we do things.'

'No?'

'No! Even if I *could* cripple my competitors beneath the abettors' notice, it's hardly worth risking Our Lord's Acclaim for, now is it? Especially when we can both get patronage.'

While this last part is technically true, we're statistically less likely to succeed with more competition. Seventeen of us compete for five places at most. Who wouldn't want to better those odds? No doubt admissions for the graving conspectus will be as much a trial of sabotage as of graving, and to the most ruthless, wiliest victor go the spoils.

However, it's the first part that deserves more scrutiny.

'What do you mean, risking Acclaim?'

'Well, forgive me for pointing out the obvious, but treachery goes against several Radiant Principles. It'd be cruel, cowardly, and the very inverse of oneness. Too many misdeeds and I may as well take a butter knife into the arena, yes? I'd be sabotaging myself.'

I narrow my eyes at her. 'Then why do you want to practise?'

'Why does anyone?' Lourdes cocks a brow. 'I've never had the chance to train with a Prey before, and by the sounds of it, I may never get to again. I daresay we've got things to learn from each other.'

Either Lourdes has massively overestimated my experience or this is some other trick I can't yet identify. 'Like how to lose your spire?'

Lourdes grins. 'The underdog-from-Preyburn act isn't going to work for me, I'm afraid.' *Act? Do people really think I planned it?* 'But something tells me you've got more than that up your sleeve. So what do you say?'

'I... will think about it.'

'Excellent!' She gives me a friendly clap on the shoulder. 'Come find me when you're ready, yes?'

She heads on into the common room to join some friends of hers, an entire bevy of them, and I scurry back to my room with the pastries.

At the desk, I flip open my textbooks and notebooks, and their mouldy yellow-paper funk whacks me in the nose. I suppose Withersham makes you nose-blind to it, but here in St Penderghast's, it's impossible to ignore.

Because my ink cartridge needs changing, I'm covered in green stains before I've copied the first glyph. There's more ink on my hands than I scratched into my notebook. It looks like I offended a squid.

Limbridge's gift has taken on a malignant aura, buried beneath the clothes in my unpacked suitcase. No doubt it resents being spurned for my old, leaky pen, and the fact that I still haven't written my mentor a letter. Why aren't I using it again? Oh, yes – because of what she said. Although now Alastair's said the same, maybe it wasn't the cruelty I'd thought it was.

Except, I'm *not* a piss-poor graver. I know I'm not, so it makes no cocking sense that people keep telling me so. Alastair told me to analyse people's motivations, and about the funding Withersham will get if we earn a place at Penders. He too stands to benefit if I give up graving. By his own admission, neither he nor Limbridge can be trusted on the subject.

But Mortritis said no. I'm not going to audit her conspectus, and her words whisk up my gut acids until my chest burns. So why am I still here writing glyphs instead of asking the housekeepers to arrange a carriage? It wouldn't be too late to reach out to my back-ups, but the thought of going back to Preyburn now doesn't exactly excite me – not only because I'd be leaving Alastair in the lurch, although that is a factor.

It would feel bizarre to leave now, never knowing how far I could've gone, whether I would have won Edusa's patronage and my place at the Commonwealth's most prestigious college. It would be something I'd always wonder about, and quite possibly be haunted by. I crave a haunting as much as the next girl, but not this sort.

Moreover, what if Limbridge and Alastair are right? What if I'm not going to be a graving master and I'll never get satisfaction from the cohort, no matter how hard I try? All I will have achieved is messing up my own life, giving up a viable career for nothing. Now that Mortritis has turned me down, that seems more likely than ever.

Maybe I ought to just let it go. Can I do that? Even though I know exactly what the cohort will say about me, and the thought of it turns my blood molten?

What will my parents say? At least one of them was prepared for me to be a scion's bastard, and even paid for the privilege. Possibly, they both did. If so, they must have been prepared for it to come out someday.

If I were to have a decent spiring career, I could afford them a new house outside of Crippleditch. A cottage where they could live in peace, away from the community's vitriol. Even in Glimwick, if that's what they wanted.

I set down the pen and go to clean my hands. When I return to my room, I burrow through my suitcase until I find the pouch. I'd almost forgotten how fine the pen is. It's perfectly weighted in my hand. Using one of the new cartridges – Balverian Lavender – I tear a page from my notebook as neatly as I can.

Dearest Limbridge…

The nib glides across the page, every blue stroke a dream.

***

I need to speak to Alastair. I've already left it too long.

I don't look forward to the tongue-lashing I'm going to get, the burning black stare and palpable disdain, but I have to apologize. We have to clear the air before the next stage.

I'm ready to face him. My headache evaporated after lunch, which means my body's overcome the poison I poured into it. I take a deep breath, trying to release some of the pressure that's been building at the back of my throat, and rap my knuckles against Alastair's door.

A moment later, he opens, and every word I'd prepared flees my brain in panic. It's like opening a door to the all-consuming abyss, all light and warmth dragged into the void of his cold and lifeless presence. His arm's free of its sling and his black-glass eyes fix on me, waiting. A loud, awkward silence follows.

Just when I'm starting to think it's never going to end – that we will stay right here in this hallway, staring at each other with unsaid words hanging over us, for eternity – he speaks.

'I was about to come for you. Edusa's summoned us to his apartments.'

The last I heard his voice, it was wild with anger. Now, it's recovered its usual stiffness – but that only means he's composed himself. In many ways, I preferred the hiss-shouting to the terror of the unknown.

'*Us?* What for?'

'His message didn't say.'

Alastair steps out, closing his door behind him. His face gives nothing away, placing my nerves firmly on edge as he leads us to the staircase. I ascend to the very heights of Dunchester House muted by his silence. Even as I furiously rehearse apologies in my head, my tongue lies heavy in my mouth.

A dour-faced manservant admits us to Edusa's apartments. I don't begrudge him his dour face; he must suffer greatly in the spiring master's service. He invites us into the vestibule, across a large silk rug threaded with Edusa's sigil: twin spires crossing blades over a Choir bell. We proceed from one ostentatiously furnished room to another riddled with tawdry patterns and expensive trinkets... and some rather gorgeous trophies.

Eerian heads glare invitingly amongst all the frippery: eyes, teeth, and curious appendages, taxidermized and mounted against the brocade wallpaper. When I pass a particularly impressive creature, I can't help but stop to admire it. Its entire head is mostly maw, and its maw is a veritable maelstrom of ridged pink gum and handsome fangs. I don't recognize this charming beast from my textbooks.

I test a fang's cruel point against the tip of my index finger and it rewards me with a bright jewel of blood. I get goosebumps.

'*Hal...*'

For a moment, I imagine the eerian growling my name. Alas, it's only Alastair. I remember myself, and the manservant waiting for me with joyless patience. My finger stops bleeding as eagerly as it began, and I follow our guide 'til we arrive at a balcony. The view of the grounds is predictably spectacular.

Slightly less predictable is Edusa. He poses on an actual throne with his back to the view. It's an obnoxious yellow gold and floridly carved with eerians. Their eyes, teeth, and claws gleam with encrusted nacre to match the fabric's cream-and-gold-thread damask. One gloved fist props up Edusa's cheek while the other grips a spire so overdecorated, I wonder if it can actually be used. A second spire, this one sheathed, leans against the throne.

Just because it isn't snowing doesn't mean it's warm enough to sit outside, yet Edusa's only protection from the elements is a very tight pair of leather trousers, calf-high boots, and a ridiculously floofy, floor-sweeping fur coat in plum brown. He goes bare chested, flaunting rock-hard pecs and abs that could grate even the toughest Prey cheeses. He's cartoonishly muscular – I'll give him that.

I hear a soft scrape behind me and turn to see an oily-haired man in the balcony's corner, shivering and scowling with concentration. He's half hidden by an easel and canvas, presumably painting Edusa – or something *like* Edusa, if he's responsible for the hard-jawed fabrication outside the games hall too.

'Aha! Just the accord I wanted to see!'

The sheer magnitude of Edusa's voice startles me. It was made for the arena and other large spaces; in close quarters, it overpowers. They can probably hear him all the way down to the ground floor.

He rises merrily from his throne with no consideration for the man trying to paint him. Then again, I suppose he needn't sit still if the artist's going to make half of it up anyway.

'I've a *magnificent* surprise for you.' With a flourish, he lifts the sheathed spire high into the air before deftly twirling the hilt towards me. 'I know you'll put it to good use, my little Prey hopeful.'

I object to being called *little* anything, but I stifle my annoyance and take the spire from him. Touching the hilt gives me a static shock, just like the ones I used to get off the dorms' old radio with the dodgy wiring – not painful, just a surprise.

'Thank you,' I say, testing its weight in my hand. 'It's—'

'The Might of Our All-Glorious Lord.' He reverts to his imperial pose with almost mechanical accuracy, his own highly wrought spire angled towards the stone floor. 'It was only a matter of time before your old one broke. Ordinarily, I'd demand a replacement from your school, but Preys aren't known for their spire-making, and I can't risk a repeat incident.'

Struck by a thought, he bellows at the artist: 'Speaking of repeat incidents, make sure you're getting my cheekbones!'

'Of course, of course!' the artist replies with a false, nervous laugh that's meant to reassure. 'I surely couldn't miss them! Such *masterful* cheekbones!'

This, I suspect, is the only correct way to answer if he values his employment.

Satisfied, Edusa returns his attention to the subject of my spire loss. 'Once may win endearment, but twice wins an eyeroll.'

My gaze flicks from Edusa to Alastair, wondering what he makes of this. First a private summons to Edusa's apartments, and now a gift. Why the special treatment?

'Fortunately for you, Edusa is as famed for his generosity as his spiring prowess and animal magnetism,' says Edusa. 'This is but one of a wealth of spires I've been gifted over the years. Go ahead – take a look.'

Slowly, I draw the spire from its sheath and study the craftmanship as if I know the first thing about it. 'It's a fine spire,' is all I can think to say, which would be obvious to anyone. There's more luxury in this spire than there is in all of Crippleditch. Spiring masks cap the S-shaped crossguards, a Choir Knot engraves the pommel that tops the hilt, the crockets along the blade are needle keen, and the knuckle-bow's vainglorious design rivals Alastair's in swagger.

'*Fine* is the word,' Edusa agrees. 'Not Helel's best work, I'm afraid.'

Now Alastair speaks: 'I thought it looked familiar.'

'I should hope so!' Edusa flashes a dazzling smile. 'Did you know your spire was part of a pair? The Might of Our All-Glorious Lord, and the Cunning of Our Dark-Crowned Lady.'

Bolstered by Edusa's presence, I risk a look at Alastair. 'I didn't know your spire had a la-di-da name.'

Edusa gives a shout of laughter, as if my ignorance delights him. '*All* spires have a la-di-da name.'

'Well,' I say, 'surely I'm the last person that should have a spire with *this* name.' I, like all Preys, do not even refer to Oldrac as *Our Lord*. There is only Our Lady and Oldrac.

'The Cunning was given to me by Papa as an insult,' Alastair says, his jaw a taut line. 'He thought it fitting, since I took such an interest in Our Lady.'

Edusa chuckles. 'Yes, that certainly does sound like Aiden.'

'Maybe we should swap?' I say.

'Out of the question! Barb or not, Alastair's spire has become a part of him, just as yours will become part of you. You may as well ask to swap legs. Besides, the Cunning is a better fit for him.'

No arguments there. He's a better fit for the Might too.

'And?' I say, lifting my gaze to Edusa's. 'What is it you want from me?'

'That should be obvious,' he replies, smirking. 'I want you to keep entertaining my public for as long as victory allows.'

I recall what Limbridge said in her office: *Your successes will be their successes.* With a thrill, it dawns on me that Edusa thinks we have what it takes to *be* successful. He wouldn't waste time and resources on us otherwise. It's not generosity he has, but commercial wit. No doubt the spire will be snatched away the moment victory *dis*allows us.

'That's not all,' Edusa says.

He produces an envelope from some recess in his enormous coat, handing it to Alastair. I watch him break the wax seal, unfold the creamy white paper inside, and scan its contents. It could be my imagination, but there is the tiniest upwards quirk to the left corner of his mouth before he passes it to me. It's a cordial invitation to Edusa's soirée in wanton, looping script, addressed to the accord of Halen Kilchoir and Alastair Bartholomew Faulton.

'As I mentioned in orientation, I throw a party for Oldsfall every year for all the spiring circuit's major players.'

'Why would you invite us?' I say.

Alastair glares at me for asking what he must think an obvious question. Luckily, Edusa finds my lack of knowledge charming.

'I need to see how you're received by my fellow luminaries.'

'Right,' I say wearily. 'Another test.'

'Needless to say, your invitation is conditional on winning your next stage.'

I thought pupils would get a reprieve over Oldsfall, some space in which to breathe, but what I'm hearing is that our attendance is compulsory. Assuming we win our next stage, I'll be forcing smiles for Edusa's entourage and scrabbling for conversation. Exhausting, but not nearly as difficult as what needs to be said between Alastair and me at some point today.

That point comes right after Edusa dismisses us. We leave him to pose while his artist tries desperately to paint the fantastical majesty of his employer's cheekbones as he imagines them. Once we're on the other side of those double doors, we're in the hallway, alone together in dread-thick silence once again.

'Look,' I say, cracking at last, 'I'm really very sorry about what I said last night. I'm even more cut up over how I've behaved over the last year or so. Especially this business with Flaypenny. You have to know that if I had any idea what she was up to—'

'I know. That isn't your fault.'

'But spreading the rumours *is* my fault. I know how it feels to be on the receiving end, everyone making stuff up about you behind your back. And you're right about our feud. I haven't done anything to mend it, so... I'd love it if we could move past all the nastiness.'

Alastair's eyes are too intense to look at for longer than a few seconds. I have to keep taking refuge in staring at the floor.

'Does that mean you've decided to stay?' he asks.

'I can't see much benefit in leaving. I won't pretend I've given up on Mortritis.'

'Hal, really. You have as much chance of becoming a lauded graver as I do of becoming a fen heron.'

'No offence, ghoul face, but I can't take your word that I'm a piss-poor graver. I need to hear that from a higher authority.'

'Fine. I can appreciate that, I suppose.'

'My devotion is even stronger for having met her. If I quit admissions, we'll never breathe the same air again.'

The roll of Alastair's eyes is so exaggerated, it immediately reminds me of her. 'Your blind infatuation with my aunt is abhorrent.'

'There's nothing *blind* about it.'

'Well, what words would *you* use to describe someone who worships a woman they know nothing about? Because I'm keen to be generous.'

'If it's generosity you're about, help me convince her to trial me.' Alastair just stares at me, so I go on. 'There must be something I can do. I just have to work out what it is, and in the meantime we have to win our place here. Although...' I look down at the Might. 'How I do that without Acclaim, I don't know.' I feel no closer to achieving Acclaim than I did in Limbridge's office, and as I've yet to come up with a plan to win over Mortritis, I'll need more time.

'For that, I'm working on a short-term fix.'

'Go on.'

'There's a technique that would allow you to wield Acclaim through our accord. My brother suggested it, but I'm not sure if or how it will work. I need to consult with him further.' He stops walking and looks at me with total attention. 'Was there anything else?'

'I don't think so.'

'Really?' he says, the blush creeping up his throat. He must catch me looking, because he rubs at his collar. 'Nothing else was said last night that you'd like to address?'

'You might need to give me a hint.'

'Another?' he mutters. Then, more loudly: 'Forget it.' He closes his eyes for a few seconds and then opens them again. 'I've plans to see my brother this afternoon. Perhaps I'll see you at dinner.'

I can only watch as he walks off. When he turns the corner, disappearing from sight and also my thoughts, my attention returns to the spire in my hand. I draw back the sheath for a second, unselfconscious look, without the weight of Edusa's anticipation and Alastair's judgement upon me. With its scalpel-sharp edges and thistly, fang-like crockets, everything about it screams *eerian damage!* Even with its stupid name and Choir branding, I look forward to seeing the Might in action.

16

A TRICKY MANOEUVRE

The next morning, I go to the library's graving floor. There's a bell or so before I need to meet Alastair and Tieran for training. If I fail the second stage, I will have missed the opportunity to gorge myself on rare graving books. I need to make the most of it while I still can.

Today, as I vanish into the stacks' shadows, I'm after books on the Condemner. Withersham's library is sorely lacking on the subject, as is every library in the world, but I've heard St Penderghast's lacks *less*.

I peruse the spines, plucking titles from the shelves until I find one that grips me too hard to let it go: *Script of the Abyssal Gods: Parsing the Glyphic System* by Mortritis Moppeton. It's no surprise to see that name here; breaking down the glyphic system to modernize its capabilities is her specialism.

I plant myself on a luxuriously cushioned sofa and disappear for a while, turning each beautiful cream page with reverence as I inhale the ink's faint bitterness. We know next to nothing about the Condemner, despite his importance to our history. Without this umbral figure, Our Lady would never have leapt from the firmaments to our world, giving Oldrac no reason to come here either. Then there would have been no spirers and no gravers.

Glyphs, the Eternal Spite, pulp – every facet of graving owes its existence to the Condemner's sanity-mangling gift of knowledge. In her book, Mortritis describes him as an *eldritch atrocity* – words that thrill to the marrow – grasping Our Lady's mind from the abyss. Her brilliance must have been rare indeed to snare his ruinous attentions. One can't help feeling a little jealous.

The book is so hideously brilliant that when second bell strikes, it feels like I just sat down. With a grudgingness that verges on physical pain, I drag myself from the sofa and return the book to its place, promising to return for it later. All too soon, I'm trading the library's sweet, gentle darkness for the bright, gruelling cold.

I'm halfway to Dunchester's main building when I hear the crunch of another's steps nearing in the snow. I glance over to see dark, cropped hair and a Prey graver's uniform coming towards me. Her face has a slightly starved look to it that has nothing to do with gauntness and everything to do with her huge, dark eyes. She stares at me like someone mesmerized, and for a moment I can look nowhere else.

'Mortritis said I'd find you here,' she says.

With this, she earns more of my attention. *Mortritis sent her?*

'I'm bidding for her patronage,' the girl goes on. 'She said I might like to speak to you. I'm Viler.' She proffers a hand gloved in burgundy leather. I shake it, curious but wary. She has a firm graver's grip.

'Hal,' I say, slowing down only a little. My eyes are stinging from the dry cold and I can't wait to get inside. Viler must be suffering with the Glim weather too; she shoves her hand straight back into the pocket of her smart wool coat.

'What part of Preyburn are you from?' she asks.

'Crippleditch. You?'

'Wutherweir.'

The capital – a far cry from my hometown, which is practically out in the hinterlands. No wonder she looks so well put together. Excepting the crust of snow, her boots look smooth and clean as polished bone. And, I can't help but note, her uniform includes pleated trousers for girls, as it bloody well should.

'I assume your scion's heritage is paternal?' she says.

'How did you know?'

'Oldracian women rarely agree to handshakes.'

I bristle instantly. She means an entirely different kind of handshake to the one we just did. I don't hear any Ransley-style scorn from Viler, though, only shy interest and a Prey accent that, after some time surrounded by Glims, could be a comfort. However, her cheerful and exact speech reminds me of Withersham's preceptors teaching the pronunciation of different glyphs. She speaks with that same false, word-perfect brightness, as if this is a listening and comprehension task for which her lines are memorized.

'Oldracian men need only commit to a matter of minutes,' she says, 'whereas women must be more involved, shall we say.'

'Is it common in Wutherweir?'

'Oh, yes. Oldracian flesh is a means to an end all over Preyburn. It has a phenomenal rate of conception, and fortifies the mother's body through the birth. Of course, almost one hundred per cent of Prey children by a scion become gravers. You're an exceptional case.'

Again, no note of derision; Viler's tone has shifted from interest to carefully restrained excitement. There's a hungry gleam in those enormous eyes. Even Alastair's never looked at me quite so hard. At first I think it's attraction, but that word doesn't quite fit. She seems to want something else from me.

'You seem to know a lot about this,' I say.

'It'll be my thesis proposal – demystifying Oldracian flesh.'

'I thought the Council outlawed that sort of research?' Which, given the history of experimentation on scions before the truce – all of it quite involuntary – is understandable.

'Precisely why we have a caveman's insight on all this,' Viler continues in that same bright tone, belying the illicit territory into which our conversation has led us. 'People get very cagey about it, but Mortritis isn't one to let antiquated rules foil discovery. With her help – and, hopefully, yours – people will get over the taboo. *Everyone* should want to know what really makes a scion, and what makes a graver.'

Ah, so *that's* why she's tracked me down. She wants me for a guinea pig.

Under different circumstances, I'd be flattered to get such attention from a girl like Viler – intelligent, well dressed, and charmingly creepy. Not to mention the fact that Mortritis clearly favours her. But now, with frightening clarity, I see her looming over me with a maniacal grin and a syringe as I struggle against the straps holding me down.

Now would be the time to extract myself from the conversation, but Mortritis sent her so I can't be rude. Besides which, I'm curious.

'I thought it was down to pulp,' I say, frowning. 'The child has to consume it regularly, and in enough quantities to suppress Oldrac's flesh.'

'And how do you explain cases where the body begins to reject pulp?'

Cases like mine. I think back to what Alastair told me about his parents. His father married his mother, a graver, to prove the strength of his lineage.

'The Oldracian flesh is too strong for pulp to overcome,' I say.

Viler mock-grimaces and waves a hand, as if the theory is a bad smell she can waft away. 'Egoistic superstition. Plenty of scions from flouncy bloodlines have illegitimate children who became gravers, not to mention the *legitimate* children who succumbed to compulsion.'

Ah, now this I've at least read about. Compulsion drives scions to consume pulp, just as Oldrac was driven to Our Lady. It becomes a craving they have to fight.

'Just because there's a correlation,' says Viler, 'doesn't mean there's a cause.'

'You must have a theory. If not quantity of pulp or quality of lineage, what makes the difference?'

'Delighted you asked.' Viler smiles, but I don't enjoy it. I still haven't seen her blink. 'Mine is a study in behaviourism – the impact one's psychology may have on Oldracian flesh.'

'You think a god's hereditary material can be impacted by *psychology?*'

Viler's look tells me she's seen this reaction many times, and isn't knocked back in the slightest. 'I lack the data now, but with Mortritis's help and more case studies, I intend to prove it.'

'Case studies like me, you mean?'

'There's really no need for that look. I'm not hoping to get you on an operating table. I would never dream of dissecting you. You're far too valuable – too *exquisite* for that. I only want to observe and interview.'

All this said with the nervous passion of a girl professing love. I can't deny I'm intrigued, both in the research – this might be the most interesting proposition I've ever received – and Viler herself. If people don't creep you out a little bit, what's the point in getting to know them?

Unable to hold her all-encompassing stare, I drop my gaze to the snow. 'Sorry, but I don't fancy going under the microscope much more than the scalpel.'

Viler winces, visibly heartbroken but not quite ready to give up.

'If the joy of discovery doesn't move you, what about compensation?' she presses on, hounding me to the main building. 'Pud, or something more remarkable? You must be missing electronics from home.'

'You've brought electronics across the border?' I say, in tones of *Are you mad?*

'My mother's developing a dampener to stop scions interfering with electronics. It's a prototype, but it mostly works. *Mostly.*'

'Let me think about it,' I say, but only to get rid of her. As much as I'd love an electric kettle and a radio, I can't risk getting caught with contraband. My position here is precarious enough as it is.

At the doors to the main building, I pause. When I half-turn back to Viler, her hopeful gaze is almost too much to bear.

'When people's bodies start rejecting pulp, how do they overcome it?'

Viler blinks five times in quick succession, then resumes staring. Now, she uses my least favourite expression. It's the one Alastair used before we auditioned for the abettors, the one Limbridge used after her pep talk: grim pity. In a soft voice, she says, 'You'd have to overcome your personality. I'd say you're too far gone to turn around.'

I push through the doors, kicking myself. I shouldn't ask questions if I don't want to hear the answers.

But for all Viler's confidence, she said it herself: there simply isn't enough research into this to answer conclusively. Just because she hasn't seen it done doesn't mean it isn't possible.

Inside the vestibule, I find Alastair waiting for me – *spying* on me from the frost-glazed window.

'You've got a fan,' he remarks.

'In a sense. She wants to study me psychologically.'

'At long last. I've always said how you manage to delude yourself so thoroughly ought to be studied. You're a psychologist's wet dream.'

I scowl at him. 'What do emotionless lumps of stone know about dreams, wet or otherwise?'

'I know how to tell achievable goals from fantasies, which is to say, more than you.'

'You always find such imaginative ways to say you want your teeth on the floor.'

He turns from me, leading the way down the hall with a leaden voice: 'Threats of violence go against our ceasefire.'

Alastair and I warm up in one of Dunchester's umpteen courtyards while snow gathers around us like dust. St Penderghast's wouldn't know simplicity if it had been married to it fifty years, but this particular courtyard is lighter on decoration. Spirers use this ample space, framed by gallant arches, sculptures, and stained glass, to train in.

Our breath puffs in the air. It's even too cold for the wall fountains to work; the carved, marble mouths of hares spit nothing into the gilded bowls beneath them. The unevenness of the snow says it has a natural floor rather than a paved one, but with weather like this, it won't make much difference. The ground is frozen hard enough that if a head hits it, it may as well hit stone.

As we finish our warm-up, three pupils I don't recognize wheel an enormous gilded crate in through an even larger set of doors. They all hold spires, and their garb is unique: black from boot heel to collar with bullion gold embroidery. Amongst the customary cream and robin's-egg blue, you couldn't possibly miss them.

'You're saying *Alastair* can give me Acclaim?'

'Share,' Alastair corrects. 'Not give.'

'Our Lord teaches fellowship in all things,' Tieran says. 'As he shares his power with his disciples, so they may share that power in turn. Of course, a spirer can only ever hope to achieve a glimmer of Our Lord's power.' Tieran nods to me. 'So you'll receive a smaller glimmer of that from Alastair.'

'Tieran ran me through the theory yesterday,' Alastair says. 'All that's left now is practice.'

'And who are these?' I say, nodding to the strangers in black.

'Stage warders,' Tieran replies. 'Spiring conspectus upperclassmen, fourth years and higher. Once you've proven yourself, you'll be assigned warder duties.'

'They wait in the wings at every stage,' Alastair says, 'ready to save the spirer and fell the eerian if it proves too much for them.'

'Yes, I imagine tickets would become rather tough to sell if an eerian climbed out of the arena to savage the spectators.'

Tieran dismisses the idea with a wave. 'Oh, that hasn't happened in *years*.'

My eager gaze returns to the gilded crate. 'So what are we fighting today?'

'Let's give this technique a whirl first,' says Tieran.

At his brother's gesture, Alastair takes a focusing breath. That's all the warning I get before Acclaim strikes his spire. I don't avert my eyes fast enough, much less block my ears, so the incandescent burst blinds and deafens me.

I've barely had time to blink the vision spots away when Alastair says, 'Ready?'

'Do I look ready?' I snap, taking one hand from the Might's hilt to rub my eyelids.

Tieran speaks with the cheerful indifference I've quickly come to hate him for. 'You'll get used to the glare. Deep breaths. Go ahead, Alastair.'

The light dulls from Alastair's blade, and at the same time intensifies in mine. There's nothing gradual about it. The Might rouses as though shocked from a deep sleep with a bucket of ice water.

With an ear-popping crack, Acclaim rushes into my body. Every muscle, including my heart, seizes with panic and surging, overwhelming strength. It doesn't feel painful per se, but it is entirely too much.

My stomach lurches, and next thing I'm bent double, melting the snow with hot bile. Alastair was right to insist on leaving breakfast until after training. Even as the Might dims, I keep trembling and gasping for air.

I become dimly aware of a warm hand rubbing circles into my back, and that it belongs to Alastair. I might feel awkward about this oddly familiar gesture if I wasn't so busy feeling wretched.

The sound of Tieran chuckling away does not lessen my pain.

'It's good fun, isn't it?' he says. 'Not to worry. Everyone's first time is like that. Breathe through it and don't panic.'

Easier said than done. I wish the stage warders didn't have to be here as extra witnesses to my struggle. No doubt they could all do this drunk if they had to.

Pulling myself upright is no longer a simple task; random muscle spasms mean my abs cramp of their own accord. I smear the back of my glove across my mouth, too shaken to glower at Tieran. 'How do you bear it?'

He grins. 'I enjoy it. You will too, once you're accustomed.' He snaps his fingers at Alastair. 'Again.'

'Not yet, give me a—'

A second crack overpowers me, the Acclaim all but glancing off Alastair's spire before it strikes mine again.

My heart stutters. I grit my teeth, fighting for control as violet light flails every which way. Tieran and Alastair watch with blunt shadows twitching on their faces. They aren't moved by my struggle or the Acclaim crackling about, gouging the snow wherever it strikes.

This must be how it feels to stick your fingers in a socket – like being fried inside out. Before long, I'm on my knees, heaving from a raw throat as snow burns through my spiring breeches.

'Have you considered,' I rasp, 'that maybe I'm not meant for this?'

'What do you mean?' Tieran says.

'It's clearly rejecting me. It knows I'm a Prey.'

'Acclaim isn't like the Eternal Spite,' Alastair reminds me. 'It's insensate. It can't reject you.'

'And even if it could,' Tieran says, 'we've just seen it on your spire, clear as day.'

'Then my body's rejecting *it*.'

'But you have Our Lord's gifts. If you can pull the pulp-flesh ancestor down on top of you, you've enough of his flesh to use Acclaim.'

'The issue is psychological.' As usual, Alastair states his opinion as empirical fact. 'Hal's convinced herself she's a graver.'

'I *am* a graver, you nonsense-broker.'

'You see? Psychologists should be bashing down your door to study your delusion.' Alastair's eyes centre on mine, glistening black. 'Brace for the cold, hard truth, because here it comes: if you can't wield Acclaim, we won't get through our second stage.'

Tieran snorts. 'You don't say! It's a miracle you got through the first without it, and an even bigger miracle that Edusa hasn't sussed you out.' He lowers his voice. 'He thinks you held it back for the drama, you know. I haven't corrected him.'

Should we be worried about the stage warders snitching? No, they wouldn't. To snitch on us, they'd have to snitch on Tieran. I can't see that playing out well for them. He's proxy to the First Spiring Master, and so pulls rank on every other pupil.

'No Acclaim,' Alastair goes on, enunciating every syllable, 'no Mortritis.'

Words that burn worse than the snow soaking into my breeches. Realizing the severity of this situation, I pick myself off the ground.

'What's Mortritis got to do with anything?' Tieran says her name like it's filthy, and not in a good way.

'Hal's obsessed with her.'

Tieran scoffs. 'Along with every other ink-sniffer in the Commonwealth. No offence, Kilchoir.'

'I have taken some offence.'

'Did my brother mention she's a vindictive brat?'

'For Hal, that's all part of the appeal,' Alastair says, his voice bitter as stout.

Tieran's voice, however, takes on a teasing lilt. 'Feeling territorial, are we, brother?'

Alastair gets a murderous gleam in his eye, but Tieran's smug self-confidence is too powerful, even for him. Tieran must think Alastair wants to keep me away from their aunt out of jealousy, and I suppose it's only natural. Anyone would get possessive of Mortritis's attention.

'You talk about Mortritis as if she isn't the most beloved, celebrated graver of our age,' I say hotly. 'I'm hardly the first person to—'

'Is it so very difficult to understand that we don't share your doomed infatuation?' Alastair snaps, which he rarely does. The stress of it all must finally be getting to him. 'Can't you shut up about Mortritis for *a moment?*'

'Who brought her up?' I counter.

'Tripped *gods!*' says Tieran, yellow eyes flashing. 'Withersham's preceptors might've stopped class so you could pull each other's pigtails, but I certainly won't.' He signals to the stage warders on the courtyard's far side. They approach the gilded crate, setting about a series of heavy iron padlocks.

'Tieran,' Alastair says in warning tones.

'You said the issue's psychological. I agree – she's overthinking it.' Tieran nods to the crate. 'A little peril ought to help her Oldracian instincts kick in.'

When the stage warders remove the last padlock, one wall of the crate drops like a drawbridge. All I see inside is shadows.

Something shifts within as the stage warders fan out, forming three points of a triangle. Whatever happens, the eerian will not be allowed to leave.

Alastair runs his eyes over me. 'Is it wise to start before Hal acclimatizes? If she gets injured the day before our stage, there won't be time to heal.'

Tieran backs out of range, giving me the floor. 'If she gets injured by the practice dummy, she's past hope whether healed or not.'

My gaze stays on the crate. If nothing else of merit happens today, at least I will have seen a new eerian.

I expect a beast, but what crawls from the shadows does so on hands and knees. There's nothing human, however, about the way its head snaps back and forth on its neck. Unable to swivel its painted eyes, its whole head has to turn to take in the courtyard. The rest of its face – brows, nose, and mouth – is painted too, all arranged into a disturbingly gleeful expression.

Ulcerated puppets parody the Choir's faithful. Where its skin cracks, diseased flesh bubbles out. Adding insult to injury, they are the weakest, dumbest eerians to exist, yet difficult to break permanently. No wonder spirers like them for practice.

Eventually, the puppet settles on the closest target: me. Once free of the crate, it jerks up onto its toes as though helped by invisible strings. It stands twice the height of its former cage.

Alastair hovers a few paces behind me. 'Ready?'

'No,' I groan, but slip my mask on all the same. I just hope I won't throw up again.

I take stance, loosening my knees and raising my spire. It could be my shaking arms, but the Might feels heavier than my old spire.

The puppet half totters, half glides towards me, promising violence with its drawn grin and forever-gawking eyes. It moves with an odd weightlessness, as if some invisible puppeteer hovers over the courtyard, guiding its actions with giant hands.

'I meant what I said before,' Alastair says. 'You can achieve Acclaim. Not just like this – directly from Our Lord.'

Never has the idea seemed more ridiculous than right now, while I stand sick and shuddering from its touch.

Alastair backs off all the way, abandoning me to the puppet as hideous, rushing power takes my body again.

My opponent quickens its shambling dance. I'm anything but prepared, dumbly squinting past the light as it appears next to me.

It twists its torso left in a painfully telegraphed wind-up that I'm still too blitzed to react to. I can only brace for impact as it starts to twirl the other way, limbs spinning.

Alastair steps in to parry the puppet's arm with the Cunning. The lightless blade fails to cut; it just knocks the puppet off balance, giving Alastair time to follow up. Throwing his torso sideways, he angles an explosive boot-stomp into its hip. I can't help but be impressed by his flexibility. He's always had better range of motion than me, but he puts the work in.

The puppet goes flying, giving him plenty of scowling time. He's so unthreatened by this creature, he hasn't even bothered with his mask. It's a look that says, *Don't embarrass me in front of our future cohort.* But even resentment can't dull my panic. My own furious breaths are harsh in my ears.

Then Alastair's face is right in front of mine, his bare hand clasped to the side of my neck, hot against my skin. He applies next to no pressure, yet his hold is tight as the grave. I can't look away.

'Deep breaths,' he keeps saying.

I want to obey, but I can't focus on anything. My heart's pounding to the point of pain.

But then Alastair's voice sinks to blacker, strangely hypnotic depths. I have to breathe deeply. I *have* to. My shrivelled lungs have to expand, taking in air until full. And with each lungful, my heart slows and the all-over shuddering eases. Even my vision sharpens, adjusting to the wild, slashing light.

'That's good. Keep breathing, and listen.' Alastair's thumb traces back and forth, just grazing my earlobe. In the moment, I can feel nothing else. 'When a spirer shares their Acclaim, Our Lord doesn't intervene,' he tells me, all other sound hushed. 'Whether you consider yourself a true spirer or not makes no difference. Put it out of your head. The only thing that could stop you wielding Acclaim is you.'

I always hate to admit it when Alastair's right, but this time there's no denying it. He's taken Oldrac's will out of the equation. I don't need to embody the Radiant Principles. I only need to persevere.

'Now,' he says, 'dispose of the puppet.'

He releases me as if from a spell. I frown as he falls back, confused by the lack of him. The air is cold on my neck where his hand had been.

But there's no time to question it. The puppet's coming for me, and now, I see it clearly. Now, my muscles have ceased gripping of their own accord.

I force another deep breath and prepare to take it on myself. I'm back in control.

This time, when it strikes, my spire is the one to meet it. It's a terrible swing, nothing clean about it, but thanks to Acclaim, it goes fast and hard.

The Might slides through the puppet's wrist like paper. It cuts *nice*. There's barely any resistance – which brings its own problem: I put way too much force behind the strike, and stumble forwards.

The puppet's severed hand shatters on the ground like a thrown plate. The body shambles out of range, writhing like a possessed tongue in a pantomime of upset. This gives me time – time to recover; time to realize that the overwhelm of Acclaim has eased. My body feels almost numb to it now, the Might oddly light in my hand. The seizing's stopped altogether, and I'm focused. Intensely focused.

Discoloured flesh seethes from the hollow stump of the puppet's arm and pools in the snow, burning it away. I watch with delight as reptilian eyes pop open in the pool.

I launch myself at the puppet. With Acclaim's speed, I easily evade its defences to slice its ankle out from under it. More flesh comes spilling from the hole, bobbled with sticky-looking eyes.

I get the dangerous thought – an Acclaim-induced delusion – that I could flick this creature aside.

The puppet lurches to the side, losing some of that disconcerting lightness to bring its head within striking range. I don't waste the opportunity. Swinging the Might over my right shoulder, I hammer it down on the puppet's painted skull. It cleaves the thing in half, and flesh speckled with eyes oozes from the split like egg yolk.

I lift my spire, waiting for it to build itself back up so we can go at it again. With this vibrancy coursing through me, I realize this is a spire's true and natural state. Until now, I've only ever fought with a dead thing, a hollow imitation of the real.

So this is why spirers love the Hallowed Game so much.

'There you go,' Tieran says. 'Your technique lacks finesse, but we'll address it later. Let's see how it goes with the two of you.'

Alastair steps forward again, his gaze flicking from me to the flesh-dribbling puppet.

'Only one of you can wield Acclaim at any time, so you'll have to pass it back and forth between you. That means switching between defence and offence depending on who has it.'

That's a worry. Ordinarily, the dangers and opportunities of the fight dictate the defence and offence. Now, Acclaim will have to decide my actions.

'It's a tricky manoeuvre,' Tieran goes on, 'but you'll impress Edusa, and the crowd, if you can pull it off.'

Alastair says, 'When you want to strike, say *pass*. I'll tell you whether I can or cannot give it. If you already have it and can go without, say *pass back*.'

'Remember,' Tieran says, 'accord sharing is all about teamwork.'

I wipe the sweat from my brow. 'Let's hope for a third miracle, then.'

***

By the time Alastair and I leave the courtyard, I'm hungry, weak, and sweaty. It takes Oldracian effort to keep myself and my spire off the ground. First stop is the washrooms, and next is the common room to eat.

As I drag myself up the stairs towards our rooms, Alastair says, 'You did well today.'

'Downed gods, was that a compliment?'

'Yes, it was. Well done for noticing.'

'What's that supposed to mean?'

'Nothing. Just forget I spoke. Again.'

'I thought we were having a ceasefire?'

'We are.'

'But you're upset with me.'

He doesn't deny it. What would be the point? If the sass wasn't enough, displeasure is clear in the tightness of his jaw and shoulders, the pronounced dullness of his voice, the eyes that won't look at me. It's taken two years, countless training sessions, and the first half of admissions, but I can now finally read Alastair's body language. Sometimes.

'Take it easy for the rest of the day,' he says. 'Acclaim use brings a sort of hangover, and we need you on top form tomorrow.'

That explains a lot – the headache, the tremors, the fatigue. My limbs feel twice as heavy as they usually do after training, and raised pink flesh veins my knuckles. My first Acclaim scars. The marks of battle are something to celebrate in Preyburn… unless they come from Acclaim, of course.

What it doesn't explain is Alastair's mood. Very odd. For better or worse, we've always been able to tell each other exactly what we think. And I remember how he helped me focus during training, his steadying words, his touch. I might not have overcome my panic without his help.

'Don't change the subject,' I say. 'I haven't meant to upset you, so whatever the issue is, let's not leave it to fester. Please.'

At last, Alastair looks at me. Seeing that I mean it, his face softens almost imperceptibly. He draws to a stop on the stairs, so I stop with him, a couple steps higher so we're eye to eye.

'The issue is, I thought we were playing a game with each other these past two years.'

'A game.'

'Yes, a game. But after last night, I started to think… well, perhaps only one of us knows we're playing.'

'Faulton, what in the abyss are you going on about?' I say, patience fraying already.

'Your selective hearing,' he huffs. 'You remember my every criticism for years, verbatim, but my praise and affection goes sailing past your head.'

And then he just stands there, staring back at me like a cat sitting next to an empty bowl. The audacity!

'To be clear,' I say, 'we could have the loveliest, fluffiest accord in the world, and I still wouldn't fall to my knees and weep with gratitude every time you tell me I did well.'

'Fallen gods.' Alastair closes his eyes and rubs his temple for a few seconds, his blush building. 'Nobody can be this dense.'

'No, I got it. Thank you for the compliment, it was sublime – best I've ever had. You're *so good* at compliments, Faulton.'

By the way his eyes harden, I know this is the cement over the coffin of this conversation.

'I'm good at discretion, but of course you've never heard of it. Nothing less than the most obvious, overplayed delivery gets through to you. I see that now.' He sighs and sets his jaw. 'Starting tomorrow, we'll do things your way.'

He turns and stalks off up the stairs. I stare after him, lost but sensing danger of some kind.

'Meaning what?' I call.

'Meaning obvious and overplayed is exactly what you'll get.'

'Threats of violence go against our ceasefire, remember!'

All I hear from the next floor up is sharp, bitter laughter.

17

A DECENT SHOW

First thing the next morning, Alastair and I consult the roster. Pinned up in the common room for all to see, a list of every pupil still in the running for Edusa's patronage lies inked on St Penderghastian paper. A savage thirty-one contenders didn't clear their first stage, leaving only seventeen to take the second today.

Edusa's signature – enormous, flamboyant, Balverian Lavender blue – marks the roster's end, not so far from the names *Alastair Faulton & Halen Kilchoir*. He surely could've posted it earlier, but naturally likes to keep us in suspense.

Alastair views the roster with folded arms and a slight smile. 'We're almost last,' he says. At my non-response, he adds, 'A promising sign. Whoever's last, that's who the crowd most wants to see.'

I nod. 'Keeps everyone in their seats 'til the end.'

'Exactly. Speaking of, we should go watch some of the earlier stages.'

This hadn't even occurred to me. I didn't see anyone else's first-round stages. After we left the arena floor, Alastair went to the infirmary and I went to my room, where I holed up until dinner. That's what I'd planned to do again today.

When I hesitate, Alastair says, 'Admissions pupils watch free while we're still being considered.'

We would have to, or else you'd never get me in there. My heart leaps at the chance to see more eerians, but do I really want to spend my day in a crowd of raucous Balverians? The answer is obviously no, but Alastair's eyes are fixed on me, waiting, sucking in all light. It's day three of our ceasefire, and he seems to have forgiven me for whatever happened yesterday. I have to show willing.

'I suppose it'd be good to check out the competition.' I do a terrible job of hiding my reluctance.

Alastair shrugs, as if our competition is neither here nor there. 'I was more thinking you'd enjoy it.' I start to object but he beats me to it, echoing my words back to me: *'No, Faulton, I'd never enjoy savaging Our Lady's creations for sport!'*

'That sounds nothing like me,' I say, bewildered at his impersonation – not only how insulting it was, but that he attempted it at all. He even managed to modulate the tone in his featureless chasm of a voice. Impressive.

Alastair has a rare, playful spark in his eye. 'Come and see what the crowd sees, Kilchoir. You may change your mind.'

'It's been known to happen,' I concede.

He looks thoughtfully at my folded arms. Then he gently takes my wrist to hold my hand up to the light like a curious artefact. He's surprisingly warm. 'This might be the first time I've seen your hands without ink,' he says, smirking.

I'm not sure how to react. All the blood rushes to the points where his skin touches mine, leaving me a little lightheaded. If I didn't know better, I'd say Alastair was flirting with me... And that I was *enjoying* it.

My face heats, but I still don't pull away. 'What's your point?'

'No point,' he says, letting go of my hand. 'Just an observation.'

He leaves me feeling mystified and a little flustered in front of the roster.

Less than a bell later, still brimming with doubt, I strike out across the grounds with him. Our spiring garb is half hidden by thick winter jackets – mine a gift from Limbridge – done up to our throats. Alastair wears a caramel peacoat, fuzzed like an apricot. The ground's hard with frost, but the sky is blue and gaping. It's given up on snow for the time being.

We take a different route into the arena this time, following a few stragglers into separate bowels. Edusa's thundering, pantomime voice echoes down from somewhere up above, no doubt playing the crowd like a flute.

Alastair leads me into a hall of food and beverage stalls. Tellers serve hot buttered rum and spiced drinking chocolate, wrinkly baked apples, and knots of warm Choir loaf. Sadly, we deliberately ate a hearty late breakfast so we wouldn't have food sloshing around in our stomachs during our stage. Instead, I buy some of the darkest, oiliest, most intense coffee I've ever tasted. At my request, the teller tips half out, then fills it back up with milk and sugar until it's drinkable.

A chilly stone stairway brings us up into tiers of curved seating. I emerge from the cool, dark interior squinting in the wintry light. From this vantage, I can see out across all St Penderghast's idyllic gardens. The hedge maze, the gazebos, the ghostly glow of lanterns frozen on the lake – it's a dizzying view.

People of all ages, stripes, and stations fill the seating, their noses pink from cold. In the front-row seats, the upper classes sit swaddled in furs and fuss, jewellery rattling at their wrists as they bring stage glasses – pretentious, gilded binoculars – to their faces. The usher guides us to our section, the one reserved for admissions pupils, so it seems we won't be joining them.

He leads us towards the masses – large families in softer, cosier dress and couples dolled up on dates. This would suit me just fine, if not for how horrendous our seats are. The usher deposits us right at the front. I'd prefer to be at the back, where I could see without being seen myself, but I suppose then we'd be farthest from the action.

The stone-hewn seat is like a block of ice burning through my spiring breeches, and Alastair and I are squashed right up against each other. You couldn't slip a penny between us. I awkwardly struggle to accommodate his broad shoulders without spilling coffee in our laps or dropping my spire. I end up just leaning on him.

Alastair doesn't seem to mind. He makes no attempt to move his body away from mine, an arm slung over the back of my seat, apparently comfortable in my personal space. But he's warm and I'm cold and he smells divine – clean and soapy, but with something like papyrus – so I let it be.

By the time we've settled, the crowd is buzzed on the three stages we missed and their energy is explosive. The mess of floppy, bleeding tendrils on the arena floor gets me itching to see what comes out of the portcullis.

But before we can have an eerian, we first need a spirer. A single copper-haired scion swaggers from the spirers' gate, chest puffed and chin high.

'Ladies and gentlemen!' Edusa thunders. 'I present to you our third contender of the day: Ransley Liverich!'

This guy again.

'Yuck,' I mutter, and Alastair's hard glare says he agrees.

We're the only accord this year. All the others fight alone, and for this reason they have less dangerous eerians to face. Whatever the rest of the spirers have been fighting, our accord can expect much worse.

I remember a hush as we waited for the ancestor to emerge, but up here the excited babble of everyone around us is constant. As the portcullis begins to clank, that turns to raucous cheering and the fluttering of miniature flags – Penders' sigil on pale blue paper – wagging in anticipation.

A levitating bell ducks out from beneath the portcullis's lifted teeth.

'He's got a tolling squid!' I say, craning to get a better look.

It should be no surprise to see these creatures here. When Our Lady crafted the first of them, she salvaged the bells from the Choir's cathedral towers, cast iron and carved with ornate reliefs that narrate Oldrac's battles with eerians. The Choir considers the use of their bells in graving profoundly offensive, so despite the squids' primitive design, they remain a favourite of the Eternal Spite. Some parts of the fen – those that bleed into the sea – are lousy with them.

What separates tolling squids from ordinary cathedral bells are the tendrils of pinkish-white viscera that replace their clappers. The bells don't really levitate; they have slimy cords of muscle to hold themselves up, pulsing like arm-thick veins and lumbering across the ground.

Until now, I've only ever seen depictions of this charming creature in textbooks. To see one in the flesh, with its sloppy movements and iron skull, is a whole new experience.

I watch enviously as Ransley advances on his foe, knowing he won't appreciate Our Lady's craftsmanship any more than Alastair does. Acclaim sparks on his blade, but I can say with confidence that it's nowhere near the strength of Alastair's.

The squid shuffles towards him on its tendrils with no apparent quickness, but Ransley keeps his distance. This is smart – tolling squids aren't very bright, but their length gives them twice the height of the average man and many times the reach. He needs to ground it, get a spire through the conjunctions – inside the bell.

The crowd groans with theatrical disgust as a tendril unfurls from the writhing mass. Ropes of mucus pull between the extending limb and the central clump, which is busy moving the creature forwards, like stretched glue.

It takes a lazy swipe at Ransley. He sidesteps.

The reek of salty death carries on the wind, prompting several people to lower Choir loafs into their laps. It smells like a mollusc plucked from its shell and left to sour in the sun.

Ransley moves in to strike on its other side, but loses confidence when he sees the next tendril untangling and backs off. The squid has plenty of them, and needs only a few to stand. The rest can grab him any time they like.

He darts aside, letting the tendril whip past him, and then back to spike it. He throws all his weight behind the motion, driving the blade through hard muscle and into a crack in the stone beneath. The creature's pinned, but another tendril comes to yank out the spire.

Ransley does the unthinkable – he abandons his spire to get out of range.

The woman beside me sucks air in through her teeth. 'What a fool,' she says.

'A costly mistake!' Edusa crows. 'Our poor Ransley's broken the first rule of spiring, leaving him all but defenceless in the arena!'

I flush with shame and clutch the Might's sheath harder, reliving the moment I lost my Withersham-issue spire. The crowd would have called me a fool too. But unlike me, Ransley doesn't have an accord partner to help him recover.

The second tendril just sort of slops all over the spire, curling itself once around the blade and squeezing. Its two sharp edges create quite a lot of blood. The tendril flinches in pain but sees no choice in the matter. It doesn't have the wherewithal to realize spires have a safe hilt.

The pinned squid begins to toll with a deep, low resonance that delights me along with the crowd. The iron of its bell vibrates, struck by some lump of anatomy on the inside.

Ransley has no choice but to dive back in for his spire… and gets himself grabbed in the process. The squid wraps multiple tendrils around him before you can say 'Rook Thumbarrow' and grips 'til he squeals.

'Ladies and gentlemen, I do believe that's a fail,' Edusa bellows, his tone neutral.

All Ransley's dreams of attending St Penderghast's are crushed in seconds.

At the word *fail*, stage warders come sprinting from hidden passages. Between three of them, they make easy work of the squid and extract Ransley from its clutches. The crowd jeers without pity as both competitor and eerian are dragged, unconscious and slime-pasted, out of sight.

'Next to face her second stage, the latest in a long and storied line of spirers! Already considered a champion at her Lordslake academy, she's come to make her mark in the major leagues! Lourdes Spendlove!'

Hearing another of the few names I recognize, I sit up a little straighter to get a better view. Lourdes, long-limbed and muscular, strides onto the arena floor. She pays the crowd plenty of attention, waving and blowing kisses in all directions. The crowd are every bit as pleased to see her as she is them.

'Why's she on so early?' I ask Alastair. 'The public clearly adores her.'

'I have two theories.' His breath tickles my cheek, reminding me just how snug we are. Somehow, amid all the excitement, I started using his knee as a handrest. Alastair hasn't said a word, but I quickly remove my hand. The vibrations of his voice rumble through me. 'The first is to get people in seats earlier. If they put all the stars last, nobody would turn up until the end.'

'And the other?'

'She wins too easily.'

As a fresh tolling squid emerges from the opposite tunnel, Lourdes executes a complex sequence of flourishes with a frankly gorgeous spire, which she then lifts high over her head. Some of the children in the crowd squeal with joy as lightning threads down from the sky to strike her spire, as if Oldrac himself answered her call from the firmaments. Her blade lights like a torch as Acclaim ripples down its length.

I gawp. 'How did she *do* that?'

'Alignment with the Principles.'

So she wasn't having me on back in the common room. No tricks, no sabotage…

'She's a bona fide goody-goody,' I say, awed.

'For the most part.'

The power this gives her is upsettingly cool, radiance and dramatic shadows streaking across the arena. Compared to Ransley's piffling Acclaim, Lourdes' is big and blinding. The static charge in the air is enough to raise the hair on my arms and nape.

She's light on her feet too, launching forwards to sever a tendril and back before she gets into trouble. The cut-off limb squirms in a pool of its own blood on the ground in a way that thrills and sickens in equal measure. For her part, Lourdes looks exhilarated – a girl doing what she loves.

When a flurry of slashes causes the squid to stumble, entrails going weak beneath it, its bell meets the stone with a clank. Lourdes takes full advantage. Stamping on it with a triumphant heel, she drives her spire up into the bell. It pierces the soft meat protected by iron, once, twice, thrice in quick succession. She backs off only when it's gone limp.

'Glory!' Edusa roars.

The crowd chants, '*In passion, glory! In passion, glory!*' and rains down applause on the victorious Lourdes. I'm no stranger to jealousy, so when that sour hunger starts to curdle in my gut, I recognize the feeling instantly. I want to be celebrated like this.

'Ladies and gentlemen, we are five pupils down! Eleven stages of violent thrills to go!'

The crowd roars and I roar with them, seized by sudden, vicious excitement.

'Disgusting, isn't it? Those magnificent creatures being savaged for sport.'

Our faces, when I twist to look at Alastair, are alarmingly close – lip-locking distance, I realize, and my whole body overheats imagining how that would feel. Even worse is the dare in his eyes, the way he doesn't pull back *at all*. He's baiting me.

I reply with an exaggerated eyeroll that only widens his smirk, and turn away before I get sucked in by those abyssal eyes. I'm so annoyed at myself for picturing his mouth on mine – the image, once conjured, proves to have ridiculous staying power – that I can't concentrate on the next stage.

Soft darkness descends over the arena, prompting stage warders to light the braziers. Before I know it, it's almost time for our own stage. As we're making our way round the back of the spectators, my nose catches what I can only describe as sinister vanilla smoke. I look around without hope of finding the source in this sea of people, then carry on after Alastair.

Apart from ours, there are only three stages left – three pupils more anticipated than our accord – all present in the waiting room, waiting to prove themselves. As in the common room, or whenever we pass each other on the stairs, they don't acknowledge me. They barely acknowledge Alastair. I wouldn't care at the worst of times, but right now all I can think about is what kind of eerian we'll face.

They must have something sickening in wait for us if it's going to top the ancestor. Something wonderful.

Before we can start warming up, Edusa himself strides in flanked by Tieran. He throws out his arms. 'Just checking up on my champions-in-the-making!' he declares.

Excluding Alastair, who is always straight as a column, everyone pulls themselves up. While our competition tracks his entrance with expectant faces, Edusa casts a cursory look round at everyone before his gaze snags on Alastair and me. As he sweeps over, a half-shoulder cape of silk velvet and shimmering gilt thread embroidery flares out behind him in theatrical fashion. He smiles as if we are great friends – as if this isn't my second time ever seeing him up close, inhaling his exorbitant cologne, moustache oil, and rich, buttery leather.

'My spies tell me you were canoodling in the audience for all to see, causing quite a stir,' he says, winking in a way that makes me crave violence. 'Inspired work.'

I open my mouth to refute this, but Alastair says, 'Thank you,' and stares at me until it shuts again.

I lower my eyes to hide my frustration.

'Now, I've had a few enquiries about you since yesterday, and I hate to disappoint. I can trust you to put on a decent show this evening, yes?'

'Of course,' Alastair says.

At the same time, I say, 'What sort of enquiries?'

'Potential clients,' Tieran says. 'We get paid to appear at events and whatnot.'

'Not only that,' says Edusa. 'Balver's best tailors have thrown themselves into a bidding frenzy to design your spiring attire. *Very* eager. They'll have to wait until you're patroned at least.'

As I look at him, his smiling eyes stare right through me, seeing only the gilt I stand to make him somewhere in the future.

'I said you can't go back there! It's only for—'

'Who's going to stop me? *You?*'

Everyone turns to see Ransley stalk in, hounded by an usher who breathes through her sleeve.

'Edusa!' he barks. The closer he gets, the clearer it becomes that he's yet to visit the washrooms. To his credit, Edusa does not wrinkle his nose as the boy advances on him. From the periodicals Alastair forced me to read, I know he's braved worse in stages past.

At Edusa's gesture, the usher chasing Ransley falls back and bites her tongue.

The eliminated spirer draws near enough to drop his voice. He still has the regular, perfect features so rarely found in Preyburn, but the effect is undermined by evil-smelling squid juice. My eyes draw down to a smear of rubbery flesh on his left shoe. When he drags a hand through his hair, it stays sticking up.

'Look,' he says, 'we must be able to work this out. There's been a Liverich at Penders every generation for the past century. Whatever it takes, you know we're good for it.' Spoken with the confidence of someone whose missteps have never seen fair consequences.

Tieran regards this intruder with a curled lip, but Edusa's smarmy grin never falters. 'Call me a ravishingly charming cynic,' he says, 'but I don't believe any amount of gilt will make a crowd of… Tieran, how many tickets did we sell today?'

'Almost twenty-five thousand.'

'…a crowd of almost twenty-five thousand forget your embarrassing defeat. How could they possibly root for you, knowing you bought your way in?'

'I can redeem myself,' Ransley says, impatient. 'Nobody will question why I made the cut when they see me smash the Crucible.'

This gets a chuckle from Edusa, yet his words come sharp as a bite. 'Dear boy, if you couldn't knock a single tolling squid on its head, how in the name of Our Ferocious Lord do you expect to *smash* the Crucible?'

Ransley's face darkens further. 'This won't stand,' he spits, pointing at me. 'It's blatant favouritism. A Prey couldn't afford a Helel spire – we all know where she got it.'

The usher cringes, Tieran glowers, and the remaining admissions pupils gawp. My grip tightens on the Might's hilt, as if someone might try to take it from me.

As the silence spreads across the waiting room like a stain, Ransley attempts to stare Edusa down. It feels like an age passes before anyone speaks.

'Some perspective is wanted here, I feel,' Edusa says, his voice surprisingly low. 'What was the first thing I told you all?'

'Winning doesn't equal success,' Ransley says. 'Which is why I don't understand—'

'Who lifts you from the dust of obscurity?'

'Well, the public. But—'

'Who featured on the society pages after their first stage? Who have the columnists and fans been talking about? Who are my clientele asking for?'

His voice builds until its loudness and cadence dominate the room in the way only Oldracian volume can. It leaves ringing emptiness behind each time he ends a sentence.

'The public guides my favour,' he says. 'They found you lacking, even before today's embarrassment. If you did, by some miracle, scrape through the Crucible? I still wouldn't have offered you a place.'

'You haven't even tried to promote the rest of us!' Ransley says. 'Why should we be disadvantaged just because we didn't crawl out of some hovel in Preyburn?'

'Right,' I say. 'I crawled out of a hovel in Preyburn, and you're the one at a disadvantage. Got it.'

Ransley's look says he'd enjoy snipping off my fingers and posting them to my family one by one, but Edusa seems tickled.

'Do you hear that, Liverich? Something *fresh*.' He waves his hand lazily. 'When you've seen the enormous success that I have, you whet your instinct for potential… and the lack of it.'

Ransley jerks as if slapped.

'Now, will you leave with your last shred of dignity intact, or would you rather Tieran rids you of that too?'

Ransley looks like he recently learned how facial expressions work and is giving them all a go. He lands on fierce eyes and a clenched jaw. For a wild moment, I wonder if he isn't going to cuff Edusa on the chin.

Tieran must think the same. 'I can tell you how that would play out for you,' he says, yellow eyes flashing. 'Not well.'

I don't need Oldracian foresight to know that, and surely Ransley doesn't either. Tieran's older and more practised, hails from a legacy of great spirers, and is proxy to a spirer so famous he goes by a single name. In the end, Ransley disappoints us both when he exhales hard and stalks off, taking his stench with him.

Edusa seems to forget about him the moment he's out of sight, smoothing a hand over his coiffed hair. 'Our interlude is almost up. The crowd beckons!' Turning to us one final time, he adds, 'Don't be afraid to tease your audience with a lovelorn look or two. Tieran – we leave.'

All we can do is watch as he struts from the waiting room. The Faulton brothers exchange a glance and a nod before Tieran follows.

'Does he really claim to see the future?' I say.

'Yes, but not very well,' Alastair says. 'He's near-sighted – only a few moments ahead each time.'

Even a few moments would give an incredible advantage in the arena – and out of it.

I stare after both proxy and preceptor. Part of me dredges up comfort from knowing Edusa will support us if we get through the Crucible, but a much larger part feels grim trepidation.

'See how he'll turn as soon as the public tires of us?' I whisper. 'It's Ransley today, but it could be us tomorrow.'

In reply, Alastair does another strange thing in what's been a whole day of them: he puts a hand on my shoulder, and in a low, firm voice says in my ear, 'We won't give him the chance to tire of us.'

Stranger still, I don't boot him in the shin. I don't even shrug him off. In fact, I take comfort in it. 'No?'

'No. First, we make ourselves indispensable to him. Then we make ourselves independent of him.' He drops his hand. 'Trust me. All you need to worry about is winning today's stage.'

It's odd to feel eased by his voice, uncompromising as gravity, the black holes where his eyes should be, but I do.

18

CRUSH, GORE, AND SCALD

The sky has blackened by the time we take the arena floor. It's been swept of snow for the most part, and huge drifts lie clumped against the edges. Fire flickers in sconces along the walls and atop ornate stone braziers double our height, making the shadows twitch. The poles are gone from the stone, leaving iron covers where they'd been affixed.

Over our post-practice breakfast, Alastair and I sat in the common room to discuss the eerians we might face next. As my gaze fixes on the portcullis, I know some horrific creation lurks in the tunnel behind, and that nervous energy turns to excitement.

Edusa's resumed authority on the judges' platform, with his proxy stood sentinel at his back. Looking up into the crowd, there are fewer empty spots in the tiered seating than last time. I suppose if you're going to watch an admissions stage, better to see the later ones, where more skilled pupils take on more ferocious eerians.

For a few agonizing minutes, there's no sound but the distant crowd-gabble and the flutter of St Penderghast's flags. Then, finally,

Edusa calls for the stage to begin. The portcullis clanks up and out of sight, and an anticipatory hush falls on my ears.

We take stance as echoes emerge from the black tunnel. The metallic screech of a knife-edge being dragged across stone, and over that, a baleful weeping.

The figures that appear chill my blood deliciously. As if in mockery of the ancestor's clumsy dance of arms, these eerians are so graceful as to look unnatural. They glide into the light, their tunic hems coasting along the floor too smoothly to hide two human legs. How they plan to manoeuvre in floor-length garb, I can only wonder.

As they near, I realize that may not be an issue. Neither clothes nor hair are disturbed by the breeze. From scalp to hem, both are the colour of ancient and uncared-for bronze, a blue-green patina mottled with black rust. Pitch tears streak down both their cheeks, and since their faces don't move the sobbing is royally disconcerting. Apart from forward motion, they're perfectly still, as if pushed by some outside force.

They each have a woman's head, a torso, two slender arms ending in two hands, and weapons. The left eerian drags what looks to be a boulder by three chains behind it – the source of that metallic screeching. At second glance, it's a hefty censer, and like chapel censers, thick swathes of incense smoke issue from the metalwork. Unlike chapel censers, it glows and smoulders as if filled with a living fire.

The eerian on the right went for something more direct: a whacking great scythe, built for war rather than cutting grass. The curved blade extends from the shaft as opposed to sitting at a right angle like a hook, making it essentially a polearm.

'Yes, my esteemed guests!' Edusa roars. 'The dreaded rusted-censer maiden, and her sister, the atrocious rusted-scythe maiden!'

A laugh escapes me. Only here in the arena would I be blessed enough to meet such rare and special creatures. *And get to battle them,* adds a voice in my head, and I give myself another mental slap. These are Our Lady's great works of art. It's barbaric to destroy them, and even worse to take pleasure in it.

Shaking free of my thoughts, I turn to Alastair. 'Rusted maidens. You know what that means.'

'What?'

'Beheadings.'

As far as Eerian Studies go, the maidens have seen more attention than the ancestor, likely due to fame. Alastair's baffled staring says he's forgotten that Our Lady sent the maidens – or some cruder version of them – to challenge Oldrac himself. He ended it by cleaving their necks. Later study of their epitaphs has proven his method the most effective one; that's where crucial conjunctive glyphs are held.

'I'll simplify things for you,' I say, with just the right amount of smugness. 'Cut the necks, end the stage. The difficult part will be getting our blades to them.' Alastair nods. 'These two were designed to work together. Let's keep them apart.'

'Divide and conquer,' says Alastair.

The maidens continue to advance on us. Every movement is smooth and decided, a thing of terrifying beauty. The greatest beauty is the kind that repulses, after all.

'I want the censer maiden,' I say. 'I've never fought anyone with a flail before.'

'Have you fought anyone with a war scythe?'

'No, but the flail looks nastier.'

'Flails are a poor choice, functionally speaking.'

I sniff. 'Our Lady understood the importance of aesthetics.'

When the first sparks of Acclaim burst from Alastair's spire, I resist the urge to startle. A light that is nowhere near the intensity of Lourdes', nor the faintness of Ransley's, lashes the blade.

'Besides, inhuman strength and dexterity helps,' I add, correcting my grip on the Might's hilt. 'Come on, then. Give me Acclaim.'

'I'm not *giving* you Acclaim. I'm sharing *my* Acclaim *with* you.'

'Semantics!'

'Not semantics; important, functional distinction. Only one of us can use *my* Acclaim at any one moment, so—'

'So we have to time our attacks, I know.'

'If you know, act like it. What's the signal we agreed?'

I grit my teeth. '*Pass!*'

'Denied,' he says flatly, advancing on the scythe maiden while I stare in open-mouthed shock.

The problem is, I don't have much say. It's entirely up to Alastair when he will and won't allow me the use of his blessing, and in the meantime I can't strike or parry, only evade.

Still sobbing as if the world is about to die, my maiden swings her censer up over her head, building momentum. Her willowy, turquoise arms don't look capable of such control, but she flicks this ball of smouldering metal about as though it weighs little. Its heaviness conjures mental images of being walloped in the gut, on the knuckles, in the face. As if the bone-crushing force weren't enough, the metal is spiked and burning. It will crush, gore, and scald all at once.

She hurls the censer at me, maximizing punch with pace. It comes smashing down next to my boot, splintering the stone.

That could've been my ankle.

Her chain's reach is alarming, outstripping mine by an arm and a half, but she needs distance to use it. It won't be easy, but if I can weasel in past her reach, I'll have a decent shot – or at least I would if I had an Acclaimed spire.

Glyphs blaze and writhe across her neck as though taunting me, daring me to strike when I've nothing to strike with. Incense smoke thickens in the air around us, filling my lungs with acrid haze, making my eyes burn. Partial blindness, coughing, and spluttering do not help my form. The maiden's movements blur as she advances on me, twirling the censer's chain like a damned baton.

'Pass!'

Somewhere in the smoke, Alastair calls, 'Denied!'

'Listen, you feculent toad-spawn! If you keep hogging, you won't have a partner to pass—'

'Granted!'

A loud crack splits my ears as the Might jolts to life in my hand. My lids snap shut, shielding my poor singed retinas from its offensively showy light. Acclaim's relentless, surging energy seizes hold of me and refuses to let go. The feeling is not at all comfortable.

The hairs on my arms stand to attention, skin prickling as I fight to remember... What was I supposed to be doing?

Edusa's laughter rattles around my head. 'It appears our Prey hopeful and exiled Faulton seek to show off the strength of their accord tonight!'

The censer comes flying towards me again, and lucidity with it.

I sidestep, blinking tears from my ruined eyes, letting the stone absorb all the censer's momentum. I have as long as it takes the maiden to recover from the impact to dart in.

Moving with the jittery haste of a girl who's overdone the coffee, I lance her waist with as much force and speed as I can muster – which, with Acclaim on my side, is considerable. And unlike before, when my Withersham-issue spire rebounded off the ancestor's limb as if I'd whacked it with a branch, this time the blade pierces the skin. Great swaggering whips of lightning come jagging out every which way, spiking right through me. I should be brain dead and disintegrating, but by Oldrac's blessing I'm intact.

'To share Acclaim successfully demands utter accordance!' Edusa bellows on. 'They must be two halves of a redoubtable whole!'

Here's another curious thing: even when I'm a spire's distance from her, the maiden looks just like a tarnished bronze statue. Her body makes none of the movement that would be natural for a thing alive – there is no swell as she inhales, no recoil when she's hit. Yet the spire pierces tunic and skin as easily as it would a meringue. Bits flake off her like eggshell around the entry point. Dark green blood seeps out and fizzles to nothing from the white heat of Acclaim.

Her plaintive blubbing rises to a howl that's almost comedic in its drama. I might be chuckling if she weren't hurling the censer in an arc towards me. Blazing spikes claw the scaling from my left shoulder, lighting it up with pain. Her swing's so vicious that the momentum makes off with her, allowing me two quick jabs into her spine.

In case I thought getting inside her reach was still the way to go, the maiden pulls the chains shorter, tightening the arc of her censer. She catches me off guard, clouting me in the calf.

There's a visceral crunch as flesh, bone, and cartilage pound together, the spikes tearing on their way in and out. I scream. My knee cannot help but fold as the force of it knocks me sideways onto the ground.

'Pass!' Alastair yells – not a request, but a demand – and the Might dies in my hand. The light dulls like the sun setting in rapid time, leaving colour spots flitting across my vision in the resultant darkness. A downward blow from the censer will mean the end. That Alastair would rip my only defence from me in the moment I need it most is evil at best, and at worst, poor strategy.

Half blinded by suffering and smoke, I throw myself to one side. My leg and shoulder howl in pain together, but it's all I can do to roll, scrabbling from the trajectory of her follow-up swing. Alastair's many things, but a poor strategist isn't one of them. *Something must be wrong.*

'Oh dear! Our exiled Faulton may have bitten off more than he can chew with the scythe maiden! And our Prey hopeful has also fallen afoul of the censer maiden!'

As soon as I try to put weight on my leg, I know I'm in trouble – the kind of trouble I haven't feared for two years as half a scion's brat. While my body tries to recover from Acclaim, it won't heal any other injuries. I wielded Oldrac's blessing for all of a moment, and now I tremble from scalp to toe, muscles spasming against my will, guts threatening to purge. Decent form is out of the question, the pain so vicious in my leg that I can only hobble. I've got no option but to back off, half dragging my broken leg along with me. The censer maiden pursues me single-mindedly across the arena, bawling her eyes out all the while.

I get a good look at Alastair and immediately see why he needed his Acclaim back. While the crowd rejoices in his volley of fast strikes, the scythe maiden parries with eerian speed, meeting every strike with a thresh of her blade. His masked face betrays nothing, but the cords jutting out of his neck reveal how hard he's pushing himself.

No matter how devastating his attacks, how quick his flurry of blows, the maiden rises to the challenge. If this keeps up, he'll simply burn out – and if he falls, I'll be quick to follow. He doesn't have any attention to spare me, to know when I need Acclaim, and when I can go without.

Reflexes dulled by suffering, I barely duck the censer maiden's next swing. The censer collides with the nearest stone brazier, knocks a chunk from it, and ricochets. Happily, it takes the maiden off balance, giving me more time to get away from her. I limp over to a brazier and support myself against it.

'Bring the scythe maiden towards me!' I call.

Alastair's voice comes strained and panting. 'The plan was divide and conquer!'

'Right now, they're dividing and conquering *us!*' I say, eyes on the recovering censer maiden. 'How can we co-ordinate if we can't see when each of us is attacking?'

Alastair gives some grunted reply, but he evidently agrees because he parries the scythe maiden's blade with enough force that he can get distance, sprinting towards me. Because of this, he sees my maiden winding up her next strike.

'Pass!' he calls.

The Might kindles like a star in my hand, wrongfooting the censer maiden, who can hardly halt the momentum of her heavy censer mid-swing. I duck the chains and drive the spire through her tunic, into *her* leg. *Insults demand answers.* I know I've done serious hurt when an uproarious wail rises.

The censer maiden wobbles like a spinning top starting to fall. I time my exit so I don't get walloped by chance, staggering out of range.

Alastair shouts, 'Pass!' and as the light drains from me, the all-over pain returns with a vengeance. With the power of Oldrac's Acclaim, this agony had been numbed, both a blessing – allowing me to do what needs to be done, injuries be damned – and a curse, driving me to worse trauma.

Alastair gets within reach of my maiden's still-swinging censer with his own maiden on his heels. Fortunately, neither of them seem to go anywhere in a hurry. He raises the Cunning over his shoulder, hands tight on the hilt, and swings right to left.

The blade catches the censer like a cricket bat, with a crack of lightning I feel in my bones and enough power to send it careering back on her. That the spire didn't simply snap in two says absolutely nothing about Helel's work and everything about the power of Acclaim.

The censer maiden, who had seemed the incarnation of poise, now completely loses control of her weapon. In an attempt to still herself, she plants her feet (if that's what she has under there), but the censer keeps circling, wrapping her up in its chains.

She might be bound, but her sister's right behind her. We have only a moment.

'Pass!' I say, because Alastair's recovering from his Oldracian blow.

'Granted!'

I summon all my strength and halve the censer maiden's neck – a deliciously sinister feeling.

The crowd clamours as a lush fountain of blood leaves the stump. Her head tumbles from its perch to thunk into the stone and the chant of *'KIL-CHOIR! KIL-CHOIR!'* hits my ears.

Edusa's voice rumbles across the arena: *'Glory!* One ghastly, shrieking maiden down! But we still have her formidable sister to go!'

I watch, mesmerized, spire poised in the air over my shoulder. I'll treasure this memory for as long as I live.

Then I say, 'Pass back,' and the torture resumes, buckling my leg.

Alastair's upon the scythe maiden. His strikes are so fast, his spire doesn't even seem to change position. It's dizzying to watch. Even without my injuries, I couldn't hope to match that speed. With a pang, I realize there's no point passing back to me.

Worse still, if it's a test of stamina, the scythe maiden will outdo him. His Acclaim scars continue to multiply, spiking out of his collar, reaching for his face like the claws of Our Lady. I'll bet his entire body's covered beneath his spiring garb.

It's burning him out.

My gaze returns to the beheaded censer maiden, her motionless body twisted in chains on the ground, the censer smouldering next to her...

I think furiously. I mean, that's an *eerian* weapon. If I find the strength to lift it, I will have broken another rule on spiring etiquette, but I'll have something I can use.

While Alastair struggles valiantly against her sister, I roll the censer maiden's body free of the chains. Steeling myself for this Oldracian task, I plant the Might in the frozen dirt between cracked stones. If I fail to lift the censer in front of all these people, it'll look pathetic indeed.

There's one other problem with this plan, which I realize as soon as I seize the chains. I hear my own flesh sizzle like meat on a grill, feeling pure white pain as the metal burns into my skin like the nibs of a hundred graphia. Of all the days to forget my spiring gloves!

Rather than rebuking me, Edusa sounds tickled by my efforts. 'You see that, Balver? The resourceful quirkiness for which Preys are known! But how will this rather *exotic* strategy play out for her?'

The searing agony proves impossible to ignore, but when I heave on the chain, the censer lifts. Jaw locked, I half carry, half drag the censer towards Alastair's giddying fight. I'm wreaking havoc on my leg, but flesh and bone can be recovered. Admissions can't.

'Alastair!' I grit out, drawing his attention.

He sees and instantly understands. Using what I suspect to be the last of his strength, he parries the maiden's scythe with a brutality that knocks her my way, then traps it with the crockets of his spire hooking onto her blade's neck.

'Now!' he shouts.

That's my opening. She'll easily escape his hold, but not before I heave up the censer, simultaneously bludgeoning her hip and tearing every muscle in my core.

She goes down hard, head smacking the stone. Her temple explodes in eerian flesh shards, glancing off Alastair's mask as he takes *his* opening.

The Cunning plunges deep into her chest, eliciting a baleful scream. It cuts off abruptly when a successive slash takes her head. The resultant lightning deafens and blinds me.

'*Glory!*'

Past the ringing in my ears, I hear another, fiercer cheer from the crowd.

'FAUL-TON! FAUL-TON!'

Alastair stands triumphant but brittle, his mask sprayed with emerald blood as he faces me. He looks magnificent – like a demon warrior, fists rigid and shaking around his spire's hilt as he heaves for breath. I look away in a state of shock.

Somehow, both maidens lie stiff on the ground.

It takes every shred of willpower I have to limp back over to the Might and jerk it from the dirt. The leather-bound grip feels like a cheese grater against the raw, bloody skin of my palms.

I badly want to take the censer maiden's head as a keepsake – how gorgeous would that look on a mantelpiece? – but I couldn't possibly carry it. In fact, if not for all the people watching, I might like to cry.

'While delightfully unexpected, I'm loath to reward the jilting of one's spire for an eerian weapon...'

Alastair and I turn to stare up at the judges' platform in unison.

Edusa rises slowly to his feet, still talking. 'It isn't strictly against the rules, but then again, it isn't strictly *spiring*...'

He drags out the moment as long as he can, which I wouldn't mind if I wasn't in more agony than I've ever had to endure. It's been years since I felt so... mortal.

Finally, he throws his hands out. 'Oh well! I'll allow it!'

The crowd noise rears up all around, and I spit out a molar. It must've been knocked loose when I fell.

Alastair comes over to offer himself as a crutch, which I accept until he goes to take all my weight off the ground.

'Don't,' I say, but he only scoffs.

'You're not planning to walk on it?'

'I can't be carried out of the arena. It's embarrassing.'

'Don't be pathetic.'

I glower through the pain as he scoops me off the ground. The crowd noise rises to a roar, punctuated by several whoops and whistles.

'You wouldn't like it if I did this to you,' I hiss.

'I would if I thought the crowd wanted to see it.'

My face burns worse than my hands as he carries me back towards the passageway, as if carrying his new bride over the threshold of the Faulton estate. This image will haunt me for years to come. It'll be splashed all over the periodicals come morning.

Which is, of course, exactly what he intends.

The penny drops.

'Earlier, when we went to watch the stages – that was for the crowd's reaction too, wasn't it? You wanted everyone to see us together, to think we were...'

I stop. I cannot say the word *canoodling* out loud.

When Alastair doesn't reply, I muster a shaky laugh. My head thunders with barely subdued fury. 'And you call *me* pathetic? I'm not willing to debase myself for—'

'As per usual,' Alastair intones, 'you are so deeply invested in one pitiful sapling that you've failed to notice the surrounding forest. When Edusa said he wanted a decent show, what do you think he meant?'

'Obviously he meant for us to smash the stage the way Ransley thought he'd smash the Crucible.'

'It's like you're not even listening half the time. Spiring is only *part* of our performance. The rest of it is—'

'Our great love affair?' I say, disgusted. 'Is that truly what the spiring fans want to see?'

'This might have escaped your attention along with everything else, but things are different in Glimwick. People laud romance and pageantry above death and gore.'

'Well, of course you do. You're all insane.'

Alastair acquiesces once we're out of the crowd's sight, setting me back on the ground. He shepherds me along to the infirmary, where I spend the next few bells in excruciating pain.

———○———

Instead of practising glyphs, I while away the day's remainder by watching the progress of my hand blisters, worrying the new molar that emerges with my tongue. Glyph practice is out of the question; I couldn't even hold a pen at this point.

If only blisters were the worst of my troubles. The Acclaim scars are thickest and sorest where I gripped the spire's hilt, though they make inroads up my arms and shoulders, jagging across my chest like outstretched fingers.

Alastair hasn't fared any better; I was right when I'd guessed he was near his limit. Sleeves folded back to his elbows reveal a network of thorny, pale pink scars branching up his forearms. They tangle from the wrists down, leaving his palms and fingers more scar than unmarked skin.

The nurse checks my knee to make sure it's reset itself properly. Oldrac's flesh usually does, but there have been accidents, things that heal wonky and have to be broken all over again. While he works he shoos away Alastair, whom I then watch through the frosted glass, pacing back and forth, until I pass out.

My sleep is lamentably shallow, disturbed by pain and aftershocks. Some residual Acclaim sparks in this muscle or that, prompting weak spasms. I suppose it hasn't fully left me yet.

When I come to properly, a new molar has reasserted itself in my gums, and my hands are a normal colour again. Alastair's in the chair next to my bed. His arms, no longer scarred, are folded loosely over his chest as his gaze bores into the floor.

As soon as I stir, he meets my eye with a look that tests my nerve. It says I'm about to be lashed for bad behaviour. But instead of laying into me, he places a hand dangerously close to mine on the bed. I watch as though it might suddenly set fire to the sheets. Even my sleep-addled brain knows he's about to say something intense.

'I can't have you thinking it's all for show.'

My voice comes hoarse from sleep. 'What are you droning on about now, vile revenant?'

'I'm not pretending feelings for you. It's just that I wouldn't usually put them on display for an audience.'

'Faulton,' I say, flushing, 'you must realize this has come from absolutely nowhere?'

He scoffs, leaning back to run that too-close hand over his golden hair. 'It *really* hasn't. It's just that subtlety is wasted on you.'

I glower at him, sitting up to test my healing leg. 'Is it, now?'

'Yes, and not only that – I told you outright during our argument the other day. You chose not to hear it.'

'What? No, you did *not!*'

'I said, *I care about you.* What did you think I meant?'

I can only frown at him. I don't remember that at all.

Alastair shakes his head. 'It's my fault,' he says, almost to himself. 'I thought you knew what I wanted and feigned ignorance to torment me. I should have known it was as authentic as ever.'

'Alastair, I don't—' I break off, unsure what to say. *Is he being genuine?*

'You don't *what?*' he presses, but my brain's stopped functioning.

He waits to see if I'll recover enough to give him a complete sentence, but I've got nothing to say for myself. The silence deafens.

'I'll simplify things for you,' he says at last, visibly chagrined. 'The periodicals print false accounts of our great love affair because they know it sells. We'd be imbeciles not to play into it, regardless of how you feel.'

I bristle at his tone, equal parts patronizing and domineering. Despite the insult, I'm glad to be back on familiar ground with him.

'What exactly are you asking of me? Because if you think I'm going to hang off your arm, simpering like a lovestruck fool, that goes *well* beyond the terms of our truce.'

He sighs out a curse. 'You don't need to hang off my arm and simper. Just try not to look quite so sullen and disgusted the next time we're in public together. Can you manage that?'

'I don't see why it's all up to me.' Even to my own ears, I sound like a petulant child. 'Have you considered being charming or likeable?'

Alastair only stares me down with his twin voids. The silence intensifies every moment, until I finally relent with a huff. 'I'll do my best.'

Never breaking this ruthless eye contact, Alastair rises from his seat to tower over me, stiff and uncompromising as a monolith. 'And you call *me* cold-blooded.'

With that lovely bit of vitriol, he stalks over to the door, jerks it open, and vanishes into the night.

19

THE BEST POSSIBLE CHANCES

The next evening, Alastair and I make our way down to the games hall, where Edusa's soirée is in full swing. It marks the first day of Oldsfall, a four-day holiday for the anniversary of Oldrac's fall from the firmaments. It ends on the day of the Crucible.

We've been promised a grand affair, so Alastair's worn a complete set of rings for the occasion. He can't leave them alone, twisting them around and around his fingers. I never imagined his nerves could be worse than mine.

I say, 'Will it be that bad?'

He replies in a low voice, wary of anyone who might be coming up or down the stairs. 'Would you believe me if I told you this evening is more a threat to us than our last stage?'

An alarming thought, especially now that only eight other admissions hopefuls made it past the second stage, slashing seventeen places down to nine.

'How so?'

'Remember what I said to you in the carriage? About guessing people's motivations?'

'I remember.'

'Good. Yes, the guests are here to enjoy themselves, but they're also here to judge whether we have star quality. I haven't seen scrutiny like this for a long time. You haven't ever.'

'So? Edusa's always banging on about my Preyburn charm. He likes to think of me as a provincial hick, just like he plays up your exile.'

Alastair frowns. 'We need to be more than passing novelties.'

In keeping with Prey social graces, we've both pretended to forget the more awkward parts of our little chat in the infirmary. Sweeping our demons under the rug, where they can feed on our fears, growing in virulence until they escape at the worst possible time – that's the Preyburn way.

For my part, I still can't tell if he was being genuine about liking me. The more distant I get from it, the more baffling it becomes, but more likely it's another manipulation. Perhaps he thinks he'll be able to control me if we start sleeping together – to keep me in admissions.

Maybe he would, says an errant voice in my head. *Maybe he's just that good in bed.*

By the stars, where do these thoughts keep coming from? And why couldn't I bring myself to tell him I wasn't interested? It shouldn't matter whether he meant it or not.

I can't fret over this now. I need to focus.

The games hall needed very little decoration to make it soirée-worthy, but of course spirers must push things to extremes. Voluminous flower arrangements swell from man-sized vases; elaborate candelabras host twenty candles each; the porcelain floor has been polished to a sheen so severe that it becomes a mirror. There are several dramatic fireplaces which had been unlit the last I came, and each one is large enough to stroll into without bashing your head on the mantel. The domed glass ceiling is dark with snow.

Alastair told me to expect food, so I expected some sort of buffet. Instead, uniformed servers circle some eighty guests and a harp player with gold trays of fizz and delicate treats, hunting for half-empty glasses or plates.

There are few familiar faces. Among them are the eight other pupils left in admissions, Lourdes included; the abettors who selected us; Tieran; and our host. Among the people I don't recognize are those St Penderghastian preceptors who aren't accepting new pupils this year. There are twelve in total, six gravers and six spirers, each with a proxy beside them.

As we walk in, Alastair indicates one new face after another, listing names. 'Gladwina, Laudred, Cassander, Therese, Dracen, and of course all of their proxies. Adoro Heartmaster, Valorie Spyrewell, Ottie—'

'I didn't expect to see preceptors from the graving conspectus here,' I say, nodding to a group of people who are unmistakably gravers. Naturally, I've read the names of every preceptor on the conspectus but haven't yet matched them to faces.

'It's irrelevant to their conspectus, but a party's a party,' says Alastair. 'The ladies are Preceptor Elda Hagpest and her proxy, Ordelia Dolwright. The gentlemen are Preceptor Silas Pyrewicket and his proxy, Mord Ogleby.'

Some stand chatting, some dance, and the rest conspire on chairs in candlelit corners. All wear their riches.

Edusa had outfits delivered to us for the occasion, and it's a good job he did because provost knows there's nothing spilling out of my suitcase that would've been appropriate. If not for the detail, what we wear could be described as a jacket, trousers, and shoes. Mine are dark blue with golden, beaded fen herons embroidered across the chest and along the sleeves and legs. The lining is silk twill of a pattern that evokes the firmaments. The jacket buttons down the left side, like a spiring jacket. Alastair's clothes are inverted in colour, primarily in cream and dark blue with shimmering gold embroidery, Glim hares replacing the herons.

Just when I think we've managed to slip in without his notice, Edusa extracts himself from his guests and struts over. Not to be outdone by anyone, he wears a cream dress shirt that gapes from throat to hips, exposing an undershirt made of gold, netted beads.

'There you are! My champions-in-the-making!' he says. 'Fashionably late – *resplendent!*'

What follows is a dizzying carousel of high-society faces. Edusa sweeps us from one batch of esteemed guests to the next, proving Alastair worried for nothing. We don't have to do much talking. Edusa spouts witty anecdotes, reminisces over scandalous events of soirées past, brags about his own feats of athleticism in the arena, and recounts amusing but false accounts in the periodicals.

He's supporting a few false accounts of his own, namely this whole narrative about our accord. I overhear him describe it to an heiress, her dress frothing with taffeta: 'The feisty Prey girl struggling to make it as a spirer, the thoroughbred scion committed to exile… a chance encounter, an unthinkable, forbidden romance…!'

At first, the truly painful part is how the guests are lapping it all up. Then Alastair begins leaning into it. He stands as close as physics will allow, picking an imaginary piece of lint off my shoulder, brushing his hand over my waist. Suffering takes on new meaning. I need every bit of willpower not to glass him. If only anyone in this room understood… But then we might lose their interest, and with their interest, their support. Whenever the urge for violence starts to rise, I remind myself that this is for my benefit. If they prefer to think of me as the lovestruck fool, I have to let them. I have to keep the sullen disgust off my face. It's for Mortritis.

There are several columnists from the society pages here, and an artist. He roams the party, pausing in select spots to commit what scenes he can to paper with pen-and-ink vignettes that will be used to complement their articles.

The carousel of guests wheels around again, bringing Alastair and me into a circle with one Lord and Lady Cofferspyre. They've travelled all the way from Thundermark in the Storm Grounds to be here. Edusa introduces and then abandons us, swaggering off to see how Lourdes is faring with his other guests.

'We wouldn't expect you to know this,' the Lady says to me, 'but Cofferspyre is an old, *very* old spiring name. Even older than Faulton.'

'Oh, right. Fantastic,' I say. *Was that meant as a barb?*

'I expected to see Priel here tonight,' Alastair says, covering for me. 'Your eldest came to admissions this year, no?'

Lady Cofferspyre's smile sharpens. 'Even after all that time in Preyburn, you have an excellent memory. I'm afraid our daughter failed her first stage.'

'Oh. What a perfect shame.'

Alastair's faux-surprise does nothing to soften the Cofferspyres' rage, thinly masked by genteel smiles.

'Her time will come.' Lord Cofferspyre's eyes settle on me, his tone halfway threatening. 'Apparently this is *your* year. What an impression you've made.'

'You can't open a paper these days without seeing your name printed somewhere,' the lady goes on. 'I never expected to see a Kilchoir at admissions. No doubt your skills are *highly* impressive in Preyburn.'

'We've never been to Preyburn, because... well!' Her husband breaks off, chuckling. 'One hardly needs to justify that statement.'

Bristling, I say, 'My skills are highly impressive everywhere. That's why I'm here.'

The Cofferspyres keep smiling at me with too many teeth.

'Well, you certainly are *here*,' the lady agrees. 'Edusa always knows how to spin a good story. Skill matters, of course, but as we've seen this year, the story is what really counts.'

'And what a story!' chimes in the lord. 'The society pages are milking it dry, and I have to say, your latest vignette in the *Balver Chronicle* was a special treat.'

'Wasn't it just? It takes great confidence to utterly ignore the fashions and simply throw on whatever takes your fancy.'

'So tell us: how *does* a Prey come to possess Oldrac's traits?'

My mouth opens, then closes again. Whether verbal or physical, fights in Preyburn are usually brawls, not assassinations. We don't hide our insults with pretend niceties. Powerless to insult them like I would Alastair, or with my fists, I've been totally defanged. The Cofferspyres keep staring while my urge for violence rises to new, irresistible heights.

Sensing this, Alastair grips my hand and squeezes to the point of pain – magnificent, distracting pain. He chuckles, half amused and half scornful. 'I should think it happens the usual way. You have children of your own, so hopefully I needn't go into detail.'

The Cofferspyres chuckle with him, sweet and false.

Because the world isn't entirely devoid of mercy, Edusa returns and steals us away before I do something I regret. He looks delighted to see us hand in hand. I try to shake Alastair loose, to no avail.

We leave the Cofferspyres looking horribly smug to join a new ring of faces. When I catch a circling server's eye, he practically teleports to my side to unload whipped cheese and fresh cherries on toast into my hand.

'Looks like you just went a round with the Cofferspyres,' says a husky voice.

I turn to see Lourdes at my shoulder. 'That we did,' is my grim reply.

'Ghastly people,' she mutters. 'No wonder Priel failed out, poor thing.'

'Doesn't badmouthing people go against the Radiant Principles?'

'A few unkind words aren't going to tip the scales, especially when Our Radiant Lord would agree with them. He upholds compassion, lest we forget. The Cofferspyres don't know the meaning of the word.'

Alastair clears his throat.

'It's all right, Alastair,' Lourdes says. 'I'm not trying to step in on your date. Just saying hello, yes?'

'Hello,' Alastair says. *Frosty* doesn't quite cover his tone, but Lourdes is undeterred.

'And to compliment your second stage, you little show-offs. The Acclaim sharing, the carry offstage – it all went down a treat.'

I keep searching for sarcasm or insincerity in her words, but I can't find any. Having seen her spire, benevolence clearly pays off.

'Part of me wishes the abettors had put me in an accord,' she says wistfully. 'I would've loved to spire the rusted maidens.'

When Alastair says nothing, I say, 'Thanks. Your stage was… quite impressive.'

'It means a lot to hear you enjoyed it.' Lourdes flashes her winning smile again, slightly raising her glass to me. 'Do let me know about practice, won't you?'

She saunters off to schmooze Edusa's guests, as familiar with the evening's trials as an eel in the fen.

Alastair says, 'You've spoken before?'

'Apparently not as much as you have. It seems like she knows you.'

'In a roundabout way. Our older brothers are good friends.'

'Would she have ulterior motives, inviting me to practice?'

'Not the kind you're thinking of. Lourdes is a tediously straight arrow in every area but one.'

'Which is?'

'She stirs up relationship drama to excite the public.' Alastair's face is pure distaste. 'That's how she makes up for her boring wins.'

'What? And you think she…?'

'It's possible she offered in the spirit of oneness, encouraging fellowship and the like, but equally possible she didn't.'

'She's flirting with me,' I say, hardly believing it.

Alastair's voice drips sarcasm. 'Keenly observed.' I realize he still has my hand when he tugs me towards him, dropping his voice. 'How are you coping?'

His overcurious gaze and the warm press of his skin dredge up memories of the infirmary. I have to look away from him to banish them. 'The conversation is exhausting, but the food almost makes up for it. What about you?'

'I'm decent. I attend one or two events like these in Copperfont every winter, whichever invitations Papa declines. People are always curious to hear about my time in Preyburn, but there isn't usually so much inquisition.'

'Well, thanks for fending off the Cofferspyres.'

'If you find yourself alone with them, phrase your insults as compliments and keep smiling.' He offers a smile of his own, but a wry one. 'With that sharp tongue, no doubt you'll take to it.'

'Prodigal Faulton, Prey hopeful!' Edusa pops up out of nowhere. 'One moment of conspiratorial whispering is mysterious, but two is off-putting! Remember this is a *party!*'

Instead of flouncing off again, he stays to supervise our interactions with his guests. I should be on my best behaviour, but I'm still privately stewing in my rage over the Cofferspyres, imagining every foul thing I would've liked to say.

I only have eyes for Mortritis, of course, but Gladwina is undeniably, fearsomely gorgeous. She wears an equally gorgeous coat, but in true spiring fashion there's wildly too much of it, sloping from her bare shoulders. Her proxy, Adoro, hasn't left her side all night. He's painfully smug in her company, and who can blame him?

New guests make their way into the games hall. Everyone turns to level untamed stares at them, murmuring to whoever happens to be beside them. I turn to see a lady with pitch-black hair, slicked back, and an ankle-length gown of elegant detail. Her skin is as clear and smooth as a pane of glass, her nails double the length of her fingers and filed to skin-coloured points. She's flanked by Tieran and four other boys – bronze-haired and chisel-featured, the eldest no older than fourteen – who survey the party with imperious, black-glass eyes. I know exactly who they are.

When Alastair claps eyes on them, his whole body goes rigid. He squeezes the stem of his wineglass 'til it snaps. This is not his fault; the glassware in this room has all the strength of spun sugar. Alastair barely notices as one of the servers dives in to relieve him of the pieces.

He strides across the games hall to meet his family.

'Goodness,' says Preceptor Gladwina. 'Is that Drasilla Moppeton and her boys?'

Edusa answers first with a knowing look that is incredibly punchable. 'It is indeed.'

'I had no idea she'd come tonight. I thought Alastair was estranged by order of Aiden Faulton.'

'You're quite right! But when I reached out to let her know how well he was doing at admissions, Aiden gave her leave to attend.'

As quite literally everyone in the games hall watches, Alastair reaches his mother, takes both her hands, and smothers them with kisses, a thousand times more reverent than he was with Flaypenny. Drasilla watches him with a mixture of joy and heartbreak. Her scarlet-painted lips are moving, but she's too far away to hear.

Gladwina's eyes widen. 'Will Aiden be coming?'

Edusa shakes his head. 'You know Aiden – he cannot be seen to yield. It's one thing to send your representatives, quite another to make the trip yourself.'

Still gripping her hands, Alastair presses his lips to each of Drasilla's cheeks as she turns her head for him, and then her forehead. Then Alastair's brothers descend upon him with cheek-kisses and hugs of such crushing intensity that I wince. Tieran looks to be glowing. It would be strange for Preys to lavish such affection upon each other, both in public and outside of it. Again, I'm reminded of the night I brought up the incident with Flaypenny to Mortritis, lacking the sense to realize I was reopening a wound.

'Of course,' Edusa says, 'if Alastair keeps going as he has, no doubt a *father*–son reunion is on its way to us. Won't that be a sight?'

As Edusa continues to pass me around his guests like a cheeky cigarette, my eyes keep flicking back to Alastair's family reunion. So does the conversation. Every new face introduces themselves by gushing to Edusa over what a pretty picture they make, how heartened they are. I listen to Edusa tell the same story about Alastair's exile enough times that I could repeat it word for word.

I get a welcome reprieve when Mortritis appears in a gown I cannot help but gawp at. Intermittently sheer and black lace of a sensuous pattern, she is both covered and exposed from jaw to floor. The skirt flares at the knees in a mermaid cut, accentuating her hourglass figure. I forget all about Gladwina.

She greets her sister and nephews with countless squeezes and kisses. I've finished a full glass by the time she gets round everyone and am desperate to speak to her, but wouldn't dream of interrupting.

I remember, with a pang of guilt, that I neglected to practise glyphs today. I push this feeling away; it's pure paranoia. One day won't make a difference.

The guests are merry, some merrier than they want to be, and the whole scene has begun to degenerate. Guests stumble over their own skirts, spill drinks, and begin to bellow at each other. Many more wineglass stems will be snapped before the night is through.

The other admissions pupils, bar Lourdes, have clustered around Tieran. I don't need to hear what they're saying to know they're blowing smoke up his arse, and he's enjoying it immensely.

Some preternatural sense, some weak remnant of Oldrac's prophetic abilities, makes me turn towards the entrance as two familiar figures walk through it.

The woman shuffles with slow determination and the help of a silver-headed walking cane. The man probably couldn't outpace her if he wanted to. He has florid cheeks and a hard, round belly honed through years of consistent drinking. But hard bellies and florid cheeks can't compare to the look of a laywoman who took pulp. There's no mistaking that withered look, as if all vitality has been sucked out of her through a straw – hair silvered like twine, bones poking at skin that appears starched and chalky, like dry rice. Even her eyes are flat, a dull grey inside whites of an unhealthy, pinkish hue. This woman is thirty-eight years old but could be pushing sixty.

I'm vaguely aware that my mouth has dropped open. My pulse rises to a sprinting pace as I take in the odd pair, so *very* odd when you consider their dazzling surroundings. I look at Edusa, if only to confirm what I'm seeing is real, and the sparkle in his eye tells me it is. He's ready to see some drama, and like always, he'll get what he wants.

Ignoring the glances of interested guests, I hurry across the room to greet my parents. I move a bit too fast, in fact, so that when I stop in front of them, I haven't thought what to say. My mouth opens and closes like an eel snared from the fen. No words come to me as they take me in from toe to scalp, patently unimpressed.

When was the last time I saw them? It must have been months ago, when I visited Crippleditch in the summer. In spite of the distance, I've learnt more about them since I came to St Penderghast's than I did in all the years before; my parents never confide anything if they can help it. The secret knowledge manifests as a prickle along my scalp. It feels somehow shameful to know what I now know about my mother's hardships – shameful, and wounding.

Eventually, I manage to say, 'Mother… you're here.'

Her lungs make a coarse, rattling sound on every in- and exhale, but this is normal. 'So I am,' she says, smiling tightly as she soaks in the scene.

I hadn't thought Edusa would invite anyone I knew. Alastair's family are important people in Glimwick, the kind Edusa would want to be seen at his party. My parents, on the other hand, are unknowns.

What looks terribly fashionable and urban in Preyburn simply looks bizarre in Glimwick. I'm reminded of the abettors when they came to Withersham, how they looked torn from an old storybook. The reverse is just as jarring.

Mother's bundled in her best furs, the cut and hue too straightforward for Glims. Where I've seen fur here, it's always been dyed some fanciful colour. In the way of a displeased, long-haired cat, it makes Mother's gaunt frame appear much larger than it is. Father wears a brand-new suit, his paunch testing the strength of his shirt buttons' thread. The shaving-cream aroma he exudes doesn't quite drown out the smell of pub carpet at night's end.

Unlike the Faultons, there won't be any cheek-kissing or cuddling between us. It's not how we do things.

'Are you sure you're well enough to travel?' I ask.

'It's a bit late for that now.' Mother looks brittle as petrified wood but hasn't lost her bite. 'I wanted to come, so I came.'

'Well, let me get you a seat at least.'

'Stop fussing. If you want to be useful, fetch me a stiff drink. I'm gasping.'

Mother has only to utter the word *drink* and a server pounces with a tray of Balverian lavender wine. This is certainly not what she had in mind. It's light and sweet, and there isn't enough alcohol in a glass to get a pulpmoth tipsy. Father takes two, putting one into Mother's free hand.

I'm still trying to think what to say when Alastair intercepts us.

'Mr and Mrs Foulblood.' He respectfully uses our middle name, bowing low. 'Alastair Bartholomew Faulton, Hal's spiring partner.'

Mother's smile widens, her lip paint cracking. 'Oh, but of course.' Her voice becomes sunnier, less coarse. 'My daughter's told me all about you.'

Needless to say, I've never said one word about Alastair to either of them. In my letters, I redacted everything connected to spiring classes.

Alastair returns with another lie: 'Likewise. A pleasure to finally meet. I hope the journey from Crippleditch wasn't too taxing?'

'Oh, not at all.' Mother waves this away, reminding me how small and fragile her wrists are. 'I spent the time admiring your gorgeous country.'

'My wife and I are quite enamoured with Balver,' Father says, also putting on a voice.

The conversation goes on in this contrived fashion, while I stand silently squirming. This is exactly how everyone behaves around the sorcerous circle of Crippleditch, desperately keeping up appearances.

Eventually, Alastair excuses himself to return to his own mother. He makes the mistake of touching my elbow before he leaves. His fingers are light as a pulpmoth's wing, but Mother's hawk eyes track the gesture. She stares hard after him for a moment, then says, 'Actually, I will sit down,' in her normal, businesslike voice. 'We ought to chat privately.'

I lead her to a relatively darkened corner at the room's edge, where a loveseat and several armchairs face each other. Father eases Mother down into the loveseat's velvet cushions and sits down next to her, belly resting between his thighs. I take the armchair, knowing the interrogation is about to begin.

'So,' Mother says, 'when were you going to tell us?'

The still-fading Acclaim scars prickle on my neck, prompting me to nervous-itch. The other admissions pupils flaunt them as a badge of honour, but for me a love bite would be less humiliating.

'I didn't want you to find out I had Oldrac's flesh.'

Mother looks half baffled, half amused. 'And you thought performing for crowds was the best way to hide it?'

'I never set out to spire, I swear. Alastair agreed to introduce me to Mortritis so I could audit the graving conspectus if I came to admissions.'

Father nods to Alastair. 'He hold up his end?'

'Yes,' I say, shrinking farther into myself at the memory. 'I met Mortritis, but I… She may take some convincing.'

My parents exchange shrewd looks. I flick anxious glances between them, knowing I'll be forced to admit exactly how that conversation went.

Instead, Father says, 'He can't seem to keep his eyes off you.'

Well, yes. Alastair's been watching me with the interest of a cat stalking a fen rat, but it probably isn't what Father thinks. 'He'll be curious about our conversation because… well, he was the one who told me about…' I take a breath. 'Why didn't you tell me I was a scion's?'

Mother replies first with incredulous laughter. 'Why would we say anything unless it came up? Especially when it seemed we'd wasted our pud.'

Father downs what's left of his drink and abandons his glass on the floor. 'It's sod's law, really. We pay all that, and our daughter can't even make the first graving set.'

'But why go through with it in the first place?'

Mother sighs as if this should be obvious. 'When you first start taking pulp, your chances of conception are one in fifteen. When you diddle a scion—' I cringe. '—they're one in one.'

'You were our fifth attempt, sweetheart,' Father says.

'Your *fifth?*'

'I couldn't keep taking pulp much longer. After one stillbirth and three miscarriages...' Mother draws in another rattling breath. 'Your chances get less every time.'

This said with the level of raw emotional power that most people would use to complain about an empty coffee pot. When it comes to hiding pain, my mother's a professional. That's how Preys must be. Giving in to grief only softens you up for your enemies to bleed. Depressions and vulnerabilities are Glim privileges.

As my fingers begin to tingle in my lap, I realize I've been holding my hands tight enough to pale the knuckles. It takes effort to let go.

'I'm so sorry,' I say, hating how weak and ineffectual my words are. 'I had no idea what... that you'd been through all that.'

Mother scoffs. 'Don't act soft! It happened; I dealt with it. End of story.'

'Few can afford it round Crippleditch or Withersham,' Father says, splaying his palms. 'But we're not the first.'

'Beatrice Bylepuddle fakes her symptoms. She was sharp enough to try Flaypenny first. Hardly took pulp at all.'

So it *was* Flaypenny they saw. The words pull at my stomach, but I fight to keep the nausea from showing on my face. 'So... who was the scion?'

Mother grimaces. 'Some work-dodging Giltbank, cut off by his family. He needed pud to gamble with.'

An image of this Giltbank scion invades my mind. He's not unlike many of the men in this room, but with a fretted look to his well-bred features. Uneven copper stubble, the shine worn from him. He would have been as old as my mother can expect to live – older, no doubt, and with over a hundred years still left to go. I see them disappear, grim-faced, into Flaypenny's cottage together, and my stomach revolts so violently that I cannot even think to follow them.

Mother startles me by letting go of her cane. She leans over to take my hand in her papery one. She smells like wet fur and cherry cough syrup, sweet but medicinal.

'I won't pretend it was cheerful, but if we play this right, it will've been worth it. So tell us: has he tumbled you yet?'

'Fallen gods,' I spit, ripping my hand away as if her skin scalded me.

'No need to be embarrassed. We're family.'

'No! A thousand times no!'

'Good. We wouldn't want him losing interest too quickly.'

'But don't leave him too long on the hook.' Father wags a finger. 'Pretty-boy toffs like him can afford to be fickle. If you don't put out, best believe the next girl's waiting with wide-open legs.'

'Give it a rest,' I hiss, but he points out some of the admissions girls. They are looking at Alastair the way girls do, smiling and whispering to each other. 'The only thing Alastair wants from me is Edusa's patronage.'

Mother scoffs. 'Don't be so naïve. He's a man and a Glim. He wants everything – to have his cake *and* set a house on fire.'

'Edusa's patronage *and* a sticky truncheon.'

My gorge rises. 'He's faking it for the society pages. They want to see romance, so he gives it to them.'

'He'll be faking the romance all right, but not the leching,' says Father. 'It's sure he fancies you.'

'You know what I fancy? My career.'

Mother pushes out a humourless laugh. The sound comes on every inhale, like a door swung back and forth on rusted hinges. It makes me feel as though my skin's being stripped away. It's almost a relief when it turns to a wet, ragged cough.

'Oh dear,' she says once she's recovered. 'You haven't thought this through, have you? Who's to say you'll even pass admissions?'

'Believe it or not, I'm actually a decent spirer,' I say, stung.

'Even the best spirers can fail, sweetheart,' Father says. 'Failure's a luxury we can't afford.'

'If Alastair drops out, he'll spend a year gallivanting on his parents' pud, and then he'll go spire for St Caladyne's. He's set for life, no matter how badly he fudges it. We need to do everything we can to better our odds.'

'But what about graving?' Panic climbs my throat and spills from my mouth. 'Kilchoirs *do* get onto the graving conspectus here, you know. Mortritis's own rival was a Kilchoir. If she lets me audit—'

'You've got more chance of convincing a heron to lay square eggs than you do of becoming a decent graver. Besides, graving won't pay the bills like an allowance.'

'So… what? You want me to…?'

'No need to act the innocent with us, love,' Mother says. 'You understand. Scions are more virile than scarlet fever. Once should be enough, provided you time it right.'

'But this goes against everything Our Lady stands for! We'll be outcasts!'

'*Our Lady?*' Mother sneers the words.

'It's that school,' Father mutters. 'Stuffing their heads with Glim twaddle.'

'Everyone pays lip service to that daft Glim cult to get pulp. If the Choir realized we were false believers, they'd have us in for deceiving them. We thought you'd figured that out.'

I hate the way they're looking at me, that poisonous mix of pity and contempt. They think I'm the biggest idiot to come out of Preyburn, and the feeling deepens with every question I ask. But I have to ask, because I'm nowhere near understanding.

'If you don't believe in Our Lady, how do you explain eerians, and graving, and—'

'We've more important things to worry about.' Mother's voice says I'm exhausting her. 'If Our Lady resents us doing the things we need to live, she's not worth believing in.'

'Oldrac's flesh doesn't just give you kids. It gives you prospects,' Father goes on. 'Graving limits you to the military. What happens when the war ends? Given that any thought?'

No, I hadn't given that any thought. But of course, they're right. With the war ended, Preyburn will have satisfied its duty to the Commonwealth, and with satisfaction comes redundancy. What's graving without warfare? An incredibly morbid waste of time and resources. Perhaps a sign of some psychological disorder.

My parents' words blur as a sissing sound fills my head, the wordless rambling of electrical noise. Unable to look at them, my gaze finds Alastair. He stands with Edusa and Tieran, surrounded by family members and spiring socialites, all smiles and civilized chatter and clinking glasses. A Faulton family reunion looks like something to savour. A Foulblood family reunion looks like... well, this.

Alastair's glistening black eyes centre on mine through the crowd. The sissing noise snaps off, abandoning me to Mother's rasp.

'When did you last bleed?'

'Stop talking,' I whisper. 'This is *heinous*.'

Father looks baffled that he could have raised a daughter so ignorant of the world's workings. Mother, on the other hand, looks as if *I've* said something obscene. As she sucks in a fresh lungful of air, her outrage hangs suspended above me like an axe.

'I suppose you feel hard done by? Well, I'm sorry I had to give my life's savings, my pride, and my health to give you the best possible chances. Compared to everything we sacrificed to get you here, what we're asking is a sunny day's picnic.'

I can only drop my gaze to the floor as my whole body burns with shame. It's true; she's given everything to get me where I am. I don't simply owe her my abilities. I owe her my life.

It makes me ill to think of what she's had to go through, what she'll continue to go through until death. The least I can do is provide her the best life I can for as many years as she has left. The fact I can't bring myself to give up *my* life and pride to do it proves my selfishness.

But what they're asking doesn't just affect me. They want me to deceive someone, to bring a life into the world, all for a bloody allowance. I won't do that.

I'm summoning the courage to tell them so when a smoky voice reaches us from across the room, turning our heads.

'You really must stop being so aggressive, poppet. It's unsightly.'

20

THIS ⊕NE WILL
C⊕ST Y⊕U

Mortritis stands with Drasilla, maybe ten paces from where we're seated. I'd been so focused on my parents' wicked words that I hadn't noticed them drift our way. Now everyone within earshot is watching, even though some pretend not to. I've seen enough brawls at Withersham, so I wouldn't have needed to hear words to know trouble's brewing.

'Who's being aggressive?' Drasilla also fails to keep her voice at normal volume. 'All I said was that your research borrowed some key points from my own.'

'Oh Drusie, let it go. It's been how many years? Besides, you needn't worry yourself about silly things like research now – you've a household to look after! The guest bedroom won't redecorate itself.' By all measures, Mortritis looks as though she could flick Drasilla across the room if the mood took her. Petite little Drasilla only comes up to her sister's chest, but doesn't look cowed in the slightest.

'You really must stop being so bitter, darling,' she says. 'It's unsightly.'

Mother leans in to Father, muttering, 'Moppetons,' under her breath. He nods, smirking as he dries sweaty palms on his suit trousers. I hurt more from our earlier conversation than I did after the last stage. I sit reeling in silence, light-headed and furiously relieved that they've found something to distract them. I would've taken an earthquake if that's all fate could have offered me.

'Bitter?' Mortritis's laugh sounds like knuckles of ice clattering together. 'Whatever gave you that impression?'

'Oh, come now. You'd trade every last one of your accolades for what I have.'

'Cripplingly low self-esteem?'

'A husband, six bright, beautiful children, an estate...'

'Don't confuse the situation, poppet. That's the *Faulton* estate you're crowing about. You just decorate it.'

Drasilla's face draws taut with anger.

Mortritis takes a sip of her drink, then goes on. 'Your children too, adorable though they might be, are all Faultons. Not one graver among them.'

'Our Lady's gifts spurn the flesh of Our Lord, Morty. I can't pervert the laws of nature any more than you can.'

'Oh dear. It's like you've forgotten how to be a Moppeton altogether.' With her free hand, she gestures grandly to herself. 'Perverting the laws of nature is what we *do*. We both know none of them followed in your footsteps because hubby forbade it – and when hubby gives you an order, he means business. Look what happened when you disobeyed him last time – my poor nephew, exiled for five long years.'

My gaze finds Alastair in a cluster with his brothers, oblivious to the scene playing out behind him.

'Although, I suppose five years is but a blink as far as Aiden's concerned. How old is he now? One hundred and sixty?'

'You are a vicious bitch, Morty.'

'Why not do yourself a favour and step back, poppet? You're so close, I can smell the vomit on your breath. You always were a messy drunk.'

Drasilla does not step back. Her face only contorts further.

Mortritis says, 'Any bitterness between us is yours. Certainly, you've never cared for accolades. If you did, perhaps you would have pursued that promising career instead of a geriatric Faulton's estate.'

My gut twinges.

'But I have something *you've* always wanted but will never bargain out of your husband: a bright, beautiful graver son.'

'You can't possibly value him that much, or else you wouldn't have subjected him to Mother's demented experiments,' says Drasilla. 'You always thought yourself the favourite, but really, what sort of parent uses their own flesh as a guinea pig?'

'I'm far from a guinea pig, Drusie, as is my son. The pulpmoth caterpillar who is freed from his cocoon by a man's knife rather than his own struggle emerges helpless. So does the child who comes of age all trussed up in his mother's coddling. Tieran is a prime example.'

With that, Mortritis takes a celebratory sip of her drink. But Drasilla soon recovers from the blow, a slow smile creeping across her mouth.

'You know, Morty, I think you're on to something. Only it's not bitterness that gets me whenever I think about your Kiel, it's guilt. About something I never told you.'

'You're an incontinent drunk? Poppet, we know.'

Drasilla lifts her voice now, apparently wanting other people to hear. 'I also bedded his papa – your Kieran.'

A sudden watchful silence falls over the groups nearest as more heads turn towards the quarrelling sisters.

Mortritis replies with a vicious smile, as if delighted by this admission. 'Oh, Drusie. How very *you*. What else do you have to offer a man but flesh?'

Drasilla keeps on as if she hadn't spoken. 'He was mad over me, and for a time I felt the same. That's why Aiden was so upset about Alastair. Kieran pursued me for years after we broke up, and even though I made my feelings clear, Aiden worried Alastair wasn't *his*.'

'Really? A paternity scare? How inelegant.'

'It's been eating me up, knowing the night of the Winter Formal was the night I ended things. He was terribly upset, but then there you were, keen for my sloppy seconds...'

'Good grief. You couldn't honestly think he preferred you?'

'Quite a few of us knew about it. My friends and I were all there, watching you lead him away. I would have told you sooner, but we've had our ceasefire and I didn't want to—'

Mortritis's free hand lashes out like the jaws of a viper to make a fist in her sister's hair. She still wears her vicious smile while Drasilla yelps in pain. Mortritis yanks her down to waist height, managing to keep her own drink level as Drasilla's tumbles from her hand.

All the Faulton boys turn in unison. What must be the fiftieth glass breaks against the porcelain as Drasilla tries to extract herself from her sister's clutches.

Mortritis sneers, 'You're nothing but a rich man's brood mare,' still without spilling her drink.

That is, until Drasilla's boys join the fray.

Everyone but Alastair gets involved; he looks on, mystified, while his brothers try to wrest the two apart. Nobody else in the room even pretends to do anything but gawp. Lourdes looks downright horrified, but a few of the preceptors merely look weary. They've clearly seen it all before. A server waits with a broom, anxious to clean up the broken glass but not stupid enough to enter the mêlée.

There's a rare spark of mirth in Mother's dull eyes as their yelling drowns out the harpist. 'Glims like to pretend they're a cut above, but look at the state of them.'

'No better than the scum of Preyburn at last call,' Father says.

Finally, a co-ordinated effort by the boys tears Mortritis from her quarry. It takes all five of them to wrench her off, fury twisting their features. Tieran looks positively ballistic.

'You do so *love* to make mistakes,' Mortritis says, letting some of Drasilla's black hair drift from her fingers. 'And just like your little misstep with hubby, this one will cost you.'

Drasilla whimpers from the middle of her boys. They've formed a protective barrier around her. Her chest heaves while tears pull eye powder down her cheeks in dramatic black streaks. Mortritis takes a moment to fix her with a glare that could rust metal before marching from the games hall.

I've spent years fantasizing about Mortritis in combat, but in my imagination it was never quite so bleak.

⎯⊖⎯

Not long after her sister's exit, a tearful Drasilla is escorted from the party by no fewer than all of Alastair's brothers. Eventually, my own mother reaches her limit too. She rarely travels far these days, and now looks liable to give way. I won't pretend it's anything other than a relief when she announces they'll return to the Balverian inn Edusa's put them up in.

'Our ride leaves early, so we won't see you again before we leave.'

Alastair takes up her hand, brushing her craggy knuckles to his lips. 'It was a pleasure. Do travel home safely.'

'Thank you, Alastair.' Mother wears the false, bright smile she came in with and is no doubt dying to retire it. 'We hope to see you in Crippleditch sometime.'

I always used to think the Crippleditch community would be ashamed to be seen consorting with Glims. Now I know better. People care less about pride than about getting by. If Alastair came to visit, my parents would parade him around for all to see we've got links to the Faultons' deep pockets.

I stand in sullen silence, feeling utterly drained as Alastair shakes Father's hand. Then, finally, they're gone and I can breathe again.

Although it's now the middle of the night, many of Edusa's guests look as though they're just getting started – there is raucous laughter, weaving feet, and various states of undress. I heard the top-tier scions can sometimes struggle to get drunk because their livers are so good at resolving poisons, but this lot have done a marvellous job.

Alastair turns to me and says, 'What's the matter?'

'Why were you all over my parents like that?'

He frowns. 'They're your parents.'

I don't know what to say to that, but I could always say something mean. It might make me feel better. But in the end, I say, 'Is your mother all right?'

'She will be, once she sleeps it off,' he says ruefully. 'Drink doesn't agree with her. I don't know why she lets Mortritis goad her into it.'

I lapse back into silence, remembering what I'd overheard. I can't reconcile Mortritis Moppeton – graving master, goddess, icon – with the woman I saw tonight bickering with her sister, over a man of all things.

But then, I suppose it wasn't really about a man. It sounds like they have a long history of one-upmanship, and a man was just another pawn in their game. I daren't tell Alastair what I overheard for fear of causing more family drama.

He surveys the partygoers with a grim look. 'Shall we take a walk?'

'A walk?' I echo, as if this is a word he's made up.

'We could take in the grounds.' Both our gazes slide to the windows, and the snow piled high on the ledges. 'Or stroll back to our rooms. I want to leave, but I don't think I could sleep just yet.'

I gesture for him to lead, and we make our way towards the exit. I wonder if we should say goodbye to Edusa, but then I look over and see a second fight has broken out between Ordelia and Adoro, with Edusa looking doubly delighted. I decide against it.

We lower our voices as we leave the bright glamour of the games hall for the dimmer, slightly more subdued glamour of the hallway outside. Alastair still has a glass of something non-alcoholic in his hand, his other buried in his pocket.

'The last I saw Mama was in the summer,' he says. 'We didn't even know whether the abettors would come to Withersham. Now, my place here is so close, I can taste it.'

'So your father's said he'll…?'

'Exactly. Mama says I'll have my old room back at the house.' This *house* he speaks of will no doubt be the lavishly appointed estate his mother mentioned, the Faultons' ancestral home in Copperfont. 'We'll spend Fall Days together. We'll go to all the tournaments. I've already missed so much.' The melancholy in his voice startles me, and I look over to see his eyes are shining. 'Five years of birthdays, funerals, communions… I've been cut from the picture for so long, I don't know whether I'll be able to fit back into it.'

'Of course you will,' I say firmly. 'Your mother and brothers were overjoyed to see you.'

'Things are different now. I'm practically a stranger to them.'

'But that'll change once you have your place. You'll get to know each other again.'

'Maybe.'

'It's brutal, what your father did. And such an overreaction. To be honest, I can't really get my head around it.' I sigh. 'You didn't deserve it. I hope you know that.'

'Thanks, Hal.' After a moment, he says, 'And what about your parents? How were they?'

'Oh. Well.'

My face burns thinking about all the disgusting things they said, most of which I'd never dream of telling Alastair. Hearing what they think of me was humiliating enough.

Alastair frowns. 'They seemed to be all right about the spiring, but then I... Not to pry, but it looked as though you weren't getting on.'

'We spoke about Flaypenny. It *was* Flaypenny, by the way.'

Alastair nods. 'I see.'

'All this time, I thought they'd be ashamed to learn I wasn't my father's daughter, biologically speaking. But it was a choice. They decided it was worth the Choir's support.'

'From what I've heard, lots of other Preys draw the same conclusion.'

'They don't even mind that I'm becoming a scion because they – *we* – have more opportunities. They just don't believe I'll make it as a spirer.'

There's a pause. Alastair sets down his now-empty glass on the nearest windowsill.

'I don't mean to offend,' he says, 'but what would they know about it?' At my silence, he adds, 'Unless they have some expertise I'm unaware of, why would you trust their opinion on the matter?'

'Whether I trust their opinion or not, they are my parents. They sacrificed a lot to get me here. I have obligations.'

Alastair's face hardens. 'What do they expect you to do? Drop out of admissions?'

'They've not asked for that. They just don't believe I'll see success.'

'You know who does?' He begins counting on his fingers. 'Limbridge, for one. The abettors, for three. Edusa, renowned champion; Tieran, his proxy; provost knows how many spectators; and me, who knows you—'

A shadow crooks round the corner and hammers a fist into Alastair's stomach.

The strike comes hard enough to bow him, all breath knocked out in a grunt. He drops to one knee, and vicious instinct surges up within me. I move without thought.

Leveraging Alastair's shock, our assailant follows the first strike with another. I intercept, grabbing the stranger's shirt, using his momentum and my strength to crack his head against the wall's ornate moulding. There's a nasty finality to the sound his skull makes before he goes slack.

Naturally, this is just the start of it. Three more strangers come creeping from the hallway's sconce-cast shadows like so many spiders. One of them, obviously the pack leader, isn't quite as strange as I'd like. I recognize his sneering face instantly.

'I thought rejects had to leave the grounds after they failed?' I say.

'We've more right to be here than you do.' Ransley's voice is dark and bitter. 'That they even let you compete is a mockery.'

'Tell that to Edusa. Oh, except you already did and he told you to sod off.'

'Edusa's blinded by the gilt he stands to make off your novelty,' says the boy at Ransley's left elbow. I'm pretty sure I've seen him in the common room, but if I ever learned his name, I didn't retain it. Same for the other one. 'He's put profits above the Hallowed Game's integrity.'

I snort. 'As if anyone would care about spiring if there weren't profits involved.'

Beside me, a just-recovered Alastair rises to his full, intimidating height. The squared shoulders and hard line to his jaw says he's ready for what's coming.

'Strange to talk about integrity when you're skulking around, throwing dirty punches. You do realize none of this foolery will get you back into admissions?'

The three rejects reply first with a scouring glare. I can practically taste their resentment.

'We're under no illusions,' Ransley says. 'We know we won't be attending St Penderghast's this year… but neither will you.'

I look him up and down. 'You want to put Edusa's favourites and a Faulton out of the running? The *nuts* on you.'

'Insults demand answers,' Alastair recites. We exchange looks of gloomy understanding before he turns back to Ransley. 'For all you scorn Preyburn, you'd fit right in at Withersham.'

This is, apparently, too much for Ransley to hear.

He launches himself at Alastair. The two other rejects take his lead. Only one comes for me. Ransley and the other target Alastair. I'd say this is good strategy, since he's easily the more threatening of us. I might take comfort in it, only he's trained to fight with a spire. How many bare-handed scraps has he seen? I've seen more than could be called fair.

When I miss a left-handed punch, my nameless reject catches my wrist. I boot him away with a well-angled heel to the chest, the seams of Edusa's fancy trousers tugging at my groin. The stitching, the material – none of it was made for anything more vigorous than the Preyburn Balter.

We manage to get each other in a mutual headlock, arms tight around each other's necks as we wrestle for control. From here, I see Alastair caught between his two assailants. Ransley stomps his heel into the back of his knee, buckling it.

While my accord partner falls for the second time in a fight that's barely begun, a silver flash appears in Ransley's hand. I shout a warning to Alastair, but it spikes down, into the join of his neck and shoulder, venting a rush of arterial spray.

A victory strike if I ever saw one.

21

A PREY WAY OF SEEING THINGS

When he realizes he's been stabbed, Alastair's eyes go wide with disbelieving fury. The rejects have only to watch as he lurches away. He clamps a hand over the wound, but the blood is relentless. It keeps pumping out between his fingers.

In Preyburn, a neck wound like Alastair's spells death. As he's a scion, half of me hopes he's just being dramatic. As he's trying and failing to get up, slipping in a puddle of his own blood, the other half learns better. He's out of this fight.

This grisly sight gives me the extra push I need to manoeuvre out of the headlock. I hook the nameless reject's ankle out from underneath him and he goes crashing to the floor.

'*Such* integrity,' I snarl, booting him in the guts. 'Knifing your opponent in a fistfight, you peeling serpent!'

'Nobody said this was a fistfight, *dog*,' Ransley replies. The lack of originality in this riposte is an insult all by itself.

In case I had any faith left, Ransley gives Alastair a good hard shove that puts him down on the crimson-stained carpet for good. The sight of my accord partner beaten and bloodied on the floor sends my heart into frantic overdrive. *Nobody* beats Alastair.

To make matters worse, the guy I smashed into the wall is slowly coming to, his expression dazed and violent.

There is absolutely no chance I can win a four-on-one fight, but I can't go down without one. As my gaze shifts from one reject to another, fists up, it's not about whether I can somehow save myself. It's about how much damage I can cause before they best me.

Ever eager to lead, Ransley takes a crossways swipe with the dagger. I snap to the right, seizing his wrist and forearm with both hands, as well as delivering a cheap shot – my shin to his groin. He swears blood, doubling over in pain. This cheers me up for all the time it takes for a nameless reject to step in.

He kicks me in the abdomen so effectively that my torso flips forwards, legs flying backwards 'til my face plants into the ground like the heavy end of a see-saw. The impact bends my neck past its limit. I feel a sickening crunch – broken vertebrae – that leaves me utterly paralysed.

My heart beats hare-quick in my chest. As Ransley circles me, the only part of me able to move is my eyes. He wants to make sure I can see him and his dagger, still wet with Alastair's blood.

'How long do you think it will take your nose to grow back?' he says, lips peeled from his teeth. 'What about an eyeball?'

Maybe longer than I have before the next stage, which will seriously hurt my chances… assuming I even make it to the next stage. He's definitely going to torture me, but he might even be demented enough to murder me.

I track the blade's movement as he advances, my face half-smushed into carpet, drool leaking from my mouth.

Alastair shows better signs of life. As Ransley passes him, he reaches out to snag his ankle with a strengthless hand. Ransley kicks this off as if shaking out his trouser leg and doesn't even bother glancing at him.

The nameless rejects roll me onto my back, and I can do nothing to stop them. I can't even talk. Panic clogs my throat, each breath barely scraping past it. At least in the arena, we have stage warders to protect us if we fail. There's nobody watching out for us here.

But as Ransley looms ever nearer with his evil, sneering face, marking the pieces of me he's going to slice out, someone behind him politely clears their throat.

Ransley and the rejects turn to see who's appeared behind them, and all colour drains from their faces.

'I had to see it to believe it,' says Tieran, stepping into the light. 'I didn't think anyone would be so thick-witted.'

Ransley straightens, brandishing the dagger like he means to use it.

The nameless rejects baulk.

'Fallen gods, Ransley, are you serious?'

'Don't! It's as good as striking *Edusa!*'

Tieran looks at Alastair, laid out in his blood puddle. His voice takes a sharp edge as he strides forwards, causing the rejects to flinch.

'You've already struck me. Defied my preceptor and *maimed* my brother.' His gaze locks on Ransley, alive with righteous fury. 'And your second stage was a disgrace to the Hallowed Game.'

Tieran cracks his knuckles for effect, and I'll admit a little thrill goes through me. He's without his spire, no doubt returned from sorting out Drasilla. Still, his eyes blaze yellow, reminding us all that he's far from weaponless.

'You've forced my hand.'

How do you fight someone who knows every move you're about

to make against him? I certainly don't know, and I have a feeling these crazy idiots don't either.

Ransley, being the craziest and stupidest of the bunch, strikes first *again*. Tieran pushes this aside with the most unimpressed look you can imagine, more withering than the abettors.

But Ransley proves he's not completely useless when he twirls the knife by its hilt, gripping it rear-handed to spike back at Tieran's face.

Unfortunately for him, Tieran not only deflects this but uses the motion to twist Ransley's arm around and behind his back, forcing his head down. Ransley staggers forwards, all command gone as Tieran shoves him flush against the wall.

Instead of opting for a nice, clean smash, as I had, Tieran presses one hand to the back of Ransley's head and *drags*. His scraped cheek paints a rainbow across the wall with blood, which might be one of the most beautiful things I've ever seen.

Ransley falls to the ground and stays there, huffing in pain.

While I'd love to follow the rest of the fight from start to finish, soaking in every detail, I still can't move my neck. Even rolling it from left to right is out of the question. All I know from my limited view is that Tieran's flinging the rejects up and down the hallway like misbehaving playthings. Every move is as slick as if he and the rejects had choreographed them together. Skulls bounce off his fists, elbows, knees, boots, and every available surface. The rejects' howls of pain remind me that even a pampered bonbon like Tieran can have some goodness to offer the world.

I strain my eyes to look at Alastair. His chest's moving up and down, which is a relief. There's too much jammy red to see how much of the wound has knit together, but at least it's stopped squirting.

When a nameless reject decides to cut his losses with a frantic bid to get away, Tieran catches him at the corner, where Ransley stays slumped… and uses it as a fulcrum to give his arm an extra bend.

All too soon, with every reject incapacitated in one way or another, Tieran circles back to Ransley. It hurts to say anything Tieran does is impressive, but *I mean!* Not a single bead of sweat marks his brow.

He stomps on Ransley's arm with his boot heel, making the reject's mouth holler and his hand spasm around the dagger's hilt. Tieran takes it, holding it up to the light and twisting the blade to examine it from all angles.

'Needless to say,' he mutters absent-mindedly, 'you needn't reapply for admissions next year.'

Something strange happens. A crackling sensation takes my body like a seizure, every nerve firing. It's like static shock times a thousand. A burning smell fills my nostrils, and a visceral crunch in my neck makes me gasp. Everything snaps back into excruciating focus. But at least pain is a move in the right direction.

My body's listening to me again. Screaming at me, but also listening.

I move my neck gingerly at first, taking in the bloody carnage around me. Hard to believe this guy, all handsome boyishness and elegant clothes, is the cause.

'Who cares about admissions?' I say, shaking something fierce as I drag myself off the ground. 'Call the constabulary.'

'The what?'

'Whatever passes for law enforcement around here! They should all be in *prison*.'

Tieran frowns. 'Well, naturally I'll tell the abettors, who will tell the provost.'

He makes his way over to Alastair, heaving him up off the ground. Stringy, bloody bile trails from his mouth as he climbs unsteadily to his feet. His body moves woozily, but his eyes are wide open and painfully alert.

'The provost is the ultimate authority here,' Tieran says. 'Their punishment is Her Sagacity's decision.'

'Let's hope she makes it a good one,' I say, with no lack of bitterness. 'We could have died.'

Tieran scoffs. 'Hardly. They just wanted to scare you. There isn't a trace of pulp on that blade.'

'I don't see how—'

'Get Alastair back to his room, won't you? I still need to deal with the situation here.'

The way he unloads Alastair onto me makes him seem like a light thing. Alastair is, in fact, a comically heavy thing, and all the heavier for my injuries. I hook an arm around him, and although I struggle to take even some of his weight, the insistent knock of his heartbeat reassures me.

'Are you all right?' I ask him.

Strong but shaking fingers curve around my side. 'No. Are you?'

'He'll be fine,' says Tieran. 'I'll wager his ego hurts worst of all.' He pats his brother's cheek in a move I'd call patronizing. 'A cup of tea can only help matters. Keep him awake for a bit – he'll heal faster.'

'Have you seen the carpet?'

'Yes, definitely ruined. I got a bit carried away.' Tieran rubs his chin as he takes in the mess. 'Not to worry. The Liveriches will pay for a new one.'

'I meant look how much blood Alastair's lost!'

Tieran studies his brother's neck. 'Once the wound is closed, which it already has, it's a simple matter of blood replenishment.'

'If it took him a day to heal a broken arm, how can a cut blood vessel take moments?'

'His broken arm didn't threaten his life.' Tieran looks hard at me for a moment, as if trying to work out if I'm being deliberately stupid. 'Scions' bodies don't function the same as other people's. Life-threatening injuries heal faster because they can't afford to wait. You really ought to know this if you're going to spire.'

I clench my teeth together hard enough to make the molars ache. I vaguely remember Limbridge saying something about this, and it chimes with the healing rate of my own injuries, most recently my broken spine. But to save face, I tell him, 'We didn't study scion biology at Withersham.'

'And remember, Alastair's a Faulton, not a—' *A handshake baby.* Tieran catches himself before he says it. 'He's pure-fleshed, is what I mean. Made of sterner stuff.'

I know this is meant to comfort me, but I only feel irritated. My gut instinct is to argue more, but I end the conversation with a muttered, 'Right. Thanks for intervening.'

'It was my pleasure.'

The floor curves under my feet as I stagger off with Alastair, leading him round the corner and up the stairs. Despite shivering and panting like he might give way any moment, he doesn't trip once – which is a blessing, since I don't think I've the strength to heave him off the floor.

'I think my neck broke back there,' I say.

I don't necessarily expect Alastair to respond, but after a moment, he goes, 'I doubt you could heal a broken neck in the time it took Tieran to thrash Ransley's troupe.'

'But Tieran just said we could.'

'He said *I* could.'

I hold my tongue, too exhausted to fight about it. I know it doesn't make sense – that a hybrid like me could heal so rapidly – but I also know what I felt. What I *couldn't* feel in those terrifying moments when Ransley came at me with the dagger.

I manage to steer us back to our dorm. As we reach our floor, images from the last time we walked back here rush into my mind uninvited – the argument I've done my best to get over.

Alastair fumbles with the lock for a moment before I lose patience and take the key from him. The way he staggers through the door tells me he shouldn't be left alone. Tieran told me to keep him awake, so I follow him inside.

His room is like my room, but immaculate and with all the furniture reversed. Instead of two armchairs, there's a two-seater. Alastair immediately collapses on it, chest heaving, head flopped back to stare at the ceiling. Thanks to the housekeepers' diligence, the fireplace beside him is already roaring.

'Don't close your eyes,' I say, and with what looks like an Oldracian effort, he pries them open.

I knew, even before I came in, that there would be no clothes spilling out of his suitcase. He will have slotted that away somewhere, every item lovingly organized in the armoire. He's made use of the shrine table too, with personal items sitting beneath the portrait of Oldrac that's mirrored in my own room. It would be rude to touch, but I can't hide my interest. There's a scroll held in place by a yellow ribbon, several votive candles, three of Alastair's wax-seal rings, a bowl of fresh figs, a cameo of his mother, and another of a silver-haired man with a forbidding face that I assume is his father. There's a clear resemblance in the knife-like cheekbones, the strong line of his jaw, and the humourless expression. I'm likely biased, but this is a pitiless face, a face for whom condescension is as natural as breath.

I tear my eyes away to see Alastair's are closed. Tieran said he'd heal faster if I kept him awake.

'Alastair – no!' I snap my fingers twice as if he's a dog, which works a treat. The indignity gives him the strength to lift his head and glower at me. 'I'm making tea.'

Given the simple reversal of our rooms, everything I need – kettle, mugs, black tea – is easily found. As scions can't use electric kettles, water has to be boiled over the bloody hearth. The kettle hooks onto a hanger made of ornamented iron, suspended over the fireplace. I dread to think what sort of primitive nightmares the cooks must face in the kitchens.

I miss Preyburn's electronics. Keeping what modernity we had was one of our conditions for joining the Commonwealth, although it limits scions' travel across Preyburn. Even the idiot Glims could see how difficult and embittering it would be for Preys to give up modern technology.

Naturally, war with the Ascendancy has hurt our progress. The Zsietians are known for their industry, and we're mostly cut off from that now. I say *mostly* as there's a thriving black market for Zsietian tech in Preyburn for those who can afford it. Nevertheless, though more sophisticated than Glimwick's, some of Preyburn's gadgetry would seem primitive to a Zsietian today.

I glance over at Alastair to see his eyes closed *again*. I have to get him talking.

'Remember what I was saying before?'

'Before?'

'About my parents.'

He licks dry lips, frowning as he lifts his head to look at me. 'What about them?'

That got his attention.

'Even if I become the greatest spiring champion who ever lived, Mother will never get her health back. They expect me to ensure their hard work pays off, and the chances I can do that by spiring are low.'

Alastair takes a few laboured breaths before he replies in a chafed voice. 'But it was your mama's decision to try for a graver. Being born isn't something you should have to make restitution for.'

'Something else they said really threw me,' I say, nervous to repeat it – and to Alastair of all people, the most religious person I know. 'They called the Choir a cult.'

'A cult?'

I hand Alastair a steaming cup of black lavender tea. He tries to sit up a little straighter as I take the cushion next to him, wincing. Seeing him so weakened unnerves me.

'They said they only pretended to believe in Our Lady to get pulp, and keep pretending so they don't get punished. They said it's like that for everyone in Crippleditch.'

Alastair considers this over a sip of his scalding-hot tea, which he takes without reaction. Then he says, 'Do you know why the Choir only sends pulp to the faithful?'

I shake my head.

'Our Lord's Principles are moral guidelines, and they think anyone who follows them is more likely to share their values – prudence, strength, compassion, et cetera.'

I scoff. 'That's worked out well for them.'

'Quite. They should do more to verify who's actually receiving their pulp.'

I look down into my own cup. If the Choir were more diligent, there's no way my parents would have made the cut.

'I don't think they appreciate how far removed Preyburn is from their message,' he says.

'Or maybe that's less important to them than training gravers for the war.'

'Possibly,' he says with a shrug. 'Withersham's a strange case, its own bubble. Unlike laymen, gravers witness Our Lady's power, so they have to believe in some of the Choir's teachings. But they're still Preys with a Prey way of seeing things. Everyone at Withersham worships Our Lady over Our Lord, and thinks Glims do the reverse. They're supposed to be upheld as one, antithetical but accordant forces. They're supposed to be balanced.'

'Are you trying to convert me, Faulton?'

He startles me with a chuckle – a sound I feel in my own chest.

I don't remember hearing him laugh in a way that wasn't mocking before. Sadly, the chuckling stops as suddenly as it begins, cut short by his pained wince. 'Why? Is it working?'

'Not really,' I say, anxious to refocus on something else. 'Firstly, some Glims *do* worship Oldrac above Our Lady. Your father's one of them.'

'He's not the rule, but yes, that's true.'

'Secondly, you say Preys have put a false spin on things, but are you sure it isn't the Glims? When have Preyburn and Glimwick ever been equal? We've always been under your boot heel.'

'I couldn't agree more,' Alastair says, surprising me. 'It's not a *false spin* you have. It's a perspective, and I don't blame you for having it one bit. There are a lot of things I'd change about the Commonwealth, given the chance.'

We go on talking long after we've finished our tea. Just as Tieran predicted, Alastair improves visibly. The colour returns to his cheeks and he becomes... well, *less* animated. A healthy Alastair is a rigid and composed one.

Before long, he's in better form than I am. Usually, I find his voice a chore to listen to, but right now it's a narcotic. My body shouldn't have recovered as quickly as it has, but I must still have a way to go. Everything feels slow and heavy.

Our conversation couldn't be more innocent, but what's unsaid hangs in the air like incense, thick and pervasive. What began as a respectable distance between us shrinks as we draw together. He smells like sweet, soapy woods and blood – an irresistible combination. He keeps looking at my mouth, my neck, my ink-free hands, in a way that says my parents were right about at least one thing. I tell myself I imagined it, and then he does it again, a flush stealing up his throat. A blind man could see what's going on here, and yet I couldn't.

I think that awful reunion with my parents just opened my eyes to it – *the leching*, as Father so tastefully put it. Evidently Alastair meant what he said in the infirmary and wants something more than a ceasefire – and why should that be so hard to believe?

No doubt Alastair would enjoy any manner of submission from me, carnal or otherwise. I'd enjoy the same from him.

The sourness I felt before, when he performed affection for onlookers, has disappeared. It's the fakery that rankles, the scrutiny that discomforts.

Of course, I'd sooner gut myself with a dull blade than admit all this to my parents. Their wants have nothing to do with pleasure, which, if anything racy did happen with Alastair, would have to be the reason it did.

I watch the firelight sparking in dark eyes that are watching my lips move in a trance. After his chilling eldritch voice, enough to give me goosebumps all by itself, Alastair's eyes are his best feature. Black and inevitable.

My mother's voice replies, *Scions are more virile than scarlet fever. Once should be enough.*

A full-body flush jolts me back to my senses. Suddenly he's too close, his gaze too heavy. What if once *was* enough? My life would be utterly derailed.

I can't let that happen. I'm not going to be my parents' pawn – a brood mare.

And I have to remember, this is Alastair we're talking about. Alastair, who infuriates me half the time. If I really wanted a playmate, I'd find a suitable option like I did in Crippleditch, someone I can see casually and won't get stuck with if our interests dwindle or turn sour.

I need to go, take myself to bed.

Alastair startles when I say this. His eyebrows furrow. 'Now?'

'Yes, now. You're back to normal, and I can hear the birds.'

He rises as I rise, trailing me to the door. 'Is that really why?' I half-turn to look at him like the strange thing he is. 'I know it can't be easy, but you have to forget your parents' doubts. They don't know nearly enough about spiring to offer worthy advice.'

I give him a look. 'Are you worried I'll creep off back to Preyburn when your head's turned?'

'I'm worried you're going to overthink. What you'll do after that, I don't know. Your commitment tends to waver.'

'I'm deeply committed to Mortritis. I'm not going to lose my chance with her for anyone.'

Alastair looks far from reassured. 'Just don't pull the rug out from under me. You know what I have at stake.'

'Faulton, this is the blood loss talking. If I have any thoughts of leaving, you'll be the first to know.'

Apparently, this isn't the right thing to say either. In an unbelievably bold move, he smacks his palm on the door to stop it from opening. 'What are your plans for Fall Day?'

'No idea,' I say, folding my arms.

'Come into the city with me.'

'No thanks. I don't know how people can even pretend to celebrate in this cold.' The weather has been pretty but vile. I used to think Withersham's sultry fogs were bad, but I never had to dread them like I do perpetual snow.

'You won't be cold in the crowds with a hot scotch in your hand.' Seeing my nose wrinkle, he adds, 'We've been to Balver's celebrations before – we'll show you around.'

'Who's we?'

'Me, my brother, and his friends.'

'Ha! *No*. And especially not so you can keep an eye on me.'

'You'll have fun.'

'I'd have more fun paddling in the salt fen with paper cuts between my toes.'

'You will have fun. I'll make certain of it.'

I'm less interested in fun than I am in getting through admissions, but that will be in limbo still.

It's the first time since I arrived that I've thought about leaving the grounds. I always could, same as everyone else, but with my glyph practice, I haven't had much chance.

We don't really go in for Oldsfall in Preyburn, but in Glimwick, it's meant to be the event of the year. Oldrac's scions pay for and organize the whole festival. It's a competition between the families — whoever can contribute the most cements themselves as the richest and most powerful.

'You know the best thing about Oldsfall in Glimwick?' Alastair locks eyes with me in a way that stills. 'The food stalls. Roasted meats, artisanal confectioneries, spiced hot chocolate with fluffed cream, baked cheese apple bowls—'

'What's that?'

'An apple, hollowed out, stuffed with cheese and herbs, then baked 'til the cheese goes all gooey inside.'

'Wow. That sounds bestial.'

Alastair smirks. 'You won't eat better anywhere in the Commonwealth.'

My stomach responds instantly, the traitor.

'*And,*' he says, 'there won't be a dining service at the college. They expect everyone to be at the festival.'

'So my options are the best food in the Commonwealth or nothing at all?' I sigh. 'In that case, how could I refuse?'

Alastair's victory smirk is infuriating. 'I'll knock for you at fifth bell.'

22

A GOOD FIRST IMPRESSION

I wake the next morning feeling deeply stupid. All Alastair did was look at me, and I acted as if sex was moments away, and motherhood a few moments after. I'm so lucky he can't read my thoughts. I blame tiredness and also my parents for pouring poison into my ears.

Also in my defence, my parents aren't the first people to make that scarlet fever joke. Everyone says that about scions, but of course protection exists. Even the proudly tech-averse Glims don't think themselves above safe sex and contraception. If Alastair and I were going to—

By Our Lady, *of course* we're not going to. I'm being ridiculous.

When I've returned from the washrooms, one of the housekeepers has made the bed and set an envelope on top. I open it to find a summons to Thumbarrow inside – from *Mortritis!*

I make myself presentable, head buzzing with questions, and strike out across the gardens. Outside, it is almost cold enough to freeze the tears in my eyes, so I've more than one reason to hare across the snow.

When I arrive at Mortritis's office, there's no answer. After a long stretch of silence punctuated by the occasional gloved-knuckle knock, I test the handle and find it's unlocked. I poke my head in. The only life in the room comes from the blazing maw of the fireplace. As I was invited and there's no seating in the hallway, I let myself in.

It would be a lie to say there isn't any snooping, but I don't touch anything. I scour the spines on her bookcase, noting several rare editions of titles by lauded masters. The upper-right corner has been dedicated to personal interests, bawdy tales with salacious names that make me blush to read.

On Mortritis's desk, a newspaper called the *Balver Oracler* lies open at the society pages:

> *Yesterday evening, Balver's top socialites and a slew of spiring luminaries put on their spiffiest winter gowns for Edusa's notorious Oldsfall Soirée.*

My eyes catch on an illustration of two figures hand in hand, gazing into each other's eyes.

> *Admissions favourite Alastair Faulton, recently returned from exile in Preyburn, attended for the first time this year with Preyburn national Halen 'Hal' Kilchoir. Although the pair represent a little-known Prey school called Withersham Hall, their debut stage against the pulp-flesh ancestor is considered to be one of the best St Penderghast's admissions has seen in recent years.*
>
> *The seemingly starstruck Kilchoir was 'giddy' around her Glimwickian accord partner in Dunchester games hall, spies told the* Oracler. *The pair were later seen leaving the party hand in hand and quite alone.*

*An alleged eyewitness claimed: 'Alastair had his hands all
over Hal. They're clearly having it off with each other.'
While the* Daily Stance *co-signs this and 'confirms' the
two are courting, Edusa had this to say: 'A man of honour
could never betray the confidence of his pupils... but as a man
of romance, the tension between them is simply an agony!'*

Struggling to believe what I just read, I skim the article again – no,
I read everything correctly. You'd never catch that dopey expression
on my face, and I know for a fact we weren't holding hands... except
the memory of Alastair's hand squeezing mine as the Cofferspyres
had a go hits me with aching clarity. Well, the rest of this is *definitely*
lies. Apart from Edusa's quote, of course.

Tripped gods, what if my parents see this? They'll probably have
it framed.

After that, there's a vigorous dissection of the 'tiff' between
Mortritis and her sister. I hope that's all she read, and not the bit
about Alastair and me. Fortunately, none of their so-called spies
seem to have grasped what their fight was actually about. Or perhaps
they aren't allowed to publicize such foulness. I set the paper back
down with a grimace. Even this hollow gossip wouldn't get printed
in Preyburn.

Elsewhere on the desk, a map of the Commonwealth has been
rolled out and pinned at each end with paperweights. She has
marked, with crosses of what is undoubtedly Cognac Brown ink, the
Collegiate Pentad, the emblem of the Council that, with heavy input
from the prelate, governs the Commonwealth. The provost of each
regnant college counts for one fifth of it. While the Winter Grounds
has St Penderghast's, the Ascent, the Verge, the Storm Grounds,
and the Cradle all have their own colleges in their own capitals. St
Penderghast's is the best, of course, a fact that is proven time and again

through league tables and intercollege mêlées. Spiring was their only focus to begin with, but when Preyburn joined the Commonwealth, the Council established a graving conspectus in each one.

I'm admiring the cartography – the beautiful paper, the elegant script – when I hear a scuffing on the carpet behind me. I turn to see a shadowed man filling the doorway in a hulking, double-breasted wool overcoat. He steps forward, slipping off his gloves, and I take a step back. My hands feel suddenly empty, missing the grip of my spire.

'How I detest these Balverian winters,' he says, brushing past me to reach the desk. 'And to think – another three months freezing our tits off. Why do people live here?'

In the twitching light of the fire, I realize he's younger than I first took him for. He could be a third or fourth year. Moreover, I'm certain I've seen him before.

If he recognizes me, or is surprised to see me where Mortritis ought to be, he doesn't show it. He rattles the handle of her desk drawer and sighs when it won't budge. He begins rifling through what's on top of the desk itself, lifting sheafs of paper and nudging books aside, until finally he says, 'There she is,' and holds up a tiny iron key. From the drawer, he pulls out a pouch of tobacco and papers to roll it in. I haven't seen the like since I left Preyburn.

'Smoke?' he says. I shake my head. 'Mind if I do?'

'Not if I can open a window.'

'Have you been outside lately? Do you know how cold it is?'

'I need my lungs for admissions.'

He groans. 'A *crack*.'

I open the window a crack, and by the time I've turned around, he's at the drinks cabinet. He unstops a decanter of amber liquid, sniffs, grimaces, and tips some into a cut-crystal glass.

He takes a seat in Mortritis's office chair. With him behind the desk, rolling his cigarette on top of her beautiful map, and me stood in front of him, wondering who in the abyss he is, it feels like he's the one who summoned me.

'You're not one of her pupils,' he says, not lifting his gaze. He pinches tobacco from Mortritis's pouch and sprinkles it into the cigarette paper, and little brown twists scatter over the fenside towns that border the Greater Fenlands.

He has long aristocrat's fingers, that could also be thief's fingers if not for the clean, square nails and rings. The first is silver and shaped like spinal vertebrae; the second has an intaglio wax seal like Alastair's, but I can't make out the sigil.

'Are you?' I say.

'I am indeed.'

A proper graver. An exceptional one, worthy of Mortritis's patronage. There's a louche quality to him that seems innate and utterly at odds with the clean-cut presentation. The mouth is full and rich – suggesting depravity – yet the hair, black as liquorice whirls, is cropped close to the scalp, suggesting utility and discipline.

This sharp-faced, handsome stranger runs a pink tongue along the edge of his cigarette paper – and that's when it clicks. This is the boy I caught getting off with another in the library, who made me feel like *I* was the one caught. Thank the stars he doesn't recognize me.

'So what are you in for?' he says, pressing his cigarette into shape. 'Graves or spires?'

'Officially, it's spires.'

'Are you any good?' He takes a Prey-made lighter from his coat pocket, smirking like he has a secret. 'I suppose you must be if you're here.' He moves out from behind the desk, exhaling smoke. 'Come and sit down, will you? You'll make a boy nervous, looming over him like that.'

I get the impression even the provost would be hard pressed to make him nervous, but I pass through swathes of vanilla smoke to take a seat by the fire. It's the same seat I had last time.

The stranger sheds his overcoat, revealing a Prey-made jumper of thick, plaited plackets of yarn. 'My family's big on spiring. I don't think my aunt's missed a single Grand since seventeen. She even married into it.' He pauses to take a drag and, on the exhale, says, 'But you're a Prey, no?'

'What gave me away?' I joke, knowing how odd I must look in spiring garb.

'Mama and I lived in Preyburn not so long ago, down in Holyhalt. Everyone here tells me I have an accent now.'

I don't hear it. To me, he just sounds like a Glim. 'Did you like it?'

'Well, let's see. Everyone was uptight yet vulgar, scheming yet moronic, with advanced technology and a backwards outlook.' He gives a wolfish, trickster grin. 'I loved it.'

'When you say your mother,' I begin slowly, 'do you mean Mortritis?'

His grin widens. 'Mama Mortritis, yes.'

But of course. Now that we've said it, the intaglio of his seal ring is dark blue to match the field on the Moppetons' sigil. More telling than that are his features. Mortritis will have given him that height, and just look at his face. He *is* Mortritis, but much younger, and much more male. Imagine being the son of the world's greatest living graver.

I say, 'You're not Kiel?'

'Why?' His eyes narrow. 'What's she been saying about me?'

'Nothing,' I say, my voice shrilling.

'Fallen gods, that woman,' he mutters, at the same time as the door opens and Mortritis ducks her head under the doorframe. I jolt up like a child who's been caught scribbling on the walls, and Kiel pretends to glare at her. 'How can I make a good first impression when everyone knows me before I meet them?'

'Kiel,' Mortritis says in surprise. She sniffs. 'I see you've found your way into my good tobacco.'

Kiel doesn't look a bit guilty, or like he even knows the meaning of the word. Mortritis closes the door behind her, gesturing for me to sit back down. I lower in time with her hand.

'And met Hal.'

'Hal.' He says it slowly, as if considering the taste. 'Is that her name? She's been very evasive. Revealing nothing about herself, yet knowing provost-knows-what about me...'

'Don't be silly, poppet. You know I'd never speak ill of you.'

'That's just the thing. You can't tell the difference between ill and healthy. No doubt you've revealed something shameful.'

Mortritis waves this notion away. 'If Hal thinks any less of you for the manner in which you were conceived, then she's not the sort of person you want to know.'

Kiel has no reaction to this except to shiver, wrap his coat more tightly around himself, and exhale smoke until his edges blur. He's clearly heard it all before.

I watch the cigarette smouldering in the dark and can't believe I'm looking at Mortritis's own son and her proxy – someone much more than an exceptional graver.

Mortritis says, 'Hal, thank you for coming.'

'Of course.'

It's difficult to bring this image of Mortritis to terms with the woman at the soirée last night, yanking her sister to the floor by her hair.

'I called you here because I spoke with Edusa last night.'

My face heats, and all the more intensely for Kiel's scrutiny. 'You did?'

'I did. Well, it'd be more appropriate to say we spoke very early this morning. I caught him on his way back from the soirée.'

'What soirée?' Kiel says. 'Why wasn't I invited?'

'Edusa's soirée. It was all the spiring crowd – you would've hated it. As I was saying, he's consented to let me trial you without any repercussions.'

'*He did?*' I say. 'Why? I thought spiring was a jealous mistress.'

Kiel snorts, smoke arcing from his nostrils.

Mortritis says, 'He was in incredibly high spirits.'

'But he can just as easily take it back,' I say.

'He most certainly cannot. He swore to Our Scarlet-Tressed Lord in front of multiple witnesses. I made sure of it.'

My toes curl in their boots as I drop my gaze to the carpet. 'What about Drasilla?'

'You needn't concern yourself with my sister. She's a big girl.'

I fall silent, knowing this is the aftermath of their squabble, a punishment for the nasty truth Drasilla revealed to Mortritis last night. Either she wants to hurt her, or she no longer cares if she does.

But I can't afford to get all moral about it. I was beginning to wonder if I'd ever get the chance to prove my worth to Mortritis, and here she is, offering me the floor.

'Preceptor, I don't know how I could ever thank you enough.'

'Don't be silly. I do this for my benefit. I need all the decent gravers I can get.'

'Wait,' Kiel murmurs, looking between us. 'You're going to trial her?' To me, he goes, 'Aren't you here to spire?'

'She's a Kilchoir who wants to audit my conspectus,' Mortritis says.

Kiel rests his gaze on me. 'You do know Kilchoirs rarely make the cut?'

'Your father did.'

'He was the exception, not the rule.'

Mortritis says, 'Did Hal mention she's in an accord with your cousin Alastair?'

'I had no idea. You poor thing. Your fortitude must be legendary.'

Mortritis sighs. 'I wish you'd put this childish feud to bed. It's just embarrassing.'

'What's embarrassing is Alastair's social skills. I've squeezed better conversation out of the donations.'

'You might find you have more to talk about now he's spent a few years in Preyburn.'

'Doubt it. He's a good-looking boy, but he doesn't know how to have fun.'

He watches me over the top of his glass as he sips from it, a gleam in his eye that says, *I do.*

'Alastair's many things,' I say, 'but he never bores me.'

Not anymore.

'Try wearing a blindfold the next time you hang out with him.'

'I'd still disagree. If he really bored you that much, you wouldn't bother to bitch about him.'

Kiel smirks. 'Have I touched a nerve?'

'*Children,*' Mortritis says. 'Two of my pupils expect us downstairs for the trial. We'd best be getting on.'

My heart leaps. 'You won't regret giving me this chance.'

Mortritis smiles. 'Oh, I never regret anything, poppet. It's all part of the fun.'

23

A DISGUSTING
TRAVESTY

Mortritis leads us through the towering set of doors that mark entry to Thumbarrow's training hall, a cavernous, hewn stone chamber. Her heels echo off the floor and walls like distant thunder. It has a sensible floor, as Withersham did – wear resistant, able to bear the weight of heavier effigies, and easy to clean messes from.

But this is still Penders, where we are never without ostentation. The painted firmaments swirl across the ceiling, gold stars seething in a vaulted navy sky as Our Lady leaps towards Preyburn with the nebulous shadow of the Condemner whispering in her ear. Since Our Lady shared very little of him with her followers, artists usually depict the Condemner as dark and amorphous as possible. Well, excepting a particular group of girls at Withersham, who liked to depict him in carnal ways – prose as well as drawings – that would no doubt horrify the prelate.

There are no windows. The room's light comes from a circular hole at the centre of the roof's dome, and sun falls through it like a white, hot spotlight.

Two boys clad jaw to heel in the smart, rich fabric of the graving conspectus turn to look at us through the slitted eyes of gravers' masks, while to their left atrophers smoulder in a claw-footed fire bowl. These two are dressed for battle, or, more likely, training. They come equipped with gravers' belts, their Compendiums and graphia holstered in firm leather at each right hip. As a graphium is a Prey-made tool, it would be contraband in Glimwick if they had them for any lesser purpose.

Farther back, where I almost didn't notice her, is another figure. I recognize the smart coat and burgundy leather gloves first and the huge, hungry eyes second. Once Viler sees I've spotted her, she gives me a big smile and a manic wave with a notepad. A stranger might mistake her for an obsessive fan.

It seems Mortritis wants to measure me against her favourite admissions pupil. Well, bring it on.

As we draw closer, the boys stand to attention, the very picture of lockstep discipline. Moving in concert, they tuck their masks under their left arms to salute Mortritis with their right. Their eagerness to please is a visceral thing.

'Good morning, boys.'

Even their reply has perfect synchrony: 'Good morning, Preceptor.'

Mortritis draws to a stop, her gaze falling to the ten bodies on the stone in front of them. They lie naked but for their faces, which are covered by cloth shrouds, and are arranged in two five-pointed stars, heads together, feet angled out.

'Oh, boys,' Mortritis breathes, her voice soft as smoke. 'You've done an *exquisite* job.'

'Thank you, Preceptor.' The boys' faces do not soften but they do turn as pink as beet-pickled eggs. Despite their hawkish airs, they are helpless to stop the blush from conquering their faces. From their starched collars to the roots of their martially short haircuts, it's clear they're gagging for the measliest drop of her praise, and who can blame them?

I also survey the bodies. Back home, nobody touches a donation except the graver who claims it. So what keeps it from rotting? Not a damn thing. If it spoils, it's burned like any other corpse. It's an incredibly wasteful system that doesn't cost chapel workers the time, energy, and materials needed to preserve them.

I recall Crippleditch Chapel's mortuary, a berth of souring corpses with rot growing like black moss on their skin. All will have been left lying at some odd angle, blood pooling wherever it may, and unshrouded. Faces without shrouds add the exciting possibility of expulsion splatter, a creamy froth that builds up in the lungs to squirt from the mouth and nose.

But the training hall brings none of the smells that, to me, are synonymous with graving. There is cold, humid stone, yes, but where is the fungus, soil, cheese, human waste, and post-mortem intestinal gases? Instead, there is only sweet incense and soapy, aldehydic freshness.

Any graver should be thrilled to find donations so pristine. When I think of the messes the Crippleditch pastoress had to take care of, it's little wonder the job turnover was so high.

'First is a test of glyphic aptitude,' Mortritis says. 'You and Kiel each have a half-bell to create a witherbrute from five bodies. Then, you will test said effigies against each other.'

My heart drops into my gut. I thought she meant to pit me against Viler. Kiel's a third year, not to mention her son and proxy. How can this possibly be fair?

'Then why's Viler here?' I say, even as the girl bores rapt holes into my back.

'I said she could observe,' Mortritis says. 'I hope that's all right.'

'Of course.' It has to be all right because Mortritis said so, but a mix of stress and envy tightens my voice. If Mortritis is already helping Viler collect data for her thesis, she must see something special in her, or at least in her research.

The research that says I'm doomed to fail as a graver.

'Hal, I appreciate there's a difference in experience level here,' Mortritis says gently, 'so your trial will be open book.'

I keep a fixed gaze, even though my mind is unravelling. I hadn't even imagined it could be closed book! I don't have all 1,063 glyphs memorized!

At a gesture from Mortritis, one of the first years steps forward. He removes a graphium and the very latest edition of *The Compendium of Glyphs* from his belt and presents them to me. I seize each like a salvation. The second steps forward to present me with a mask.

My thoughts are at war. It isn't fair to put me up against Kiel, and I should say so. But if I do, I'll seem ungrateful for the chance I begged for or, worse, lacking confidence in my abilities.

She's offered this trial on a whim. Since she can rip it away from me just as easily, I'll have to grit my teeth and muscle through. I fit the mask onto my head, inhaling a whack of mentholated lavender that makes my eyes water, and fasten the backstrap. Fallen gods, I've missed this.

I must be demented even to attempt this without a pulp physick, but I have no choice. If I tried to drink one now, everyone would watch me spit it straight back up.

Fortitude, Hal. It wasn't the preceptors' generosity that won you all those high marks at Withersham; it was your theory. Even Limbridge had to admit it's excellent. You can do this.

I glance at Viler. She stands with her notepad tucked under one arm, hands buried in her coat pockets, and eyes bright with interest.

I remember her words outside Dunchester: *you're too far gone*. She's come to observe my failure, but like the last time we met, I'll leave her disappointed. Two years' spiring and a touch of stage fright couldn't possibly counteract all the hard work I've put in since childhood.

'Whatever you have when I call time will be what you have to fight with. Understood?'

'Yes, Preceptor.'

'Boys.' Mortritis turns to them. 'Stand by in case we need you, all right?'

'Yes, Preceptor.'

Still high on her compliments and struggling valiantly to hide it, the boys retreat to a well-judged distance.

'A half-bell,' she repeats, 'starting now.'

My hands have already begun to tremble long before I open the Compendium. It takes them an agonizingly long time to find the correct pages; I struggle to feel the edges through my gloves.

Book- and carefree, Kiel circles his five donations as though out for a summer's-day stroll. He twirls his graphium between his long fingers, whistling through his teeth as he studies his materials.

I try to focus on my own work, but I can't ignore how quickly Kiel sets to his. In my peripheral vision, beyond the edge of the crisp, pale yellow pages, he bends to take a donation's freckled wrist. The nib of his graphium glows and hisses as he presses it to the soft flesh on the inside of the donated arm. Before I even know which glyph to put where, he draws the first stroke, creating the scent of petrichor. It's so pungent, it reaches past the herb-stuffed nose of my mask.

I feel the weight of Mortritis's gaze on my shoulders as I approach my five donations, heart in my throat. I set to work with my own graphium, marking my first arm. Instead of petrichor, I smell char and salty ham – glistening pig on a spit. The smell of things going wrong.

I keep going, wanting to cry as I brand abdomens, fingers, hairy chests, assigning values to each body part. All must take their place within the epitaph.

Kiel works fast from memory. Witherbrutes are a basic creature. He will have written each glyph a thousand times. He's a proper graver.

To make sure I'm putting the right glyph in the right place, I have to keep referring back to the Compendium. I take great care to copy out every stroke precisely. A tail that's too long or too short, a curve too acute or too wide, a wonky spine, an extra flick, a missing loop – all could change the value of the glyph. The graphium stutters against the donation's skin as I inscribe its throat.

I'm perhaps halfway through the epitaph when I notice a problem that chills me. The glyphs aren't still on the page.

No, wait – I'm so panicked, I'm hallucinating. Aren't I?

I ogle the page, cementing my worst fears. The glyphs are moving. *This cannot be happening.* It is. My punishment for spiring. My body's rejection of the pulp, the glyphs' rejection of *me.* Even though I've practised faithfully almost every day... I mean, I have skipped a few days lately, but only a few, and now they snub my understanding.

Have they been moving all this time? If so, I have no idea whether the glyphs I've written on the donations are the right ones. There are no corrections in glyph work. Once a donation's marked, it's marked. I'd have to remove the erroneous glyphs from the epitaph completely, replacing the donations that hold them with fresh ones. But this isn't a battlefield. I don't have bodies to spare.

Fallen gods. What can I do but forge ahead? And try not to make any more mistakes?

Kiel's glyphs begin to wake, whispering leaves skating over brick.

A fresh wave of panic crashes into me. Kiel has already completed his epitaph. His donations shiver as the glyphs ignite on their skin.

I beg my glyphs to fix in place. Kiel's are dazzling now. I pray for Our Lady's forgiveness, but of course Our Lady does not forgive.

Kiel's glyphs begin to break down the hosts, reforming them into something new. I try to remember how they should look. Kiel's donations drag together, flesh coupling with flesh. I make it up, stumbling towards the finish line with all the assuredness of an ill three-legged mule. My heart thumps like the foot of a baby hare and I can't breathe.

But, despite what I know to be myriad slip-ups, my donations do spasm towards each other. Their flesh does come together, bone and sinew resolving into something wholly new.

Mortritis watches with a shrewd, enigmatic gaze as my effigy takes shape before her.

When the glyph-light dulls, we stand in the shadow of a behemothic, clawed biped with features both cervine and lupine – a perfectly formed witherbrute.

Beside it is a horrific mess. If I had to make a comparison, it would be to the pulp-flesh ancestor, but even that could manoeuvre itself from A to B. It was capable of base logic, of communication, of threat.

What I've created in the past half-bell can do none of these things. It is a useless, quivering jumble of flesh, a failure of such epic proportions that it inspires reverence. It is a disgusting travesty, an insult to the very notion of graving, and all I can do is gawk at it.

There's not going to be a second step to this trial. My pitiful attempt couldn't fight its way from a wet paper bag, let alone Kiel's effigy. It may not even be sentient.

I am mortified.

Kiel considers the thing in front of me as if it's a child's drawing – objectively bad, but lovable in its own way. Viler's gaze flicks back and forth between my attempt and the notepad she's scribbling in furiously, documenting my greatest shame for her bloody thesis. The first years are trying their best to keep plain, rigid faces, but I feel their smirks. They're the cohort's smirks. They always knew I was going to fail exactly like this.

Finally, Mortritis takes a breath. 'Boys, do you mind cleaning this up while I speak to Hal outside?' She waves a hand at... *this* – my attempt. 'And taking the effigy down to the enclosure?'

'Yes, Preceptor,' the boys chime.

'Kiel – thank you. You're free to go.'

There's nothing left to say. Kiel inclines his head towards his mother. The look he gives me before he leaves is tender and pitying: *Oh, you sweet little fool.* He disappears through a side door. Viler edges closer to my attempt, positively transfixed by the mess. She circles it, pen slashing endlessly across her notepad, examining every angle.

The first years don their graving masks and, using flat-jaw tongs, retrieve the atrophers from the fire bowl. I stare, frozen, as they set the glowing plates atop blobs of pink and white flesh, branding it with *ezorhox*. Where the atrophers touch, the skin turns grey and begins to rot. It jiggles a little but otherwise cannot complain.

I'm gripping the Compendium and the graphium so tightly, my fingers have lost all feeling. Instead of trying to prise them from me, Mortritis lays a large, firm hand on my shoulder. Tears catch in the chin of my mask as she steers me towards the exit.

24

THE JAM INSIDE
THE DOUGHNUT

I'm sitting in a dark, windowless room. It stinks of embers and ashes, but the gloom is a balm for my eyes, behind which a dull pain has settled.

Mortritis stands watching the fireplace with a fist against her hip. Even though my stool is right beside it, it feels like a distant sun whose heat barely reaches me.

'I hoped you both would and wouldn't succeed today. If you had, I would have had Edusa to deal with.' Mortritis sighs, as if the mere thought exhausts her. 'But I would have had potential on my hands. A double-edged sword.'

She's procured another drink from somewhere, another faceted crystal glass to drink it from. When she offers me a sip, I don't say no. I don't say anything.

'How many from my admissions group could create a witherbrute, do you think?'

I shake my head.

'All of them. With an open book, it should have been easy for you.'

I feel like a fool. I *am* a fool. To think I fought so hard for this trial, only to disappoint. How did I convince myself I was good enough for the graving conspectus? Even when everyone told me otherwise?

I take the largest gulp of bourbon I can manage, which isn't very much at all. It burns.

'Hal, why do you want to be a graver?'

The answer seems to come from someone else's mouth: 'I want to be known for something worthy.'

Mortritis takes the glass from me, knocking it back like water. 'Do you know why you failed today?'

'I lost sight of my priorities. I neglected my glyphs, and they rebuffed me for my hubris—'

'No, poppet. They rebuffed you because you've fallen foul of Our Lady's principles.'

I look up at her, something I've been too ashamed to do until now. I don't know why she's even bothering with me after what happened, nor how we got here.

I'm sure we haven't left Thumbarrow. The room has a graver's austerity. A heady cocktail of panic, shame, and disbelief addled my memories, and now the shadows around us are so thick, I don't know what they hide. The floorboards, the stone walls – it all just fades to black.

'It takes malevolence to be a graver,' she goes on. 'Spite fuels us as much as it does eerians.'

A light sparks in my chest. 'Then what about pulp? If I took enough—'

She laughs. 'Were it only so simple! I'd have a legion of Kiels. Our Lady tried her hand at scion–eerian hybrids, but pulp is incompatible with Oldracian flesh. Force it, and it'll poison you to paralysis until your body purges it.'

Deep down, I knew this. I knew Viler was right. My stomach will keep rejecting physicks, because it's infested with Oldracian flesh, made of the very thing Our Lady sought to destroy.

The spark sputters and dies as quickly as it came to life. Still doomed, then.

One of Mortritis's pupils emerges from the shadows with what looks like two dusty lumps of coal on a brass plate. She thanks the girl with a heart-stopping smile, plucking one lump between two incredible talons.

Blushing furiously, the girl turns to offer the second to me. I take it on impulse – a doughnut, velvet black, made of chocolate brioche dough, dusted with sugar. It's the size of a man's fist. I cannot even think about eating it. It sits in my hand, squidgy and sandy.

Even if I spent the next decade working at it, the chances of Mortritis taking me on as a mature pupil are next to nil. Graving masters want the prodigies, the pupils whose achievements look effortless. They want the Kiel Moppetons of the world.

As the girl melts back into the shadows, Mortritis takes an enormous bite, her eyes rolling back in pleasure. A jammy red filling oozes from the centre, over her fingers, and onto the floorboards.

'I know you don't want to hear this,' she says through a mouthful, 'but the problem is that you're too soft.'

Every muscle in my body cringes as if struck by Acclaim. '*Me?*'

'Glyphs sense their reader's nature. Our Lady knew Our Lord was an altruist at his core. She designed glyphs so that he and his followers would never be able to adopt her work – a sort of encryption.'

'The glyphs can't possibly think I'm Oldrac's follower. I don't even remember all the Radiant Principles.'

'They don't think. They *know*. Glyphs don't just see your actions; they see your constitution. You follow the Radiant Principles in your actions *and* thoughts.'

'Far be it for me to question your experience, Preceptor, but this is quite different from what I've been taught.'

'For good reason. If pupils think lack of study equals glyphic illiteracy, it encourages them to work hard.'

'You mean to say that all this time I've been working my fingers to the bone practising glyphs, desperate not to lose my graving ability, it didn't even matter?' I close my eyes and take a deep breath. In that case, I'll never regain literacy, no matter how hard I work.

'Believe it or not, Kiel faced your same problem.' Mortritis dabs at the jam in the corners of her mouth. 'He was an alarmingly sweet child – still can be, at times. But the spirit that allows him to grave so fluently today had to be cultivated. That's why I raised him in Preyburn. It's singularly well suited to churning out gravers.' She quotes the Radiant Principles: '"Harsh, brief lives breed hard, bitter hearts." Honour, generosity, compassion – sadly, these things don't help in the making of effigies.

'All my pupils would be Prey if the provost allowed it. Do you know how many times we've had this exact conversation? She wants me to make soft gravers *work*, as if I could overrule Our Lady's will if I only tried.'

The wider implications of Mortritis's claims are not lost on me. Preyburn's misery serves the Commonwealth, which has a vested interest in keeping Preyburn exactly the way it is because it breeds the hard, bitter hearts needed for graving.

I think back to the conversation I had with Alastair before that first meeting with Mortritis: *The Council and the Choir pushed you into it, a bankrupt country desperate enough to accept Glim strength for war service... and look what it's done to you all.*

But I don't have the mental or emotional capacity to get into that now. Quietly, I say, 'If Kiel overcame it, I can too.'

Mortritis is shaking her head before I've even finished. 'Children are malleable. At your age, a radical personality shift would take measures more drastic than anyone could *morally* inflict upon you… and should you really seek them out?' She shrugs. 'Unfortunately, the die is cast.'

I've never known heartbreak close to this. Or humiliation.

I might actually expire.

Mortritis polishes off her doughnut and bourbon, dusts the sugar from her palms. 'That being said, I do have an offer for you.'

I look up at her, eyes wide.

'It's not on the conspectus,' she warns. 'You wouldn't be a pupil at St Penderghast's, or anywhere, but I'll take you on as my research assistant.'

All I can do is blink at her. *A job?*

'My projects are quite endless. There'll be a lot of book scouring, some travel. You wouldn't see combat, which is entirely for the best.'

Another white-hot flush of shame sweeps over me, making me drop my gaze again.

'But graving isn't just about what happens on the front lines. Our Lady was a maker long before she was a destroyer. This will be a launchpad for your ambitions, and a lucrative one at that. In Prey currency, it equals fifteen thousand puds per year. It's advertised as a graduate position, but I think you'd take to it.'

I'm stunned. Leaving education to take up a job never even crossed my mind, but she's right. I'd never get to be a St Penderghastian alumna, never don the graduation robes and frame a copy of my degree… but so what? With the experience and esteem the position of First Graving Master's research assistant would give me, I could do whatever I wanted.

In some ways, this offers an even better opportunity than the conspectus. I'll be working directly on Mortritis's projects. So I won't see combat, which is shameful, but I'll be scouring books, reading, using my pen – things that I love.

The spark in my chest is fully aflame again, creating a warm, fuzzy glow.

But then I remember the night before – why Mortritis invited me to trial in the first place – and it quavers.

'This is about Drasilla,' I say. 'If I'm not going to be a pupil, that will mean breaking my accord. Alastair will return to exile, and she'll be distraught.'

Insults demand answers.

'I should have known that would upset you.' Her voice is neutral – not a bit perturbed at the accusation. 'The glyphs are never wrong.'

She sets her glass on the mantel.

'Naturally, you and Alastair have grown accustomed to each other. That's the whole point of accords. The provost swears up and down that it's oneness in action, but more likely it abuses your Oldracian impulse to put others' needs before your own.

'Let's forget about what Alastair wants, what Drasilla wants, what I want. Do you want to be a spirer, poppet? Or is it your Oldracian flesh telling you to sacrifice your true ambitions for that boy?

'I'll tell you now, if you go along with spiring for anyone else's sake, you'll end up resenting them for having derailed your life. Resentment will do wonders for your glyphic literacy, but that won't be much use to your curriculum vitae after seven years in the arena.'

I shake my head again. 'You don't really want to employ me. You wouldn't offer me a thing if not for Drasilla.'

'Wanting to teach my harlot sister a lesson and wanting to employ you are not mutually exclusive.' Mortritis grins. 'Drasilla's despair is just the jam inside the doughnut, so to speak.'

'Forgive me, Preceptor, but I'd have to be dizzy in the head to believe that. All you've seen me do is fail.'

'Nonsense! Do you know what I value most in a worker?'

In the resultant pause, she comes over to my stool. The closer she gets, the lower it seems to sink into the ground. All I can do is stare at her like a gormless fool while she towers over me, taking my chin in the talons of her thumb and forefinger. She tilts my face up and up until our eyes lock. She has Alastair's eyes, twin portals to the black and burning abyss.

'Subservience,' she says softly.

My breath hitches in my throat. The image of the two boys in the training hall and the girl with the doughnut come to mind. Disciplined and desperate to please, like dogs.

Mortritis lets me go, wandering back towards the fire. Feeling something wet and gooey on my fingers, I glance down to see I've squeezed half the jam out of my doughnut.

'I appreciate this is a big decision. Why don't you take some time to think on it?'

Thank the provost. If she demanded an answer on the spot, I don't know what I'd do. 'Yes... thank you.'

'Go, enjoy the festival. Come back to me before second bell in two days' time.'

In two days' time, I'm supposed to take the Crucible.

But of course, she knows that.

'My offer will hold until then, but fair warning: I have another applicant to offer if you turn me down. And if he turns me down, I have another after that, and so on. We mustn't keep them on the hook for too long. It simply isn't fair.'

'I understand,' I say, not wanting to say anything that could make her take the offer back.

'So,' she says, 'are you headed into the city to celebrate tomorrow?

Oh, you'll love it! It's pure debauchery. Not as loose as Preyburn, but even the saintliest Glims let their hair down for Oldsfall.'

I rise unsteadily to my feet, my squashed doughnut now drooling raspberry jam into my left hand.

'Do keep your wits about you, won't you? There'll be plenty of pickpockets and ruffians preying on the intoxicated.' She gives a devious smile, complete with eyebrow wiggle. 'Don't do anything I wouldn't do.'

25

THE FOG OF WANT

Fall Day's revelry starts in the pub. Tieran and his friends have been here since breakfast, so we're among the lucky few with a table, even if it is wet and sticky. The place is packed, so most patrons have to stand.

On this day hundreds of years ago, Oldrac fell from the firmaments to Glimwick in pursuit of Our Lady. To celebrate, everyone from the highest noble to the skintest commoner, locals and tourists alike has taken to the city centre in their hordes. Outside, they flow through the streets like a wide and lazy river. Inside, giddy laughter, cheering, and high, lilting music fill the air.

Alastair was right about the weather. Snow blows past the foggy windows in tiny specks, but you wouldn't think it was cold enough with all these clammy bodies clumped around us. I'm sweltering in a scarf, socks thick enough to make my boots feel tight, and a knitted jumper cocooning me under my waxed coat. When I finally relent and strip down to my shirt, Tieran's friends goggle like they've never seen breasts before, even though there really isn't much to see.

Alastair and I sit side by side while they face us, drinking snifters of brandy. Baltair, Spenny, and 'Golden' Edgar are as charming as drunk, hedonist pricks can be. Less brandy gets sloshed into their mouths than onto their own finery.

'To drinking like Preys!' Baltair roars, and they all clink their snifters together.

Tieran, I used to dislike, but now that I've met his friends, I despise him. They all operate on the worry-free vivacity of society's upper crust. Everything is a hilarious joke, and anyone who can't see that is just being miserable for the sake of it.

These are the ones who went to the Embankment, so I have to listen to them talk about that for a while – how cheap everything was, how foul the weather, all the funny slang they picked up. Every time they say *pud*, they are so thoroughly impressed with themselves, it makes my toes curl.

They talk about Preyburn as if it's their own playground. I imagine them leading a merry jaunt through the Embankment, visiting bars, gambling dens, soap rooms, being obnoxious, leaving all sorts of disgusting messes for the locals to deal with. Their talk is so infuriating that I almost forget the things I should actually be worried about. Then I hear Alastair's rumbling voice, and remember.

I haven't told him about the job offer, and won't unless I'm definitely going to take it. No point getting him all riled up for nothing.

Riled up is putting it lightly. Furious, apoplectic, incandescent with rage: these are more accurate terms. It'd be a hundred times worse than any fight we've had in the past because now we're enjoying a ceasefire, as Mortritis would say.

He's been doing some goggling of his own. It's a great deal subtler than Tieran's friends, but he doesn't snap his head away when I catch him anymore. He's been watching me the way a cat looks at a lap it plans to curl up in, giving his full attention even through the prattle of Tieran and company. The outsides of our knees press against each other, and not by accident.

Our delightful friends haven't missed it either. Alastair bears an onslaught of leering grins and winks and innuendos. Spenny is the worst of them. It's difficult to believe he's Lourdes' older brother, but they apparently share a surname and his nickname came from that.

'So Alastair,' he says slyly, 'I imagine the two of you have been getting lots of exercise in? And some spiring as well?'

It's all about as delicate as a hammer to the skull, but they're squiffy enough to think I haven't caught on. Between the five of them, I feel exposed, like a grub that's had its rock lifted up, desperate to burrow back into the damp, dark soil.

So far, Alastair's tactic has been to reply with polite taciturnity and wait for them to get bored. He's smartly dressed for the occasion, and so handsome it disgusts me. He wears a dark, well-cut peacoat and his musky, sweet-woods cologne. His hair is princely like a golden crown.

Polite taciturnity isn't going to work for me.

'I suppose that might be a clever joke if it was the first one ever told,' I say, glaring Spenny in the eye.

He replies with another, creepier grin, the armour of his gilded life too thick for my barb to pierce. 'Come now, don't get upset. We're only teasing.'

'Actually, you're being lewd,' I say.

Golden Edgar's quick to back him up, shrugging his eyebrows in a bawdy manner. 'I thought Preys appreciated a bit of lewdness.'

'Only when they're not pretending to be all prim and proper,' Baltair says, then turns to Alastair. 'She's a bit prickly, isn't she? Your Prey sweetheart.'

Now they've turned on his brother, Tieran growls out a warning. '*Boys*.'

But the lack of excitement in Alastair's voice says he isn't fazed. 'If you went to Preyburn and everyone there spoke down to you, I daresay you'd prickle too.'

His lightless gaze settles on Baltair in a way that makes the other boy itch the brandy-reddened skin at his collar. He looks to Spenny for support, and gets it.

'Pfft!' Spenny waves Alastair's words away. 'Don't cry because your big brother had to save you *and* your girl from a handful of admissions write-offs.'

Something finally sparks in Alastair's dead eyes, something ominous and livid, but my mouth sparks quicker. 'I'd like to see *you* take on five trained spirers at once, you sodden brandy sponge. You'd lose a fight with a balloon.'

He frowns. 'With a what?'

Remembering the likelihood of Glims ever seeing a balloon, I snap, 'If this ridiculous province had any technology better than a flushing toilet, you'd know!'

Spenny sneers. 'Technology you scraped from *the Ascendancy*. That's nothing to be proud of.'

Tieran slaps his hands down on the table so fiercely it makes us both jump.

'Right, everyone finish your drinks!' His tone brooks no argument. 'Let's get to the arena before all the good seats are gone.'

To my great annoyance, his friends instantly abandon our fight to knock back what's left of their brandy. Frowns and glares turn to sloppy grins as all thoughts of hostility leave their heads. They couldn't care less what I think.

As we sidle out of the booth, it's pounced on by two groups of the nearest standing patrons. A row ensues behind us as we push our way out.

Surrounded by people on all sides, we move at a shuffling pace.

Tieran and company lead the charge, undaunted by the crush of revellers, with Alastair and I bringing up the rear.

We pass market stalls of gorse-yellow fabric selling food, furs, and souvenirs. The air is thick with a heady smoke of burnt leaves and juniper needles. It billows off the bonfires and people that have been near them, the scent clinging to their clothes and hair. Musicians stand wherever their tip hats won't be kicked over, strumming joyful tunes on instruments I can't name.

Garlands of evergreen needles wrapped with ribbons web between the arches and gables overhead. Someone managed to chuck one over a grand statue of Oldrac so it looks like his feather boa. I can't help but picture Edusa when I look at it.

To Alastair, I say, 'How will we get into the arena without tickets?'

'Today's stages are free to watch,' he says. 'There's always a fireworks display at the finale.'

I'd love to see a few free stages, but as soon as we get within a hundred paces of the arena, the crowds thicken around us until we can barely move forwards or back.

I pretend I'm not being pressed up against the soft wool of Alastair's jumper and his firm chest beneath it. If that isn't happening, then my thighs must be twingeing together for entirely unrelated reasons.

The pretending becomes more difficult when some drunkard shoulder-barges me. Alastair, in an arrogant show of intimacy, puts a protective arm around me and leaves it there. Do I shrug him off? No, I don't. Do I snuggle into him a little? Yes, I do.

The consequences are almost immediate. The woman directly in front glances back at us and does a double take. After some furious whispers to the girl next to her, she cranes around to get an eyeful too. Finally, the left girl says, 'Excuse me, but are you two dating?'

'I beg your bloody pardon?'

'Are you two on a date?' the girl repeats more loudly, as if I might not have heard over the crowd. 'I say yes, but my sister says no.' She dashes a flirtatious gaze up at Alastair through her lashes. 'She thinks you're so handsome.' The girl beside her – the sister, I assume – jabs her with a fur-clad elbow, to no effect. 'She even stole one of your posters, look!'

I follow her pointing finger to the nearest wall, where posters advertise tickets to the Crucible. Sketches of the admissions pupils blazon each one. There are some of me, or rather a figure who is supposed to represent me, but none of Alastair. Overhead, I can just make out the print on a notice: *Stealing posters is a criminal fault! It carries an immediate 50-gilt fine!*

Unfazed that his posters are setting knickers aflame all over the city, Alastair musters a slight, polite smile.

Before he can say anything, I jump in with, 'Not that it's any of your business, but we've come with friends.'

Both girls look utterly contemptuous.

'*You're* public figures and *we're* fans,' says the poster thief, sniffing. 'Of course it's our business.'

My heart's going, eyes darting from face to face. I'm not used to being amongst so many people packed so close together, or being asked personal questions by perfect strangers, and I start to feel a bit overstimulated. The desire I had to watch the stages evaporates.

I must look how I feel, because Alastair slips his hand under my scarf to stroke warm fingers up and down my nape as if to reassure a spooked horse. It helps in a way, but in another it makes me even nervier, like someone's opening a bottle of fizzy wine and I'm waiting for the cork to pop.

The two nosy sisters take this as the real answer to their question – likely the real reason why he did it – and the mouthy one makes smug eyes at the other.

'Alastair,' I hiss, swatting his hand away, 'if I don't get a baked cheese apple bowl in the next half-bell, I'm simply leaving.'

Taking my threat as serious, which it is, Alastair calls to his brother. 'Tieran!' The crowd noise is uproarious, but you cannot fail to hear his thundering bass. Tieran whips his head around, as do several other people. 'We're going! It's too crowded here!'

Tieran pouts. 'You're not going *now*?'

'I'm afraid so.'

'Let him off, Tieran,' says Spenny, his voice slithering with suggestion. 'With any luck, he'll get to use his own spire before the day's through!'

Golden Edgar guffaws, the nosy sisters smirk, and a piece of my soul shrivels up and dies.

Tieran smirks too, turning back to his brother. 'A fair point! We'll be at the Ancestor's Arms after the fireworks if you want to find us later!'

Alastair leads me away, his hand wrapped around mine, which is only sensible. We could easily lose each other, and I'd have a fine time finding my way around this labyrinth without him. Even so, it bothers me that we have an audience.

As Mortritis promised, the streets are pure debauchery, not so different from Preyburn at Ersfall, marking the Fall of Our Lady. People are messy, already baffled on drink and worse things. A woman stumbles over the cobblestones in heeled boots, a man relieves himself in a flowerpot – they will be easy targets for skulduggery. But there are families too, children sitting happily on their parents' shoulders, sticky with confections.

As we're making our way through, yet another person knocks my shoulder, except this one apologizes. I recognize her voice instantly.

'Lourdes,' I say, surprised.

She turns towards me, grinning even before she sees who addressed her. Some five bodies stop with her – friends, I assume – creating a bulwark against the jostling crowd.

'Hal! Alastair!' She's either very merry or a bit sozzled. Alastair tenses beside me. 'Fancy seeing you here, having fun! I heard you got ambushed by Ransley and some of the other dropouts, but look at you! Not a scratch.'

'You should've seen us after the fight. We've cleaned up okay.'

'Shameful business.' Lourdes shakes her head. 'People like that give spiring a bad name, in philosophy *and* ability. I'm just sorry I don't have Tieran's foresight. I would've enjoyed putting them to rights.' She claps a hand to my shoulder and gives it a squeeze. I half expect it this time and don't flinch. 'Last chance to let loose before the Crucible! I'll be seeing you both in the arena. In passion!'

'Glory,' Alastair and I say, his voice dry, mine so weak she might only see my lips move.

Then, with a wink at Alastair that's devoid of lewdness but clearly irks him all the same, Lourdes vanishes into the crowd.

When we're far enough away from the arena and free to walk normally, rich, sweet smells fill the air: hot milk and caramel. At Ersfall, I can look forward to sticky sausage wheels, warm and squidgy oat bread steeped in onion gravy, steaming mounds of sherry-soaked sponge, and lots and lots of lovely stout.

Puds would be useless here; they don't accept Prey money. Fortunately, Limbridge exchanged some of my school allowance for gilts, the hexagonal coinage used in Glimwick. Not having left the grounds the whole time I've been here, I haven't spent any of it yet.

As we weave our way round the stalls, I am viscerally disappointed by the lack of stout in what is obviously a stout-drinking opportunity. It's all spiked hot chocolate, blackberry wine, and that spicy vanilla concoction Glims love so much. What I end up spending my gilts on is a cup of honey hot scotch with chilli. Its smell could peel paint from walls, and its taste is a punch of warm spices to the gut.

'I can't believe people drink this on purpose,' I say hoarsely.

Alastair's voice is teasing. 'You Preys love to tell everyone how hard your stomachs are, but when it comes to *real* liquor...'

'This isn't real liquor. It's acid reflux at a premium.' I take another eye-watering swallow. 'If it came down to it, any Prey could drink a Glim under the table. It's in our blood.'

With hot scotch heating my stomach, we pass more stalls, most of them dedicated to either booze or sweets. Booze I understand, but what sort of pervert craves spiced pumpkin soup and burnt caramel pears when they're drunk? Where's all the stodge? Where are the promised baked cheese apple bowls?

The best I can find is baked cheese pies. Alastair and I join a long and rambling queue with people shouldering through it every five seconds.

As much as I try to put it out of my head, my mind keeps circling back to Mortritis. I only have today and tomorrow morning to reach a decision, after all. I'd be crazy not to take the job, wouldn't I? It's more than I ever hoped to gain when I got on the train at Burymeadow.

I won't even have to wait four years to graduate before I can start earning, rubbing my success in the cohort's faces. And let's not forget my parents – there'll be no more gross suggestions when they hear I've got a proper job with a graving master.

I picture Alastair's face when I tell him, and the prospect of telling him that he's going back to exile, that there'll be no father–son reunion, does kill me a little. But I shove those images away. Realistically, we've been friends for all of five minutes. I can't sacrifice my career for him.

By the time we've reached the front of the queue, received our baked cheese pies, and made way for the bawdy, ravenous drunks behind us,

I've made my decision. All that's left now is to tell him. I should do it now, but I can't bring myself to say the words.

Seeing that Alastair leads me away from the crush of people, I say, 'Where are we going?'

'Somewhere you'll like. I promise it isn't far.'

Soon, we can stroll and eat without getting jostled quite so much. If not for my dilemma, I'd be able to relax. As we walk, the sky darkens enough that I hear a high-pitched whistle, followed by the first firework, exploding with a thud I feel in my ribcage.

Alastair says, 'Do you ever wonder what the abettors saw for us?'

When I glance at his soft eyes in his hard stone face, his gaze is on my mouth again.

'Didn't you hear what Mortritis said? They shove people into accords at random to please the provost.'

'Will you believe anything my aunt tells you? She discredits them because they don't bring her enough talent. Abettors don't do things *at random.*'

I bristle. 'Do we have to do this now, Faulton?'

'I'm not trying to bicker with you.'

'Good.'

We throw our empty cups and the greasy paper from our pies into the rubbish bin. There are a few people with sparklers, and I note the air has turned sulphurous with that burnt-match smell you get after fireworks.

I'm pleased to be away from the crowds. The only people who come close are a young mother and her child. She can't be older than ten. The mother smiles encouragement at the nervous child, who points her face to my shoes, apparently too shy to speak. She does hold out a piece of paper, which I take. It's one of the stolen posters, only this one has a sketch of me.

'Would you mind?' the mother says, hesitant.

I look back at her, bewildered, until Alastair bends close to my ear. 'She wants your signature.'

'My...' *Fallen gods*. This is a prime opportunity to whip out my pen, the Prelate's Archivist. 'Oh! Not at all.'

I reach into my coat pocket, ready to wow them with an eyeful of my gorgeous pen. I make sure they get a good look at the craftsmanship – they're wonder-struck, no doubt – before Alastair lets me lean on the broad canvas of his back. I scrawl my name across the poster with a tasteful flourish. Naturally, I had already swapped out the cartridge to one of Oldsfall Pine to mark the season.

Signature acquired, the child runs off with a look of shy triumph. The mother mouths her thanks and follows. I am, frankly, elated to have found another use for the Prelate's Archivist.

We keep walking, but ten minutes later Alastair slows to a stop. We're stood in the commercial district, facing one of the many shops lining both sides of the streets. This particular shop, the one he's looking at, reads Urnwell's: For the Morbid Academic. I follow him inside.

It's a bookshop, lovely and dark, narrow and tall-ceilinged, with shelves that go all the way up. A lone teller sits on a stool behind the counter, reading. He looks up as if surprised to see anyone today, but then he smiles, nods, and goes back to his book.

Alastair leads me past the counter, where a set of steep, wooden steps lead us to a much wider space underground. Down the steps, I see rows and rows of neatly arranged bookshelves.

'Urnwell's deals exclusively in graving books,' he says. 'I'm told it's a favourite haunt of Penders' gravers, although you won't find them here outside term time.'

It's gloomy and deserted, and we can barely hear the noise of outside. 'What a treasure trove,' I say.

The bookshop has an unnatural heat that, in all my swaddling, makes me feel light-headed. Heat is good. It's what Withersham's library was missing to keep out the damp. As I pop the buttons on my coat, Alastair does the same, folding his over his arm as I comb the shelves.

I pick one out, saying, 'They had a copy of this at Withersham,' as I open it. I do this gingerly, even though it looks and feels solid. 'It was mush inside the covers, so I never was able to read it.'

My heart plunges when I see the glyphs writhing on the page, but I try to hide this by presenting it to Alastair. He feigns interest for all of five seconds before his gaze returns to me. His eyes are like two thimbles of molten pitch. They've a vulturous look to them, hungry and impatient, reminding me we are quite alone down here. I thought this was a good thing, but maybe it's a very, very bad thing.

The look knocks me so completely off my stride, it's all I can do to shove the book onto the shelf and turn away. 'A treasure trove,' I say again, but faintly.

'I thought you'd enjoy it.'

As I carry on down the aisle, trying to read titles on spines, his presence takes on a physical pressure that makes it hard to focus on anything else.

'It's completely deserted,' he remarks, a suggestive lilt to his voice that draws all the room's heat into my face.

Deserted is right. He's fixed the problem of our audience.

The deeper we go into the bookshop, the tighter the knot pulls in my gut. I could tell him I've looked enough and that I want to go back to the festival – I absolutely *should* do that, especially since I haven't told him about the job offer – but I don't. I keep going deeper and deeper. As we near the boundary of the bookshop, impossibly far from the one exit up the stairs, I am jittery with nerves.

'This far underground, nobody upstairs would hear you, no matter how loud you screamed.'

I jerk my head round to look at him. 'It's really starting to sound like you've brought me here to murder me.'

'Oh, I have.' His eyes centre on mine, too intense, the blush high in his cheeks.

'Maybe we should try to meet back up with Tieran's lot?' I say, looking away.

'You do know I was joking.'

'I'd be running away if I didn't.'

'Don't you like it here?'

'Of course I do! It's glorious. But I could do with another drink. They said they'd be at the Ancestor's Arms, I think?'

'Hal,' Alastair says dryly, 'Tieran and his friends will be three sheets to the wind by now. We've as much chance of finding them as a one-ended stick.'

'Right. I suppose that's true.'

He swipes a hand through his hair. 'We can *try*, I suppose, if that's what you want. I'm just surprised. I didn't think you were enjoying it.'

The thought of going back to battle against the crowds, the sloppy drunks, Tieran's friends… trapping my fingers in a rusty hinge would be more enjoyable, and Alastair knows it.

'I wasn't either,' he goes on. 'I'd prefer us to be alone.'

I shouldn't. I *really* shouldn't.

'Now it sounds like you're going to Winter Formal me,' I say.

Alastair replies, deadpan, 'You can't Winter Formal someone in an empty bookshop. You heard my aunt. It's either the bathroom, where one of your preceptors could walk in at any moment, or the roof, where you might freeze to death.'

'Every girl's dream.'

'There are many things I'd do for you, but the thought of Winter Formalling you in a public bathroom makes me want to cry.' Still in his straight-faced monotone, he says, 'It'll have to be the roof.'

It gets a giggle out of me, but a slightly nervous one. 'Seriously, Faulton, it feels like you're trying to get into my breeches.'

Alastair reaches for my hand, but instead of taking it, he draws his fingertip along my palm, the inside of my wrist, light like a feather. 'Nothing gets past you, does it?'

If I thought my face was burning before, now it's being incinerated.

I don't pull away, which is a mistake I can't help but make. Turns out I'm just like anyone else with a pulse. When someone as straightforwardly gorgeous as Alastair goes for you, the most primitive part of your brain takes over – the part dominated by instinct – and smothers all rational thought.

Relentless, Alastair forges on: 'Do you feel the same?'

After a moment, I nod.

'Have you done anything like this before?'

In tones of *how dare you*, I say, 'I'm not a virgin.'

'Good. Neither am I.'

He falls silent, watching for my reaction. My thoughts race, unable to make sense of my own craving. I keep coming back to the sensation of his fingertip on my wrist and how good it feels. I just *want* to, logic be damned.

I slide my hand up his forearm, narrowing my eyes at him. 'You'd better not go weird on me afterwards.'

'Define weird.'

'Awkward.'

He slides both arms around my waist, murmurs, 'I won't feel awkward in the slightest,' and crushes his lips against mine with the greed of two years' wanting. He opens my mouth and I let him, mortified by my own keenness. He tastes of hot scotch, warm and maddeningly sweet. My pulse is wild in seconds.

He walks me backwards until I hit the wall, pressing into me, one of his thighs between mine. I already knew Alastair's in incredible shape, so I don't know why I'm so impressed. It makes me wonder how he'll take *my* body, none of which escapes his attention.

While my hands are less adventurous, coiling in his hair, exploring the divots at the base of his spine, his hands are everywhere in no time at all – up the front of my shirt, down the back of my trousers. He makes it impossible to feel self-conscious when he takes such naked delight in everything he finds. He makes a noise deep in his throat that sounds like Mortritis when she bit into her doughnut yesterday, and I'm no better.

Some of the sounds that leave my mouth would be humiliating if anyone overheard, and they won't stop no matter how smug and bold they make him. Fortunately, whoever told him about this place was right. Nobody's going to hear us.

But beneath this shameless display of enthusiasm, I feel deeply wrong. Not for the fact of what I'm doing, or even where, but because I still haven't told him about the job. It's a lie by omission – a big fat betrayal. He might be glad now, but it's not going to last. I'm only making it worse.

I have to tell him, even though he's immediately going to hate me. The longer I let it go on, the worse his reaction will be.

I turn my face slightly, away from his mouth. 'I think you've had a scotch too many, Faulton. You Glims can't take your drink at all.'

'You're funny,' he says, bringing his hand up to turn my face with an impatience he doesn't bother to hide. 'I'm sober as the prelate, same as you. So much for your nerves.'

He recaptures my mouth with his.

In a titanic feat of willpower, I break off again. 'I need to tell you something.'

He's undeterred, his lips moving to my throat. 'Let's hear it,' he says, his breath sending shivers up and down me.

I can tell by the ease in his voice that he thinks it's something he wants to hear. My heart sinks, knowing he couldn't be more wrong.

'Can we stop for a second?'

He freezes. 'What? I mean, yes, of course.'

He disentangles himself, breathing hard, and steps back. I don't look at him until there's a couple paces between us, and when I do, there is doubt for the first time. His mouth is swollen from mine, and he looks downright flustered.

'Look,' I say, 'I can't do this. My heart belongs to your aunt.'

He scoffs. 'If that's true, you'd better hope she never finds a use for it.'

'Meaning?'

'My aunt finds uses for everything, usually to the thing's detriment.' After a moment spent searching my face, he says, 'You can't stop tormenting me, can you?'

'Alastair,' I say, shamefaced, 'she's offered me a job.'

His gaze cools instantly. 'When?'

'Yesterday,' I admit. 'She said I wouldn't be able to keep up with her conspectus, but since I'm so committed...'

Alastair frowns, standing up a little straighter.

'What is it you'd be doing for her exactly?'

'Well, I'd be a researcher. Helping her with various projects.' It's damn near impossible to hold his gaze. Every time I look at him, I have to look away.

'I might be missing something here, but I can't see how that has anything to do with us.'

'It's a full-time job. I'd be working for Mortritis instead of studying.'

He says nothing at first. A black lake of silence wells up between us.

Then he snorts and looks away. 'You're taking it? And you've known all through today?'

'I haven't decided yet, but I—'

'Oh, well. I won't pack my bags just yet then.'

I wince. 'I'm sorry.'

'You're not sorry now, but you will be.' His face darkens. 'She didn't make this offer right after her fight with Mama by chance. She'll stoop to any depths to get revenge on the people who've slighted her. Any evil can be justified.'

'But maybe—'

'She's not doing this because you're *so committed*. She's doing it because I'll be denied Penders, and she knows how much that will hurt Mama.'

'Yes, but—'

'I grew up with this woman, remember? I know how she works.' He shakes his head in dismay. 'You can't seriously be considering this?'

'I know it's selfish, but it's the only way I can contribute to graving.'

'It isn't just selfish, Hal. It's *stupid*. You have a real shot at spiring for St bloody Penderghast's! The one thing you're actually good at!' Alastair's voice rises from low and sinister to rolling thunder.

Remembering my shocking performance for Mortritis, my skin starts to prickle.

'Why in the provost's name would you throw that away to work for a cruel bitch who only values you as a pawn in her revenge plot?'

'All my life, I've only ever wanted to be a—'

'Fallen gods, you're like a broken record!' The disgust in his voice is savage. 'Why waste my breath trying to dissuade you? I should've known you'd cast me off the moment Mortritis so much as glanced your way.'

He takes a step back, jaw tight, looking as if the fog of want has finally lifted. As if he sees me clearly for the first time, and it sickens him to think he ever let me touch him.

'You know what? Take the job. You're perfect for it. My aunt loves desperate, naïve idiots who'll follow orders without question, and an employer like her is exactly what you deserve. Do you know how she and Kiel got to such an unnatural height?'

'What?'

'If she's prepared to experiment on her own son, imagine what she'll do to you. She's going to ruin you, and I can't wait to see it.'

I watch him stalk off down the aisle. He gets maybe five steps away before a wave of indignant savagery comes crashing over me, so intense it blurs my vision. Without giving it too much thought, I snatch the nearest book from its home on the shelf and launch it at his head. This is sacrilege, of course, no way to treat a book, but it hits its target, thumping him squarely between the shoulder blades. The heavy tome has as much impact on Alastair's back as it would on a stone wall – it merely bounces off – but it's the insult that counts, the insult that makes him stop and turn, his face the very epitome of contempt.

'Did you just deliver a moralizing lecture because I won't upset my entire life to suit you?' I yell. 'You really are the incarnation of entitlement made flesh!'

I stalk towards him, still yelling no matter how close I get. It turns out I did end up screaming down here, just not in the way I'd hoped.

'It's fine for me to lose my dreams, but provost forbid you lose yours!'

'I just think that if you're going to ruin someone's life,' he snaps, 'you might at least do it for a reason that *benefits you!*'

'Your life isn't going to be ruined. Your life *can't* be ruined! As if you won't find another way to weasel back into Glimwick in your next hundred and fifty years. Why should I spend my fifty years as your stepping stone?'

'What is *wrong* with you? You're becoming a fully fleshed scion. You've got another—'

'My point, if you'll shut up long enough to let me reach it, is that you're the only one of us with means beyond Edusa or Mortritis!' I rage, getting into his face.

He rigidly holds his ground, expression tightening with every word I say. Even the tips of his ears are scarlet now.

'You've been pushing me to spire for your own self-interest, blatant manipulations since before we left Withersham! And now, because I've stopped baltering to your tune, you turn nasty! You don't have the moral high ground here, you slack-spined worm!'

'Worms don't even *have* spines, you clay-brained, corpse-bothering wretch!' Alastair snarls back. I flinch. 'See? Anyone can cobble random words together. You're not some genius wordsmith. You're a *clown.*'

'And you're a bastard in every sense of the word! Your sodden mess of a mother told Mortritis so herself at the soirée. That's why your father hates you. That's why you were drawn to graving. You're Kieran Kilchoir's son, not his.'

For a moment, I can't believe the poison that just flew from my mouth, that I've thrown this at him like Drasilla threw it at Mortritis. My heart thunders as I wait for his reaction.

First comes the incredulous fury. Then a hatred that goes well beyond contempt, lips pulled thin as a stitch. Finally, and most terrifying of all, overblown, scathing laughter.

'You really are thicker than a castle wall,' he says at last, 'and truly, *truly* pathetic. Do you think you're the first to repeat this nonsensical rumour to me? If I was the son of a Kilchoir and a Moppeton, where would I have gotten my ability to heal? Papa may have worried when I was a child, but he couldn't possibly believe it now. He hates me because I challenged his authority.'

'It sounds like that's how it goes in your family – one authority, not to be challenged. No wonder my free will dismays you. If I was your mother, I'd just fall in line, wouldn't I?'

He lets out a little huff. 'Of course you'd drag our argument down to a slanging match about our mamas. Insults for the lowest common denominator, and another glass house you shouldn't throw stones from. I've met yours, don't forget. A pitiful, social-climbing false believer who'd sell her own grandmama to get ahead in life.'

'Her grandmama is long dead, Faulton. In case you've forgotten, we don't live that long in Preyburn. So much for your compassion. Scratch the surface, and you're just another Ransley Liverich.'

'Don't misunderstand. I have great compassion for her circumstances. But the way she cast you aside, ignoring you because she thought you a dud? Beneath contempt. My mama has her faults, but at least she loves me.'

I recoil a little. 'Of course my mother loves me, you fen-rotten parasite.'

'No wonder you're so desperate for Mortritis's attention, to prove your worth to someone. The closest you've come to love is Limbridge, and even she sold you out for funding.'

I glower at him, so hot it's as though I'm being immolated. I want to hit him so badly, but it wouldn't go down well. My fists would probably bounce straight off him like that poor book did. Still, it takes Oldracian effort to keep them bunched at my sides.

'*Your* mother only loves you as much as your father allows,' I say. 'She couldn't even get you out of Withersham. And as for the desperation bit? Chasing the acceptance of a father who disowned you for a quarrel you had as a child? There's a glass house for you.'

The look Alastair gives me is a drained one. 'That you believe I want his acceptance only goes to show how much you don't pay attention.'

'Then what?'

'Oh, Hal.'

Instead of giving me a real answer, he takes a step back, disengaging, to sigh long and loud. I watch the fevered tension leave and the icy composure return. If only I could detach myself from my anger so easily. He sounds deeply disinterested when he says, 'Every time you start to wonder why life's worked out so miserably for you, I do hope you'll remember this.'

Then he turns on his heel again, as if it's no longer worth his time to fight with me. I can't say that he's wrong, nor can I find the will to follow him. In the end, I stand rooted in anxious misery, shaking like an autumn leaf.

26

THE WRONG ANSWER

I greet the next morning wide awake in bed, which, considering where I could have ended up after the festival, is not a bad place to be. I made my way back to the grounds yesterday evening to a chorus of cries and screams and thudding starbursts in the smoky sky as gold sparks showered the arena. It was beautiful.

Where Alastair got to amongst it all, I don't know. Would he have stayed out to drown his sorrows or come directly back to his room? There was no light under his door when I got to mine. It's possible he decided to up and go before I speak to Edusa, to see his mother before he has to leave.

But no, that would be out of character. He won't leave 'til he's given me a good whipping. It'd be better if he *had* gone. When I picture his hate-filled eyes, my heart clenches. It's been doing this all night. My sleep was so brief and disjointed, I wonder if I slept at all.

I wish they had radios in Glimwick, so I wouldn't have to listen to these thoughts. Soon, the remaining admissions pupils will start preparing for the Crucible. The thought of seeing anyone in their spiring gear, ready to take on the world, turns my stomach to lead.

Where will Alastair go now? He's not allowed back to Glimwick, but what's there for him in Preyburn? Committing him to exile will probably haunt me forever, and all the more so because I imagine this is the last we'll speak. He deserves his reunion, but in the end, that's really down to his father, not me.

This is why the glyphs rejected me. I'm thinking like a Glim when Preys don't have that luxury. I need to look out for myself – be selfish, like Mortritis said. Alastair wants to reconcile with his father. *I* want to be Mortritis's research assistant, to prove my worth.

If the cohort and my parents had been present at my trial, oh how they would have laughed.

Fallen gods, I'm doing it again, fretting over what everyone else is going to make of my actions more than myself. It seems impossible to try to strip that all away. I hate to admit my love of graving is anything so shallow as a need for cachet, but now I'm clearly not as talented as I thought—

Another full-body cringe ripples through me. Now that I've had my uselessness confirmed by the world's most respected graver, researching for Mortritis doesn't excite me quite so much as it would have back in Withersham. What other people will think of the opportunity is exactly what makes it valuable. What could look better on my curriculum vitae?

Spiring. A disconcerting thought that pops into my head straight away. Outside Preyburn, there's more prestige to be had in spiring. More value, opportunities, and pud. Better than scribbling away in the shadows on someone else's projects.

But just because I'm not going to be a graver doesn't mean I have to be a spirer. To spire means to stay on at St Penderghast's as a pupil, but I can always go back to my parents' house in Crippleditch...

I remember Mother exhaling in my ear before she left, digging her fingers into my arm. Telling me not to mess up. They only want me back at Crippleditch with a scion on the way, or else they'll bring the abyss upon me.

No – going back to them isn't an option.

With a sigh, I throw back the covers and heave out of bed. I emerge from my room, coming face to face with the door to Alastair's room. It looms sullen and silent, and I quickly turn down the hallway for the common room. Stuffing myself with pastries can only improve the situation.

'*Kilchoir!*'

I stop dead, blood icing at the deep, bellowing voice. I'm not nearly ready to face Alastair, I've no idea what to say, but I also won't outrun him. With no choice but to turn around, I try to still my nerves and do just that. But it isn't Alastair's unnerving symmetry that greets me, twisted with rage. It's Lourdes.

'Admit it. I had you, didn't I?' she says, grinning as she approaches. 'You thought I was Alastair.'

My attempt to smile feels more like a grimace, and I'll wager it looks like one too.

Lourdes appraises me. Her smile, which at any given moment dazzles so hard one must squint to look at it, disappears like the sun behind clouds. 'What's happened?'

What to tell her?

'Alastair and I… fell out.'

'Ah.'

For a dreadful moment, I think she's going to ask questions, and worse still, that I'll answer them. That once I start explaining the situation, the words will keep falling out and tears will join them, until she has the whole humiliating story.

'Well, there's only one thing for it,' she says instead. 'Let's get you to the courtyard, pronto.'

'What for?'

'To my knowledge, there's no better way to banish the doldrums than training.' Before I know it, she's steering me back towards my room with a hand on my shoulder, dazzling smile returned. 'Besides, we're due a practice session, yes? We'll be nice and limber for the Crucible.'

I won't be attending the Crucible.

This thought stays in my head, though my mouth refuses to speak it. Mute and obedient, I grab the Might, then follow Lourdes to the courtyard where Alastair and Tieran taught me about Acclaim sharing.

A few inches of fresh snow cushion our steps and cinereal clouds seethe overhead, threatening to pelt us with more. I would've liked the courtyard to be empty, but no such luck. Every contender is here to train before they attempt their final stage.

Enormous crates collect snow at the courtyard's fringes, while the other six admissions pupils battle their contents: ulcerated puppets in various states of disrepair. Several stage warders supervise the training from a safe distance.

To our right, three girls sit huddled on a carved marble bench. When one sees us enter the courtyard, she elbows her friends, and they all sit ramrod straight. Naturally, they're here to watch Lourdes.

'I'll get us a puppet.' Lourdes is about to make her way over to the stage warders, but I stop her.

'You should know that I...' I probably shouldn't tell her this, but it's Lourdes. She wouldn't snitch. 'I really don't have Oldrac's Acclaim.'

Lourdes takes only a moment to absorb this revelation. I expect horror and questions – *You came to admissions without Acclaim? Have you lost your wits?* – but all she says is, 'You little daredevil! Not to worry. We'll share.'

Moments later, she returns from a brief chat with the stage warders. Three of them set about the locks on one of the unopened crates.

'They usually like hordes of eerians for the Crucible,' Lourdes says, 'so I propose we start with techniques that hit multiple targets at once.'

Hearing the word *techniques*, I say, 'I fear you may have overestimated my ability.'

Another ulcerated puppet crawls free of the newly opened crate, its neck snapping back and forth as before. Lourdes puts two fingers in her mouth and whistles for its attention, waving as its head snaps towards us.

'I most certainly have not,' she says. 'I saw your second stage.'

As the puppet jerks upright, Lourdes smooths both hands over her hair, as if it ever escapes the iron grip of her pomade. Even the vile Balverian snow slides straight off it like a duck's well-preened back.

'Wild, forking strikes like that are pure spectacle for one target but fantastic for keeping lots of attackers off you *and* circulating damage.'

Lourdes draws her spire from its sheath, letting me see it up close for the first time. Needless to say, it is ridiculously fine, the pommel engraved with what I assume to be the Spendlove sigil: a bolt of Acclaim striking through a gilt coin.

I'm still admiring her spire when my own jolts to life. It takes me several moments to overcome the initial shock, the panic of it. I already knew Lourdes' Acclaim would be stronger than Alastair's, but I simply wasn't prepared to feel it.

'All right?' Lourdes says.

I force deep breaths of the sharp, cold air. 'Fine.'

When my mind calms, so does my body. I adjust my grip on the hilt and loosen my knees as the puppet approaches.

On my first strike, I understand what Lourdes meant. The Acclaim lashes out hither and thither in a show that *is* pure spectacle against a lone enemy. Some forks hit the puppet, but the rest hit snow and air.

'Just like that!' Lourdes shouts, circling us.

Bolstered by her praise, I try for another, more powerful strike. As the puppet and I fight on, Lourdes keeps close enough to review our movements, but far enough that it won't engage her.

It turns out she was right, as I imagine she often is – beating down a physical enemy takes my mind off the intangible ones, for the most part. In those moments when the puppet stutters overlong or retreats, my worries inevitably creep back in.

The more I think about it, the more it kills me to leave St Penderghast's today, forcing Alastair to return to Preyburn alone. What if he resorts to Flaypenny to get by? The idea chills me, but what he does isn't my business. I should be thinking about me, about my life.

Spiring's too much of a gamble. What if I don't get very far at all? What if I fail admissions, having passed on Mortritis's offer? I'll have nothing.

Mortritis is the sensible bet. All right, so I won't be what's traditionally thought of as a graver. I won't be following my effigies out across the battlefield with rifle and dagger. So what? Mortritis won plenty of medals on the field but didn't earn the title of graving master until long after. It was eerian research and effigy design that made her.

After a half-bell or so, Lourdes calls, 'Let's try a focused strike. Right now, the Acclaim follows your movement. It needs to follow your will. Give it some direction.'

'How?'

'I find it helps to visualize. Imagine Acclaim flowing from hilt to tip through the blade, then out in a straight line.'

When I attempt this, the Acclaim does straighten out a little. What begins as multiple forks concentrates into one, albeit briefly. It quickly reverts, splaying in all directions. But even briefly, the concentrated strike catches the puppet in the chest with enough force to smack it down into the snow.

'Perfect,' says Lourdes, even though it was anything but.

Her Acclaim drains from me, leaving cold emptiness behind. My spire grows heavier as I stand puffing clouds into the air, but I still have strength. The strain of our training won't hold me back in the Crucible.

Lourdes comes over to give me a congratulatory clap on the shoulder. 'You need to work on precision, yes? Not only to save your strength, but to extend your reach. When your Acclaim's strewn across multiple branches, those branches are weaker and shorter. When you focus all your strength into one branch, or near enough, your strikes can go farther and hit harder. Watch.'

Lourdes lunges with her spire, and a giant, retina-searing strike cracks across the courtyard, splitting the puppet open and thrilling her fan club. They gasp and clap while the puppet's limbs twitch, glutinous flesh drooling from multiple scorched cavities. The largest sits in its torso.

'After that,' Lourdes goes on, 'we'll look at manipulating the branches' shape. You'll have noticed Alastair twists his Acclaim like a whip. Acclaim whips naturally, but controlling its direction is another matter. It needs precision *and* a prolonged surge of power.'

'You're nebulas ahead of me,' I say, as shamefaced as I am awed.

Lourdes cocks a brow. 'How long have you been training?'

'Two years.'

'Two years,' she echoes. 'I've had expert training since I was a tot, yes? You've come a miraculously long way in limited time. That proves natural ability.'

I'm only a little embarrassed to admit how this compliment thrills me. I've heard it before, but from suspect characters. This is *Lourdes*, repeating what Limbridge tried to tell me at Burymeadow Station.

'Work to hone it,' she goes on, 'and we'll train as equals one day soon.'

'You'd make a stellar preceptor.'

Lourdes flashes her handsomest smile. 'You flatterer,' she teases.

To my horror, my cheeks burn.

Biting back grins, Lourdes' fan club elbow each other on the sidelines as if subtlety is their great nemesis. All through training, they've watched us with blatant interest, no doubt dissecting every interaction. I remember what Alastair told me about Lourdes stirring up relationship drama to make up for her predictable wins. For her sake, I hope this gives them something to chew on.

'Lourdes, I have to go,' I say.

Her smile turns wry. 'Tell Alastair I said hello, won't you?'

'If I'm still here after the Crucible,' I say, taking my first steps towards the exit, 'I'll teach you everything I know about eerians. To say thank you.'

'Oh, hush. I'll see you at the offer ceremony.'

As I backtrack through the labyrinthine hallways, my thoughts are as quick as my feet. I've realized something.

The problem with *not spiring* isn't just that I'll regret turning my back on Alastair. I'll also regret not competing. Not because of Alastair's exile, or Limbridge's disappointment, or even Mother, but because I'd never know how far I could have gone once I'd stopped trying to wedge myself into the graving conspectus and polished up my natural skill set. All the nightmarish eerians I'd get to meet and bleed. The rush I'd feel, fighting in the Crucible.

When I picture myself thrashing the competition in front of a roaring crowd – Edusa's congratulations, Limbridge's face when she opens my notice of acceptance to St Penderghast's – that's where I get my fuzzy feeling.

Finally reaching my room, I push through the door and cross to the desk. The Prelate's Archivist sits by my notebook, now mostly filled with doodles of many-limbed ancestors and wailing rusted maidens.

I pick up the pen and tear out a page.

Storm clouds are brewing as I make my way to Thumbarrow. I hear the scrape of metal against frozen earth as groundskeepers shovel clumps of snow from every path to the arena. Soon, the crowds will be flooding in to fill every seat. Of the admissions events, the Crucible – the finale – is always going to be the most popular.

A shudder tightens my skin as I cross Thumbarrow's threshold. It's cold enough to freeze the tits off a heron, but that's not the only reason why.

Mortritis is exactly where she said she'd be, in her office.

When I enter, she smiles, ignoring the fact of my spiring breeches and boots beneath my jacket. Her shrewd eyes can't have missed them any more than one can miss a foghorn in a library, but still she smiles and beckons me over to the desk.

'How did you like the festivities?'

'Oh – well, I saw what you mean.' I give a sheepish smile, my heart pounding as I draw nearer. 'Not so different from Ersfall back home.'

She looks as though she may not have been to bed yet. Of course, she's no less intimidating or gorgeous for the unbrushed hair, stale makeup, and shadowed, red-rimmed eyes.

She nods to a crisp, pale sheet of paper on top of the desk, stamped with the Moppeton family sigil – three unsmiling gravers' masks –

and a quite beguiling pen. 'The contract. It's all standard practice, but please do take a moment to read through it. Feel free to ask any questions.'

With effort, I pull my eyes away from the salary. *That's a lot of pud.* 'Preceptor...'

'Once you've signed, I'll brief you on some of the projects I have under way. You can start today – did I mention that? You'll be renumerated at month's end.'

'I can't accept your offer.'

'Don't be silly. Of course you can.'

'I'm sorry. I can't.'

Mortritis dons a concerned expression. 'Oh dear. This is about Alastair, I suppose? He's really done a number on you.'

'I'm sorry. As grateful as I am to be considered, I can't commit him to exile. You're right – my nature's too Oldracian. I'll never forgive myself.'

'Do you imagine he'd do the same for you?'

I shrug. 'Maybe not. But this is about me. *I* couldn't live with it.'

'I see. You've made your mind up?' Before I can answer, she goes, 'Oh poppet, are you *sure* about this? You've been desperate to work with me this past week. By the sounds of it, you've wanted it your whole life. Are you certain you aren't making a great big mistake? You won't see an opportunity like this again.'

'I'm certain.'

Mortritis sighs. Her breath smells like smoke and liquor, but coming from her mouth, I don't mind it one bit.

'Well, I can't say I'm surprised, but I am disappointed. If I've learnt anything in life, it's that people like to think they make decisions based on logic when what really drives them is feeling.'

I can do nothing but stare at a corner of the desk, unable to meet her gaze or deny her words.

Mortritis squeezes my shoulder. Her touch is warm and reassuring. 'Your heart's made up. I can see that. I can keep throwing reasons at you, and you'll keep deflecting, but...' She sighs. 'In terms of what's best for you, I'm afraid that is *objectively* the wrong answer.'

In the next moment, the hand that had been on my shoulder wraps around my throat. I jolt as the air's squeezed from my windpipe. The pressure of her grip intensifies as my boots leave the carpet.

'You can't say I haven't tried to be charitable,' she says, ignoring my nails as they claw at her hand, her wrist, and the sleeve of her jacket. 'It's not as if there weren't a hundred graduates better suited for the job.'

Her eyes stare emptily as mine water and my throat bruises and I try, uselessly, to kick her away.

It occurs to me, blearily, that a great many people would pay good pud for this treatment from Mortritis. Here I am, getting it for free.

My arms stop listening as my strength leaves me and the room darkens. I barely feel the ground when it hits me.

'You won't be spiring today, I'm afraid.'

27

THE BLACKEST WAY

I lie down on the carpet, its coarse weave pressing against my cheek. I try to move my limbs, but I'm not sure that I do. I'm prone and paralysed, melting into the ground.

Mortritis's voice is somewhere far away, muttering to itself. She wrenches my head back by the hair, pours grey-tasting sludge into my mouth until I choke. Not all of it comes back up. Some of it slides down my gullet to pool in my gut like poison – which it is.

I drift in and out of the world as I'm dragged and kicked and rolled across the ground. She takes my arms and legs and bends them to impossible angles. Her hands feel enormous and absurdly strong. I can do nothing as she folds me up like an ulcerated puppet and crams me into something wooden, however I will fit.

Then there are no hands on me, only the hard wooden sides of my box and the lead in my gut and the pressure against my windpipe – a boot heel. I suppose I live here now.

I don't feel discomfort. I hardly even feel pain.

That melting feeling takes my body again. I am dissolved into sludge, and slowly, over centuries, solidified.

My wooden box has long since rotted away.

Now, there is dense fog of a milky green, silky, copper-coloured mud, the malodour of things living and rotting together all at once. Where else could I be but the Fenlands?

The fog's a veiling miasma that makes me feel dirty just walking through it. Worse still, there's no Fenway to direct me. I have to pick a route and hope it leads somewhere.

With a deep, fortifying breath of putrid air, I start slogging through the muck. That guggling sound I hear is the tide. It creeps back into the fens like a sly thing on its belly, the Bitter Sea come to smother the mudflats in their sleep. The ground swells beneath me like rust-coloured sponge. If I don't find safety, I'll be hip deep before I know it – and that's not my only problem.

I hear strange eerians lowing in the distance. All manner of nasties call the fens home – things that slither, things that scuttle, things that bite. Clouds of midges chitter at the sedges, and more than once I'm startled by a giant fuzzy white pulpmoth flapping through the fog. Their black-veined wings are as wide as my handspan.

At the very least, I'm not cold; the fen holds an unnatural, sticky warmth. Before long, fresh sweat stripes my forehead.

The ominous wail of a fen heron seems to summon shadows in the fog, their edges blurred until I draw closer. Cecilia stands reading from the Compendium, as before. Ramshaw and Stripthicket inscribe the glyphs on a five-pointed star of donations, as before, although this time Gretch joins them. Kiel is the one to oversee proceedings. He wears no graver's mask, just his hulking great coat and the knife-grin that splits his face in two.

The donations are in a bad way – skin ravaged to patches by fen lice, flesh infested with pulpmoth larvae. Pulpmoth caterpillars eat necrotic flesh, so laying their eggs in a corpse host means guaranteed food for the hatchlings. I can see the skin ticcing of its own accord, with what looks like writhing white moss spreading across their abdomens.

Unlike before, the donations lie unshrouded, and all five crane their necks to get a good look at me. Their eyes are cloudy and pale, as the dead's ought to be, but they see me – *know* me.

Even in their poor condition, each one is undoubtedly Mother. I'd know that grading stare anywhere. Five sets of Mothers' lungs rattle in concert, wheezing in the fog that was always so hazardous to them. The cohort take graphia to her flesh while the reeds sing with strange, terrifying insects all around us.

The glyphs begin to dazzle, their light dancing strangely upon the haze as the Mothers spasm towards and corrode into each other. The cohort shrieks with laughter. Their heads tilt back and back as they watch their effigy grow.

The burgeoning flesh mass finds the limit of what can be made with five donations, and ignores it. Something impossibly large looms above us all, shrouded in ghostly green.

I turn and run, although naturally I can't. There's no running in waist-high fen, only a frantic, exhausting scramble.

A creature heavier than the ancestor slams into the ground beside me, creating a wave of primordial fen slime with the force to knock me sideways. It curls over my head, sending me under. I resurface, gagging, smearing mud from my eyes to see what it is.

A boot. It looks very much like one of Mortritis's boots, although the heel itself is the size of a marble column. From somewhere far above me, her monstrous, caricatured laughter echoes in the clouds.

'Mortritis!' A male voice, even more thunderous than hers,

interrupts. 'What have you done with *my* admissions pupil?' This said as if she's borrowed his favourite piece of jewellery. 'If you've damaged her right before the Crucible...'

Cracks of lightning strike the fen around me in a strange pattern, briefly illuminating the murk. It reminds me of last night's fireworks, the violet bursts and smoky remnants they left behind.

'I have done with her whatever I damn well please, you buffoon,' Mortritis replies. 'She's signed a contract for a position as *my* research assistant.'

'That's a lie,' says another male voice. 'She came here to turn it down.'

Mud banks in front of me, pressed up by some foulness beneath. I brace myself for fresh peril, but a young man emerges. His face is a spiring mask with eyes of the abyss; his body is marble flesh. He should be caked in fen slop, but it recoils from him the way oil does from water. He has the aura of a mythical eerian hatching, or a deadly flower grandly unfurling its petals, and yet I battle the fen to reach him as if he is sanctuary.

'Oh, beloved. For your sake, I wish that were true – honestly, I do.'

'We wouldn't play your games even if we had time for them,' says another, more dislikeable voice. 'Where is Hal?'

'Here, see for yourself.'

'That has to be the laziest attempt at a forgery I've ever seen,' says the abyssal-eyed statue, his lips still. 'I suppose you were in a rush?'

'Don't be preposterous!'

'*This* is what Hal's handwriting looks like. In her own hand, she told me she was coming to turn it down.'

The hands scraping through the muck towards the boy are wizened thin, and not from the water. This isn't my body; these aren't my hands; they are an old – tragically old – man's hands.

'You've not a leg to stand on, Mortritis.'

'She may have come here with that intention, but she couldn't bring herself to do it. She's a Prey, in the end – she'd have to be a dimwit to turn it down!'

The mouldy, festering air makes my lungs too heavy to breathe. The ground slides beneath me, the tread of my boots trying and failing to grip silky fen mud, but I finally reach the boy...

And he snaps down on me like a trap.

Irresistibly strong hands force my shoulders down into the fen. Some of it gets on my tongue, thick and gritty. He doesn't even seem to notice that I try to fend him off, my head submerging as he says, 'Hal *is* a dimwit.'

Opening my eyes takes Oldracian effort. The wood grain swirls before me, pulses like maggots squeezing past each other. Rows of spiny teeth open and open.

'But of course you're upset, poppet. It hurts when you want someone very badly and that person chooses to leave you behind.'

'He's not your poppet. As if we don't know you've done this to get back at Mama, dragging my brother's accord into your stupid fight. This is exactly your brand of petty.'

'You'd even go so far as to offer your job to a girl who's not qualified. You can't stand to be second best, and now you've done something to her. We know you have.'

I try to push it off, but the heel presses down more firmly on my throat. It feels like an iron weight sinking into clay, pushing the cartilage of my neck inwards, changing its shape.

'Hurtful, boys. Very hurtful. Moreover, baseless. Hal's not here. She left right after she signed. If you're so certain I've done something to her, you'll need to find out where she's gone first. There can be no crime without a body, so to speak.'

Speak...

I can't speak. My tongue's swollen to fill my mouth, blocking my air.

'I am going to find her. And then, dearest aunt, I'm going to come and find *you.*'

'Gracious, Alastair. You'd threaten your poor aunt with violence? Perhaps you are your papa's son after all.'

'The provost will hear of this, Mortritis. Whether the girl signed willingly or my proxy's assumptions are right, you can't just filch my prospects. This insult will not stand.'

'I assure you, I am *quivering* in fear. Fallen gods, how will I sleep tonight?'

I hear a whole army of bootsteps retreating, leaving me behind. I try to push the boot heel off again, but it's too heavy.

I try to call them back, but all that comes out is a thin, garbled sound. There's no way they could hear me – but the abyss hears all.

'What was that noise?' it demands.

'Oh for provost's sake,' Mortritis says, impatient. Her boot becomes crushingly heavy. 'There was no noise. Hurry up and get out of my office. I have work to do.'

'I heard a noise.'

Mortritis huffs loudly, but not so loud that she drowns out a second garbled noise forced past her heel.

There's an age of silence.

Then, the unmistakable scrape of spires leaving their sheaths.

Mortritis laughs. 'I'm sure it won't be the first time you hear this, but you can put those skinny little things away. You won't be needing them.'

'My dear, what spirer *hasn't* heard that retired old joke?' Edusa says. 'Now move away from the desk.'

For a moment, I wonder if she will. But then the pressure on my neck lifts. I rake in air, like breathing in jagged chips of ice. The shadow lifts and is replaced by a new one, dry and woody and familiar. His face looms over me, square and huge.

'Hal,' he breathes. *Yes… that is my name.* His face is a spirer's mask and his eyes are raging pits of darkness. 'What did you do to her?'

'Will you please relax? We were celebrating her new job and she had a bit too much to drink—'

'You cannot possibly expect anyone to believe that!' Tieran snaps.

Strong hands untangle the mess of my arms and legs, hauling me from my wooden box. Once I'm out, I see it's not a box at all, just Mortritis's desk. I feel boneless, and my head lolls on my neck.

'You pulped her,' says Alastair, wrapping me in his arms, holding me against him like something cherished. There's no softness to him. He feels solid, just lean muscle and bone, but I do like him better than the desk. I try to say so, but all that comes out is a slurred groan.

'Mortritis!' Edusa's Oldracian voice reverberates in my gut. *'Before the Crucible?!* You sabotage me deliberately!'

'Edusa, you ridiculous peacock, please, please shut up. You've got this completely wrong.'

'Take her to the arena!'

'Are you sure she'll be able to—'

'Do as I say!'

My vision blurs as I'm carried from the room.

———⟶———

It takes years to get to the arena. The path sways as if we're walking the deck of a fen boat. There are people, and they all stare at us with eyes like saucers. We have to stop several times so I can vomit grey sludge into drifts of snow. I'm on my hands and knees while Alastair holds my hair in his fist.

'I should've let her have you,' he hisses through his mask. 'Really, I should have.'

'I'm sorry,' I say, again and again, while I vomit and shiver and sob. Grey bubbles from my lips and nose. My hands are red against the snow. Whether they're numb from the cold or the poison, I don't know.

'Put your fingers down your throat,' Alastair demands. When I whimper like a child, he says, 'Do it, or *I* will. If we've got any chance of spiring, you have to get all of it up.'

I do it, my fingers like icicles. My throat keeps clogging, the pulp dragging up from my stomach like mud. As I retch, as my breath comes in shuddering gasps, Alastair talks. His voice comes from everywhere and nowhere.

He says things like, 'That's it,' while rubbing warmth into my back. 'Keep going.'

But he also talks about Mortritis. 'You forget how well I know her. She and Mama have been trading penalties since before any of us were born.'

Throat raw, insides gutted, I let out a little moan and move onto the dry heaves. When he's confident there's no more to come, Alastair smears pulp and bile from my lips and chin with his bare fingers, gentle and rough at the same time. I'm disgusted *for* him.

'They stockpile acts of vengeance like ammunition and bring them out when they'll cause the most pain, or whenever they've taken a hit themselves,' he says, grunting as he hauls me up. I will strength into my legs, gritting my teeth at the pain. 'Mama brought me into the world, but Mortritis… You don't have a good reason to worship her like you do. Renounce her.'

Far away, beyond the walls, the crowd roars.

I squeeze my eyes shut, tears streaming from them. When I open my eyes again, I'm not outside. I'm sitting in the arena's waiting room with Alastair beside me, putting icy water to my lips. It soothes my gullet and chases away the sour taste of bile.

He still hasn't taken his mask off.

'I've seen the hold she has on people. But she's not real. She loves *no one.*'

My head swims. Willing strength into my arm, I manage to pick it up and flop it over his thigh. If I tried to pick up a spire right now, the hilt would slide straight through my grasp.

He glowers at it for a moment, like it's a disgusting slug. Then he takes my cold, numb hand in both his fever-hot ones and brings it to his mouth. His mask-lips are warm and soft against my fingers. He's close, and his voice is an urgent whisper: 'Renounce her and avow me or I swear, I am gone.'

'I do renounce her.' The breath rattles in my chest. I sound like Mother. 'I will uphold our accord. I'm sorry… I really did go to turn down the offer…'

'That much is obvious,' he mutters. 'Otherwise, I might have some questions about why she pulped you and folded you up under the desk.'

'I'm going to make it up to you.'

'How?'

'We're going to win the Crucible.'

Alastair lets out a sour laugh. 'Bold words for a girl who had to be carried here. You're in no state to make me any promises.'

I manage to squeeze his hand, but weakly. 'You won't have to carry me in the Crucible,' I say again, my voice thin. 'Oldrac's flesh will resolve the pulp, and we're going to win.'

'I hope you're right, for your sake.'

'I know. Your mama will be after me the rest of my life.'

'I'm not talking about Mama. I want to say that I'm better than my parents, but it'd only be words. You know what I realized yesterday?' He pauses, as if I might possibly know the answer, and I give a little shake of my head. 'I realized their flesh is my flesh. I spent all night thinking up the blackest way to punish you. If we lose the Crucible because of this, I don't know whether I'll be able to forgive you.'

I squeeze his hand more forcefully. 'It won't come to that. I swear it.' I experiment by trying to pull myself away from the wall, only to slump back against it. Still, it's more than I could do a few minutes ago. 'How long until our stage?' I ask.

'All the other pupils have gone already. Tieran said they'll give us as long as they can, but they can't delay forever. The crowd's getting restless.'

'So how long does that give us?'

'A quarter-bell or so.'

I nod. Seeing the concern on his warped mask-face, I say, 'Plenty of time. You know how fast I heal.' I pick up the water and drain the rest of it, hoping I can speed things up a bit more. 'How does the Crucible work, exactly?'

'Usually it's one big mêlée. They let in eerians by the horde. All one type, or specific combinations of types that work well together.'

'Sounds brutal.'

'It will be. Only one of the seven other pupils has passed – no guesses who.' He shakes his head, mortified by our odds. 'We mustn't lose sight of each other; we'll be more vulnerable if we're separated. We stay together. We watch each other's backs.'

'What happens if one of us goes down early and the other lasts 'til the end?'

'It's happened in the past. It'll be up to Edusa to decide, but usually he rules against offering them a place.'

'Right. No passengers.' My voice sounds halfway normal again. I curl my toes and release them, then flex the fingers of my free hand. They might just be able to hold a spire. I can now feel how hard Alastair grips the other, enough to cut off blood flow. I wriggle my fingers a little and he seems to realize this as well, easing off.

'Do you really think you can do this?' he says. 'Be straight with me. Don't tell me what I want to hear and let me take you out there to get slaughtered.'

I lock my jaw. My back teeth could be about to crack open, every muscle twining, but I heave to my feet and hold there. 'We aren't going to get slaughtered.'

My head spins, but I don't lose my balance.

Tieran comes up to us with a grim expression. 'The provost's sent the fifth abettor to find out what the hold-up is – the frostiest yet.' He casts a critical, none-too-friendly gaze over me, then looks to his brother. 'We need you now, I'm afraid.'

Alastair nods and rises from the bench. 'We're ready.'

28

IN PASSION, GLORY

Alastair and I emerge from the tunnel's shadows into the snow-dulled light of the arena. The crowd noise is roaring; spectators of all kinds have turned up for the final stage of admissions.

So has the bad weather. The wind ruffles my spiring jacket and the clouds I saw earlier have drawn in to circle the arena like black vultures. They make good on their storm threat, spitting out the first pellets of hail. When these start to bounce across the stone, rainshades bloom like powder-blue roses over the crowd.

Fortunately, I have my mask to hide what is probably a dazed expression, and I needn't keep freaking out about Alastair's face anymore because he's now wearing his – truly.

I'm barely keeping it together. It feels like I've been eviscerated. The arena walls grow and shrink, darken and lighten. The poison fog from Mortritis's office continues to haunt me, clotting and roiling about the arena. I know it isn't really there, yet it proves impossible to ignore, obscuring my vision of the crowds.

A bank of fog peels away to reveal a statue planted in the arena's centre, facing the portcullis on one knee with its head bowed. Alastair strides over to it immediately; any change to the arena must be investigated. It's undoubtedly connected to the stage.

I go after him. It's difficult to know exactly what shape the statue takes, since beneath a human, marble-carved head, fabric robes in cream, gold, and powder blue drape its body, flittering in the breeze.

Along with the spirer's colours, a spirer's mask shields its face. It's a thousand times more ornate than ours, made for decoration rather than function, its hard planes aswirl with intricate patterns. Despite this, there's no spire in either of its enormous hands.

Alastair brushes what looks like an ecclesiastical scarf – the kind worn by members of the Choir – with his fingertips. Words have been stitched along the silk with gold thread.

"'Render the state to which everyone and thing aspires,'" he reads, "'and in return, I will render glory.'"

I stare at him like an idiot. Needless to say, I'm not in the best headspace for riddles. It takes all my focus to walk in a straight line.

Alastair moves to the back of the statue, grabbing the material to hold it still. Twin tears disfigure the robes – except these holes are too precise to be tears. Their edges are clean and deliberate, exposing equally deliberately crafted holes in the statue's marble body.

'Oneness,' Alastair says, his voice almost swallowed by the hail. 'Render oneness.'

He turns, and I follow his gaze to the judges' platform. Joining Edusa and Tieran is a figure both familiar and obscure. I've seen her likeness many times in the periodicals, and there's scarcely a room in Dunchester that doesn't have her portrait in it. It's the first I've seen her in the flesh.

The provost of St Penderghast's sits enthroned on her judge's seat, her expression imperious. She's a barrel-chested woman with a face I'd call daunting. As the provost of a college famed for spiring and graving, her robes reflect both conspectuses. They have all the gilt metal intimidation of the gravers' uniform and all the gold-embroidered drama of the spirers'. But it's the bizarre headpiece that marks her as the provost from any angle and distance, a mighty horned halo that must wreak havoc on her spine, though you wouldn't know it from her regal posture.

Flanking her are the two abettors who came to Withersham: Credencia and her hat-loving partner, straight as twin pillars. The very people who offered us this accord, here to see whether they were right to do so.

The provost waves a magisterial hand, and I startle at a loud cranking sound. The portcullis begins to lift.

Alastair and I fall into stance, spires angled towards it.

For what feels like an age, there's nothing to see, nothing to hear but pelting hail and ripples of anticipation through the crowd. I squint at the opening, my head throbbing, ice sliding down the back of my collar.

Slowly, a pale and pulsing liquid seeps towards us along the deep channels in the stone, like treacle poured into gutters. It's slightly yellowed in the light from the braziers, giving the impression of candlewax drippings in motion.

When I focus my hardest, I see glyph-light streaming beneath its ever-changing surface, but it's faint and blurry. Whether my glyphic literacy has completely degenerated since Mortritis's trial or it's the complexity of the epitaph, I can't say. In any case, I have as much hope of interpreting its glyphs as I do solid inkblots.

Edusa is silent. The crowd is silent.

When the mushroom smell of decay wads in my nostrils, I know it at once. My heart sinks.

Alastair follows its slow but certain progress with his gaze. 'What's this?'

'Primordial grave pulp,' I say weakly. 'The Blood of Preyburn.'

'What does that—'

'Think of it as a lesser manifestation of the Eternal Spite. It carries the very essence of Our Hollow-Hearted Lady.'

'This… ooze?'

'It's what she used to construct the earliest eerians. Just keep striking and don't let it inside your head.'

A pointless thing to say. As if we could stop it.

'The primordial,' I try again, 'uses psychological warfare as much as physical. It'll try to demoralize you.'

We watch as the paleness streams around us to fill every last crack in the arena's hail-thrashed stone. Once it's spread out, covering as much ground as it can, it begins to build upwards.

Looking at pulp after it poisoned me is like seeing a seafood buffet the day after eating spoiled prawns. What made my nose wrinkle before now strikes terror in me.

Alastair steps back as a river of sallow gloop twists upwards through the air like a waterfall in reverse. It rolls up and over itself until it reaches my height and more, a towering, malformed candle. The hail dimples it, and is swallowed by it.

Unwilling to wait any longer, Alastair calls Acclaim to his spire. I squint, turning my head slightly. *Why don't spirer's masks come with bloody eye shades?* The crack of Acclaim lightning echoes the storm heaving above us, making it sound near and far at the same time.

What is at first amorphous soon takes on a more defined human shape – one we both recognize. A wax copy, subtly pulsing like an arrhythmic heart. It has an angelic face, smooth and slightly greasy, framed by waxy whorls of hair. If she were the real thing, these would be blonde. When her mouth moves, I hear Pastoress Flaypenny's disembodied voice, innocent as milk, deep inside my brain: '*Do you know how much you could make, Alastair? Eight hundred puds a pop.*'

Alastair's jaw is a taut line, his body stiff.

The resemblance would be superb in some places, if it weren't so horrifically warped in others. Her left arm is thin as bone while her shoulder bulges like a pulpmoth infestation. Every bit of Wax Flaypenny is pale enough to write on, except for the eyes, which are black as fish eggs.

She steps towards Alastair, palms splayed in petition. 'You wouldn't need your father anymore. You wouldn't need anyone. You'd have independ—'

'Don't listen!'

I lop off the head with one hard swing. I could've gone lighter for the same effect; the waxen flesh has all the resistance of candle cake. The head dives for the stone with a dull thud, softens, and slides back into the cracks.

Alastair stares at me. 'How did you do that without Acclaim?'

Having totally forgotten that little necessity, I stare back. 'I don't know, but it worked.'

The next copy is already forming beside me. I whip around to see another curd-white woman looming. The wax glasses and corvine features leave me feeling like I've missed a step on the stairs.

The lithe, warped muscles of Wax Limbridge's face slither about until she looks equal parts disappointed and disgusted. 'We had such high hopes for you, Miriam and I.'

She turns to glance over her shoulder, where a second copy forms no more than five paces behind her. Wax Miriam looks at me like something contagious, white lips dripping down her chin to puddle on the ground.

'If we'd known you'd fail everything you try your hand at, we never would have wasted so much time and energy on you,' she says.

'*Wasted* is the word,' Wax Limbridge agrees.

I lift my spire again, aiming for the neck. Wax Limbridge evades with contemptuous quickness. I'm still working the lethargy from my muscles.

'You're as bad at spiring as you are at graving. What a pity.'

'I'd set you up in the cottage with total privacy,' Wax Flaypenny says. I back away from Wax Limbridge and Miriam, getting enough space that I can see Flaypenny's re-formed in front of Alastair. 'It could be over in less than a minute! Not bad for eight hundred puds, wouldn't you say?'

Alastair swings for her. Wax Flaypenny casually swats the blade away with her stick arm and cracks him in the skull with her other, bulging fist. I wince as his head snaps back on his neck.

'You wouldn't need to do anything *extraneous*,' she goes on, her smile beseeching. 'You don't even have to speak to them if you don't want to...'

'Pay attention when I'm talking to you!'

Wax Limbridge slams her fist into the base of my throat with enough force to send me rolling across the ground.

'Hal!' Alastair shouts.

'I know!' I choke out. *I deserved that.*

I right myself, gasping but determined not to get caught on the ground. I tighten the grip on my spire. *Focus.* There's a pulsing, buzzing sound in my ears that is almost certainly a hallucination from the pulp in my system.

Alastair gets over his shock at seeing Flaypenny so hideously recreated and unleashes a tide of blows on her. His Acclaim lights up the fog, but it's wasted effort. She slinks out of range as if they're teasing each other.

'You might find you enjoy it,' she says. 'I know how lonely you've been.'

Alastair rushes her again.

Wax Limbridge and Miriam block my path to him. They are sinuous like pulled toffee, every movement skin-crawlingly wrong. I'll have to blast my way through them. Alastair and I need to stay together.

More primordial swells from the cracks in front of me. I whack it to no avail. Before it's hardened into shape, it's like cutting cream, swallowing every wound as if it were never made.

Instead of waiting to see who it becomes, I launch myself at Wax Miriam. We need crowd control. The more copies there are on the field at once, the less chance we have to win.

I strike from above with my lightless spire, landing a blow that cleaves her in two. The two halves bend to either side, curling in on themselves like citrus rinds. The stink of grey death is strong enough to turn my stomach.

Wax Limbridge comes for me like something unspooling – a flurry of hand-strikes. I narrowly avoid them, getting enough space for a cross-slash that splits her chest. Her knees fold like runny paste drizzling over itself, and the rest of her follows.

I turn to see Wax Father flanking me.

'Stupid girl,' he says. I leap away from his fist, pivoting round to face his blobby visage. He looks like he's been bobbing for apples in boiling oil. 'How could I've raised such a stupid girl?'

I charge, throwing my weight into another cleaving blow... and miss completely. Wax Father punishes my mistake with a hard punch to the back that feels like he dropped a boulder on my spine.

'He's not going to wait forever. Girls like you are plentiful as fen rats, and the next one's waiting with open legs.'

I stagger out of his next strike's path, avoiding it more by luck than skill.

'Let's face it, he's your best prospect in life. You're not the sharpest knife in the drawer.'

I swear, if Alastair hears any of this, I'll die of embarrassment before anything else.

Oh, dear Lady, can the *crowd* hear this?

I fall back, manoeuvre myself around so I'm at least edging towards Alastair. He's got his hands full, fending off a triple assault from Wax Flaypenny, Drasilla, and Edusa. His Acclaimed blade does just as much damage as my un-Acclaimed one. That should be a good thing, but—

Wax Father streaks after me. I dodge strike after strike, each one closer than the last. In the background, wax versions of the cohort mix with the graving pupils from my trial. They don't even bother to attack. They just point and laugh, their mouths stretched too wide.

Wax Stripthicket's there, one eye swollen like a boil. 'You should start being nicer to Alastair. Then the only kind of labour you need worry about is the kind you do on your back. Could you manage that at least?'

'A Faulton's brood mare.'

Wax Mortritis springs up beside me, her breath stinking of carrion.

I whirl on her, lashing wildly. She holds every shot in eye-rolling disdain – 'It's the best you can hope for, poppet!' – then counters. Long talons slice past my neck, less than a finger from my carotid artery.

A blow from Wax Father knocks me sideways. Wax Mortritis pulls back for a death-strike when Alastair storms through them both like a gale.

'I see what you mean,' he grunts.

I can't think what to say, because a new pus-pale fountain wells up to take Mother's hunched-shoulder shape.

'What you have to understand,' she says, 'is that Preys are like so many fleas living in a dog's fur, sucking its blood to live.'

This version of Mother is slick as fish, chopping at me as if her hands were blades. She overreaches and I sever her elbow. I would've followed up with a finisher, if not for Wax Father getting in the way. The pair of them fight as a team.

'Honesty, compassion, forgiveness – people like us can't afford them.'

When she's close enough, I pike her in the head and yank the hilt, flicking off the top of her skull.

'Ungrateful wretch,' she says, voice thick with incredulous fury as she sinks into herself.

In a brief reprieve, I turn to Alastair. 'I would love it if we could both just ignore everything they're saying and never speak about it.'

'Deal,' he says.

A new Wax Mother gushes up behind the last, swivel-eyed and retching up her words. 'I used to be able to cross a room without getting out of breath. I used to be gorgeous! You sucked the life from me *and gave nothing back!*'

The copies rise faster than we can thrash through them. I carve up a Wax Tieran and another spurts up to take his place.

'I wanted to love you again, Brother,' he says earnestly, 'but you've come back all crooked. Preyburn's tainted you, blackened your heart.'

Alastair lunges for him and he sidesteps, slipping past his defences like a knife. 'We don't fit anymore. Preyburn's where you belong.'

Wax Tieran clouts Alastair in the stomach, but I bury my spire in his face. He sludges to the ground while Alastair splutters through a quick recovery.

We fight on, an ocean of wax rising and falling in waves around us. I feel the sweat veining my forehead, the furious knock of my heartbeat, the last of my energy leaving me. The primordial is as lithe as ever, its copies loose-limbed and frisky, while I seem to move with all the gusto of a tranquillized snail.

'I'm sorry to say this,' I huff, 'but I don't think we're hurting it.'

I desperately want to be told I'm wrong, but instead Alastair says, 'I know. I'm just trying to keep it off us while I figure out what that statue's for.'

All we're doing is tiring ourselves out. We can't keep this up forever, especially with the primordial coming thicker and faster with every figure we knock down.

A Wax Aiden Faulton surges forward, stunning Alastair so fiercely, his Acclaim dies.

'Leave it!' I say as Alastair recovers. 'You're draining yourself for no reason.'

'There's plenty reason.'

I hear the truth in it instantly. The loss of Acclaim leaves an emptiness in the air, a dark stillness that chills. I never imagined I'd say this, but I feel exposed without it. The fog-stuffed arena seems to cave in around me... but then Alastair's spire rekindles, disbanding the shadows.

'You couldn't possibly be my son.' Wax Aiden looks at Alastair with horror, as if his son were a knife stabbed through his own gut. 'No flesh of mine would ever *dream* of graving! It's an evil practice; it breeds virulence and misery. I won't have that poison around my family.'

Wax Drasilla weeps. 'I'm sorry, darling. You were always destined to be cold and spiteful.'

'Emotionless,' says a strangely familiar voice. My blood curdles when I recognize it.

I spin around to see a Wax Hal advancing on us. Her face writhes as if the skin hides larvae instead of muscles.

'A soulless abomination. A creepy, dead-eyed—'

Repulsed, I hit her with everything I've got; the blade slices her crossways. I leave her to be swallowed back into the mass, because of course, Wax Alastair's here to have a go.

'Well, that was pathetic. You are a deeply deluded individual, Kil—'

Alastair rages, 'Shut *up*,' and strikes his copy down. 'There's no end to them.'

'There will be an end,' I say, heaving for breath. 'Just keep going!'

'No – there won't be. I've figured it out.' Alastair pauses, panting. 'The statue is an Icon. A holy effigy, powered by Acclaim.'

I'd scoff if I had the energy. When the Choir creates effigies, it's *holy*, but when Preyburn does it, it's dark sorcery.

Alastair goes on with doom in his voice. 'That's a keyhole in its back. Our spires make the key together.'

'So we have to give up our spires? Put them both in—'

'It's powered by *Acclaim*, Hal. It wants two Acclaimed spires.'

'*Two?*' I whip round to look at him, eyes bugging. 'So we're done for?'

Alastair locks his rueful gaze with my horrified one. 'I think that's the only way to hurt the primordial, yes.'

The look in his eyes, the tone of his voice – both read despondence.

'You're not giving up?' I say. 'That's just the first theory we've come up with!'

'Of course I'm not giving up,' he snaps, but I don't believe him.

He doubts we can win.

With Alastair at my back, we take wave after wave of primordial ooze, a sea of liquid black eyes, pale wax faces, and barbed words. Even with the two of us working together in perfect accord, filling every gap in each other's defences, he's right – there's no end to the copies this thing can create.

Wax Aidens, dismayed. 'An embarrassment to my name – a poison.'

Wax Edusas, bewildered and pitying. 'You're just a novelty.'

Wax Kiels with pulsing grins. 'This is what a *real* graver looks like.'

Seething Wax Mothers and disappointed Limbridges and cajoling Flaypennys blurring into one roiling mass.

They don't call it the Eternal Spite for nothing. It's been here, steeping our lands, for centuries. It will be here for centuries more. Alastair's theory must be right. How could we ever hope to win without holy help?

I steal a wounded glance at the Icon, knowing Oldrac will never grant me Acclaim. A Prey with a hard, bitter heart...

But my thoughts jerk back to the aftermath of Mortritis's trial. If the glyphs really can see one's constitution, if they believe me to be Oldrac's follower in action and thought, then maybe... maybe Oldrac could grant me Acclaim.

But really, since she pulped me, every word that's ever left Mortritis's mouth lies in doubt.

It must take heroic effort for Alastair to keep his Acclaim going throughout this onslaught, but he does it anyway. I feel held by it; strengthened and protected. He's had to shoulder this all by himself, halfway carrying me through admissions.

Everything hurts. The urge to give up and let the waves take me only grows in power. But if I do that, we lose everything. So I fight on, overwhelmed by the stink of carrion bloom, denied range or breathing space. An endless nightmare of throbbing wax horrors, splitting and braiding together again.

'I can't last much longer!' Words I never thought I'd hear from Alastair's mouth. 'If we can't win, we only delay the inevitable. Better to forfeit and—'

'Downed gods, *no!* What a suggestion! After everything we've been through to get here?'

'I don't like it any more than you do, but... this is futile.'

'Stop that! No forfeits until we know beyond doubt there's no other way to win! I'm *with* you!'

Alastair doesn't miss a beat. 'I'm with you, too,' he says, and the words pull my heart a little because I know he means them. 'That's not in question.'

Wax Aiden rears up on him at the same time Wax Mortritis pounces on me.

'Too nice to be a graver,' she says. 'Not nice enough to be a spirer. The limbo of mediocrity.'

I plunge my spire into her chest for what must be the fiftieth time, and almost fall straight through her. It feels like I hit water, but then she seizes my wrists with her wax hands. They feel like cold, sweaty icing against the exposed skin above my gloves, but their hold is as firm as a vice.

'Oneness is an illusion,' she seethes. 'You abandoned Our Lady's truth for a dirty con.'

Her hideous eyes fix on mine, and I can do nothing but stare back. I'm trapped in time as the features contort around them, a face I no longer recognize.

'Oldrac has to judge deeds because he can't see hearts,' says the primordial. 'Our Lady can. *I* can. Your false accord doesn't fool me.'

'What's false about it?' I spit.

'A true accord goes both ways.' A spark of light from below its writhing face throws visceral, twitching shadows across it. 'Yours doesn't.'

My lip curls. This is the Blood of Preyburn, a craven manipulator like Mortritis, like Mother, like the cohort.

I don't admire their ways. They *horrify* me.

As I stare into the primordial's face, repulsed less by its eldritch visage than its malevolence, I realize they were all right. Especially Limbridge.

Turns out I'm a spirer after all.

But the primordial isn't done trying to crush my spirit. 'Just wait 'til you see what he's—'

The Might jolts to life, unleashing a storm of Acclaim inside the primordial. I feel it like a thunderclap in my chest. The creature lights from the inside, exploding in my face.

I stagger back, eyes shut tight, arm shielding my head, buffeted from all sides by frenetic Acclaim and greasy wax-splatter. When I dare to open them again, I can only stare at the Might in shock.

That familiar, surging power grips my body again, this time with a fanatic's intensity. Blessed numbness erodes the aches and pains that had almost grown too much to bear. Strength returns to my body and clarity to my mind, more than I've ever possessed. Now my pulse runs quick not with exhaustion and fear but with hope.

This time, the Acclaim comes to my spire direct from the source. Oldrac lends me the strength I need to finish this.

'You did it!' Alastair says, breathless.

Oldrac gave me his blessing. I have Acclaim.

A moment's marvelling is all I get before more primordial figures come slithering and winching towards me.

Even though Alastair's right next to me, I shout to be heard over the primordial's raging voices. 'We can't let it delay us any longer!'

'Agreed!' Alastair shouts back. 'Let's push through to the Icon.'

Realizing we now have a chance to win, the primordial stops toying with us. The wax copies fuse to make grim amalgamations. I watch with frightening clarity as the wax cohort becomes one churning mass with Wax Kiel's head bubbling out of the neck.

I don't let them get close. With a slash of my blade, Acclaim snaps in answer, welting holes through their wax bodies. *Wild, forking strikes... fantastic for keeping lots of attackers off you* and *circulating damage.* The smell of burning candles thickens the air as they melt in on themselves, but it's no cause to celebrate. Wax Edusa's already charging us with Aiden sloping off one shoulder, an arm coming from an arm and both of them grasping.

We blitz our way through a gelatinous tide, dodging each strike to reach the Icon. The radiance and tumult of *two* Acclaimed spires in close quarters is almost unbearable, but my whole body thrums with strength.

None of our attacks stop the primordial. We can only slow it down. Every wax copy it hurls at us is merely another distraction to keep us from the Icon. It'll keep roiling and clotting and taking new forms until we're spent.

Oldrac's strength may be godly, but my mortal body can only take so much of it. I imagine a new scar forming on my skin with every strike and wonder how long I have left.

As we near the Icon, the primordial forms a lumpy stew of faces twice my height. Several mouths become one giant gaping hole that opens wide to swallow us – no, to scare us away.

We strike together, our dual Acclaim twisting and knotting to blaze craters in the primordial's waxy visage. What isn't blasted away sags into the ground, giving us space to vault over it. When we reach the Icon's back, we have only moments before the primordial regroups and catches up to us.

My gaze meets Alastair's, both of us panting as we line the points of our spires up with the Icon's back. To give up this power seems dangerous and absurd with the enemy converging, but we're desperate.

Alastair's masked face conveys nothing, but I see it all in his eyes. The fight's stripped him of the vile imperiousness that's always marked him. Naked of pretence, I just see… him.

'Now,' he says.

Moving in almost perfect accord, we plunge our spires, the Might and the Cunning, side by side, into the Icon's bowed back.

Once half the blades are in, some inner mechanism activates. It drags the rest inside with a creaking grind until only the crossguards remain. Our spire hilts stick out like the wind-up key behind a toy soldier.

I cast a fearful look back at the onrushing wax avalanche, but a sudden cacophonous roar stops its flow.

A cascade of lightning strikes the Icon, too focused to be anything but divine, and *keeps* striking it. The hail ceases and the arena turns white as this light-pillar blasts straight down from the firmaments. It crashes into the Icon and torrents out across the ground, troubling the stone beneath my boots, dispelling the fog, melting every blob of lymphatic ooze in a ten-pace radius.

Slowly, surely, the Icon animates, rising from its kneeling pose to tower over Alastair and me – an awesome sight; stood up, it's even bigger than the ancestor. It's slow, however, where the primordial is fluid and fast.

The firmament's lightning wanes, and with it, that terrible roar. My poor abused ears keep ringing in its wake. The primordial, giving up on its unflattering lookalikes, coalesces into one formless body, unleashing a monstrous gargle all the while.

The Icon turns its colossal head, observing our foe through the holes in its golden mask. I read pure contempt in its cold eyes and lifted chin.

It lifts both fists. I can already tell every strike will be like this one, unfortunately telegraphed by plodding slowness.

The primordial charges in all its amorphous fury. Glutinous limbs and faces and eyes gain sudden, horrifying definition amid the mass, tumbling over each other. They're swallowed up again in the next blink, like shapes folded back into dough.

There's another flaw to the Icon's design, which strikes Alastair and me almost instantly. He sinks to his knees, teeth gritted together, and I can't help but join him. I taste copper. Scars flow like river systems along Alastair's neck, and mine. I feel them running all over me like lava in my veins.

The power leached by the Icon takes us to the precipice within moments. If not for the humiliation that would follow, I'd simply succumb, wallowing and twitching on the ground. Lamentably, we have a crowd, a preceptor, and a provost to impress.

When the Icon hammers into the ground, Acclaim surges towards the primordial. It has an altogether better effect than either of our spires did; a tidal wave of bilious gunk goes smashing against the arena walls.

The stench of burning wax fills the air. The Icon's Acclaim must be hot enough to destroy it. With every strike that follows, more of the primordial dissolves.

My eyes blur with tears as wave after wave of wax teeth try to devour the Icon, only to vanish like butter in a skillet. It's as powerless against the Icon as our spires were against it.

We're so close, and yet so far. I've hit my limit. I wasted too much time and strength on the primordial's copies, and now I—

A gloved hand grips mine. I blink away tears to see Alastair's unfastened his mask, revealing a sweaty, pink face. Acclaim scars have scaled his throat, forking all the way up to his eyes. He's smiling. *Lost his mind at last.* I won't look any better, but with trembling fingers and a great deal of focus, I manage to get my own mask off.

He's saying something, but the fight's too loud to hear him. I have to lip-read.

'We won.'

I strain to follow his eyeline. A single globule of grease bobbles on the ground. The Icon raises a mighty heel and stamps on it. It bursts like an abscess, Acclaim crinkling out across the ground to fizzle every last pearl.

Thank the stars.

As soon as I see the primordial's no more, I lose the will. My Acclaim dies and the Icon petrifies where it stands, glaring down at the spot that had held the last slippery pustule of our enemy. Both spires halfway eject with a loud and final *thunk*.

Alastair's first to rise, and so helps drag me to my feet. It feels like I've been deboned, but he holds me up with an arm hooked round my waist. After all that chaos, the crowd-roar sounds dull and far away.

Before we turn to face the provost, Alastair turns to face me. I stand dumb with shock as he thumbs what is probably blood from my lip and pulls me in against him. I lean on him the way drunks lean on walls. My face tucks into the hollow of his throat, his chest pressing on mine with each panting breath. Despite fatigue, his exhilaration comes off him like heat and I finally start to absorb it.

We won.

We break off from each other to bow for the provost. Edusa slaps his gloved hands together over his head, but Her Sagacity taps her fingers against the back of one hand.

'In passion, glory!' Edusa shouts, and the crowd takes up the chant.

We withdraw our spires from the Icon as though they've tripled in weight and exit the arena to whistles, roars, and thunderous applause. I get as far as the tunnel's shadow before I bend double and throw up. Alastair's hands and voice keep trembling as he rubs my back, whispering comfort and praise. He can't believe it either.

As long as I live, I may never manage another slice of candle cake.

29

AN ARC OF BRIGHT VERMILLION

The next morning, I wake when Edusa has another ceremonial outfit delivered to my room, which I'll be wearing for the next several bells. The last thing I want is to be paraded from luminary to luminary all day. But I can hardly complain when, at the end of it, Edusa will announce his offer to Alastair and me.

I spent most of yesterday in the washrooms, scrubbing dried sweat, blood, and primordial grease from my skin. It could take weeks before I feel clean again. I didn't see Alastair, although I did knock for him. There was no answer at his door, so I retreated to bed and fell directly to sleep.

Now, when I hear knuckles against the door, I open it to find Alastair all scrubbed up. His hair, which had been smeared across his scalp with wax, is all clean again. There's a nasty bruise on his temple and another on his cheekbone, but they won't last.

'Fallen gods,' I say. 'I thought we had more time.'

'We do.'

Something about his expression and the low timbre of his voice makes the skin prickle along my arms. 'We do?'

'Yes.' Alastair moves into the room, prompting me to take a few steps back. 'And I hear the view from the roof is thrilling.'

My breath hitches, but then I analyse his impish grin. 'Very funny.'

He laughs a rare, genuinely joyful laugh, a sound I cannot help but marvel at. With his bottomless well of a voice, it sounds positively demonic. 'I wanted to speak before you go down. How are you feeling?'

'Like death,' I reply, 'and not in a good way.'

'You only have to last until Edusa announces himself as our patron. It'll be a few bells at most.' He pauses, two inkwells of Cosmic Black staring into me. 'Congratulations on achieving Our Lord's Acclaim.'

'Thank you,' I say hoarsely.

Alastair twists one of his rings around his finger, still looking at me in a way that makes every inch of skin hot.

After a pause, I say, 'What will happen with Mortritis?'

'I wonder. Any punishment the provost metes out will be laxer than we'd like, and not for lack of will. My aunt remains a powerful woman with many advocates, especially in pro-military circles.'

'She'll come after us again,' I say, not even questioning it.

'I don't doubt it. But she'll need to move carefully. We have our illustrious patron, and a small amount of celebrity now. She'd be stupid to attack directly, and she isn't that.'

I nod, unsure whether that's any comfort. I'd prefer a direct attack than one that leaps from the shadows to take me by surprise.

Alastair's ring loosens from his finger. He wasn't toying with it but twisting it off. He gestures for me to hold out my hand, then presses it into my palm.

I frown at it. It's the one with Oldrac's face, alabaster like our masks – a miniature sculpture in ring form. 'What's this?'

'A thank you gift.'

'Oh.' I squirm. 'Even after what happened with Mortritis?'

Alastair smiles, but it doesn't comfort me. It's the smile of someone who knows things you don't.

'Papa's here.'

A moment passes while I wonder whether I heard correctly. His face, filled with fierce excitement, tells me I did.

'Downed gods! Really?'

'He's asked to meet me in private before the offer ceremony.'

'Alone? Will you be all right?'

'Perfectly.'

Searching his face, I don't see any fear. Far from it, in fact – he's giddy with anticipation, his usually guarded features open. I've never seen him like this before. He's a different man.

Maybe it's because he isn't used to smiling for happiness, only for cruelty, that he looks so disconcertingly sinister. Instead of sharing in his joy, my skin itches with a sense of wrongness.

'You've given me everything I've wanted these past five years,' he says, a slightly unhinged glint to his eye. 'I'll never forget it.'

After a moment's staring, I clear my throat. 'I don't know that I deserve that, but thank you anyway.'

'Oh, you deserve every last drop of it.'

Despite his weird intensity, to know I'm forgiven brings overwhelming comfort.

As if to prove all's forgotten, he pulls me into an embrace. We stand there a while, holding each other tight. I listen to his breathing, the steady thump of his pulse, and a rush of affection swells in my chest.

Finally, he pulls back to hold me at arm's length. His bright black eyes fix on mine, their message inscrutable. I move forward to kiss him, and am so relieved when he meets me halfway. I loop my arms around his neck, bringing us flush as he kisses me back, firm and slow.

His hand slides from my hair to my throat and down until his palm rests against my breastbone. It's like he wants to know how hard my heart's beating for him.

He eventually breaks off, cupping a hand to my cheek. 'I'll see you, Hal.'

'See you...'

My nerves fray further as he turns and goes, partly for the loss of him, but also for the scale of what he goes to do. The father he hasn't seen or spoken to since their devastating row five years ago is suddenly moments away.

How old would Alastair have been when he was exiled? A child of thirteen, with no hope of knowing the consequences his rebellion could have. I can only pray that now, five years on, he's better equipped to handle his father's temper. I will be *very* upset if Aiden crushes his high spirits.

I'm strangely cold as I make my way down, as though Alastair took the sun with him. A shadow clings to me even here, in the obnoxiously bright lights of the games hall; even now, as Edusa pounces on me.

'Toeing the line between fashionably late and *rude!*' he proclaims. 'I have some guests just *dying* to be introduced. But before that, there are some delightful Prey women here to see you. Over by the confectioneries.'

I glance over to see a woman with dark glasses and her glad rags on. She's amusing some lady luminaries, no doubt with embroidered tales from darkest Preyburn, with a glass of Balverian lavender wine in her hand.

I'm over there like a shot.

'Limbridge!' I fling my arms around her before she even has a chance to turn around, inhaling her scent of oiled leather and musty moss. 'I can't believe you're here!'

She pats my head, saying, 'My dear, I never miss an opportunity to say *I told you so*. In person is best.'

I pull away from her. 'Yes, well—'

'Quite the show you put on, you and Alastair.' She lifts her glasses so I can see the beady eye she's giving me. 'You're looking very... *happy*. My goodness, whoever could have seen that coming? I must be some sort of Oldracian oracle.'

I feel the tips of my ears heating up. 'Limbridge, really.'

'Oh, don't get all fussy, dear. I'm only teasing.'

She gestures to the woman beside her – it's Prefect Miriam. With half a tiny, jiggly cake in one hand, she seizes mine in the other and shakes as if she means to yank my arm from its socket. She's looking a bit pink in the cheeks, so I don't take offence. Especially since I owe her an apology for my hypocrisy with Alastair.

'Well done, you!' she squeaks. 'You've done Withersham Hall so absurdly proud!'

'Not to mention better funded than we've been in decades,' Limbridge says. 'We've already started on the renovation plans, you'll be pleased to know.'

My eyebrows shoot up. 'Just how much did you get for our admission?'

Before she can give me an answer, Edusa sweeps in. 'My dear ladies, I apologize but I must steal young Halen away for a moment.'

'Of course, of course,' says Limbridge, happy to be saved. 'Hal, we expect you and Alastair back to cut some ribbons and won't take no for an answer.'

She and Miri lift their glasses, and we leave the two of them chatting.

Under his breath, Edusa says, 'Quickly – the guests *must* be distracted from this catering disaster!'

He introduces me to some of these esteemed guests, then abandons me to deal with this disaster nobody else seems to have noticed. I stumble my way through a conversation with them for several minutes. At one point, I catch the eye of Preceptor Laudred's proxy, Valorie. Although we don't know each other, she smiles, lifting her glass to me.

Across the room, I see none other than Lourdes, fiercely grinning. I try my hand at a polite excuse, which the guests gracefully accept, and make my way over to her.

As soon as I'm within reach, Lourdes' hand takes its preferred spot on my shoulder. 'Look at this! We made it, yes?'

'Are we the only three who made the cut?'

'We certainly are. The rest will be licking their wounds in the infirmary, poor things.'

I shudder to think how they must feel, and how easily that could have been us.

'So, classmates before long. I might get that eerian study session we talked about.'

'I look forward to it.'

Lourdes dazzles a little harder and gives another shoulder squeeze. 'Good man!'

She moves on to Preceptor Gladwina, the glamorous centrepiece in a nearby cluster of guests. Out of the corner of my eye, I see one of the servers tumble into the room. My gaze might have slipped straight past him if not for his face as he snags one of the senior servers, a busty, officious-looking woman. It's the face of someone who's accidentally set a house on fire.

His lips move furiously as he relays some frightful problem, and apparently his terror is catching. I watch the senior server's face contort too and know that this is not the catering disaster Edusa mentioned. It's a *real* disaster.

Some Oldracian instinct drives me to leave and investigate. As the server and his senior bustle from the games hall, I follow. Moving through the long, bright hollows of the corridors fills me with a cringing dread. They stop outside one of the many private salons that outfit Dunchester House.

The senior server pushes her way in through the unlocked door and stops dead. I don't bother to hide myself, staring past their heads into the room beyond.

Tieran kneels on the carpet. The tendons in his throat are tight as bowstrings. His chest heaves with every breath, his face scarlet and crooked. Grief looks as unnatural on him as joy looked on Alastair.

'No, no, no, no...'

A man's head rests between Tieran's hands. In front of him, the man's body is splayed out on the carpet.

I know immediately who this man has to be. I saw a wax copy of him earlier today, and before that, a portrait on Alastair's dresser: Aiden Faulton. His skin is leathery, his hair white, and a wheelchair sits bereft by the table. Since scions struggle to age, he must be practically primeval.

I can tell by the awkward angle of his arms and legs that he's fallen unconscious, and then, by the divorce of head from neck, that he is dead.

I slip past the servers, who don't react to me at all, and look around. There's no one else in the room. It's just Tieran, gasping for breath, and the dead old man.

My eyes widen in horror as Tieran jams the bright, raw flesh of his father's neck repeatedly into the base it was severed from, hoping it'll mend itself.

'Come on... come on!'

I don't know whether that's ever worked. In Preyburn, you get all sorts of stories about what does and doesn't kill a scion. One thing we can all agree on is the help of pulp in such matters. Once you've crippled their unnatural capacity for knitting themselves back together, they're no more invulnerable than the next target.

My gaze follows an arc of bright vermilion wine along the carpet. It stains the plush wool fibres, roughly from Aiden's hand to the cloven-footed table leg that stopped the wine goblet's roll. I take a deep breath in, and sure enough, it smells grey.

Tears stream down Tieran's face as he tries and fails to stick his father's head back on. The servers decide not to intervene, content to stare and be aghast.

'Tieran,' I say, my throat tight on the word. 'Tieran, it's not working. His flesh isn't bonding.'

Now that I'm closer, I can see the bone-pale liquid oozing from Aiden's severed gullet. He had pulp forced down it, just as I had yesterday.

'Because you'd know,' Tieran snarls. 'You didn't even know how scion healing worked until I explained it to you.'

'But you said scions' bodies heal grislier injuries faster. By that logic—'

'*Stop talking!*'

I look away, at the wheelchair. Aiden's body's capacity to heal must have been waning if he'd needed it. Even before he got pulped, he was vulnerable.

But I can't expect Tieran to listen to *me*.

To the servers, I say, 'Fetch Edusa, please?' in a rather brittle voice, and they immediately disappear. Any excuse to get away from the horrors of this room.

Tieran heaves a gasp. He finally gives up bumping his father's head and neck together, but that's not to say he's done manhandling the corpse. He wraps both arms around the head, hugging it to his chest like a teddy bear stitched out of old man's skin. His shoulders wrack with sobs. 'I can't believe he... How could he do this?'

'Who?'

Tieran gets to his feet. He and his father's severed head turn to face me, one set of sightless eyes and one set of livid, glistening ones. There is unmistakable violence in the rigid line of his shoulders and jaw. Remembering the mess he made of Ransley and the nameless rejects, I take a step back, but Tieran presses in further, hissing through locked teeth.

'You *know* who.'

30

A HAPPY LITTLE FOURSOME

We stand in the unabashed luxury of Edusa's office. Tasselled drapes frame the tall arched windows, gathered in scarlet cords. Outside, snow lies inches thick on the grounds.

Edusa's favourite portraits of himself hang from every available space. This includes a triumphant, life-size nude in oils hung above the mantel so you're staring at his member as you walk in. Technically, he wears a crimson velvet bathrobe, although it's completely open. The fact that it can distract me at a time like this is a testament to the artist's talent. Whether the artist exaggerated his anatomy, as they all seem to do for his chin and cheekbones, I'm happily not in a position to say.

Fixing my eyes on the carpet, I say, 'How can you be certain he did it?'

Mortritis rolls her eyes up to the ornate ceiling roses. She's taken up an armchair by the fireplace. With one long leg crossed over the other and her head propped on her fist, she has the air of someone desperate to escape dull conversation.

Kiel speaks in his guttural rasp. 'She's right. Innocent people *always* flee the scene of the crime.' It's hard to say whether he's smiling, but I hear it in his voice. He perches on one arm of his mother's chair. Despite the waist-high flames behind him, he's again hulking in his coat.

'They might,' I say, heat growing in my voice, 'if they thought they'd be falsely accused. Or it could've been self-defence.'

Kiel looks amused, but Tieran stirs at this. He's also taken an armchair, albeit one that's as far away from Mortritis and Kiel as it can reasonably be. His face is still damp with tears as it twists into a sneer.

'You're not suggesting what I think you are?' he says, fighting to control his breath. 'Papa only came to welcome Alastair back into the family.'

'Maybe the conversation didn't go how he planned. Maybe they—'

'He could barely *walk!*'

'If Aiden wanted his son killed,' says Edusa, standing a step from his proxy, hands clasped behind his back and brow furrowed, 'surely Preyburn would've been the cleaner place to do it?'

Kiel nods. 'You can't cross a room over there without bumping into a butcher for hire. Enterprising folk, the Preys.'

I throw him a dirty look, but he doesn't even have the good grace to notice. He's digging a lighter and pre-rolled cigarette from his coat pocket, but when Edusa snaps, 'Ah-ah-ah! My sanctuary is a smoke-free area,' Kiel makes a fuss of tucking his lighter away. The cigarette stays, held firm but loose between his fingers.

My hands tremor gently like they did during my trial. I've been struggling to keep myself together these past few bells. Terror lurks beneath the surface like a monster crawling up from the bottom of a dark lake, waiting to strike. Reasoning keeps it at bay.

To Tieran, I say, 'Look, I didn't know your father—'

'Exactly.' His voice is a low hiss. 'So why don't you be quiet?'

I recoil.

The two abettors – Credencia, as bald as an octopus, and Laurentius, beneath a hat as tall as the day is long – stand solemn in their precise Balverian tailoring.

'This is all speculation,' says Laurentius. His fashion choices make more sense under Balver's soaring ceilings than they did in Withersham's cramped ones, but his hat still looks bizarre. 'There can be no certainties until Alastair is brought in for questioning.'

Tieran fixes the abettors with a yellow-eyed glare. 'Did you know this would happen?'

'*Tieran*,' Edusa says in the warning tone of a man whose hound is about to do something naughty like rub its behind on the nice rug.

'It's all right, Edusa.' Credencia dons a tolerant smile. 'The boy is grieving.'

Tieran drops his eyes to the carpet, choking back a sob as if these words have redoubled his pain.

Mortritis lets out a theatrical groan. 'Is this going to take very long?'

Laurentius steps towards the centre of the room, his bejewelled hands open and his gaze on me. 'As Alastair's partner in accordship, you must answer for him.'

I start. 'What do you mean, *answer for him?*'

'You're in an accord. You are liable for his actions.'

I let out a sharp, nervous laugh. 'You're not serious? You'll charge me with the murder of a man I never even met? What good will that do?'

Fallen gods, I'm about to lose everything. Not just Alastair and St Penderghast's but my freedom.

Tieran looks me up and down. 'How do we know you weren't an accomplice?'

'What in the golden firmaments are you basing that on?'

'You're in an accord together.'

My voice rises to a shrill. '*So what?*'

'Hush, Tieran,' says Mortritis. 'You want someone to point the finger at because you're upset. The likelihood of Hal conspiring in a murder plot and then hanging about to be arrested is slim to none.'

Tieran rubs a puffy red eyelid with his knuckle. 'Now you defend her? After you had her pulped and stuffed under your desk?'

'For the last time, you entirely confused the situation. And I fail to see what one event has to do with the other.'

'What *I* fail to see,' I cut in, 'is why you're all so certain Alastair did it. Who's to say nobody else was in that room – someone who's taken him?'

'Hm,' says Edusa. 'Not impossible, but they'd struggle to drag the boy from the grounds without anyone's notice.'

'We've examined the area and interviewed the staff,' says Credencia. 'We found no evidence of other involvement.'

I reply through locked teeth. 'Just because you haven't found the evidence in the *first bells* of looking doesn't mean there's none to be found. You're not even constables!'

'I beg your pardon?'

'It's a Prey title,' says Kiel. 'Constables enforce laws.'

Credencia's voice is thick with disdain. 'We are *all* things to Her Sagacity. That includes law enforcement when the situation demands it.'

'But without present-day science to analyse the evidence, how do you know you're enforcing them correctly?' I say. 'Why don't we get professionals in from Preyburn with the proper tools?'

The abettors stare as if this is an outrageous thing to say.

'Present-day science may not be required,' Edusa says. 'If it's a case of someone drugged with pulp, Aiden wouldn't even be her first victim this week.' He cuts his eyes to Mortritis, who is bouncing her stiletto-heeled foot to keep herself awake. If anything, she and her smirking, rough-mannered son look bored by the charge.

'Oh, my. Accusations without proof?' She drops her voice to a stage whisper. 'Are you sure that's wise, poppet?'

'Three people found my prospect paralysed in your office. I'd say the proof is ample. Wouldn't you?'

'If I was going to take up poisoning people, don't you think I'd have the wherewithal to space them out a bit?'

'Several people have accounted for Mortritis's whereabouts when the crime was committed,' says Laurentius.

'That proves nothing,' Edusa replies. 'She has plenty of tiresome suck-ups ready to do her dirty work.'

'It was Alastair,' Tieran spits. 'He never forgave Papa for his punishment.'

I feel sick. Hideously sick.

'Are you really going to put me away for this?' I say faintly.

'Not necessarily.' Credencia adjusts her collar. 'In the Oldracian spirit of compassion, the provost has decided to acquit you and allow you to keep your place at St Penderghast's, assuming Edusa is willing—'

Edusa makes an exaggerated scoffing noise. 'Surely you jest? The only thing that grips the public harder than a romance is a murder mystery! We'll have Balver by the throat for years to come. Of course I'm willing.'

Tieran flares his nostrils but remembers to keep his mouth shut this time. He simply glowers at Edusa's back as another tear slips from his eye.

'*Provided*,' the abettor says pointedly, 'you meet one condition.'

'Which is?' I say, hope opening in my chest.

'You find Alastair and bring him back to stand trial.'

Shit. I've got more chance of building a cathedral out of cream.

'I have no idea where he's gone. And even if I did, how could I hope to overpower someone Alastair couldn't?'

'Assuming Alastair has been taken,' Kiel interjects. 'And on the almost certain chance that he hasn't, she might struggle to force him back here if he doesn't want to come.'

Laurentius looks impatient. 'We weren't suggesting you'd go alone.'

Credencia looks from Edusa to Mortritis. 'A scion has been murdered in our demesne. One you each have close ties to.'

Mortritis scoffs. 'Now that *is* a stretch. Out with it, Credencia. What's the real reason for dragging me up here? Or is this just your latest method for wasting my time?'

The abettors don't so much bristle as grow multiple poison-tipped spikes.

'You could stand to be more cooperative,' Credencia replies in a crisp tone. 'Particularly given Edusa's accusations. Don't think Her Sagacity has dismissed them simply because this matter takes precedence.'

'Oh, please. Edusa has no proof, and Her Sagacity cannot possibly take his word on anything. The man's never told a story without embellishment, and he's always hated me.'

Edusa barks out a laugh. 'You flatter yourself. I could no more muster any hatred for you than Our Lord could for an insect.'

'The provost is well acquainted with your history,' says Laurentius wearily, 'as well as Edusa's flair for storytelling.'

'Is it my flair for storytelling she's afraid of?' Edusa says, an eyebrow cocked. 'Or the backlash from Mortritis's cultists?'

Since the abettors decline to answer this, I have to conclude that he's on to something. Alastair did warn that the provost's punishment would be laxer than we'd like.

'In the spirit of oneness,' Credencia goes on, addressing Mortritis, 'Her Sagacity offers a chance to atone for your misconduct towards Edusa and his charges.'

'*Misconduct?*' I say.

'A chance to atone for misconduct he imagined?' Mortritis says. 'How generous.'

'Understand that unless an honest effort is made on your part, this incident will reach the Council. Her Sagacity trusts you to restore Edusa's faith, and hers, by ensuring Alastair is fetched back.'

Mortritis gives a false, tight smile. 'And how would Her Sagacity like me to do that?'

'Either you will accompany Hal, or your prox—'

'Kiel,' Mortritis says, 'you're up.'

Kiel shrugs. 'At least it will be warmer.'

I stare at the abettors, dismayed. 'You're not sending me off with the son of the woman who—'

'Edusa,' says Laurentius, as if I hadn't spoken, 'as patron to both of the accused, Her Sagacity asks the same of you.'

'As much as I'd love to go on a jolly adventure up and down the Commonwealth, I couldn't possibly. I have an *abundance* of important matters demanding my personal attention.'

'I want to go,' Tieran says. 'He's my brother. He murdered my papa. I should be the one to punish him.'

'You will do no such thing,' says Laurentius, affronted. 'Alastair's punishment – his *guilt* – will be determined by the Council at a fair trial.'

Tieran's face says he disagrees, but his mouth says, 'Yes, Your Learnedness.'

'What happened is obvious.' Mortritis sounds exasperated, as though she can't believe we're still belabouring the point. 'Alastair's spent the last five years stewing in resentment, dreaming wet about the day he'd pay back the man who condemned him to squalor. He played the game for as long as it took to get Aiden in a room, and not a moment longer.'

Hearing this, my fist squeezes of its own accord. Alastair's ring cuts a jagged circle into my palm.

Kiel hasn't stopped smiling, or shivering. 'I'll be the first to hold my hands up and admit I was wrong about him. He's got hidden depths after all.'

'That makes no sense,' I say. 'All Alastair wanted was to get back to his family – back to Glimwick. Killing his father gives him the opposite, forcing him to go on the run.'

Mortritis sighs. 'I fear this has gone over your head. Sometimes people say things that aren't the truth. These are called lies. Alastair *said* he wanted his family back, but what he actually wanted was revenge. See how that works?'

'I don't believe—'

Kiel picks up the thread. 'If he'd told you the real reason he wanted to pass admissions wasn't to get a place but to murder his papa, would you have gone along with it?'

'Obviously not!'

'There you go. He lied because he had to.'

'Alastair isn't like that. He's all about oneness and logic. He'd never sacrifice his family and future to get back at his father.'

'It was all a veneer, poppet. Spite is my area of expertise, don't forget. Beneath that collected exterior, he's as wrathful as they come.'

'Then why couldn't he read glyphs?'

'Who told you he couldn't?'

'He did.'

Mortritis makes a face that says, *There's your answer.*

'Hidden depths indeed,' Kiel echoes, smirking. 'He must be lightning in the sheets to have you wrapped so tight round his finger. But then, the strait-laced types always are.'

Instead of shoving him backwards into the fireplace, which would be the correct response, I close my eyes and take a deep, deep breath. I mustn't lose my temper, even though everything they say is so false and sleazy it makes me burn.

Murdering his father in cold blood. Leaving me to take the blame. Abandoning everything he's spent the last five years working towards. All things Alastair would never do, no matter what these lunatics think.

Something else must have happened, and with archaic Glim science, we've almost no way of finding out what. Unless, of course, we find him.

'All of you, please,' says Credencia, pinching the bridge of her nose. 'In-fighting gets us nowhere.'

Her colleague nods, hat bobbing. 'Her Sagacity predicted emotions would run high in the wake of such fresh tragedy.'

'To ensure the provost's will is carried out to the letter, she too sends a representative.' Credencia pauses, not for effect but gathering her resolve. 'Myself. I will accompany you on Her Sagacity's behalf.'

Laurentius winces in sympathy.

In the resulting silence, my eyes double back over her outfit. It's hard to imagine this haughty individual travelling anywhere that isn't richly outfitted. She'll be wanting some sensible shoes for a start.

But then, I did see her first in Preyburn, shuddering with distaste at everything her gaze came across. She can't be looking forward to this any more than I am.

Kiel cuts the silence with his knife-like voice. 'A happy little foursome.'

'This is all well and good,' says Edusa, 'but without any notion of where Alastair's scampered off to, this may take some time. I *will* need my proxy back at some point, you know. Preferably before term starts.'

Now it's Credencia's turn to look offended. 'We have a great deal more than a *notion*. I have seen him at Our Lady's Last Stand in two weeks' time, and plan to intercept him there.'

'There's a spot of good news for you, Tieran.' Kiel cocks his head. 'You were dying to go last year. Now's your chance.'

Tieran stares at him. 'My papa, your uncle, is dead. Does that mean anything to you?'

'It means I'm being sent to Our Lady's Last Stand to fetch Alastair. Don't you listen?'

'Your papa, his uncle,' Mortritis says, 'was a miserable ghoul who should've shuffled off years ago.'

If I'd thought she'd be on her best behaviour after the incident earlier, I couldn't have been more wrong.

Tieran's face darkens. 'How dare you say that? Mama's in *pieces*.'

The very air around him seems to pulse with fury. The Moppetons appear unaffected.

'I imagine she'll get over it rather quickly, assuming the old codger remembered her in his will.'

'Mortritis, *please*,' says Laurentius. 'Why exacerbate the—'

'Then she can start courting again,' Kiel says. 'Won't that be fun?'

Mortritis nods, smiling. 'A wealthy widow, none too fussy with her affections – you'll have a new papa in no time. Dry those tears.'

I look at her now and wonder how I ever worshipped anything so nakedly evil.

Just as Tieran looks ready to combust, which seems to be exactly what Kiel wants, Credencia clears her throat.

'I believe we've arrived at a consensus? If so, we should prepare to leave immediately.'

Kiel shrugs. 'I've already said I'm keen.'

'Yes,' Tieran grits out.

One by one, they all turn to look at me askance, as if I might opt for prison instead.

31

THE CONCEPT OF FORWARD PLANNING

Limbridge surfaces outside my guestroom later than I'd like, a glass of wine in one hand and the rest of the bottle in the other. She looks militant in a double-breasted trench coat made of creaking brown leather that falls past her knees, with gloves and boots to match. She strides in without needing an invitation.

'What a perfect cock-up,' she says, settling into an armchair beside the fire. 'The abettors wouldn't know evidence if it kissed them. Eschewing modern technology is all well and good until you've a murder investigation on your plate.'

I close the door behind her, my head throbbing. 'I don't know what happened, but there's no way Alastair murdered his father.'

Limbridge looks grave and not entirely innocent.

'What?' I say, bristling instantly.

She produces a letter – slightly rumpled, its wax seal broken – from a coat pocket and holds it out between two fingers. I take it.

'How curious,' I say, staring her dead in the eye. 'The envelope clearly says, *To Hal*, and yet it's been opened.'

'Oh, stop it. What if it had contained crucial information that couldn't wait until I found you privately?'

'Why was privacy an issue? And where did you find it?'

'Alastair handed it to me in the games hall, brazen as you like. He said it was for your eyes only.'

'So naturally you wedged your nose in as soon as you could.'

'Hal, if snooped-at post is anywhere near the top of your list of things to worry about, I suggest you rethink your priorities. Read it.'

I don't need to be told twice.

My dearest darling Hal,

Apologies that this has to come by pen. I really would have preferred to tell you in person, but predicted* it wouldn't be possible to get back to you after I saw Papa.

(*I know you struggle with the concept of forward planning, but a prediction is a guess, hopefully based on evidence, about what will happen in the future.)

I expect you're confused. For a time, I was too. I thought we had a true accord, and that complicated things. To be candid, I never wanted Papa to accept me. I only wanted him to die. If he could die by the very spire he gifted me as an insult? Even better.

Our accord was something I hadn't planned for. A false accord is one thing, but I don't know that I could have broken a true one. Fortunately, you did that for me. Or it was never real to begin with. It hardly matters which. The point is, you betrayed me, casting me off for my aunt as I should have always known you would.

You gave me the freedom to pursue my plans without guilt. Revenge on Papa for every misery I endured these past five years.

I tell you this knowing full well this will end up in the abettors'
hands. It doesn't matter. You deserve to have the truth. You deserve to
know how I felt when you chose that witch and your pointless ambition
over me.

I won't pretend it doesn't sting, but I always appreciate simplicity.
Loyalty earns loyalty; betrayal earns betrayal.

Or, as we like to say in Withersham, insults demand answers.
Immortally yours,
Faulton

⎯⊖⎯

I spend a bell or so destroying all the furniture in my room. Limbridge watches from her fire-warmed seat, sipping wine, as if my screaming and wrecking things is a show she's paid to see. Everything lies inaudible beneath the sound of things breaking and breaking and breaking.

By the time I've tired myself out, jags of smashed glasses glitter the floor, half a bedpost has joined the logs in the fireplace, and the window leaks cold air after the kettle flew through it at speed.

My chest still heaving with every breath, I throw myself down in the armchair opposite Limbridge. I might have spent the last of my energy, but the ire keeps on roiling. It's going to roil for a long time, I fear. Maybe forever.

The letter, which I barely managed to refrain from tearing up, tremors in my hand. I sit staring at Alastair's no-frills cursive for what feels like several ages, my heart slowing but lodged in my throat. My first instinct should have been to call it false, to say the true murderer forced Alastair to write it, but it wasn't.

Through the confusion that had settled over me like a Withersham fog, memories came. The first and most recent? Our last moments in the waiting room. Didn't Alastair tell me himself how he'd realized his flesh was his parents'? That he'd spent all night thinking up the blackest way to punish me?

I chose Mortritis first and Alastair second. It didn't matter to him that I came back. It didn't matter that I helped him win the bloody Crucible.

The excitement and joy I saw in him afterwards came because he was finally about to get within spiring range of his father. I remember how he kissed me and want to strangle something. Not even a flicker of regret or indecision!

He was gloating. He knew how much worse I'd hurt now, knowing he had me in the palm of his hand yet I was simply too stupid to realize it.

But it goes much farther than that. Alastair planned this years ago. He told me to take no one at face value. *Everyone has their own motives, and it's up to you to wrest them out.* I trusted his word, and he took full advantage.

Alastair will say my negligence is to blame, and he's slightly right. I mostly blame him for being a shitheel.

Limbridge's creaking coat as she tops off her glass reminds me that I'm not alone in this room. She sits watching my face with that same grave expression, her lips purpled by wine.

I fish Alastair's ring from my pocket. The fact he used this one and not countless others to seal the wax on this letter is no accident. What I'd taken as a nice gesture was, in fact, a giant middle finger.

'So he's a father-slaying viper,' I say, rolling the ring between the pads of my thumb and forefinger. 'A double-faced, carrion-breathed vulture...'

'Yes. It would seem that way.'

'He duped me.'

Limbridge doesn't say anything to this, nor does she need to. The humiliation and shame sears hot enough to cremate.

Back in Edusa's apartments, I defended him to anyone who would listen. I picture Mortritis's and Tieran's triumph – hers gloating, his bitter – when I hand this letter over to the abettors, and want to vomit.

'He's getting exactly what he wanted,' I say darkly. 'He's won the game I didn't even know we were playing.'

'No whining, please,' Limbridge says. 'It's whining *or* property damage, and you already chose the latter.' She pushes her half-empty wineglass into my hand, keeping the bottle for herself. 'Nobody wins a game until it's finished, and thanks to the provost, you've the means to keep playing.'

I flap the letter. 'Will they even want me along once they see this?'

'In what sense?'

'It proves we weren't in cahoots, doesn't it?'

'If only! Alastair could have written it to exonerate you in return for your help.'

'Tripped gods,' I spit.

Limbridge studies me over the rims of her glasses. 'Anyone would think you didn't *want* to go after him.'

'Aside from the company I'll have to keep in the doing, nothing would bring me more pleasure. It's just that I don't fancy our chances of success.'

'Whyever not? Alastair's got graft, I'll give him that, but you've a graving prodigy, a spiring prodigy, and an abettor with Oldrac's foresight behind you.'

'And what if we can't find him? What if Oldrac's foresight is wrong?'

'Preyburn's bounty hunters seem to get by perfectly well without it.' Limbridge swigs as if the bottle contains water. 'Follow Credencia's lead and you'll have your place at St Penderghast's back.'

'And you'll have your payout from them,' I add bitterly.

'Half our payout now Alastair's gone rogue,' Limbridge corrects me without a flicker of shame. 'Renovations on the boys' dormitories will have to wait.'

I slump back in my seat, letting my arms hang over the sides. 'Ugh.'

Limbridge props her cheek against her gloved fist, skewing her glasses a little. 'I know it's tempting,' she says, looking me right in the eye, 'but promise me you won't do anything rash.'

'Might you be more specific?'

'Killing Alastair. Or allowing him to be killed.'

'*Limbridge*. If you think—'

'I don't, but people have shocked me before, both with their wrath and their stupidity.' Another swig. 'This isn't just about Withersham, you know. What happens to you matters to me. If you defy the provost, either by defection or failure, you'll answer for it. Promise me that no matter what, you bring Alastair back fit for trial.'

'Yes,' I say. 'I promise.'

We stay like that awhile, Limbridge swigging and somehow never getting drunk while I stare at the snow blowing past the broken window in bleak contemplation.

Into the silence, I mutter, 'I'm so glad I didn't sleep with him.'

END

GLOSSARY

THE FALLEN GODS, THE FIRMAMENTS, AND BEYOND

The Abyss: A realm of infinite darkness and cold, thankfully separate to the mortal realm. Home to unimaginable horrors, of which the Condemner is only one.

The Condemner: A powerful, eldritch entity of legend. Bestowed two cosmic gifts upon Our Lady: the knowledge of glyphs, and insanity.

The Firmaments: A celestial paradise in the sky. Domain of Oldrac, Our Lady, and their elusive kin.

Oldrac: A mythic, godlike being, titled Our Lord by his worshippers. Fell to earth many centuries ago to restore Our Lady to the firmaments.

The Choir: The dominant religious organization of the Commonwealth, governed by the teachings of Oldrac and Our Lady. Responsible for the invention and distribution of non-lethal pulp physicks.

Oldsfall Festival: An annual celebration of Oldrac's arrival on earth, the second of two Fall Days in the Commonwealth's calendar.

The Radiant Principles: The core tenets of Oldrac's teachings – honour, compassion, prudence, courage, honesty, loyalty, faith, and most importantly, oneness – and the religious text that elaborates upon them.

The Prelate: The Choir's revered leader, a precious relic from Oldrac's earthly rule.

Our Lady: A mythic, godlike being who fled from the firmaments to study glyphs on earth. Her true name, Eero, is so rarely used as to be forgotten.

Ersfall Festival: An annual celebration of Our Lady's arrival on earth, the first of two Fall Days in the Commonwealth's calendar.

The Reunion War: A centuries-long war between Glimwick and Preyburn, driven by the fallen gods.

GRAVERS

Practitioners of sorcery that comprise the Commonwealth's military. Gravers transform corpses into undead monsters for use in battle. Once a derogatory term coined from 'grave robbers', now a mark of status.

Atrophers: Metal plates carved with *ezorhox*, the glyph of atrophy. Used by gravers for the rapid destruction of unwanted effigies.

Conjunctions: Glyphs that connect eerians to the Eternal Spite, and vice versa.

Donations: Corpses donated for use in graving. Donation is a privilege afforded to every Commonwealth national from birth, except for scions; Oldracian flesh is worthless in graving.

Eerians: Wild monsters made of pulp and corpse-flesh. Although eerians were originated by Our Lady, the Eternal Spite recreates her designs most faithfully.

Effigies: Undead monsters made from human corpses, created and controlled by gravers.

Epitaphs: Glyphs arranged in sequence to create and control eerians and effigies.

The Eternal Spite: A fundamental force in nature created by Our Lady, also called the Blood of Preyburn. It replicates her eerians from corpses and pulp, while gravers channel its power to create effigies. *Our Lady is gone, but her spite is eternal.*

Glyphs: Expressions of eldritch power represented as symbols, bearing some manner of sentience. They possess many wonderful abilities, most of which relate to dead flesh.

The Compendium of Glyphs: A discursive record of every glyph known to gravers, of which there are currently 1,063. A #1 bestseller in Preyburn.

Graphium: A pen-shaped hand tool used in graving. Creates sorcerous heat, with which to inscribe glyphs onto corpses.

Grave Pulp: A valuable medium of the Eternal Spite, exclusively and naturally produced in the soil of Preyburn. Empowers gravers when certain conditions are met, but poisons scions without fail.

Pulp Physicks: Pulp mixed into liquid for ingestion. Only the Choir knows the formula for non-lethal physicks.

Pulpmoth: A pulp-corrupted moth species whose larvae feed on necrotic flesh. A perfect nuisance to gravers.

SPIRERS

Professional eerian-slayers who perform for crowds in arenas. Their sport, known as the Hallowed Game, is by far the most beloved in the Commonwealth.

Acclaim: Divine lightning granted by Oldrac. Fortifies scions who follow his Radiant Principles. Ravages glyphs, pulp-flesh, and electrical gadgetry.

The Grand Mêlée: A spiring competition held every five years to determine the Commonwealth's greatest champion.

The Might of Our All-Glorious Lord, and the Cunning of Our Dark-Crowned Lady: A duality of spires forged by Ivo Helel, esteemed spire-maker. Like all spires, they are designed to channel Acclaim.

Scions: Distant derivatives of the mythical Oldrac, according to common belief. Each one stands to inherit otherworldly traits, such as enhanced strength, healing, and dexterity.

Stage: A violent performance of spirer versus eerian in an arena.

Stage Warders: Senior spiring pupils, duty-bound to supervise their juniors' training and stages. Will only intervene in cases of mortal peril.

LOCATIONS

The Commonwealth: The united provinces of Glimwick and Preyburn. Sequestered from the rest of the world by its people's dangerous and unnatural abilities.

- **Glimwick:** A formerly minor nation, partial to snow, that rose to prominence when Oldrac endowed its people with godlike abilities. Formed of five regions: the Winter Grounds, the Ascent, the Verge, the Storm Grounds, and the Cradle.

  - **Balver:** The capital of the Winter Grounds in southern Glimwick.

    - **St Penderghast:** The most prestigious of the five regnant colleges, where spirers and gravers train.

      - **Dunchester campus:** Where spiring preceptors and students board and train. St Penderghast's arena is located here.

      - **Thumbarrow campus:** Where graving preceptors and students board and train.

- **Copperfont:** The location of the Faultons' ancestral home, and much-contested site of Oldrac's arrival.
- **The Embankment:** The city that joins Preyburn to Glimwick. This thriving hub of entertainment, not *all* of it sordid, is a popular destination for Glimwickian tourists.
- **The Fenlands:** Uninhabited wetlands that cover vast swathes of Preyburn and beyond, saturated with pulp and lousy with eerians.
- **Preyburn:** The once-home of Our Lady, the province of Preyburn is synonymous with graving and sullen weather.
  - **Burymeadow:** A tiny rural town, where Withersham Hall is the highlight.
  - **Crippleditch:** A slightly larger rural town, where Hal's parents live.
  - **Withersham Hall:** A military school that trains gravers from the ages of eleven to eighteen.
  - **Wutherweir:** The capital city of Preyburn.

Our Lady's Last Stand: The site of Our Lady's final battle with Oldrac many centuries ago, and of pilgrimage by spirers in the modern day. The deadliest eerians can be found here, for those brave or silly enough to go looking.

Zsietian Ascendancy: The closest nation to the Commonwealth, and one it is currently at war with. Possesses formidable technology, at least by the Commonwealth's standards.

OTHER TERMS

Abettors: Personal stewards to the provosts. Scions gifted with a fraction of Oldrac's divine foresight.

The Council of Provosts: The Commonwealth's leadership. Each provost governs one of the five regnant colleges and the region that hosts it.

Gilt: The currency of Glimwick.

Pud: The currency of Preyburn. Whilst originally slang, short for 'pudding', the term was eventually ratified by the Council.

CONTENT WARNINGS

Necromancy: death, dead bodies, & body horror

Fighting: violence, blood, gore, & injury depiction

Poisoning & emesis as a result

Neglect & emotional abuse by parents

Bullying

Manipulation of a child by an authority figure
(off-page, before the story begins)

Miscarriage & stillbirth mentioned
(minor character)

Murder

Alcohol use

ACKNOWLEDGEMENTS

First and foremost, thanks to my agent John Baker, AKA the Small God of Hype, Julie Gourinchas, and everyone at Bell Lomax Moreton. John, you blew me away with your enthusiastic vision for this project and helped me realise ARVA's true potential. Your contributions are too many to name in full, but I distinctly remember you called for 'some sort of bar fight', which became one of my favourite scenes. We've had a ridiculously smooth run of it so far, and I look forward to developing more creepy/violent/ saucy projects together.

I have many people to thank from Daphne Press, but I'll start with my lovely editors, Davi Lancett and Cat Aquino. From our very first meeting, I knew we would make an excellent team, and I'm beyond thrilled with the way ARVA has turned out. Not every author gets to say they have editors who listen to and collaborate with them on the level that you do, so I feel very lucky indeed.

I'd also like to thank Daphne Tonge, without whom none of this would be possible, and the broader teams at both Daphne Press and Illumicrate, with whom every interaction has been a pleasure: Caitlin Lomas, Tori Moss, Ellie Thomas, Genn McMenemy, Bianca Roberts Crook, Katie Gray, Bec Bentliff, and Zoë McGee. The publishing industry is not an easy one, so please know that I appreciate everything you have done to bring ARVA from vision to reality.

To ARVA's typesetter Adrian McLaughlin, copywriter Alan Heal, and proofreader Dan Coxon, thank you for all your hard work turning the manuscript into a fully-fledged book. I felt quite emotional seeing my words looking all mature and professional on the page after you had worked your magic.

For ARVA's gorgeous art and design, my profuse thanks to Jane Tibbetts, Tommy Arnold, Tom Roberts, and m.emityy. You handled my suggestions with the patience of saints, and I couldn't be happier with everything you have achieved for this project. I feel honoured that ARVA was able to grow from your creative talent.

Thanks to my friends and writing group, the creatively titled Writers' Workshop: Sianez, Sophie, and Amanda. You've nurtured the earliest and most bewildering renditions of ARVA, and all my other writing besides. Without a doubt, this book would not be what it is without your sage counsel.

Thanks to my teachers at Kingston University's Publishing and Creative Writing MA, with special mention to Emma, James, and Clare. The MA facilitated a major turning point in my life, not least the meeting of the aforementioned wonderful writing friends and agent. Had I not started this course, my sprint to publication might have been more of the crawl I had prepared myself for.

There are many more people who contributed to ARVA indirectly. They have supported me through some of my most troubled times, and I feel privileged to call them my friends. As someone who is reasonably good at hiding their anxiety, they have helped me more than they are likely to know.

Thanks to Hannah F, my best friend of over a decade and overall lovely human; thanks to Lucy and Lizzy, who buoyed me through the first difficult years after I moved to London and beyond; thanks to Phoebe and Zoe, fellow movie aficionados who I was also lucky enough to meet on the Publishing MA; thanks to all the friends I met through the Tower of Terror and the Best Ladies group; and thanks to Hannah S, Victoria, Will, and Donncha, the housemates who were with me when the first motes of ARVA's story began drifting into my brain.

Thanks to my incredibly understanding partner, Milos, whose many embarrassing pet names I have solemnly sworn to omit. You have endured endless rambling about ARVA with an encouraging smile and always give me exactly the reactions I hope for when I enlighten you on the monster romance genre (humorous bafflement), so you're basically perfect.

Last but not least, thanks to everyone who has supported ARVA as a reader. I wrote it for me, but I also wrote it for you.

ABOUT THE AUTHOR

Danielle Knight is an avid fan of gothic fantasy, romance, and horror, which will become all too apparent for readers of her debut novel, *A Rather Vengeful Accord*.

After receiving her MA in Creative Writing and Publishing from Kingston University, she moved into digital sales for a children's publisher in London. She mostly spends her time watching anime, playing video games, and typing various arrangements of words.